THE NATCHEZ WOMAN

BY ALICE WALWORTH GRAHAM

The Natchez Woman

Lost River

The Natchez Woman

BY ALICE WALWORTH GRAHAM

DOUBLEDAY & COMPANY, INC.

Garden City, New York, 1950

The characters and the incidents in this book are entirely the product of the author's imagination and have no relation to any person or event in real life.

To Richard

⤳ Chapter One

Of course I had known Mark all my life. He was older, just Arland's age, and belonged to her crowd. He was only a name heard now and then, a casual glimpse on the street or among a group of other people. The first time I was really conscious of him was at Arland's wedding.

She was married the spring after the Armistice, and looking back I can see how her wedding marked the end of an era. It was a big, old-fashioned entertainment, done on a grand, elaborate scale. The aunts had taken infinite trouble in decorating the church and the house and the garden, in summoning caterers and making out menus, and going over lists. There was champagne, plenty of it, but nobody got obviously under its influence. They wouldn't have dared. Afterward, things began to change. People didn't take so much trouble over decorations, and they began to drink more.

That night everybody seemed to feel we were getting back to the usual tenor of our ways, just as we'd wanted to get back to the good old days before the boll weevil and the good old days before the Civil War. We weren't going to get back, but we didn't know it then, and Arland was married in the style and manner of her young ladyhood.

She's a few years older than I am, and was my ideal Young Lady. Her mother, Aunt Margaret, died when Arland was fifteen. Aunt Margaret had been a semi-invalid for years, but though she became worn and fragile looking, she didn't give you the impression of an ill woman. She always sat upright, even if propped on pillows, and there was life in her eyes and snap and sparkle in her talk, and she never referred to the state of her health. She was a power in our family and in the town, and during her life "Margaret thinks" and after her death "what Margaret would have thought" were the standards of behavior for a long time.

When Uncle announced the engagement and approaching marriage of his daughter, Anne Arland, the aunts and all the kith and kin

1

planned and gave the wedding "as Margaret would have wanted it."
After it was over and Arland and Tim had gone and the candles were
guttering, and Aunt Tee was delicately wiping her eyes with a lacy
handkerchief and nibbling at the cake icing, the aunts chorused,
"It went off beautifully—just as Margaret would have wanted it."

I loved Arland. Claire—Cousin Olive's daughter—was mean. She
always made me feel like a poor relation. I was shy and didn't have
pretty clothes, and felt inferior, but Arland gave me presents and tried
to draw me into the rosy aura of good times and romance that always
seemed to surround her. I remember her coming-out party, and her
beaus, and the dances she went to, and her clothes. When we remi-
nisce, Kitty looks at us as though we were describing the habits and
feelings of some strange race on another planet. Even to me it's like
another world.

The time before nineteen fourteen seems as set and changeless as
a picture in a frame. It rolled slowly and evenly, I suppose because
I was young, and when you're young time doesn't show itself quick
and rushing as it does when you're older and you feel that it hurtles
you along. My life followed a routine. I did the same things, saw the
same people—I never thought they would change or grow older or
move away or die. Our town seemed forever shut off in its groove of
thinking and believing and living—a good deal different from the rest
of the world. With its kinship to the rest of the South, of course. Yet
it wasn't the South of New Orleans, or Charleston, it had its peculiar
flavor. It was Natchez, and nothing else.

Yet the outside world seemed caught and fixed too. Pick up a book
of that time. It seems immutable in its assumptions of morals and
manners. Pick up a magazine, say of nineteen five or ten. How set
and serene it shows everything. Civil War diaries, memoirs of court
life, charming illustrated articles on Provençal towns or Italian gardens fill the pages. They radiate a mild beneficence, their exhortations
or their tremors are all on problems that never came to a head or
don't matter any more. I've never found a breath of warning of what
was really looming up. A set calm seemed to pervade that world, when
it was hurrying to disaster, just as the stars look fixed in the sky, when
all the time, on fire, they are plunging through space and dragging
their helpless satellites with them.

The only big event I can remember was the *Titanic* going down.
Years later, when we were talking about it, and what a shock it was,

Arland said it was the last time all the world felt alike about something. Or mourned the same thing. Because not long after was the war, and there were allies and enemies, but nobody ever seemed to get back into being just human beings again.

I was restless and bored and dissatisfied with life then, when I was young. I was hungry for excitement, and longed for something to happen. Now I'd like to relive it all again, and savor how pleasant it really was, when I was eleven and twelve and thirteen, and Arland was a little older. No, I wouldn't—I didn't like being young, and if I went back, I'd be just the same as I was. There ought to be some guiding spirit to whisper, "Enjoy what you can while you can, because it won't last—won't re-form in the same pattern." There is. But you don't listen. You can't. You only listen to experiences, sometimes, when it's too late anyhow.

I see that space of years as an endless afternoon. There were summers and winters, mornings and nights, but my memory holds it at afternoon, on a summer day. The sun stands fixed in a dim blue sky and warm light trembles through the leafy shade. The children are playing and the men strolling home from their businesses, conducted with easy-going leisure and interrupted by frequent excursions for coffee and hobnobbing with cronies up and down Main Street. The women, "dressed for the evening" in light colors and stuffs, holding parasols and carrying large palmetto fans, would slowly proceed in groups or in pairs, on foot or by surrey, to sit with Aunt Em or Aunt Tee.

At Uncle's there was a hammock on the shady end of the gallery, and on those long summer afternoons—we always said "evening" for any hour after four—a group of young men and girls would gather. They would talk and laugh, and somebody would start playing a mandolin, and they would sing. There was always a big pitcher of lemonade and a plate of cookies. I'd usually be in the garden at the side of the house, playing moodily with a stack of paper dolls, yearning to be grownup too. I'd hang around, munching on the pile of cookies I had secreted to fortify myself, and stringing four o'clocks on a long grass stem. Even now when I catch a whiff of four o'clocks, I can hear the tunes of those old songs.

Arland went on buggy rides with her beaus. Once, in her enthusiasm for the day, and the season, and possibly the young man, she picked masses of Cherokee roses. When she came home she swelled and puffed and puffed and swelled—she'd picked poison ivy too. Right at the time she was supposed to be Claire's sister Edith's bridesmaid. Edith was married with only seven bridesmaids, and the young man from New Orleans, designated as Arland's special prey, had to console himself as best he could. The blue taffeta and rosebud-sprinkled tulle hung empty and ghostly in the armoire, while Arland scratched and moaned, and I sat beside her, wishing Claire had ballooned with poison ivy instead.

I was always at Uncle's prowling in the kitchen, licking up raw cake dough, raiding the pantry for a delicious brew known as blackberry shrub, or poking around in Arland's room, devouring the candy her young men sent, studying all the names on her dance programs— I was thrilled at the one where Tim had masterfully taken all the waltzes—Romance—or experimenting with her manicure things on my own stubby nails. That red cream stuff they used before the day of liquid nail polish fascinated me.

One morning I came early, before breakfast. At the door I found Arland's pink pointed satin slippers. Her dress hung over the banisters. On the landing was a frilled petticoat run with pink ribbons— farther up was another. At the door was a corset cover. On the floor of her room were the corsets themselves. Arland was sound asleep with a huge pink rosette still stuck in her hair. That dance she had been to the night before, and to which I hadn't gone, always loomed in my mind as the most delightful entertainment ever given in this world.

Tim had one of the early automobiles. Arland would put on a long cloak and a hat with yards and yards of navy blue chiffon veiling wound around it and floating from it, and go chugging off with him, bowing and smiling the length of Main Street, with everybody stopped in their tracks to gape and envy.

Girls read George Eliot and Mrs. Humphry Ward—Arland still refreshes herself by an occasional dip into *Lady Rose's Daughter*—and worked miles of tiny scallops on petticoat flounces and underbodies and pillowcases, and kept memory books. Arland and Claire, when they were little girls, cut colored plates out of *The Birds and Beasts of North America* and pasted them on a screen. We thought it was beautiful. It was years later before we realized a sacrilege had been committed.

Hats were important. You might, and frequently did, have a dress run up by the sewing woman, but you put out on your hat. It was an edifice of size, all covered with flowers and ribbons and feathers. Everybody who was anybody went to Miss Florence for their hats. The mirror there must have been specially made to flatter, or else it was Miss Florence herself, who so reverently placed the creation on a mound of hair, then stepped back, hands clasped, to murmur and coo.

Every day Arland agreed to meet Bess Barrett—Bess Denton she was then—at ten o'clock on the cathedral corner. She reached the spot at twelve, but as Bess never got there until noon either, it didn't matter. Then they ambled slowly down the street on the prowl for beaus. They always found them too. People dressed up for the "evening." Arland and Claire and Bess had embroidered organdies and batistes worn over pink or yellow slips with wide satin sashes to match. When hobble skirts came in, Arland had one, in spite of Uncle's mirth. It was pink flowered organdy with a pink taffeta hobble. I couldn't wait to have one, but I never did. Arland was fond of it too. The day the house caught fire she stood around, wringing her hands and crying. All she saved were Tim's letters—he was off at school—and the hobble dress. It didn't matter, since the neighbors dragged out everything else and the firemen soon put out the fire. The only damage was to the roof.

We all loved Holly Trees. It was set at the end of the street in a great stretch of lawn and garden, with a vegetable patch and a meadow beyond. It's brick, painted white, with a row of columns across the front, and furnished inside with the sort of elaboration Aunt Margaret had loved. The only thing the house lacked in Arland's eyes was a bed like the one in *Wuthering Heights*.

On the night of her wedding the house was massed with pink and white candles and pink and white flowers, and the garden was all in bloom and hung with Japanese lanterns. There were eight bridesmaids and I was one of them. The youngest and shyest. We wore cream-colored lace over pink satin and I wore a big pink rosette over each ear. They kept slipping sideways and my slippers were too tight.

Tim had just come back from overseas and was still in uniform. He was handsome, tall and wide shouldered, with a high fresh color, black hair, and snapping black eyes. He was in uniform, but it was merely decorative then. The war was over and people were longing to forget it all and go back to the old ways, so pleasant and leisurely.

Tim and Arland had been in love a long time. Everybody thought it was all so romantic. We were encouraged to be romantic, or rather sentimental, and to cherish letters, and locks of hair. We were never told anything about passion. I wonder now what the aunts thought was the motive force behind some of the stranger scandals that lurked, and sometimes blazed, in our midst. Of course we learned that some people and some things weren't "nice." Our school, where we learned *Marmion*, and Father Ryan's poems, and some other things, was up on a hill and overlooked the red-light district—several rows of little houses with names over their doors. They were presided over by some-one named Imogen. Massive in tight corsets, tight laced shoes, her hat wide as an umbrella, her face painted, she sometimes paced the length of Main Street, shepherding her girls, all dressed up too. Then people murmured and whispered. No one could have been more out-raged—not even the aunts—at postwar manners than Imogen herself. She had to leave town—she said society women had ruined her busi-ness.

Arland and I read rather a good deal. If a book had belonged to Grandfather, and had a dull enough cover, the aunts concluded it was edifying. Our libraries were old-fashioned, but there were lots of books, and we were bound to catch glimmerings of ideas and feel-ings and ways besides those the aunts stressed. I wasn't very old be-fore I began to feel that Aunt Em was going through life like some-one trying to read *Hamlet* with the part of the Danish prince left out.

But before I had many theoretical ideas about passion I began to experience the sensations.

Arland's love for Tim was so much more auspicious than mine for Mark. The Laidlaws were a fine old family, and they had some money. Mr. Laidlaw was Uncle's partner, and Tim was the gayest, the best-looking, and the most promising young man in town. All the girls were in love with him, and all the old ladies. In spite of the solid phalanx of beaus Arland collected, she never cared for anyone but Tim, and the aunts went around saying, "Isn't it sweet? Just like a story in a book with a happy, happy ending."

Everybody was at the wedding, young and old. The boys just back from the war, and all the old standbys. And guests from out of town, and all the vast family connections. There were scads of aunts. Aunt Em—I lived with her in the original Elliston house on another street —was an old maid. Aunt Augusta and Aunt Annabella were married and lived away. But they came. Then Aunt Ada, another old maid, and Aunt Tee. Aunt Tee was a widow. She lived in a funny little house crammed with heavy furniture and family keepsakes and lost in rose vines. Her sons were grown and had moved away, but they also appeared, the sense of clan strong in their breasts, in spite of having lived in the North. Because she was a widow, or for some reason, Aunt Tee never appeared officially at any large social function. She had shown herself at church, fluttering a lace handkerchief against her frilly lashes, then she had vanished. One little group after another would eddy out to the back room where she had ensconced herself, drawn by nods and whispers. They would beg "Oh, Teresa, do come out!" "Ssh!" she would whisper back, "I can't." Then they would gather and laugh and gossip and have the best time of all, feasting together, getting a little tipsy, and commenting on every single soul.

Aunt Tee had been a great heartbreaker herself, usually engaged in rapid succession to first one person then another. One of the fiancés died, and a cousin of ours took Tee off to some summer resort. The cousin soon wrote home, "Stop harping on 'that lonely grave'! Things are perking up." Aunt Tee came back engaged. I don't know why she mourned with so much fanfare, but her clothes were soft and trailing and becoming and her ways coquettish.

Bedelia said "Folks sure has turned out," and they had. The old families appeared in full force, coming from the big dilapidated antebellum houses hidden along the country roads, where they sequestered themselves among ancestors' portraits and heavy tarnished silver and long-drawn-out feuds with one another and family skeletons in closets—a kind of existence that gave them full scope to develop all their inherent peculiarities. Arland and I were nearly, or distantly, related to most of them. Maybe all.

"We're like trees in a grove," she said. "We've stayed in one place so long our roots are tangled."

Miss Faust was there, wearing long white kid opera gloves. Their newness and whiteness were startling, and caused a commotion. She looked like a bunch of old corn shucks, and on her rare appearances in town was dressed in what looked like the kind of sacking you use on cotton bales. And Mr. Durly's whiskers were trimmed. Something never seen before. Mr. Durly and Miss Faust lived together in a tumble-down old house not far from Rosemont. The road was almost impassable, and the house itself clung precariously to the edge of a ravine. There was a pond forever shadowed by drooping live oaks—a regular dank tarn out of Edgar Allan Poe.

Mr. Durly had wanted to be a painter but had lost the use of his fingers in an accident. Now he spent his life roving about in the woods and often sleeping in nests of leaves he made for himself, or up in trees. He and Miss Faust had a long-standing state of ill feeling for Miss Kate Lennerd, because the Durly goats scavenged about in the closed and sacred and unseen precincts of Rosemont.

The three Querrell sisters had come too. They were tall and were decked with old Persian shawls and old flappings of lace. One wrote poetry, one wove—some kind of mysterious work, like the Lady of Shalott's web, and the other one played tunes, quavering them out on an obsolete-looking instrument, I think it was a spinet.

Their house had been built in the days of the Spaniards, with winding stairs leading up on the outside from the brick lower story. One wing had fallen in, and a tough and resilient oak was pushing up through the remains of the roof on that side.

Everybody was fond of the Querrell girls, and people groaned but bought Cousin Medora's poems—they were on themes like the love of somebody—De Soto—for an Indian damsel. People went out over the truly hair-raising road to hear Cousin Laura play, and took care to cosset the old dears' delusions that they were world-famous.

Mrs. Van Delevan was conspicuous in all her diamonds and bright pink brocade. Her cheeks were painted as pink as her dress. Diamonds blinked through swathings of tulle and her neck appeared through the drifts like a gaunt and weathered cliff veiled in fog and set about with lighthouses. She was enjoying herself at last.

"Poor Sally," somebody sighed. "She was such a lovely thing." At fifty and sixty she enjoyed herself. But she hadn't at sixteen and twenty and twenty-five. She'd married old Mr. Van Delevan to save her family. Mortgaged to the hilt, they'd gone on giving parties and taking European tours and wearing Paris clothes until they couldn't stave off the crash any longer. So there was nothing to do but toss sixteen-year-old Sara to Mr. Van Delevan. He was supposed to die shortly. But he lived and lived and lived, careful, so careful of his money. When he died, she was sixty. Here she was, like an old, old grasshopper wheezily racketing after the frosts had come.

Mr. Selwyn was on hand, and so was his sister. They lived in the same house. "But never a mumblin' word," according to Bedelia.

They never spoke after they quarreled about a will. Miss Constance had at last put electricity in the house, and the first time the lights were turned on Cousin Charles stalked through the house with a lighted candle in his hand. He was supposed to be very well off. "Maybe so," Bedelia commented, "but he jest a'sets on his richness."

People said he let a certain necessity—it was about a mile from the house, in the golden age before the war style—decay so badly that one dark cold night he fell in the cesspool. But you wouldn't connect such an adventure with him if you'd seen him at the wedding. His hair and his mustache and his manners were so glossy. He had a way of making you feel pleased with yourself without ever actually paying a compliment. When you were with him you thought here is certainly the ideal gentleman of the old school. He was quite nearly related to us.

Every night Cousin Charlie Selwyn loped over the hills by the river road to see Miss Katie Lennerd at Rosemont. His horse was the most ambling and ancient in the world. Rain or shine, tornado or blizzard, he betook himself to Rosemont. He'd been going for forty years.

Miss Katie didn't show herself at the wedding. She never went anywhere; nobody knew why she secluded herself. It's strange when you think what a big part she played in my life I can remember seeing her only once or twice. She had been a great beauty when she was young, and when I saw a tiny woman, dressed in the full skirt and high-collared blouse of the early nineteen hundreds, I was disappointed. Until I noticed her eyes, set in hollows, but still brilliant. The ghost of her loveliness and glamour still clung to her, and haunted me.

She had been educated in Europe, and presented at various courts, and all kinds of dazzling people had wanted to marry her, but for years she had lived shut up in Rosemont, seeing no one but Mr. Charlie Selwyn. She was considered very rich, and we often speculated about the size of the Lennerd fortune and why she ignored all the world, including her own family. Alec and Michael and Mark Lennerd were her nephews. Alec and Michael were brothers; Mark was their cousin.

Miss Jessie Bryerson was also conspicuous that night, wearing maroon velvet, in spite of the heat, and a weird arrangement on her hair. I finally diagnosed it as a crochet mat stuck all over with those colored balls you see on Christmas trees. When sandwiches were passed to her she helped herself daintily, then stuffed everything she took in her bag—only it wasn't a bag, it was a reticule. Just last week she'd scooped up all the gold fish out of the fountain in the Confederate Memorial Park and borne them off in her umbrella. The U.D.C. ladies were indignant. They boiled but they decided just to restock the fountain and not confront Miss Jessie, who had been known to rout whole organized brigades of ladies by her complete sang-froid. Uncle said they ought to be glad she left Marse Robert's horse under him.

"Miss Jessie gave me a funny old cookbook for a wedding present," Arland told me. "Between the strange ingredients and the 's's' like 'f's' it might as well be written in code."

I didn't care for Miss Jessie. Serene and smiling, she used to sidle up when I was at a party, grimly grouped with a bunch of wall-flowers, and in her lovely fluty voice ask, "Girls, why ahn't you dahnc-ing?"

There weren't any good roads around town, and there's never been a through train from anywhere here, or from here to any part of the globe, and people certainly did live their own lives. That night I wasn't interested in all these people. All I wanted was to be perfectly beautiful and have a wonderful time.

I envied Arland. There was Tim, the ideal hero, safely returned to her. What could keep them from living happily ever after? I was watching the bride and groom and I was by myself, a little on the outside of things. Of course I "belonged." In those days money didn't matter in our town. What mattered was having had plenty of grand-fathers and great-uncles in Confederate gray, and I had shoals of them. I was an Elliston.

Aunt Emily was always saying, "Remember, Jane, you're an Ellis-ton." Being one was supposed to support you through every trial and tribulation. But at the time I was stranded between two eras. I was too young to accept or fit in to Arland's sweet pretty-girl atmosphere. Besides, it didn't suit me. Neither the clothes, nor the ways, nor the mental climate. And I hadn't found my own.

So at the wedding I rather stood around, until Arland herself noticed me and made me come over to the bride's table and stand right by her while she cut the towering cake. Then I saw Mark, right opposite. He was just back from the war, too, but not in uniform.

He wasn't very tall and he was very blond, but it was not a fresh blondness. His hair was light, but it looked as though it had been burned to colorlessness by the sun. He had clear gray eyes, so clear and light they made the pupils look intensely black. His eyebrows were thick, darker than his hair, and his skin was dark, deeply and evenly tanned. It was strange to see anyone so blond who suggested coolness so little. On the contrary, he reminded me of one of those hot, sultry summer days that burn on with a sort of incandescence and end with thunder and lightning.

When he turned his head, I could see the scar, a narrow silvery line, running from his temple, barely touching his cheek, going behind it and ending in his neck. He had been flying with the French before we ever got into the war.

Tim had all the outer garnish of a hero, the uniform, with decorations. The attitudes, and all the stories of what he'd done and all he'd seen. He hailed and was hailed by everybody up and down the length of Main Street, and had given talks for all the clubs. He had been brave, he had promotions and medals to prove it, but he was the exciting and glittering part of the war. The band-playing, flag-waving part. He somehow never suggested it had been dark and bitter too. But I knew then and there that Mark had struggled through some of the worst of it. He had come home and taken off his uniform and had nothing to say for himself. I looked at the scar and had a faint inkling of what it might really have been like, the long casualty lists and the long time out of normal living.

When I looked at him, I think I realized we could never go back and pretend everything was the same and forget it had ever been. I looked at him and didn't want to go back. I was through with all things past. I wanted to go ahead, into the future, with him.

Arland called him over and he came and stood near us. "Here, Jane"—she put one of the satin ribbons in my hand—"pull. All the bridesmaids must pull."

We did, and I got the thimble. Everybody laughed. I didn't like it. I didn't want to be an old maid. I absolutely would not be. Claire got the ring. Arland began slicing, and the sugar cupid trembled, its sugar wings shook, and it fell from its frosted temple.

Mark said, "That's not bad luck, I hope."

Arland shook her head and kept on smiling and looking happy. I looked at Mark, but he wasn't paying any attention to me. He wasn't

11

sharing any of the noise and excitement either. Like me, though he was in the midst of things, he was apart from the group.

I began to talk to him, asking him the usual senseless banalities. My intense consciousness of him made me shyer than ever. When I asked him if he was glad to be back, he didn't give me the accustomed answer.

"You think you want to be, more than anything. Then you get restless. You don't seem to fit in. Then you look back at the war—and miss it."

He lived in the old house below the hill on a nook of land pushing out into the river. Wishmore Point. It was good rich land but a dreary house. Like mine, Mark's parents weren't living now. He lived with his uncle, Mr. Jeff Lennerd. Mr. Jeff planted cotton by fits and starts and drank whisky mighty steadily. It wasn't much of a life for Mark, but if he took the place out of Mr. Jeff's hands and really worked with it, he might do well with it. I asked him if he intended to stay, and trembled at the thought that he might go off again.

"Reckon so. Now I'm here. The place sure needs a little regular attention. Besides, I don't know what else to do with myself."

He had a troubled, brooding look on his face. I turned the horrid little thimble in my hands and threw it under the table and pressed my foot on it and mashed it flat.

"It must be strange to come back and find everything jogging along in the same old way."

For the first time he really seemed to notice me.

"I wish you'd tell me about it," I hurried on, struggling to hold on to the attention he had at last focused on me. "What it was like, what really happened."

He smiled a little. "Would you? Most people want to forget it all. Not that I blame them. I'll show you some pictures sometime—if you really want to see them."

I said I certainly did.

Arland left to change her clothes, rustling toward the house, her lace and illusion veil catching against the bushes, her long satin train swishing after her like moonlight, a scent of lilies of the valley and roses following her. All the bridesmaids ran rustling and twittering behind her, being as foolish as possible. She went in the house and up the steps, and paused on the landing to throw her bouquet. Claire wanted it and tried to shove me aside to get it, but Arland threw it straight at me. I caught it. I remember the smell of the roses and lilies, and the creamy curled convolutions of the petals and the tininess of the little lilies, and the feel of the satin ribbons, and the sense of triumph over Claire, and the excitement—a premonition of things about to happen.

I suddenly had courage. When Tim and Arland had driven off and Aunt Em said, come, Jane, Mrs. Lews is waiting—we were always dependent on the vehicles and consequently the whims of other people—I told her Mark Lennerd was taking me home. I had already learned that things I wanted to happen to me didn't of their own accord, so quick, before my daring left me, I went up to Mark and asked him if he would take me home.

He said, sure, glad to—come along. A waiter was passing with a tray of champagne. I took a brimming glass and drank it all without stopping. Mark laughed. "Careful with that stuff, my dear child, you'll have a head." And he steered me off to his tin lizzie. I hoped he'd want to ride around, but he didn't. He took me on home. It seemed very short. He didn't say very much either, and beneath what he did say I caught a preoccupation with his own thoughts.

He was twenty-three, but the scar down his face and what it meant made him seem old, so much older than I was. I longed with all my heart to have him tell me and nobody else all that had happened to him. Everything. I could feel it and share it and plunge into it. Everything that had happened to him must belong to me, too, and all that would ever happen to him. I wanted to tell him all about myself and all I thought and felt and hoped. I was wild to dramatize myself and be a supremely interesting creature to him. I didn't know how, and I must say I had scant material to work on. I just sat there, saying a few commonplace things anyone could have said, and always did.

I wished I could be like Claire and Arland. They knew how to flirt. When I listened to them and their beaus they sounded like silly geese. Claire was full of foolish chit-chat and Arland hardly talked at all. It was a well-known fact that the worst mistake any female being could make with a man was to give the slightest inkling she had a ray of sense or an idea in her head. What you wanted was a great deal of fluffy hair on top of your head and nothing inside.

It seemed to me those girls filled the bill perfectly, since they mostly said, "Oh, shucks, I never——" and filled the intervals with

13

giggling. Arland played the piano, and with her more sentimental beaus quoted poetry by the yard. She did a great deal of listening, too, with a rapt air, but how can you listen when somebody isn't telling you anything?

And Mark wasn't. Then we were at the house. Too soon. He took me to the door, thanked me for going with him, said good night, gave my hand a little pat and a slight squeeze, and drove off. I tiptoed upstairs and Aunt Em said, "Jane, is that you?" and I went in and kissed her good night and went to my room.

Everything in the house was just the same, old and quiet, but I had changed. Aunt Em's small snores came from across the hall. She snored daintily, as if she never forgot she was a lady, and an Elliston. She never knew whether to say she hadn't closed her eyes all night, as if there was some particular merit to the experience, or whether to say I'd waked her every time she dozed off. Sometimes she told me her dreams. They sounded singularly dull, cluttered with everyday happenings. I think they would have baffled a psychoanalyst.

I couldn't sleep. I felt wild and all keyed up. The champagne had made my head ache. I was in love. People say you can't be at first sight, but I know better. I felt the shock and the impact. I had a sense of absolute certainty, but I wasn't happy. I knew Mark wasn't thinking of me. Why should he? I had no talent, no particular charm, and though not bad-looking I was not brilliantly pretty, and had none of the assurance of thinking I was, which often works just as well. Yet it never occurred to me I couldn't get what I wanted. I have never had any complexes. Things don't come to me twisted and disguised, fished out of some dim subconscious. They blaze at me stark and unmistakable. I knew what I wanted. I wanted Mark to hold me in his arms and kiss me until I was dizzy. That and more.

It wasn't like Arland's being in love with Tim. I was aware of that at once. It wasn't what I'd been led to expect—a respectful wooing from some eligible young man. After he had "paid attention," in the words of the aunts, and "rushed" me, in the words of Arland's crowd, for a sufficient length of time, my heart would gradually begin to flutter until I gave a shy consent. After which, I would arrange the articles in my hope chest, show a ring, and have wedding bells and all the conventional apparatus of Romance. You weren't supposed to feel anything until the wheels were well turning.

This was different. I'd craved attention, I'd craved something

14

vague called Love, but I'd never known what it was to want someone. This was heavy and fierce. My body was full of new and violent sensations. A door had been opened, showing me an unknown world, dark, flame-shot.

I sat in the window, in the dark, still holding Arland's flowers in my hot hands. To this day the gentle perfume of roses and lilies of the valley carry for me a connotation of sensuousness, a memory of intense desire.

I stayed there until the morning star showed in the sky. It, too, looked different. It didn't look serene and silver as it did shining over the river on fall and spring evenings. It flared sharp-pointed and mocking and malign, vivid through a dull orange haze prophesying a heavy brazen day. Its dazzle was running flames, as though Venus had set heaven and earth on fire.

≈§ Chapter Two

I didn't see Mark again until Tim and Arland were back from their honeymoon. It had only been a short trip because Tim had gone into politics and was running for Congress. I hardly even saw Arland after she came back home, she was so busy helping Tim, entertaining people who might be useful to him, writing letters, and making out lists. I went with her once or twice to go ask people to vote. She did very prettily, always saying the right thing, and remembering how many children they had, if they had any. I envied her, because she was so much a part of Tim's life. They were married, and her existence was woven into his. I longed to be a part of Mark's life, and what could I do but sit and wait for him to notice me?

I used to say I didn't want to stay here in this town and just vegetate, I used to be ambitious and want to go away to school and learn something and get a job and have some sort of career—what I didn't know, since I didn't seem to have any particular sort of talent. Now all of that was over. I wanted Mark and nothing else.

If Tim won his election, Arland would have an interesting life. She would go to Washington and meet all kinds of people, and know everything that was going on, and have a wonderful time. Once I would have envied her, but now nothing would induce me to leave this town where Mark was, where I might see him.

I didn't see him, but I heard about him. It seems he had a fight with Clem Burgess on the excursion boat. Everybody thought it was because of Ludie Daniels.

Cousin Olive was buzzing about it to Aunt Em. They were sitting on the front gallery rocking back and forth. Aunt Em trailed a scent of cologne and she was vaguely mulling over her crochet, some grayish lavenderish sort of bed sack. She was tangling her thread and dropping her stitches. Aunt Em was neat but she had a fumbling way of working that always got on my nerves. I think I'm efficient because she never was. I used to take things away from her and do them myself

16

rather than watch her uncertainties. Every now and then she dropped her crochet and picked up her fan and waved it about. We weren't supposed to have any mosquitoes. It was one of Aunt Em's illusions about the house that she never felt a mosquito. Mosquitoes on the sacrosanct Elliston gallery? No indeed. Nor did she ever see a fly. Or hear a mouse.

Cousin Olive frankly slapped her substantial ankles. She was a large, substantial woman, handsome, with a decidedly good opinion of herself, a commanding way of stating things, and a knack of transforming the most unsubstantial rumor into gospel fact. Her house was next door, large and ugly. It seemed to stand on tiptoe and peer in the street to see what was going on. Cousin Olive had once had a husband. He had been president of the bank and the bank had failed and they had lost all their money, and he had killed himself. A lot of men had killed themselves that year when the bank failed— the "bad year" people sometimes called it.

Cousin Olive had been "bearing up" bravely ever since. It was a woman's duty to "bear up" when her husband's business or health or affections failed. According to my opinion, Cousin Liv has strutted about being a brave, noble, dutiful Christian woman for years, and has had a pretty good time being it, but everybody else thinks she's suffered.

She'd married off large, blank, bland Edith, and was now trying to get Claire off her hands. I don't know why it is that women with the poorest opinion of their own husbands are in such a hurry to get their daughters married, but I've noticed it time and time again.

Cousin Olive was saying what a good time Claire had had on the boat. "Simply rushed off her feet." The boats went up and down the river, and had dances lasting from eight to midnight. I'd always longed to go, but had never been. Nobody had ever asked me. Aunt Em didn't approve anyway. She'd heard there was so much drinking and people danced in such a peculiar way, all these new dances, and there was such a Low Crowd.

"All Claire's bunch have started to go, so I have to let her. Mark Lennerd got into a fight with that Burgess boy."

"Burgess, what Burgess?" Aunt Em demanded. She had to place everybody within the framework of their family connections.

"You know, Em"—Cousin Olive was patient—"Clem Burgess's son."

"Oh yes, rather plain people. That's what I tell you, Liv, a fight!"
She was shocked, but she wanted to know all about it.

"Claire says somebody heard Mark tell the Burgess boy if he ever
opened his mouth he'd kill him next time. It was something to do
with that Ludie Daniels. I suppose Mark was jealous."

"Daniels? Never heard of her, Liv."

"You have, Em. Old Sheriff Daniels' daughter. You know he was
elected when they had that reform ticket. They say all the men are
wild about her. No better than she should be either, from all I've
heard." She turned to me. I was sitting on the front steps. "You know
her, Jane."

Aunt Emily wondered what Mark was thinking of, to go with a girl
like that, from such very plain people.

"Claire says Mark used to go with her lots before he went off to
war. He evidently does still, if Clem is a rival and they went so far
as to fight over her."

I thought I'd burst. Of course I knew Ludie by sight and hearsay.
She was rather smallish, and lusciously curved, with beautiful legs
and ankles. She always wore her dresses cut very low and she had the
whitest, roundest neck. I wanted to wring it. She'd been on the boat,
disporting herself, and Mark had gotten into a fight on her account.

I'd seen the boat from the top of the hill. It looked like one of
those square cardboard boxes I used to fix with isinglass windows.
I'd stick a candle inside and light it and drag it up and down the side-
walk in the dusk. The boat had glittered at the river's edge. The
calliope had ground out its tunes, sharp and jerky, charging the
heavy summer air with its excitement. It held a sort of thick, vulgar
promise, like street fairs and circuses—noise and life and crowds and
raucous joys. It was sad, too, as if none of the gaiety would last
very long. It was sad for me, because I was out of it all, sitting in the
dull safety of the old Elliston house. Shiny, tinkling with loud brassy
tunes, spangling the water with lights, the boat had drawn away from
the shore. It was a little island, detached from the world, its glow
quivering in the murky Mississippi and its music echoing back from
the lonely willow-lined banks.

Mark had been on it. I could imagine the spotlight shifting over
the mass of dancers, picking out his face pressed close to Ludie's. I
bet she'd worn that bright red dress, the silk taut over her round
breasts, her neck so white, her eyes so black and impudent, her hair

black and richly curling. He'd fought over her with another man. It made me feel wild and strange, drunk, too, and ready to fight with her because of him.

Arland says she can't understand jealousy. She says she wouldn't want anyone who didn't love her. If they stopped loving her, they could go, and good riddance. But she had Tim. She was married to him, and consequently, in my code of belief, safe forever. We were brought up on the live-happily-ever-after theme. Women married and then grew placid and contented and cowlike with husband and home and children. There was never any restlessness, any longings for something else. You were fixed for life.

But I didn't have Mark. And when you love and want a person so much, when a voice, and a touch, the very look out of their eyes means your life and breath—to know they are giving all you want to somebody else . . .

The mosquitoes buzzed. The dried grass and shrubs on the lawn lost their color. A bed of zinnias, their stems rusty from the drought, their petals curling at the outer edges as though they had been fried, had a hot burst of color in the late sunlight. When the sun left them they faded out.

"I'm afraid Mark's turning out to be wild," Cousin Olive said. She bent over her hemstitching. She was making pillowcases for Claire's hope chest. Claire wasn't engaged yet, but she would be. Cousin Olive would see to that. A girl had to be prepared. I didn't have a hope chest, or hopes. Aunt Em always said I'd be single, like herself.

"I hope he won't take to drink like poor Mr. Jeff." Aunt Em sighed. I whipped her work away from her—she was looking for some dropped stitches and not finding them—and fixed it up. Mark was an orphan like me. He lived down at Wishmore with his uncle, Mr. Jeff Lennerd. In spite of the fact that the land was so good, Mr. Jeff had never done well with the place. For one thing, it always overflowed when the river rose. Some years you couldn't make a crop at all, at least that's what Mr. Jeff claimed, but I always thought if he'd stirred his stumps as soon as the water went down, he could have made more cotton than he said. But he didn't really care what happened to the place. He was glad for the river to rise, then he could retire in peace to the attic of the old house and let the Mississippi rare. He always ensconced himself with plenty of corn whisky for company, and the whisky sloshed inside him and the muddy water sloshed outside. Snakes slithered through the drift and willows, and once, he said, a big water moccasin came all the way to the attic and curled up on the bedpost and looked at him, but it might, he admitted, have been a vision.

Years ago he'd had a long-drawn-out lawsuit with his half sister, Miss Kate, over the Lennerd property and the will. Poor Mr. Jeff came out the little end of the horn. Wishmore was all he got out of the Lennerd plantations and property.

"It's a sin and a shame the way Jeff Lennerd drinks," Cousin Olive said. "No wonder Martha had to leave him."

Mr. Jeff had been married once, briefly, and it was like the good ladies to leave the subject of Mark and go back to the separation of Mr. Jeff and his wife, and who cared now? But they always went back.

"Of course there's always been something pretty queer about Martha too," Cousin Olive mused. Miss Martha, though she was Mrs. Jeff Lennerd nobody called her anything but Miss Martha, sewed for people. She chopped and ripped and pinned in scowling silence, and nobody dared complain. They grumbled, but they kept on going to her, because they felt sorry for her.

"Well, Olive, you know her family—why, they aren't even Natchez people." If you belonged here you could get away with murder. Of course people speculated about Miss Kate and Mr. Charlie Selwyn, and talked about Miss Jessie Bryerson's exploits, and the probable relations of Mr. Durly and Miss Faust, shut up together for half a century out in the woods, and all the café-au-lait ladies set up by Mr. Van Delevan, but all these things had gone on so long a sort of tolerance had sprung up.

"Martha certainly ruined my lilac voile, such pretty stuff too. And she was snappish, quite snappish, when I suggested she do something about the fit of the collar."

"She messed up Claire's taffeta too. Claire wanted to wear it tomorrow night. I suppose everybody'll be down on the bluff to hear Tim speak. What are you going to wear, Jane?"

"Something Miss Martha's hashed up, I guess. I always do." I didn't have anything I wanted to wear, and I longed to be beautiful and well dressed. "I haven't got anything decent."

"You have your bridesmaid's dress, dear," Aunt Em pointed out.

"I can't wear it on the bluff. Besides, I don't like it. It's a sissy dress."

20

"It was certainly becoming to Claire." Cousin Olive went on with her maddening complacence. "But she's tired of it. She goes out so much she runs through her evening dresses. If you have no other way to go tomorrow night, Jane, Claire'll pick you up."

I knew Claire fussed and grumbled about having me tag along with her and her date, and how I hated it. I'd walked with Louis Sender at the wedding, but he hadn't paid a bit of attention to me at any of the parties. Not that I cared, except Arland's theory was you ought to make yourself agreeable to all the boys, so you'd look as if you were having a wonderful time. Then you'd probably land the one you did want. "Gather all the fish you can in your net, and gently throw back the ones you don't need." I wished I'd worked on it sooner. Claire was always saying, "You ought to have your own crowd, Jane, you're too young for our bunch." But I didn't belong anywhere.

"Everybody says Tim's sure to win," Cousin Olive was saying. "He ought to. He's certainly a fine, fine fellow. Arland's done well for herself. Such a wonderful war record."

"Mark was flying and fighting before this country ever got in war," I pointed out.

Cousin Olive and Aunt Em didn't say anything to that. They didn't want to think about the war any more. We'd won it, and Tim's decoration looked very nice. They never stopped to think anybody might be changed inside by going over there and fighting, by the blood and mud, and boom and crash of the guns. They expected "all our fine boys" to come back and be just the way they were when they left, and for everything to go on as though nothing had happened.

I couldn't stand listening to them any more, so I got up and left. Tomorrow night—it might mean a lot. I'd see Mark, and I felt I had to make some headway with him. There I was, young and untrained in any art of luring, and scrawny and dowdy. How could I hope to hold a candle to the knowing and lush Ludie? Somehow, someway, I'd have to get him away from her. She was beautiful, and I didn't know how I was going about it. Someday she might be full-blown and sloppy and fat, but now she was in her prime. But she wasn't going to have him, if I had to kill her.

I wandered down the drive and out of the gate, and along the street, through the hot dusk. I was lonely, and I was jealous. Everybody else was busy with their lives, but I had none of my own. There was a scent of dry, freshly mowed grass. Mr. Bramley was still watering his azaleas. The clematis on his fence made bunches of little white feathers. Lights began to shine in windows. Mrs. Farris came to her door and called, "Tomm-ee, co-me on ho-oome," and far down the street Tommy squawled back, "In a min-itt," and went on roaring and yelling with that bunch of little demons. Mrs. Farris prided herself on her Motherhood. She had four children, and you heard murmured details about the obstetrical production of each of the four—very harrowing—of course not meant for Virgin Ears, and, I thought, extremely dull. She got 'em born, but she didn't know how to manage them or bring them up. I hoped my life wouldn't turn out so dull I'd have to dramatize myself by a continuous repetition of all the more ungainly aspects of having children.

Mrs. Casey came out on the gallery, smiling, freshly dressed, to meet Mr. Casey. She didn't pay much attention to her children. She was a Perfect Wife, and "Mr. Casey says" and "Mr. Casey thinks" made up her conversation. I saw into the Twombly library. "Young Judge" Twombly, seventy, but distinguished from "old Judge" Twombly, who was ninety-two and of course wonderful for his age, was reading a newspaper under a lamp with a green shade and looked simply ghastly. Farther down, at the Everetts', a card party was breaking up, with women chattering and giggling together.

I turned the corner and went down a less familiar street. A pretty woman, must be Mrs. George Elton, was putting a baby to bed in an upstairs room. There were white lambs skipping on blue wallpaper and she was laughing and the baby was gurgling. Mrs. Elton was Young Married Domestic Bliss. She made a big to-do over it, but the baby was going to have George's eyes, set too close together.

I went on and on, to another part of town. There was the big old Ilman place. Mrs. Ilman kept boarders now but still talked about the Better Days she had known. She seemed reconciled to the Better Days being behind her. She was neither efficient nor brilliant, and she never seemed to try to be any different from what she was. Dreary life, with some old men and old females on the dilapidated gallery, just sitting and rocking.

Then the houses were smaller, and closer together. I went on until I came to the house where Ludie lived, and I stopped in front of it, but on the other side of the street. It was a long, narrow brown house with an empty overgrown lot on one side. A big umbrella china tree spread its branches over the bare side yard. There was hardly any front yard. Ludie's father was dead now. He'd been a wiry little man, in politics, always declaiming against this or that. Like a lot of people of such ilk, he didn't seem to see what was going on under his own nose, though I must say the scandal about Ludie had seeped out after his demise. The older sister had married and lived out West somewhere, and the big handsome, burly, sullen-looking boys had left town too. I vaguely knew Mrs. Daniels, a small fidgety, chatty sort of woman. She kept close at home. Maybe she didn't know Ludie was wild. Maybe she was only glad her daughter was beautiful and had men crazy about her, and didn't care what people said. They probably didn't say it to her anyhow.

I waited, and I saw lights flare in the back side room. Two windows gave on the street side, two on the empty lot. Very convenient. Ludie could sneak in if she got home too late. I was sure it was Ludie's bedroom because I could see college pennants on the wall. I was sure there'd be a clutter of autographed pictures of movie stars, and I had a glimpse of a Kewpie doll, with tinseled cerise-pink skirts. A shadow took shape as Ludie herself moved through the room. She came to the window and I caught a flash of white arm as she pulled the shade down, then she became a shadow again, moving about. Getting ready for a date. I had to find out who with, so I stayed.

After a while a car drew up. It was Mark's flivver. He got out. I saw his yellow hair under the street light, and the smoke from his cigarette and its glowing tip. He was whistling "Smile the While." He ran in the gate and plunged up the steps and I heard him knock on the door and then go in without waiting, as though he were perfectly at home in that house.

After a short time they came out together. When they were under the light it struck me how physically they set each other off. He was so fair and she was so dark—they were biologically made for each other, and for a wild, lawless love—the amour est enfant de Bohème sort of stuff—the kind I knew nothing about, except by feeling and instinct.

He held the car door open for her. She got in, and he did, still whistling that cloying, sickening, sentimental tune, and they drove off.

A luscious half of a moon hung in the sky, lighting their way and laughing at me. It's no use describing what I felt. You've either been in that fix and know what it's like, or you haven't, and it's no use telling the sensations, because you couldn't understand. I knew I was sick and tired of my own safe, tight, dull world, and wanted to get into theirs, or rather to be with Mark, in his, with Ludie pushed off the edge of the horizon.

At that moment I knew I was sick and tired of being a virtuous virgin.

The next night, waiting for Claire, I fidgeted in a frenzy of impatience to get out of the house and down to the bluff where the excitement was gathering. I looked around the parlor. The house had been built around eighteen-forty. It was stuffed with shabby furniture and portraits and miniatures of the Ellistons. The wallpaper was faded and the curtains were darned and the floor was worn and so was the rug over it. The clock didn't keep time, and the gilt had faded off the vase on the étagère. Once a big family had lived here. They'd had lots of slaves and lots of plantations strung up and down the river. The house had been a symbol of their power and their power had been real. Now nothing was left but an echo. Aunt Emily clung to it. I didn't. What was the use of always hearing that money and power had once been in the family, if you didn't have any yourself? She says I have no feeling for tradition. She loves this house and the family. She's contented with things as they are, but then she's always been so damned placid.

You can see, even now, how pretty she must have been as a girl, though now she looks like a flower pressed in a book for a long time. She's still vain—she likes the smallness of her feet, the fragility of her health—not a thing wrong with it; everything about herself pleases her. She always admires most her own physical type, the pink-and-white Dresden figurine sort of woman, just as she admires her own virtues, particularly Contentment with Your Lot. As though any contented person ever achieved shucks.

Of course she's been awfully good to me. When I was just a little thing my mother and father were killed in a tornado when they were visiting over in Louisiana, and she's brought me up. But I baffle her. Because I was skinny and rather mousy in coloring she expected me to be delicate and docile instead of healthy as a weed and just as stubborn, and she's never been able to see why I was always wanting more than I had.

On winter evenings Grandfather used to sit here by the fire and tell long stories of rides and battles. I didn't pay much attention, I was too young, but Arland did. She remembers it all, and was able to tell it to the generation after us. Grandfather had talked with Lee and fought with Stonewall—their eyes shine, and they begin those "if onlys" so dear to Southerners, going back and rearranging and winning for themselves the lost war.

I never wanted to go back and live in the past. Restlessness and change had set in, and I welcomed them. I wanted to belong to my own time. Impatient, I glanced at the clock, then remembered it never ran. It had stopped when the Yankee gunboats had come down the river and fired on the town, and it would have nothing to do with the present. Like everything else in the room, it was set to a time long gone. Its little panniered lady with her frilled china skirts held out a glazed pink hand to the plum-coated courtier bending to kiss it, and they proceeded no further in their courtship. My great-grandmother looked down on me—a fine old lady who had produced oodles of children. There seemed no possible connection between her world and mine. I wanted to make my own, and to be an ancestress myself instead of a descendant. How we'd dwindled. Newstead was the only plantation left in the family, and we wouldn't have that if Uncle hadn't worked hard and bought it back; and the oodles of children consisted now of only a few females, Arland and myself, Claire and Edith.

A car came to the door. Here was Claire, reluctantly come for me. But it wasn't. Mark stood in the door, smiling. "You know we haven't any phone or I'd have called you. Would you come down on the bluff with me to hear Tim's famous speech?"

The room receded behind me. The glorious future stretched ahead, full of promise.

❧ Chapter Three

The familiar bluff, where bums sat on benches in the sun, where high-school children danced ineptly around the Maypole in the pageants Miss Daisy Venner was always getting up, and where everybody made speeches, seemed to me a new and exciting place that night. Crowds milled around and struggled toward the platform. Lights shone and flags waved under pale dots of stars. All Tim's family and friends and backers were there, and the ones he thought would be his friends and backers in the future. Tim looked handsome, triumphant, and beaming. It was exciting, having a future great man in the family.

On the platform, Tim looked wonderful. He had a powerful, carrying, resonant voice, a perfect sense of timing, and he never looked at his notes once. He spoke briefly of the past, referred to the war, then launched into his plans for the future if he were elected. I suppose it was the usual political speech, but he put in it his own enthusiasm. He was young, he felt in himself a surge of life, a sureness of success, and it affected his audience. When the speech was over, and he was surrounded by his supporters, and his opponents, looking few and rather wilted, sidled off, I was as certain as he was that he could win. Not only this election but all the others.

Mark led me to the car. I was quiet, thinking. The crowd would surely gather down at Arland's, but I didn't want to go. Mark would be surrounded, and Claire would try and probably succeed in getting him off in a corner. I wanted to keep him to myself.

"Want to go join the gang?" he asked.

I said I didn't. "I don't either. Had enough of Tim for one evening."

I was surprised. I had never heard anyone utter a criticism of Tim before. I glanced at Mark. Maybe he was jealous of Tim's success. Yet somehow I didn't think so. Unfortunately, Mark didn't show signs of ambition, he just seemed restless.

"How'd you like his speech, Jane?"

"I agree with him about looking forward and not back. I'm fed up with the glories of the past myself, but of course there was the usual stuff about how much he's going to do for everybody, yet reduce taxes all the same."

"It would be a relief to get up on a platform and tell the truth for a change! I'd like to run for office just to get the chance. Let 'em have it straight from the shoulder—how we're next to the most illiterate state in the union, and what a farce prohibition is, except to some poor nigger getting caught making white mule and going to jail for it while all of us who drink it get by with it. Most of the farms in this state are all washed off, just red clay and mortgages. The wartime price of cotton's not going to last. There's going to be a glut of it on the market mighty soon, and the whole underlying problem of farms and plantation just isn't going to tick economically. Besides, if we spend all Tim thinks we ought to spend to help the particular interests that have taken him under their wing, then there's no way in God's heaven to reduce taxes. You can't have it both ways." He grinned. "Of course nobody'd elect me on that platform."

"You're as bad as I am. Arland's always telling me people have no appetite for the unvarnished truth and I'm always dishing it out to them and that it's tactless."

Mark laughed. "You can dish it out to me."

Then and there I decided it wasn't any use to be coy and maidenly with him. It wouldn't work. "I will," and something in my tone made him turn and look at me. Then he said, "I guess you think like everybody else that Tim and Arland are the perfect pair."

"They're awfully happy." I ached with envy of their happiness. Of course Tim, launched on a career, would need a wife, somebody like Arland. She'd be a great help to him, and she was herself so eminently marriageable. The only child of a well-loved man, sufficiently well off, but not so rich as to frighten off independent-minded young men, and Arland herself, pretty, and admired, surrounded by an aura of beaus and good times and easy hospitality—it was all inevitable. As for me, I had no one to help me but myself, and Mark had no career, and apparently no need for a wife and helpmeet.

"You know Uncle wanted Tim to run. He says our kind of people, the ones who used to run the South, don't have any power any more. We lost our money in the Civil War, then we lost political power, and all we have is a sort of vague social prestige and we won't even have that if we don't hump ourselves."

"He's sure right about that."

"Uncle's always hustled. He's had to, with my father dead and such a slew of clinging females in the family. He's glad to see Tim humping too."

"Just because he's a Laidlaw doesn't automatically make him a fine man like your uncle, though. If he had your uncle's slant on life he'd never let himself be taken under the wing of Dasheel. Never mind, I know Tim's the perfect hero for all of you gals."

"Not the only one. You're a hero too."

"Tim's got it all over me. I can't keep it up in everyday life. Tim has all the attitudes. Too bad horses went out in this war—I can just see Tim as a perfectly swell equestrian statue." He added, "Arland's never seen any other man on earth."

"You can't blame her."

"No, I reckon it was foreordained—from the beginning."

We had been sitting in front of the old Confectionery, having a drink, mine an innocent soda, Mark's a coke and whisky from a flask. He'd asked me if I wanted some, too, and when I hesitated, he'd said, "No, I reckon you better not. Don't want to take you home tight."

Then he did take me home, and I didn't know any way to stop him. When we drew up in front of the house, in the shadow of the big catalpa tree, he said "Good night, Jane," and leaned over and kissed me. It started to be a casual kiss, but I wouldn't let it be. I clung to him and kissed him hard and long. I wanted to feel his arms around me always, and the pressure of his lips, hot and dry and rather hard, so that the shape of his mouth and the impact of his kiss would never leave me, but would be imprinted on me always. I wanted all of him.

Afterward he sat back and gave a sort of whistle.

"Kiss me again, Mark." I wished he had never let me go.

"That's enough. In the house you go." And he got out and opened the door and saw me in and left.

What could I do but wait, imprisoned in my unreal everyday existence, wait until he chose to let me see him again?

I've read descriptions in books of just kissed women. When they face themselves in the mirror afterward their eyes are like stars, their lips softly parted, and they have a new softness and Bloom. If they start out homely, like me, in chapter one, they immediately "burgeon" into beauty. If they are passable to begin with, they at once acquire a Transcendent Loveliness. I didn't. When I got upstairs, and finally did look in the mirror, rather inadvertently, and while brushing my teeth, I found straggling hair, a nose all blobby and shiny, and my lips seemed unusually pale and pinched. I looked like a female headed straight into old maidhood.

I roamed around the house restless as a hungry tiger the next few days. Aunt Em commented on the sourness of my disposition. There was not a bit of use trying to tell her what I was feeling. I longed for my own mother. Nobody thought I remembered my mother and father, but I did. Little vivid pictures, separated from the context of living. One particularly—when they were driving away from the house that spring day. My mother had leaned out of the carriage and waved her flowered parasol. They had gone to visit some friends in Louisiana and the tornado had blown the house away and killed everyone in it.

Aunt Em had certainly done the best she could for me, but it wasn't the same. My own mother had been different, more alive. I might have talked to her. As far as I knew, Aunt Em had never been in love, though one of the Twomblys had once given her a canary. She'd think an emotion having nothing to do with reason, duty, respect, or even material benefit not only preposterous but "highly improper."

Tim was elected, and the night after Arland had a party to celebrate the victory. Mark called up and asked me to go with him, and I was so happy and so nervous that evening I could hardly set the table for supper. The cloth was clean, of course, but limp with years of use and washing, tapestried with fine darns. Great-aunt Emma's wedding china had a design of pale appleblossoms; the little flowers looked as though they'd been caught and pinched by a late frost and somehow matched the cold and meager food. In my house I was going to have black, strong tea, not the weak stuff Aunt Em sipped at, and I was going to eat cake as soon as it was made, bite right in while it was still hot, instead of waiting until it was stale. If only I could get out of here and into the business of real living!

When Mark came, he didn't look or act as though he remembered how he had kissed me, but I did, and it confused me and made me nervous and unnatural.

The party, too, was different from any I'd been to before down at Arland's. There were many strange faces and people from out of town—Tim's political friends. And Mr. Dasheel, that influential person who'd thrown his support to Tim, a large man with a keen eye and hawklike nose and large bay window and the professional politician's cordial pressure of the hand to all and sundry, friend and foe.

Tim's booming laugh and eager voice dominated the house, making it his. He kissed all the girls and told us all we were beautiful, led me to Mr. Dasheel himself and told him I was his favorite little cousin, and while he was doing it you couldn't help believe him.

Claire pounced on Mark and dragged him to a cozy nook and held onto him. I couldn't take any interest in what anybody else was doing and saying, and gradually I was alone. Arland was across the room, busy with some grizzled ancient from the red hills, listening while he discoursed on his own affairs and opinions. I could imagine just what they were, without listening, but Arland would really enjoy hearing about his farm and family and what he thought and why. She can't take a bus ride without learning the life histories of everybody on the vehicle. People don't bore her or arouse in her the impatience they do in me. She would make this old red neck welcome in this house, and he would have such a good time he would be repaid for the trouble of coming, and she would learn about him and his kind, and steer Tim into handling them the right way, and that would mean votes. As she went from one group to another the rather incongruous gathering welded itself together, people blended, and the party began to move under its own steam.

Then she saw me and came over to me. She gave a glance in the pantry where the servants were passing back and forth, and Aunt Tee and her cronies were whispering and laughing and nibbling happily. "Everything seems all right. Come upstairs with me, Jane, I've got a present for you."

Her room was a confusion of tissue paper and bouquets and bright new trousseau clothes. Tim's suitcase was half open—he was going off in the morning. I wondered what it would be like to share a room with Mark. I envied Arland her happiness and Ludie her beauty and Claire her cocksure ways, but I didn't want to change places with any of them. I don't suppose anybody really wants to be anybody else all over. People cling to the essence of themselves.

Arland gave me a sachet-scented package looped with ribbons. I snatched it open. It was a camisole, pink crepe de chine, trimmed with

lace and rosebuds. I was awed. I had never had any silk underwear.
Aunt Em thought it was indecent, and didn't admire Arland's trousseau silks and chiffons. A lady had fine linen. Arland watched me,
smiling, putting perfume on the tips of her ears and patting her hair
Her hair shone dark gold in the light and her dress rustled around her,
warmly roseate, a sort of sunset cloud of a dress.

"Like it?"

I nodded, holding up the camisole. "I wish I had heaps of things
like this, the way you have. I wish I looked just like you."

She laughed. "Well, if that's all you want—you do," and she stood
beside me and there were the two of us in the long mirror. Arland
has light brown hair full of gold lights and light brown eyes, gold-lit
too, and a dark warm skin with a subsurface bloom of color. She is
taller than I am, and somewhat slighter, but we both have the same
shaped faces, with wide-spaced eyes and short upper lips. My hair and
eyes are browner though.

"But you're so pretty, and I'm not."

"Why aren't you? What's the matter with you?"

"Mousy." Why mousy should imply drabness I don't know. A
mouse, brisk of whisker, sharp and black of eyes, a creature of bristling
force, has a certain chic. I looked at my straggly hair—so fine and
soft and unmanageable, and my pale lips, and decided I had none.

Arland considered me. "You don't put yourself together just right,
Jane. Here, let me fix you." She took the falling pins out of my hair,
seized the electric curling tongs, heated them, and set to work.

"You'll miss the party."

"They'll do all right; this is fun." She thrust the hairpins in her
mouth, and her quick fingers twisted and manipulated my hair until it
looked like hers instead of mine. "That's better. Now—let's see. Jane,
I don't much like that dress, do you?"

"Loathe it."

She went to the armoire and began flinging out a heap of dresses
and brought out a blue one with gold clasps, then a satin petticoat
trimmed with lace, and a pair of satin and lace stepins.

"I can't take your trousseau things; you've never worn them."

"Probably never will, either. Don't make a fuss." I think she understood what I wanted, and how I felt about Mark, but she didn't say
anything about it. She just dressed me in her fine new clothes. Then
she rouged my cheeks lightly and painted my lips. Girls didn't make

up then or weren't supposed to. They primped, in strict privacy. Why rats and pads are less artificial than nail varnish and lipstick I can't see. Arland has a story of Aunt Tee absentmindedly running a long hatpin through a rounded and imposing rubber inflated bosom while her beau looked on, stuttering with horror. The Elliston bosoms are mostly on the scanty side. Aunt Margaret used to speak disparagingly of them. "I do hope Arland isn't going to have the Elliston bust," she would fret. Arland's is all right. Unfortunately, I have something of the Elliston scrawniness in those regions.

"There! How do you like the effect?"

In Arland's soft blue dress, with my face delicately pink and my lips discreetly blooming, I did look like her.

Later on I grew less like her, even in appearance. I took to deep, sunburned effects and short hair, somewhat touched up, and long, dark red nails, but then, at that moment, after she had finished me, all our family resemblance showed plainly.

We went down. I didn't see Mark where I'd left him, and I stepped out on the gallery to see if he was out with Claire. He was just coming up the front steps, not with her, but with some man. He saw me in the doorway. My back was to the light, and he said "Arland——"

"I'm not Arland."

"Oh, I thought you were Arland." We went in together, and he kept looking at me as though he had never really seen me before. "You looked so much alike, for a minute I mistook you for her. But I remember, she had on a pink dress." I don't think he had noticed what I had been wearing before I adorned myself in Arland's brand-new blue crepe. I had left my own dress crumpled up in a heap upstairs. I never knew what happened to it, I never put it on again, and I left my old self up there with it, just like a locust tired of its old skin and wandering off from it with a brand-new one.

Before the party was nearly over Mark asked me if I'd had enough of it. "Plenty; let's take off."

This time he asked me if I had to go right home, and I said of course not, though I knew Aunt Em would be horrified if I stayed out late. I didn't give a damn.

He drove through town, then turned his flivver out on one of the country roads. There was only one headlight, askew, flaring on the bushes and ditches, anywhere but straight ahead. The road smelled of dust and dew and tall, flowering weeds. I felt queer, tense, as though only a few minutes were being given me out of a lifetime and I had to work with them, and work fast and not make a mistake. He seemed tense, too, and for a while we rode in silence. Soon he stopped the car at a hot-dog stand on the road. It was a rough-looking shack. There were red and blue and white electric-light bulbs matted with bugs strung along under the roof, and a battered sign invited you to "Dine and Dance." The creek ran near, willows along its banks, and from it a stale weedy smell of low water at the end of summer. Inside a player piano was grinding out frazzled old tunes and a few couples were whirling around.

The worn-out jangled music and the listless shuffling of the dancers passing and repassing the windows, so that there seemed to be more people than there really were, excited me, promising me all kinds of unknown pleasures.

Mark asked me if I wanted to go in for a while, and I was about to say yes when I saw Ludie Daniels in there and said no, violently. She stood out among the others, making the rest of them seem dim. She had on a red-flowered organdie dress, girdled around the waist with a wide black sash. Her dress was low in front, showing her breasts. I longed for her beauty, her vividness of black and white and red, and her sumptuous curves. Obvious and earthy and effective. I thought I was quite capable of being just as good in the clinches as she was, but she looked it, and I didn't. She swayed her hips and clung to the man she was dancing with. Her neck was so white and her mouth so thick and moist. I wanted to go away, but Mark had ordered some cokes and was dragging a flask of whisky out of his pocket. I wondered if he had come here deliberately, expecting to find her, but he seemed intent on fixing drinks.

"I need a drink. How about you?"

He poured some in a glass and I took it and drank it. It was strong and made me choke and sputter and sent fiery prickles through my nose. "Hold on. I was going to mix it." The cokes came and he fixed me another while I was still wrassling with the first one.

"Take it easy, kid." He chuckled at my do-or-die manner.

I have never liked whisky. Aunt Em used to give me mammoth doses of castor oil in a toddy, and the association persists. To this day a faint aura of castor oil hangs around even the best whisky. But I didn't want to seem naïve.

"First drink of straight corn you've ever had, isn't it? Took it like

33

a man too. Not such bad stuff. Old nigger out in the swamp makes it. I generally get wind of it when the sheriff's nosing around on his track and let him know, and he gets time to hide it."

I was watching the window for Ludie. Mark didn't seem to be paying any attention. "You and Arland hit it off pretty well, don't you?"

"I love her better than anybody. Almost. Claire's a pig."

Just then Ludie came out with some man. She passed right by the car and looked at us and said, "Hiya, Mark?" and he answered the same way. Claire paled beside her. She was beautiful all right, but she had thick black eyes without any transparency. I hated that kind of eyes and could not refrain from saying so. I wasn't smart enough to hide what I felt. "Someday she'll spread into a lot of fat too."

Mark smiled and gave me a measuring sort of look. He said he reckoned it was mighty likely, "someday," then he added, "But that's a good way off yet."

He started the car and drove a little way, then turned into a narrow side road, hardly more than a cart track through the fields and woods. The highway was graveled, but this road wasn't. Tufts of grass grew in the middle of it, and the tracks on either side of the grass where the car followed were pale in the dark with powdery dust. It wound lazily in and out, and Mark slowed the car at an abrupt curve where it twisted sharply to the bridge over the creek. "Have to watch out for this place." The bridge itself shook and rattled under our wheels. Finally the road wandered out to the even more curving one running along the bluffs and ravines by the river.

"Some beauty lasts," he said, more to himself than to me. "Time doesn't make a bit of difference."

I couldn't keep still. "Are you crazy about her?"

"Crazy about who?"

"Ludie, of course."

"I pretty well fell for her when I was a kid in high school. But I'm not any more—I mean I'm not a kid in high school." He chuckled. "I was always hanging around her. I remember when her old man died. I'd never cottoned to him. Nasal, hard-shelled hypocritical old rascal, I always thought. He was strict with Ludie, not that it did any good. She and her mother were in cahoots. Mrs. Daniels wanted Ludie to go out and have a good time, and the two of them pulled the wool over the old man's eyes good and plenty. When I brought her home pretty late after a dance, we'd skiddle across that empty lot and I'd push and shove Ludie into the window. He never knew. One night, though, he almost caught us. It was plenty late, all the roosters were setting up a racket, and he was coming in, just as we were, after raiding some poor nigger's still. I pushed Ludie so hard she went thump on the floor and I had to get down flat into the weeds among a lot of old tin cans and stay there until he got in."

It sounded as though they'd had a wonderful time—enough secrecy and danger to make it all interesting.

"When the old man kicked off at last, I felt like I had to show up at the funeral, since I'd been dating Ludie. Hot! One of those soggy days, and that house, you know where it is, crammed with people. Flies buzzed and wiggled their feet, and everybody burst into tears all together, just like turning on a faucet. I didn't have any ready— I got caught short. Queer things, funerals. I remember when old Mr. Bailey jumped in Mrs. Bailey's grave and kept hollering, 'Bury me too—bury me too,' until the undertaker got tired and started shoveling. When the first clod hit old Bailey he leaped out. In ten days he was married again." He laughed. "And there was Cousin Ben Galway, when his wife died and was in her coffin, he was out in the kitchen, kissing her overshoe, and somebody said how touching it was, and Cousin Louise said, 'Leave him be; they ain't Annie's, they're mine, but leave him be.'"

Mark seemed to be slightly cynical on the subject of people grieving for their mates, but I was interested in the Daniels.

"What happened at old man Daniels' funeral?"

"Nothing spectacular. Only Brother somebody from out of the tall timbers kept orating. Sure thought up a slew of virtues too. I'd have liked the chance to speak up about a few little items in the old man's career. But it was hardly the time or place."

"I bet Miss Ludie wasn't too grief-stricken," I said. "I gather she's managed to have herself a high time lately."

What could Mark be thinking of, hobnobbing with those people? But I knew that wouldn't stand in his way if he were still in love with Ludie. He didn't have any sense of class, any feeling at all for social values. He "ganged his ain gait," unhampered by the conventions. He wouldn't let the fact that Ludie didn't belong stand in his way if he wanted to marry her. I didn't think even her bad reputation

35

would stop him, if he wanted her enough. I had to know how he did feel right now. I asked, "Why did you get in that fight?"

"Me? Fight? At a funeral?"

"I don't mean at the funeral. That fight on the boat. I heard you were mixed up in one."

"Oh, that little dust-up with Clem. He had it coming to him."

"Why?"

"He was being damned indiscreet about something that was no business of his, and I wanted him to keep his mouth shut. Which same he'd better."

"Tell me about it."

"No. I don't want it broadcast."

"Everybody knows about the fight."

"Let 'em."

"I wish you'd tell me. I won't say anything."

"You won't, because you won't know anything." And he wouldn't say another word.

"She's no good—you know that perfectly well, Mark Lennerd!"

He only laughed. I persisted. "But she isn't. Now is she?"

"What do you expect me to say? I'm bound to declare the lady is as the driven snow. Isn't that the line? I'm bound to swear that the relations of my aunt Kate with Mr. Charlie Selwyn are pure and platonic, and have been, lo, these last forty years. I can't burst out and impugn the honor of any of these fair flowers of Southern Womanhood, can I?"

"The word's impunge."

"Lord, no, impugn. I bet it is. Never used it before. Just seen it written. Funny word, anyhow."

We were driving along the narrow rough road where the ravines cave in close, slippery, unreliable land. "This place kind of gets me." Mark's voice was low. I understood what he meant. You could feel something dangerous and wild beating through the heat and softness of the deep night. It disturbed me, gave me a challenge—I would have liked to keep the ravines from caving and straighten the road and plow and plant the hills, bring it all under control and order, and I sensed he didn't. He liked the unstable, untenable mocking something, defying any taming.

He said, "Right here, on this spot, seems to me the very depth and essence of the South itself." It was a primitive place, the deep gulches choking themselves with vines and briers and all kinds of growth, and the trees so big and tall, throwing wide black shadows, and beyond and below, the Mississippi. The tree-lined hollow to our right framed a glimpse of the river, and the water was lightened by a sheen from the sky. In an open field on the other side of the road fireflies clung to long stalks of grass.

After a while we came to a grassy hill, smoothly sloping, pointed with pines. It was protected from caving by a long tongue of flat land below, Wishmore Plantation, where Mark lived. But on the hill stood Rosemont. We passed by the gate, wrought iron, with stone pillars on each side. Shrubs and bushes and vines tangled together hid the outlines of the fence. Live oaks hid the house. No lights showed through; it was all black. In Miss Kate's hands Rosemont hid its splendors. They were almost legendary now, it had been so long since anyone but Mr. Charlie had been welcome here.

"I want that house," I said. "Think of it being shut up and going to pieces."

"What on earth do you want it for?"

"Oh, I'd do over the furniture and fix the gardens the way they used to be, and fill it with lights and people, and lots of food and wine, and give parties every night!" And to myself I said, "I want it for you and me, to live in and be happy in and have lots of children playing and yelling and then growing up and filling it with grandchildren. Then you and I can lie side by side in the little cemetery on the hill and never be away from each other—not ever."

"Somehow, down here, you can't ever feel you own anything. The river creeps up over the land, or undermines it and cuts it away, the cotton gets eaten up or rained on or burned out. You whack at the trees and weeds, and clear up some land, and the first thing you know the trees and the weeds come sidling back. I guess that's what I like. I don't want to own things, or be owned. What's the use of being bogged down by a lot of possessions?"

"Rosemont's safe from the river, and I'd keep chopping and pruning on the growth. Anyway, I want it." I wanted it for us—for the wonderful life we could have. We could make love in those big four-poster beds, and get up and wander down the garden paths . . .

"Try and get it," Mark said. He offered me a challenge. "Try and get it" is what he said, but he seemed to be saying "Try to get me—try to make me what you want."

"I mean to. Someday. When Miss Kate dies, and I'm rich." More than anything, more than riches or Rosemont, I wanted him. I was going to try to get him. Now. Not in some distant future, but now.

He stopped the car. "How're you going to wangle all that?"

"I don't know, but it's no fun to want what's easy." He wasn't easy; he was damned difficult. If I could get him, for myself alone, and for always, I would be sure of myself forever.

"I guess it isn't. But what about wanting and wanting and not getting? How'd you like that?"

"Not a bit. But I believe you get it, if you're sure. Dead sure of what it is, and hang on."

"Want to bet on it?"

"All right. I bet twenty years from now—make it twenty-five—we both get what we want most if we don't ever give up."

"What'll we do? Totter to this spot twenty-five years from now, to Aunt Kate's gate, and give an account of ourselves?"

I smiled at my own vision of Mark and myself walking arm in arm to the gate, and my reminding him of this moment, then he'd smile and kiss me, and we'd agree we'd both had what we wanted most. I knew I was thinking in terms of a romantic story, and Mark, at twenty-three, hard, sure of himself, experienced, wasn't made of the malleable material that fashioned the usual hero.

But he was smiling at me, and when I looked up at him he put his arms around me. He hesitated, then he kissed me, but I knew this time kisses weren't enough. Then he pushed me gently to my side of the car. "You do mighty well for such a nice little girl."

"I've done a lot of practicing—in my imagination."

"Also you have a natural aptitude."

"I wanted to kiss you."

"Look here, Jane, there's been a lot of romance fluttering through the air lately, making you woozy. But I guess we'd better remember you're just a kid and don't mean a thing."

"I'm no child. I'm nearly eighteen. I do mean it."

"Like this." His voice was rough, and his arms suddenly around me, holding me tight, were hard. I couldn't have broken away if I had tried, but I didn't try. I couldn't see his face, but I put my hand on his cheek, and his skin was hot to the touch, as though he had fever. He did want me, he could be wild and violent, and I wanted his wildness and violence for myself alone. He kissed me in an unrestrained, ardent, passionate way this time. Not a kiss for a child. Maybe not even for a lady, I thought, giving myself up to it with an entire lack of inhibition.

Then he detached himself from my arms, and sat back and lit a cigarette. The flare of the match showed me his face, suddenly glowing out of the dark, cut out from everything else. I knew I'd never feel for anyone else what I was feeling for him. I was right. I never have.

"You know, Jane, I'm not the kind for any girl to get serious over."

"Why not?"

"You know I haven't a thing to offer a girl. A man ought to be able to make a living, and provide a home—all that kind of thing. The sort of setup Tim and Arland have. A career in the offing——"

"Marriage doesn't mean only a lot of monograms stuck on tablecloths and towels and a dozen pieces of flat silver in everything, including salad forks and butter spreaders. Does it?"

"I don't reckon so, if you boil it down. But a lot of women seem to think so. Have you given any thought to the subject? What does it mean to you?"

"Love."

He gave me a long look, his eyes narrowing a little. The tip of the cigarette he was smoking glowed, faded a little, glowed again.

"I guess I don't know much about that."

"Haven't you ever been in love?"

"Not what you would call the real thing."

"Not with Ludie?"

"I was pretty crazy about her at one time," he admitted.

"How about now?"

He laughed. "Hell, no."

I wanted to believe him, so I did, though I didn't know if he were telling me a lie or not. "You were with her the other night," I blurted out. I felt at once it was an error in tactics, but it was said now. I added, "You passed right by me."

"Had a little matter I wanted to talk over with her." But he wouldn't tell me what it was; when I kept on questioning him he said: "Not any concern of yours, sugar."

I wondered what he really did feel about her, if he'd outgrown her, or had come home and been disillusioned somehow. I didn't think he'd have been given to any great illusions about her in the first place.

Maybe he was still crazy about her, and wouldn't admit it, feeling all the pull of a blind fascination, such as I felt for him. I knew it made no difference what he was, or what he'd done, or how worthless he might be. But it was no use in questioning him. Anyway, if he felt it, it was no use in my knowing it, since I intended to have him if I could.

"Was there anybody in France?"

"Unhumph. Attractive girl too." He was laughing at my jealous curiosity.

"Oh, so you had an affair over there."

"You never knew whether there'd be a next time—you lived from day to day, sort of."

"Why didn't you marry her?"

"She happened to have a husband, for one thing. Besides, can you imagine bringing her back to Wishmore?"

"Maybe a vraie Parisienne wouldn't think much of it, but what's the matter with it? Richest land around here."

"Have you ever seen it?"

"I've never been in the house."

"Want to come take a look at it? I can offer you some cognac."

I said I'd go, and he started the car. "Uncle Jeff was O.K. when I left. Don't suppose he's gotten in his cups since. Don't believe he has any money to buy any."

We went down the hill, down the bumpy ungraveled road to the flat land below, then over a track hardly more than a widening between the cotton rows, and up to the house. It was backed against the slope, as if it were trying to withdraw from the Mississippi as far as it possibly could. It faced the fields and the river, a low, dim, wandering outline of a house with hot murky lamplight coming from one window and all the rest dark.

I knew Mr. Jeff. Everybody knew his wanderings down Main Street, where, when drunk, he harangued all bystanders on all subjects under the sun, including free silver, seemingly unaware it was a dead duck, to people's religious duties—all this on the way to the fire-engine house where he sat by the hour. If his speeches grew too belligerent and his gestures too violent, somebody gently steered him to the jail, where he felt quite at home. When he sobered up, he made his way back to Wishmore, or went on to the fire-engine house, where he had originally intended to go, and he would be completely unaware that maybe a day or two had elapsed between the time he set out and the time he reached his bourne. He had practically nothing to do with the people in his own walk of life, but spent most of his social life with the fishermen on the riverbank and the drifting folks who sometimes moored their boats on the curve of Wishmore Point. Or else he betook himself to Mistletoe Grove and holed in with Jerry Ladd until whatever moonshine they had acquired by their combined efforts was finished.

Tonight he was on the gallery, smoking and listening to the frogs croak. In an amiable frame of mind, he asked after Uncle and Aunt Em and even had some inkling there had been a wedding in the family. He was like a lot of people in our town. They lived shut away in moldy old houses and got queerer and queerer—the characters of Natchez developed their individualities long before a lot of books came out telling you you ought to—but a certain mellowness and flavor clung to them like an afterglow. When you were with them, it was hard to believe in all the family quarrels and interminable lawsuits and exotic scandals you heard so much about.

Mark whispered to me, "Let's go in and get ourselves that drink."

He lit another lamp and led me through the hall to the dining room. I noticed the cracks in the plaster and the holes in the screens, and the cat asleep on the table, and all the dogs, sprawled everywhere and rising up with too much enthusiasm at our coming. But by lamplight and because of the mood I was in, I was only dimly aware of the house itself. It almost pleased me in its careless shabbiness. It looked as though everybody just did as he pleased and never bothered about anything. It was free of all the conventions and rules of housekeeping and living drilled into me. People used to laugh about Mr. Jeff's bed. It was too tall for his room in the ell, so he just bored holes in the ceiling and let the four posts just rare on up into the attic. Down here it seemed a perfectly natural way to deal with it.

"Do you think you ought to keep anything to drink down here, on account of Mr. Jeff?" I asked Mark.

"You don't keep it long on account of him, unless you hide it mighty well. Otherwise, it doesn't matter. Aunt Martha tried that tack of never mentioning drink or having it around. It didn't work at all. Nothing does. Nothing will. She finally couldn't put up with it any more, and cleared out. Couldn't blame her."

He got out the bottle, shooed the cat from the sideboard where it had jumped, and seized two murky glasses. He was about to pour the cognac when I snatched them away from him. "Let's wash them." He seemed a little surprised, but I whisked them off to the bare and dismal kitchen. Whenever I hear people talk about old-fashioned Southern kitchens I always think of the one at Wishmore, where Hettie, the cook, and Tillie, the washwoman, were left to their own sweet devices. It was a monotone of drab blotched gray, mold filmed, filmed, too, with splotches and spots. There was a clutter of aged brooms and mops and rags and pails and a few twisted tin things on the worn tables.

I found a thin wedge of soap and scoured the glasses. There didn't seem to be any hot water. Later, I found out there wasn't. If you wanted any, you made up a fire in the stove and heated it in a kettle.

I brought the glasses back to the dining room and Mark poured the drinks. "Watch it, Jane. Sip it. It's strong. Don't want you high on my hands. Think of your aunt Em's reaction."

But I'd forgotten Aunt Em's existence. This was another world from hers, one she didn't know. Mark sat down near me and lit a cigarette and held it between his straightened fingers. The lamplight flung the shadow of his lashes on his eyelids. The scar from his temple down his neck shone leaden in the duskiness of his skin. It marred him, and kept him from looking really young any more. His body and his nerves would always hold the memory of danger and pain, but it gave him a sort of distinction, setting him away from those who did not know. I asked him why he had volunteered.

"Oh, I don't know exactly. Lot of different reasons. There didn't seem much point in sitting safe on your hunkers and letting other people do the work for you."

I said it made a lot of sense to me. I loathed war. The war Southerners were always harping on had meant nothing but loss to us. I didn't see any sense in sentimentalizing it and its glories. As to the Germans, I loathed them and always would for setting the whole world upside down. Of course I didn't know a lot about history and nothing about economics, but why did a nation have to expand and have cotton and coal and things? It would be a lot cheaper to buy their cotton from us. God knows we were always wild to sell it.

"I took to flying anyhow," Mark said. "I had a notion to keep on with it. I wish I had now, but fliers out of the Army are a dime a dozen these days. Sometimes I'd like to try it again."

42

I said I didn't see why, when he had a piece of land to work at.

He talked about some friend of his, and showed me some snap-shots of a group of fliers taken together beside their planes. I asked what became of this boy. "Went down behind the enemy lines. On fire." I never wanted to hear about him again. I wondered how Mark felt. He didn't say. I wondered if the good times he and this boy'd had together, and then, ending, haunted him, invaded his sleep.

But it brought back the memory of the spring of nineteen eighteen, when the Germans seemed to have a chance to win after all, after all the losses and all the battles. The newsboys kept calling out extras. I would go out to the gate and listen and watch, and I had the feeling I was plunging down into deep, deep water and couldn't get back out again. I had almost forgotten, now I remembered. Mark had heard the guns roar and had looked down on the smoke and confusion, had seen the planes beside him fall, had watched the enemy zooming out at him. He had been there in it.

"I hardly knew you before you went away, but the war must have changed you a lot, Mark." It had changed even me, sitting safely at home—shattering a pattern, so that the edges never fitted back together again. He looked completely healthy. His eyes, gray, without a tinge of blue, were brilliant with life, the whites clear. His hair and lashes grew thick, and his skin was taut and unlined, the deep smooth brown of natural well-being and constant sunlight. He moved quickly, with a neat precision and economy. His perfect co-ordination was one of the things about him that pleased me most—I hated a fumbling ineptness and awkwardness. But sometimes he'd pace around a room as though he longed to escape, as if something was driving him to get clear of all confining walls, and I noticed how at times the muscle twitched near the scar. The ruling and controlling nerves themselves kept an eternal echo of past suffering.

"You find out what you're made of, I guess. Before, you wonder, then you know. You know whether you can make the grade or not. But afterward the place where you'd been seems to have closed up behind you, and the nook you expected to fit into isn't there any more. Or maybe the place is there, and it's you who's out of kilter and can't somehow find your way back in it with any comfort."

"I get sort of scared when I look at all the misfits around here. I've made up my mind I'm not going to be one of them." I sighed.

"Around here there are too many pottering old ladies who've never done anything and never could do anything useful who just sit around. They never hustle. Even if they are half starving they don't. They just nibble on crusts and go on being ladies, and having a very thin time. Look at Aunt Em——"

"What's wrong with her?"

"Nothing. Except she doesn't have any real life at all. I'd rather plunge into things and get into snarls and unravel them some which way——"

He smiled. "I guess you're right. Like a hand at cards. If you consistently overbid you're apt to do better than if you always underbid."

"Maybe your trouble is you've already lived too hard, crowded in too much in too short a space of time. Like somebody who's eaten so much spice and pepper in their food, plain bread and butter has no taste any more."

"Anybody worth their salt ought to be able to adjust. It's just that I don't have much appetite for sitting down here and planting and plowing Wishmore, and yet at the moment I don't exactly know what else to do."

He frightened me. I was so afraid he would pick himself up and go away from here. "It's a wonder with all that happened you ever did come back."

"Law of averages. Some are bound to come back. Anyhow, if I hadn't, you'd never have missed me."

"Yes, I would too." There would have been an empty place in my heart, a restless searching all of my life. I might not have known what was the matter, who I was looking for, but I would have wanted him all the same. "Lots of women have lost their husbands and lovers and sons. And lots of women have lost the men they could have loved and should have loved. Once I asked old Miss Fanny Ames why she had never married, and she said she'd never met him, he must have been killed at Shiloh or Vicksburg. And that's true, never think it isn't. The ones they never knew—they never yet loved. But that unused and useless love just kept waiting and waiting." It was sad and dangerous, that mass frustration running through generation after generation sacrificed by wars. I felt sorry for them, all those women, and exultant over them, because Mark had come back. He had come back for me, and to me.

He was listening, and looking straight at me. A flush rose to his

44

face, and his mouth quivered and changed. He had always seemed hard, remote from me, but now, deep in my own feeling, I realized how much he could feel too. I knew I had at last managed to pierce through his remoteness, down into his spirit. He was aware of me, as a person, an individual, and I knew I was right to stake everything on him.

In the pupils of his eyes I saw my own tiny reflection as though I were a part of him. Then he turned away from the light and his pupils expanded until all his eyes looked dark, and my picture wasn't there any more, only darkness. The moment was over. He had gone away from me again.

He said come along, it was late, and high time he was getting me home. I wanted to stay, but I got up and went out. Mr. Jeff had left the gallery. We had the night to ourselves, the sleeping fields and the cabins and the silent river around the curve lapping against the land, building it up here, nibbling it away there.

We drove back up the hill and passed Rosemont. At the top of the next slope, among the pines, the light of a little church shone out. The warm lamps sent a glow through the branches. The congregation were singing. Mark stopped the car and asked me did I want to get out and listen, and I said I did. He held my hand as we climbed the hill. We went around to the back of the church and sat down under the trees, facing the river. In the church the deep voices rose and fell, and the drums thudded. The darkness, the singing, and the solemn black of the pines gave the church an importance it didn't have in the daytime, when it was closed and empty.

"The brethren and sistren are coming through good and plenty," Mark said. "In there, they're to themselves, not bothered with their problems and not bothered with white people for a while."

The congregation had begun to sway back and forth and stamp their feet to the thud of the drum. We looked back and could see their shadows pitching and tossing against the walls. Their voices, some high, some low, blended together, and they were unaware of us.

Where we sat, the dark was unbroken. The ground was hard and warm, sleek and scented with pine needles. Even so late, the air was hot, but not burning any more. Beyond the trees, over the river, a river of stars was flowing. Toward the south the big constellations of winter were beginning to rise. In the midst of summer they told of change. I was happy, I clung to the moment, I didn't want time to move on, but I knew it would move on and that I must make the most of now. I knew I was happy, and to this day I remember and savor how happy I was.

"It all belongs to us," I whispered. "The hill and the singing and the river and the sky."

Mark picked up a handful of pine needles and let them fall one by one through my hair. "I like to be on the outside, off to myself."

I was solitary, but from necessity. I liked the pack, and wanted to lead it. I would have liked to be part of a group, the bigger the better, and have everybody looking up to me. But Mark didn't want to be in it, or have any part in its activities. Nor did he seem to need the security, the sense of being one with many lives.

He put his arm around me and drew my head down on his shoulder. His face, above mine, looked dark. He leaned down and kissed me, with the intensity and technique of a man who knows how to kiss. I couldn't help thinking of how much practice he'd had—Ludie, that woman in France, others too. They didn't matter now, but they had had more of him than I'd had, and kisses were no longer enough. I was learning too. I held my hands around the back of his neck, and I wanted him to hold me a long, long time and never let me go. When he did, I leaned back in his arms so he had to keep on holding me.

"Why do you stop?"

He laughed a little. "Don't you think we'd better?"

"Why should we?"

"You know why—we're hanging on the brink of being pretty damned reckless."

"Well, let's."

"Let's what?"

"Be reckless."

"No, you're too young. You don't know what it's all about."

"I can learn, can't I?"

"Look here, Jane——"

"Mark, I don't care—I'm past caring. Don't you want me?"

"You know damn well I do!" he muttered.

"Well, then——" I detached myself from his arms, and found myself lying on the ground, feeling the sleekness of the layer of pine needles and breathing in their scent. My hair fell away from its confining hairpins and spread around my head. I don't know why it gives a sense of abandon to have your hair fall down, but it does. Maybe there was something to all the moralists' objections to short hair— maybe to have your hair always hanging loose does encourage moral lapses. Anyway, all I know is that whatever vestiges of prudence or caution I had slipped away with my hairpins. I didn't care what happened afterward, now was all that mattered. His arms were around me, his lips and his body against mine, and I knew I had been made to belong to him.

A star had come up and was climbing out of the southeast. Afterward, with him lying there beside me, with his arms still around me, I noticed it. It was so bright it was reflected in a small pond, the pond cupped in a hollow of the slope beyond our hill. The water, not wide, not deep, held for a while the shine of a big sun whirling somewhere on the edge of the universe. Like my heart, holding for a while joy like fire from beyond the outer rim of the world.

⋖§ Chapter Four

According to everything I'd been taught, after having flung my bonnet over the windmill, I should have wept bitter tears into my pillow. I didn't. I crept in yawning, and fell asleep at once, beautifully and dreamlessly. The sun shining bright in my face at last woke me up. I didn't feel any different from yesterday, except better pleased with myself, and I must not have looked very different because Aunt Em didn't notice anything. She kept asking me about the party at Arland's and I kept giving her vague answers as I wandered around her room.

Mrs. Lews was taking her to town and she was dressing, giving me instructions about the quince preserves bubbling on the stove. Her bureau drawer was open. There was a pile of neat handkerchiefs in one corner and a flowered box with compartments for hairpins and those little kid curlers that look like the flowers that fall from oak trees in spring. A painted china box held the combings of her hair, which she made into discreet rats. "My own hair," she always explained. "Of course I wouldn't use false hair." She was getting her good gloves back in the box with the faded silk lining. I picked up a small paper fan and flipped it back and forth, absent-minded.

"Be careful, Jane." Her voice was muffled by the limp folds of a dark blue-and-white voile house dress she was taking off, revealing a heavily starched petticoat and corset cover. "Miss Simmons gave it to me when I was a little girl."

I put it down. She had been a careful, good little girl. She was a good woman, making the best of what she had. I had a wicked impulse to say to her, "It's too late to be careful. I've been out beyond the boundaries and it's wonderful." It would have been fun, just to see her reaction. Of course I didn't say a word. I've never set myself up as a rebel against society. A façade of invulnerable respectability often allows more leeway. If I want something beyond the limits of the established code, I just make a little sortie and retire again, un-suspected.

Aunt Em never dreamed that last night I had parted with my vir-tue, and we continued to discuss the quince preserves until she left.

I went out in the kitchen, and while the quinces bubbled in their iron pot and I poured boiling water into the jars, I meditated. I was already restless, wanting to see Mark again. And suppose he never showed up! The only thing that worried me was that I had always been led to suppose a female too ready to give all loses her desirability.

It seemed to me being a girl in a small Southern town was a very thankless business. The joys and delights of being an American girl, that free and pampered creature, were supposed to be supreme, but the actual being of it wasn't always so easy. Maybe if you were beau-tiful and rich and lived where there were plenty of men . . . But right here it was a pretty hard job. There hadn't been enough men in this town since sixty-one, and there were always lots of pretty girls who were always in competition with each other. Because of co-education and public dances I not only had to compete with girls like Claire, but with Ludie. If a girl could hold her own here, she could reign in any court in Europe and a Turkish harem besides. Maybe it was a good idea, if you wanted to marry off a daughter, to offer a herd of cattle with her.

There'd been no cattle to go with Miss Fanny Ames and Aunt Em and Aunt Ada and all the other old maids, and nobody had fended for them. There'd be nobody to fend for me, either, so I had launched out for myself.

A shadow fell across the patch of sunlight in the kitchen door. I looked up and saw Mark. "I rang the bell, but nobody answered. Where's Miss Em?"

I wiped my hands and put down the kettle of hot water. "Out."

"Good. Jane, I want to talk to you."

"Let's go out on the gallery; it's too hot in here." We went out on the back gallery. Albertha was out in the yard, hanging up the clothes. A breeze rustled in the Madeira vine, and a mockingbird who'd made a rather disheveled-looking nest in it came and scolded us. Mark leaned against the railing, smoking. I took one look at him and knew I'd been a thoroughgoing goose. He didn't think any the less of me, or want me less. He was here, and I was happy.

"Jane, I've been thinking. And I don't like this setup."

"I was hoping you'd say come with me tonight on the hill. It's going to be a beautiful night." I went over to him and kissed him slowly and deliberately. "I still feel reckless."

He laughed. "You have the courage of your convictions, don't you?" Then he took his arm from around me and began to pace around the gallery. "It won't do, sugar. You're too young, and your family and all—— No, if we want to keep on, we'd better go ahead and get married."

His voice seemed to come from a long way off. He added, "You've seen Wishmore. God knows it isn't a hell of a lot to offer. It's falling down around our ears, and there's a mortgage. You'd have Uncle Jeff on your hands—there isn't anywhere else for him to go."

He was trying to be honest and to show me things as they were, but I couldn't see anything real at all. He might as well have been talking about some place in a dream. The problems he was presenting were real enough, but he was the only thing real to me then, and Wishmore and all its drawbacks was an earthly paradise because it was his.

"You'd better think things out before you make up your mind," he said.

"I'm past thinking. And it's made up. I'll make you a very good wife." Just then I finally became aware of a fearful smell of burning and scorching. I came to, and rushed into the kitchen. The quince preserves were a gummy, sticky black mess, past retrieving. It was not a shining example of wifeliness. I didn't care, and Mark didn't notice. He soon took himself off. I was glad he did before Aunt Em came back; somehow I preferred to prepare the way before they encountered each other.

Albertha made a great to-do over the ruined preserves, and when Aunt Em came back and sniffed the air she wondered what in the world I'd been thinking of to let it happen. It would never have done to have told her the current and direction of my thoughts. After all, no lady was supposed ever to cogitate along those lines.

After a while, though, I did break the news and tell her I was going to marry Mark. Her pretty, faded face fell into separate pieces. She was astounded and unhappy and, when she got her breath, made all the objections she could think of. The Lennerds were a queer family, and I was too young; she kept repeating, "Mark Lennerd—of all people! I thought you were just seeing something of him on account of Arland's wedding. I never dreamed——" She seemed to think I must always stand on the outskirts of somebody else's big moments and never be plop in the middle of my own. Among all her objections she never brought up the one about his being so poor. We were accustomed to being poor, and took it for granted.

A long time afterward I said to Arland, "Aunt Em never had anything against Mark, yet she disapproved as violently as she could."

"Oh yes, she has something against him, but she doesn't know what it is—it's so intangible. The same thing that draws you to him, Jane. The essence of his nature is strange to her and repels her. He makes her uneasy and wary and inspires the sort of fear she'd feel if she met a wild animal sidling down the path in the back yard. When you ask her to welcome him, you might as well ask her to call to a wildcat and ask it to come sit by the fire instead of her own ancient brindled tom."

When we were first married I was happy. Kitty and her friends assume as a matter of course I brought to marriage an appalling ignorance of the facts of life. I would have, too, had Mark and I not cavorted first on the hill above Wishmore. Sometimes Arland and I are rather appalled by some of the things Kitty and the girls she knows discuss so openly. Nobody taught us anything, and our extremely limited knowledge came mostly from books in the library. I used to gulp some of the more interesting portions of *The Decline and Fall of the Roman Empire*. "Theodora unblushingly indulged in all the natural and unnatural vices. Over some of her excesses we must draw the veil of an ancient language." Then lots of footnotes in Greek at the bottom of the pages. Very provoking, when I was dying to know about the Unnatural Vices.

Kitty knows. It's the convention of her day to know. She's read books on abnormal psychology, and books on birth control, and books on the Technique of Love-making. "Of course, Mother, when you were young——" she says in a superior manner. I think she believes that if I had approached marriage armed with enough blueprints, everything would have been easy. I've never been able to learn to dance or play the violin by a series of ten easy printed lessons, and I don't believe I'd have learned about being married that way either. I often wonder if her generation are really wiser and more capable of handling their lives than we were. What used to be called Original Sin and is now Self-Expression had its fling before the twentieth century; just look at Theodora. It seems to me charts are pretty flat; it takes life and experience and a capacity for feeling, and maybe certain chemical combinations to give them color and dimension. Then, of course, Kitty knows nothing about that night on the hill long, long before she was ever thought of. To her, I am a pillar of respectability. Kitty, in spite of her education and technical knowledge, never felt like that; she's not made the way I am in certain respects. She is not violent and passionate, and unless you are, the blueprints can't really tell you about it.

I'm sure Mark never read a book on technique in his life, but he knew how to make love. Too well for my peace of mind. There is one phrase in Kit's psychology book which sounds very sensible: "You learn by doing." And he had. With Ludie, and with that girl in France, and maybe others. I was jealous, always jealous, but certainly the physical part of our marriage was wonderful. We were both young and healthy and normal.

In spite of all I'd heard about its not only being wicked for a woman to show any desire, but bad policy as well, I realized my frank ardor had drawn him to me as nothing else would have. The usual game of coyness, bafflement, and flirtatiousness would have affected him not at all, because he was not that vague lay figure, "a man," we had been told about, but Mark. An individual. My lack of all caution and prudence, my recklessness, had made him not only want me but admire me. I had walked out of my sort of world into his, where we could meet. I showed him I, too, could ignore rules he innately despised.

Arland has her own code of behavior. It is set well within the outer moat and bailey of the usual conventions, a little inner tower where she abides. If the outer fortress were besieged and knocked down, she would still defend her own little citadel. Mark has a code, too, but it is well outside all regular boundaries, like someone hewing logs from a vast forest and setting up an isolated outpost for himself. I don't have any code at all. I just want what I want.

When I think of what I felt when I heard Mark's voice outside, talking to his dogs, then heard the door open, but not close—he never closed a door behind him—and saw his shadow along the wall, and felt his hand on my shoulder . . .

It was a chilly, windy night when we came back to Wishmore. The car light shone sketchily on empty fields and dried rattling cornstalks, on the shorter brown claws of dead cotton plants spindly in the furrows. Here and there was the dot of a tightly shut cabin. Everywhere, beyond the narrow range of light, the enormous dark stretched out, on to the river itself, not only dark but deep. You felt you could stumble on in the dark and step off into the river without knowing it until you sank in the icy black water, and it would clutch you and carry you away, out of daylight, out of life forever, until you were only a piece of drift spinning in the Gulf.

Nobody welcomed us, just the dogs. Only one lamp burned, and the wind danced to itself down the long hall. But Mark built up a big log fire. I found a skillet and some eggs and bacon. We pulled up a rickety table to the blaze and ate, and drank a bottle of champagne. Some of the logs had come down the river, and the water had lapped them against Wishmore Point and left them there. They burned bright, with a quiver of violet in their upward surge. Wood from unfamiliar trees, come from another landscape. This was our own world, shut away from the rest of creation, complete in itself, and fresh and new. At least I thought so.

Afterward we stayed awake, laughing and whispering.

"I've just thought of something. Arland's clothes."

"What are you talking about—Arland's clothes?" Mark reached for a cigarette. I explained how I hadn't liked mine that night at her house, and that she had dressed me in hers. "All brand-new. From the skin out. They were part of her trousseau. And suppose she wants them back?"

"Oh, lord." Then he laughed. "But they were intended for nuptial garments, and so they were."

When I fell asleep my head was on his arm, my face close to his. I woke up before day. The fire had gone out, except for one driftwood log, still smoldering. Every now and then a thin, sighing, bluish flame rose from it, and I could see the scar going down into Mark's neck and the puckered skin where it ended, and his closed eyes, with the thick, short, upcurling lashes, like a child's, and the cut and curve of his lips. He was frowning, as if he was fighting his way through the tangles of some troublesome dream. He tossed away from me and muttered some words I couldn't catch. He was cut off from me. The house strained and creaked like a ship at sea. Shutters flapped. Rats rioted and held revel through the walls. Outside some animal gave a shriek, then was still. I felt lost and alone and depressed.

When I woke again it was full daylight. In the strong daylight the room showed itself. Mark had gone. There were dirty dishes on the rickety-legged table, cigarette stubs on the hearth. There were no curtains, and the windowpanes, some cracked, were all smeary. Tillie ambled in with coffee so strong the spoon could stand up in it, in a thick cracked cup and a saucer with a chip out of it and having absolutely no relation to the cup. Tillie wore lots of strings and brass rings around her neck, to ward off "de misery." I found out she never took them off. If she did, it would kill her. She had cut holes in her shoes to free her knobby old toes, and she wore a tall cone of newspaper on her head, shaped like a medieval hennin.

It suddenly dawned on me how much I had undertaken, coming down here to live. The house, the place—Miss Martha had not been able to stand it. My life before, if dull, had at least been simple, and this wouldn't be. I didn't really know much about housekeeping and nothing about plantations except what I'd absorbed from listening to other people talk about them. I'd just have to learn.

When Mark came in to dinner the whole place was in an uproar. I'd rooted some of the likeliest-looking hands out of their cabins and set them to scrubbing and scouring and burning accumulated heaps of trash. I had rummaged in cupboards and dragged down and dusted heaps and heaps of old books.

"What's all the bumping and humping?" Mark asked. "Looks like a tornado turned loose in here." He'd been out shooting birds. His dark skin was reddened by sun and wind, and I thought how nice he looked in his boots and old leather jacket. I looked far from the ideal bride. You know how they look in the ads—dazzlingly arrayed and smiling, gently propelling some smoothly running gadget and holding out a soft white hand for the groom to fondle fondly. My hair was straggling, my face was dirty, my hands were all gritty and drawn from the harsh powders I'd been using, and I'd made a cone of newspaper for my head, like Tillie's.

"General overhauling. It needs it. I don't suppose anybody's really cleaned it up since your aunt Martha took herself off. What will people say when they come to see us and find themselves in such an old pigpen?"

"I reckon they'll say you drove your ducks to a damned poor market." He added, "Uncle Jeff—and this place—got Aunt Martha. She stood it as long as she could, then lit out."

"I won't let it get me. Or Mr. Jeff either. You just watch. I've got him to work making a fence. He's sober today, and when he's sober he seems pretty handy. I want a garden. Look how bare it is in front here. Just hideous. And no excuse for it. I suppose we'll have to have chickens. But not so near the house. And the ones you've got are awfully stringy. We better get a good breed. Those black, doleful things look like they'd mated with buzzards. Uncle gave me a good fat check, so I'm going to do some painting and things like that."

"It's yours. Do what you want with it."

Uncle hadn't approved of my getting married so young. He told me he would be glad to send me to college. "Then, if you still want to marry Mark——" He thought it a sensible idea, having no idea what I really felt. At the moment nothing seemed more useless to me than the thought of getting an education. I told him it wouldn't be fair to take all that—he'd supported dependent females for so long —and then come back and get married.

Uncle had smiled. "You're in love and don't want to wait. Well, go ahead, child. I know when it's no use arguing."

I had no idea of leaving Mark—not for a minute, much less four long years. Leave him—— Then what would happen? Uncle was a successful man, but he had already done a lot for me and Aunt Em since my own father's death, and it was true I was tired of being a perfectly useless she-relative. I wanted my own life with Mark, and I was determined to make something out of it.

I dragged Mark through the house and outside, showing him all the things I wanted to change and improve. "Take it easy; don't bite off more than you can chew," he warned, but he was smiling. We stood looking at the house, dim in the sunshine. It had been haphazardly altered from time to time, but it still looked like what it had originally been intended to be—a pioneer's first settlement in a new country, the wild, rich wastes waiting for the right hand.

The Lennerds had built it when they had first come to this part of the world, armed with determination and a large land grant. They had made money—why not, who couldn't?—down here in those ample days. Then they had climbed to the top of the hill and built Rosemont, and set out the formal gardens around it on the pine-covered slopes. They had gone to Europe with scads of servants and children and brought back shiploads of carved furniture and large oil paintings and statues and mirrors and knickknacks. Their glory really hadn't lasted long, but it had shone with a great glare while it had. And it could be lasting yet. They had kept their land and money—at least Miss Kate had, but she hadn't chosen to make use of it. She'd come back after her lavish young days and shut herself up in solitude, letting spiders spin webs on the cornices and weeds flourish in the elaborate paths. Why? No one seemed to have a real clue to her true character.

And Mark's part of the family, losers in a lawsuit with her, had slumped down to the bottom of the hill again. There was a family tree in the back hall, drawn on sheepskin, and much chewed on by rats. It didn't amount to much, having one, if you found yourself back where the ancestors had started. I said as much to Mark.

"I wish it was back yonder in the old days and you and I had just come down the river in a flatboat and landed here, and it was all to be and had not all been. You and I would have made good pioneers."

"Pioneering's not over and done with. It's really just begun. You take a one-dimensional view, seeing it in the old terms. Look at it in the new. There're going to be a lot of new inventions and new discoveries. There's plenty unexplored, and there's the whole sky——" He had an eager look on his face.

"Haven't you had enough flying?" He made me uneasy, but I tried to think it was just his restlessness left from the war, that he would get over it and settle down.

"Enough war, but not enough flying. It's tomorrow, without any as yet known limits, Jane. Not much use my thinking about it now. but someday——"

"Get down to earth; there's plenty to do right here."

"Not worth the struggle, to my mind. Some people think so. Michael's a born planter. Hitch him to a plow and he's happy. He'll make a go of it, if anybody can, around this neck of the woods. But the whole system's crazy—all patchwork, popping at the seams."

He discouraged me. "But what else can we do?"

"Not a damn thing right now. But later on—we'll see."

"I wish we had some of the Lennerd money right now. We could put it to a lot better use than Miss Kate does."

"Been enough lawsuits in the family. Did you marry me to get your paws on Rosemont?" he teased. "If you did, I'm afraid you got fooled."

56

I'd have married the Frog Prince if it would mean Rosemont with him. I sighed, then perked up. "Oh, well, Miss Kate can't live forever and ever. We might get it yet in our ripe old age."

"Lennerds are mighty long-lived, I've noticed. And she's never had any use for Michael or Alec or me. So I reckon she'll leave everything away from our part of the family."

"She couldn't! Why, the very idea makes me boiling mad!"

"What's to keep her from it? Bet Mr. Charlie gets it all. If he outlives her. Been looking mighty droopy in the whiskers lately."

I had too much on my mind to be really interested in that old pair at the moment. "We can work hard and make our own money right down here at Wishmore."

He laughed. "We've got one hell of a chance!"

There was sound sense in what he was saying, and I knew it perfectly well, but I resented his saying it, because he really didn't care if he got the Lennerd money, or Rosemont, or finally made Wishmore into a sound, paying proposition. I picked up a clod of dirt at my feet and ran it through my fingers, crumbling it up. From the place where I had picked it, a green tip showed, a haphazardly planted daffodil or narcissus pushing through the earth for spring. This soil began to think of blooming even before winter.

It was that moment, when a faint resentment against Mark was born, that my feeling for Wishmore was born too. I looked out over the flat acres, soaking in the light—idle now, giving off a faint bluish blur from the dark loam. It was not exactly love but a sort of tenacious longing to clutch at this land, to mold it and make it what I wanted, to realize all its possibilities. Mark was mine, and the land was mine, and I was going to make them both into what I wanted. Like the pale shoot of the coming flower, I would burrow up through the earth to reach a full growth—expand into what I was predestined to be.

We went in to dinner, the old hound following. Mark didn't care two cents for Miss Kate, or the Lennerd money, or the big unused house, waiting for someone to bring it to life. Whatever ambitions he might have would never be set within four walls or four hundred acres. He didn't even care about Wishmore, I grumbled to myself. When I got the house in some sort of decent condition, and livable, I'd try my hand on the place.

I was too busy to think for the next few months. I plastered and painted and went into spasms because the hands were so slow and clumsy, but little by little things began to pick up. I had some of the furniture mended, and hounded Mark into getting a man to put new beams in the sagging back gallery. The twentieth century had walked right by the world down here. There was no telephone and no electricity, and the water was pumped from cisterns. The land itself was primitive. It had a careless lushness, and the same sort of indifferent plenty prevailed in the house. It was a change from the exact and careful meagerness I was used to. Fires roared—there was always plenty of wood—but they were troublesome, and the doors stood open anyhow, letting in the cold. I was the only one who ever bothered to close them. No one really lived in the house. Mark was busy on the place, or out hunting. I hardly ever knew where Mr. Jeff was. He stayed pretty well out of my way, because when I saw him I pounced on him and put him to work. The funny part was, he really liked to work when he got started, but you had to get over the hurdle of his awful inertia first. If I didn't pounce on him, he'd wander off and get drunk, then sneak in and barricade himself in his room in the ell.

There was always a lot of coarse food, served at odd hours, when the spirit moved Hettie to put it on the table. Uncle Jeff hardly ever appeared for meals. Mark never cared what he ate or when he ate it. Tillie would fill a plate for Mr. Jeff and put it in the safe, and he'd creep out late and eat cold mustard greens and cornbread.

The swamp seemed far from the house in the daytime, and somnolent and quiet. At night its sounds and its spirit surged right up to the doors, and the essence of its life was sinister and malign—a perpetual conflict: The rage of hunger, the flight of the weak from the strong, the noise of two creatures, almost equal, pitted in battle with each other. All of it woke and raged in the dark.

The dogs quivered and barked. Sometimes they went chasing; sometimes the sounds they heard, the smells they caught in their flaring nostrils made them seek the house and the protection of it. Sometimes echoes of their own past wildness made them go off snarling and baying. Owls hooted nearby. Possums and polecats raided the hen roost, and any silly straggler perching outside for the night never saw sunrise. Coons marauded openly up and down the back gallery. I wasn't always sure whether they'd succeeded in getting in the safe, or if it was only Mr. Jeff's foragings. All through the darkness there were paddings and scufflings, and every now and then a thin long shriek from some animal who had lost in the contest and was being devoured. In the morning there was silence. Nothing was left but the wild tracks through the yard and on the steps.

The life of the town faded out for me. I hardly ever went up the hill except on business. I didn't care about it any more, or the people, or the news. Even the news that Michael Lennerd was going to marry Joyce Delman didn't interest me much, and I didn't give my full attention to it until one afternoon when the drove of aunts descended and settled down on me. I was glad I had worked on the front room. Now it didn't look too much like a hoopoe's nest. I'd varnished the floor and painted the woodwork and built bookcases along the walls. Pot plants were shooting up along the window sills, and I'd put sprays of red swamp berries on the mantelpiece and burnished up the old brass candlesticks.

I made tea for the aunts, and everything was going along well, and they all said, why, they wouldn't have known the old place. Just then Mr. Jeff stalked past the door and, instead of going on, paused and fixed us with a glazed eye. He made us a deep bow and a horrible grimace, then, stiff as a wooden chunk, turned and walked down the hall toward his own room.

"Is he in a dangerous mood, Jane?" Aunt Em whispered.

I said probably not, and passed the sandwiches. I'd copied them from a picture in a woman's magazine, but they didn't really look much like the bright glazed illustration. However, they were edible.

"Poor Jane," Aunt Em sighed. "How can you put up with him?"

They all murmured about him for a while, and said he'd been a great trial to poor Martha until she couldn't endure any more, and they counseled me to patience.

"She was married to him, Aunt Em. I'm not. I'm married to Mark. There's a difference."

But they weren't interested in anything but Joyce Delman's marriage to Michael Lennerd. My wedding was an old story, and even Arland's stay in Washington and Tim's glories couldn't hold them, and they didn't even listen to Cousin Olive's accounts of Claire's manifold conquests of the rich and wellborn in New Orleans.

Lennerds married Ellistons, and Ellistons married Laidlaws and Gaylords and Radners. "But who are the Delmans?" Aunt Ada asked plaintively.

59

"Very plain people." Aunt Em sighed. She meant in lineage, not looks. "Jane knows them well; she's played with Joyce ever since they moved to town."

"Oh, I remember. That pretty, blond child. Do tell us, Jane."

I had a sudden importance because I knew all about the Delmans. I'd watched them move into the big ugly house around the corner from us. I'd sidled near, wild with curiosity and longing for someone to play with. Quantities of children kept darting in and out: there were eight of them. They called to each other, and squabbled, and lugged in puppies and bird cages and toys. Joyce was apart from the others—a tall little girl, jumping rope, the wind blowing her long pale-yellow hair. Arland said she looked just like a daffodil. Arland was older than I, and Claire was older and mean, but Joyce was just my age, pretty as Cinderella and placidly amenable to all my plans and suggestions.

"What is Michael thinking about?" Cousin Olive pursed up her mouth.

"Why, a pretty face and figure, Olive," Aunt Tee dimpled. "That's what they all think about." In spite of her little airs and evasions Aunt Tee had more knowledge of human nature than the others. "She'll make a lovely bride." Aunt Tee yielded to romance, while the others sighed about the break in the ranks. The old order was giving way to the new, and Michael—quiet, stolid, and conservative—was not guarding the dike.

When the aunts had gone, Mark came in. "Cat fight over?" He settled himself by the fire and poured himself some tea. He loved tea, and it always seemed an incongruous note in his make-up. He grinned at the silver teapot. Both our faces shone in it, tiny and distorted to hideousness. "You've slicked it up. It looks different from the last time I tried to use it."

"I didn't know you gave tea parties."

"Some folks dropped in. Kin of ours. They live up North somewhere. They thought they'd look us up. Uncle Jeff was on a tear and in one of his worst preaching moods. They didn't drink, so I hauled the teapot out, and Hettie filled her up, but when I went to pour the damned thing, it wouldn't pour. Come to find out, there was a dirt-dauber's nest stopping up the spout." He laughed. "Yankees have queer ideas about us anyway."

"Maybe they've got something there." Wishmore was certainly not the average smooth-running household, and if it had been anybody but Mark, it would have made a pathetic tale: shy orphan youth in crumbling old house, fishing out the ancient treasures, relics of a Better Day, struggling for the amenities and put to blushes before the no doubt conventional and prosperous Yankees, who hadn't lost the war, and therefore could still do well for themselves. But Mark hadn't given a damn. In his eyes you could take Wishmore and its contents, or leave it. He never made any apologies for it, and didn't seem to think they were needed. Neither the state of the ancestral urn nor the attitude of the guests would have worried him at all.

"You see, you needed a wife."

He didn't admit it. "Oh, it went off all right after all. Arland and your uncle happened to come down on some errand, and somehow or other she took charge and straightened out everything. Made more tea in the everyday china pot, and got Hettie to fix hot biscuits and fig preserves, and first thing you know the party was in full swing. She told the people lots of old stories—you know how she likes to tell them—and they lapped them up, and everybody had a good time."

I don't know why this annoyed me. It had happened a long time ago, before my day here. What I didn't like was the way Mark seemed to be telling me he didn't need me so much after all. I got up and told him I had to go to town. "I want to go to see the Delmans and talk about the wedding. I've got some ideas for them. They need to be steered in the right direction or it'll all be an awful mess."

"Bet you have. I see the gleam in your eye." He yawned and stretched and reached out and rumpled my hair. "All right. I'll carry you there. Reckon you'll be there till midnight, making 'em jump through hoops. But I'll wait for you. Maybe roll the bones awhile with Sam and Bob."

"Don't shoot craps."

"I won't . . . much. Got to once in a while, just to keep my hand in. Come on, let's go. So you can fix up Michael's Christmas doll."

"Don't you like her looks?"

"I admit she's got 'em, but I don't go in for that pink-and-white calm, dumb style."

I thought of Ludie's black eyes, and my heart sank a little.

"Just don't like my women placid."

"Most men do. Placid and stupid."

"I guess so. I reckon they think they're more easily managed.

They aren't, though. There's no stubbornness like the stubbornness of the stupid."

Outside there was a chill in the greenish sky. The stars were beginning to show, and in the twilight the nacissuses looked like stars too. You could catch their fresh scent in the cold air. My anger melted, and I put my arm around Mark. He looked down at me and smiled. I always loved the look of his face in a dim light. All his blondness was lost, but I could see the gleam of his teeth and his eyes.

"Jane, I believe you're a *maîtresse femme*."

"What's that? It doesn't sound so good."

"Depends on how you look at it. Highly respectable, though." He took his arm from around me.

❧ Chapter Five

The Delmans and their house had always had a sort of awful fascination for me. The children all yelled and banged and fought and pounded on the jangled piano, and wound up the wheezy victrola until it almost popped. I actually used to admire the shiny oak furniture and bead curtains rattling between parlor and dining room, but I was shocked by the bureau drawers crammed to bursting, the gray scummy water always in the bathtub, and the perpetual smell of unwashed milk bottles and didies. Nobody ever made a bed or mopped a floor.

Mr. Delman was large and handsome, and made plenty of money, but Mrs. Delman was a slattern. She must have been a beauty when she was young, but even when I first knew them, she'd lost all pretense to an outline. She'd dawdle around all day in a faded kimono, with the marabou pompons from her bedroom slippers shredding after her as she ambled from room to room. She'd eat through layer after layer of chocolate creams and read love stories just as gummy. In the afternoons she'd pull herself out of the soggy bed where she'd been lounging and struggle into her corsets. How she'd moan when she tried to make them meet! We'd have to help her lace them, and hook her into her heavily trimmed best dress, and get the shoehorn, so she could worry her poor feet into tight-buttoned bronze shoes with pointed toes and high curly heels. Then she'd douse herself with perfume and sling her feathered boa around her neck. She had beautiful hair, and she would pull it into great mounds over large rats and then slant an enormous picture hat over the bangs and puffs. Poor thing, in any weather she streamed with perspiration.

Mr. Delman used to give supper parties for his business friends: fried chickens, piled in big platters, and huge, heavy damp cakes, rich and soggy, and lots of wines and plenty of whisky, and trays and trays of spiced-up spaghetti and meatballs sent in. When the men had finished and gone away to play poker we used to fall on the leftovers and devour them to repletion. It was all so different from home where, when Aunt Em had parties, it meant weak tea and Nabiscos in the garden.

I loved Joyce in those days. She was my "best" friend, my very own, the only one I'd ever had. She would play any game I suggested and obediently admire my paper dolls and love my favorite characters just as I told her to. It was not long before her indifference to what went on in her own house shocked me. "Don't bother me," was all she ever said to the young ones when they wanted anything. Rita was the one who learned to make doll clothes and change Butch's didies and give him his bottle when he howled and blow noses. I used to help her furbish costumes out of old trash and stop the fights among the younger fry and plan picnics. As she grew up, she realized what a mess things were in and tried to help. It was uphill work, but even by the time Joyce's wedding came to the fore she had done wonders.

The Delmans always received me with open arms; that's what made them so attractive to me. They all listened to my opinions, accepted my judgment, and deferred to my tastes. Rita was eager to learn anything I could teach her. She was one of those vigorous unselfish ones who spring up without much help in a big family and somehow develop themselves. Joyce learned from me, too, but in her own way. When we were children, all she ever wanted to do with her dolls was to dress and undress them, and when she grew older that's all she wanted to do with herself. She learned to wash and comb and curl her beautiful fair hair, and to do it in current styles and imitate what other girls were wearing, and to smile at boys and dance well. What she wanted was to get out of her house, which was uncomfortable, where her mother cried and her father went stamping out in search of a little peace and diversion.

It was a shock when I found out she really didn't care for me, and all my love fell back against the bland, smooth surface of her innate indifference.

I gave a birthday party, just girls, but very important to me, and Joyce didn't come. Some boy had invited her to go somewhere, and she didn't hesitate. Nor could she see why my feelings were hurt. After that I knew I couldn't count on her, but she still looked to me to tell her what to do and what to wear.

When I went to the house that night, Rita met me at the door. She

64

was a tall, big-boned girl with bright blue eyes, shining white teeth, and a naturally high color. "Jane, we were wondering what had become of you! Come on in and talk wedding."

It was time for me to take a hand. Joyce was sitting in the parlor, in a corner, smiling and saying nothing. The furniture in that room was all knobs and whorls and juts in unexpected places, and upholstered in day-coach red plush. Like a day coach, it was apt to yield scraps of food and old banana peels and bits of trash. It was butt sprung, and when I sat down in an armchair a spring promptly leaped up and bit me. Mrs. Delman folded me in her fat arms, pressed me to her ample bosom—it felt like an eider-down puff—and kissed me gustily. She had discarded her corsets and was twiddling her toes with relief at having gotten rid of her shoes. She settled on the sofa, chewing a continuous cud of caramel and throwing the paper wrappings in the general direction of the gas log. Her kiss had left a sticky imprint on my cheek.

She began to moan and shed a few tears at the thought of losing her little girl.

"Oh, hush, Momma," Rita said with amiable scorn. "You know you're as pleased as pie Joy's going to marry Michael Lennerd, and why wouldn't you be?"

Joyce didn't have the sturdy look of the others. She was rather slight, gently curved, with pale gold curling hair, a fair fresh skin, and blue eyes—the sort of looks that had caused her since childhood to be the Christmas angel and the fairy queen and the princess in innumerable pageants. In our childhood games she had made an admirable Lady Rowena or a James Fenimore Cooper heroine. In real life, too, she maintained the admirable passivity of those ladies. She would have made a very suitable reward for winning a tournament or an excellent victim for the Indians to scalp.

Rita fidgeted. "Jane, Momma wants to wear fuchsia-colored satin. She saw it somewhere. It's got a lot of beads all over it. What do you think?"

The folds of Mrs. Delman's soft pink face puckered when I ruthlessly squelched the idea. Mrs. Delman, like nature, had a way of reverting to magenta tones unless forcibly prevented. "Like petunias," Arland said when I told her of Mrs. Delman's yearnings. "You plant them pink and white, and at first they come up that way; then the horrid little things slyly begin to streak until, the first thing you know, they're all red-purple again."

65

Well, after turmoil and argument, for the wedding I got her into soft dull powder blue with long sleeves. The younger girls made lovely bridesmaids. I'd found just the right and most becoming dresses for them, and Joyce as usual looked like an angel.

"Of course, Michael's a good match for a Delman," I said to Mark on the way to the church. "And he's a sweet old thing. But I wouldn't want him. He works so hard growing cotton all day that when he comes home or goes out he just dozes most of the time, he's so tired. If I had Joy's exterior combined with my interior, I'd have done much better. Not that I'd want to look like her if I could choose."

"If you had your druthers——" Old Lew was always saying, "If I had my druthers, gimme one of them there Shevrolics."

"If I had my druthers, I'd be another type."

"Like who, for instance?"

I didn't answer. I wanted to look like Ludie Daniels. I wished I didn't. I wished that wench didn't have so much power to make me jealous. But Ludie wasn't simply a beautiful gal of lax behavior. I sensed in her something powerful. In her way she was shrewd—nobody's fool, and if she really loved Mark—if she was not considering him as just another man in her life—she might still be a menace.

The wedding went off well. Since Joyce was more or less my job, I wanted her to put her best foot forward among Michael's kith and kin. What are kith? I wrote Arland all about it: "Everybody rallied at the last moment, and I kept a sharp eye on everything. The younger brats behaved, the food was right—I'd seen to that—and the house was so smothered in flowers you couldn't see how thoroughly awful it is, and the guests were so drenched in all that champagne they didn't notice anyway. Also, due to the champagne, most of Mrs. D.'s absurdities passed unnoticed. All the people who said they wouldn't come, came. For a while the Lennerds sort of huddled together, trying to protect the Sacred of Pastures of the established order from the tramplings of the unknown herd. You know the number and vigor of the Delmans. Then Gert got tight and snaffled Mr. D. Told him he was wonderful and the handsomest man in town. He ate it up. Mark spent most of his time in the back yard, helping Butch build an airplane."

I remember their intent faces. Butch was a dark, serious little thing then. Arland found out later that he wanted to go to Annapolis, and

Tim, in due time, pulled the necessary strings for him. He did very well, and it's strange to think of him as the leader of a task force. I used to fix the croup kettle for him—he was a frightfully croupy, sneezy child—and try to hush his yells and squalls. Many a time have I changed a didie for him, and what large doses Rita and I rammed down his mouth when he was sick the day his mother let him get all the stale pop and drink it up!

Of all the tribe only the old people and Joyce are left in town. Rita studied to be a nurse and married a doctor. When she came home on a visit once she said, "You did a lot for us, Jane. You used to make me mad sometimes—you were so bossy, but you were a big help, and Arland used to lend me books and talk to me and encourage me to go away and try to do something for myself."

The Delmans were the first American family I knew. I mean, typically American, as opposed to being typically Southern. They came from nowhere, plump down in our midst. They were of mixed inheritance: part Irish, part German, a little Slav somewhere. They hadn't much chance at home. Mrs. Delman, poor thing, was in so many ways an example of what a wife and mother shouldn't be—careless, wasteful, unable to exert any influence, exacting no obedience but only a certain good-humored tolerance and fondness from the children. Yet they did all right. They were sound in wind and limb, and they made opportunities for themselves.

When I first saw them moving into the big hideous house, I certainly never thought their family and mine would ever be united and mingled. Maybe it's just as well.

Even Mrs. Delman, in the ripeness of her old age, came into her own. Mr. Delman, after his little escapades, came back to the fold. I go to see them religiously, and Mrs. Delman makes an ideal grandmother. When I pay my visits we talk about when the children were little and look at old pictures. Arland says Mrs. D. is an example of Nature's intention; women ought to be fat and placid and fertile and have lots of children and let them go off and fend for themselves. Maybe the Delmans did well just because they didn't have the dim, leafless hedge of old traditions hemming them in like the growth surrounding the Sleeping Beauty.

Arland came home for a sudden visit in February. The first I knew of it was when I saw her standing in the door one afternoon. Her pale, soft wool dress was the color of the sleepy sunlight, and

67

she had a spray of rust-red berries pinned against her brown coat. When I saw her I knew how much I'd missed her.

We talked about Uncle. He wasn't well, and she had grown so worried about him she had come home to see for herself and make him go to a heart specialist. I tried to get her to tell me all about Washington and all the grand people she'd met and the fine parties she'd been to, but she said she'd a lot rather hear about home. "I'd give up all the parties I've been to, to have had the chance to be at Michael's wedding. Come show me what you've done to this house."

I showed her the changes I'd already made and the ones I planned to make. "Why don't you have a brick walk leading to the cistern and train the arbor over it? I love cisterns."

"You wouldn't care for the picturesque if you had to haul water. And that arbor! Mark at last got around to getting the lumber for Mr. Jeff to fix the back steps, and he built the arbor instead. As a surprise. It certainly was."

"Since he made such a carefree gesture you might as well use it. It's a dear place, Jane—has a lot of charm."

"I wish it had a better bathroom. How I loathe chill peregrinations to the w.c. I wish I could fix it up the way I really want to, but, even so, I've done too much. I see now I should have put every cent on the land and let the house go. The land's much more important. Mark should have stopped me."

"I suppose he wanted you to make yourself as comfortable as you could."

"I know, but all the same, he shouldn't have let me. The land has to come first if you're ever going to make anything out of it." I sighed. "Mark's not instinctively a planter, I'm afraid. Michael would have known better. Do you know what Joyce wanted to do? Tear down Michael's house and build a new one! Fortunately, I stopped her in time."

Arland was properly horrified. Michael's place was on the other highway, not very far from town, and on it was an old house with fanlights over the doors and beautiful mantelpieces. I went on to describe the different color schemes I'd chosen for Joyce. "It's lovely now, and when people tell Joyce how much they like it, she just smiles as if she'd done it all. She's getting rather out of hand. Gertrude and Bess Barrett, after swearing they'd have nothing to do with her if Michael married her, are now taking her up, and she's getting mighty pleased with herself."

Just then we heard Mr. Jeff somewhere outside, orating to Lew, so we slipped out before he could corner us. "He's found a still somewhere in the swamp, so he doesn't even have to go to town for it." We cut across the fields, passing by first one cabin then another. Their crooked chimneys were sighing out little spirals of smoke. Arland said they were her favorite form of architecture.

"But so uncomfortable, Arland."

"I know. If you could just make them livable but keep the same sort of roof line." She waved to a solemn-looking group of children playing in a bare space. We went on toward the levee. It was a mild day; silvery sunlight brightened and paled behind motionless streamers of cloud. The fields clicked and clacked with dried stalks and empty bolls. We skirted the edge of the plowed land, then we were wading knee-deep in a stretch of rust-colored grass. As we went, a flock of migrating warblers, tiny things, with bright eyes and soft smoky feathers, fluttered up. When we'd gone by they settled down again. We climbed the levee and walked down in a little way. It made no attempt to try to keep the water off the fields. It sidled down Wishmore Point to hold the land and keep the Mississippi from eating it up as it wanted to. The swamp rose around us, webbed and gray. Some of the trees still kept last year's leaves—powdery, ash-colored, burned out less by cold than by an intense summer. A thread of fire was already running through the cobwebby colorlessness, the maples' fresh scarlet buds like raw flame.

"Spring . . ." Arland sighed.

"Don't burble about it in this climate. It just means our pounding summer's catching up with us again."

Arland is one of those dyed-in-the-wool nature lovers, stubbornly insistent on any landscape's beauties and every season's compensations. I believe she's read all of Wordsworth, even the *Idiot Boy*.

"I might keep an eye on scenery if I lived in some placid, pruned sort of place, but here it's all grappling and wrassling."

The levee angled to the left; between its angle and the river was a stretch of cleared ground with a cabin in the middle. It was stained by floods, but looked solid. Every time the river rose, Ben and his family had to leave, but they always came back. Geraniums bloomed in tin cans in the window; there was a neat, high woodpile; a pig or so grunted; and silvery cabbages were rounding like flowers from the wet purple-dark earth—ground snatched from the swamp by the hardest.

"A skiff, firewood, and a pig is the way to live down here," I said. "Then you can blend with them. When flood comes, you pick up the pig and the pickaninnies and go, then you come back."

Just then Ben himself came along the levee, a string of fish dangling from his hand. They were cold and fluid and gleaming. He was tall and stooped, his skin matted with fine wrinkles. He spoke, and Arland talked to him and asked him about his family. He went on to the cabin and he turned back. "He and his father and his grandfather have lived here in the same old way. They struggle, God knows, but it's a simple, primitive grappling. What I want is to bring civilization down here—modernize it all: house, cabins, land—and the whole damn place fights back!"

"I know what you mean," Arland said. "I wonder who'll win, you or Wishmore."

"I will, but it's no easy job ahead."

Before we went to the house we left the levee and walked to the river, struggling through a ribbon of swamp. A frazzle of faded golden-rod and thin-petaled wild asters dwindled to the grayish edges of the bank. The ground near the river was lead-colored, grooved and seamed, strewn with dull, empty shells. The clouds looked feather-stitched in the sky.

Arland sat down on a fallen log near a cottonwood tree. She took out a thin silver cigarette case and began to smoke. She didn't yet dare to in public. When Gertrude had smoked on Main Street, a few months earlier, it had caused shocked comment. Arland wouldn't smoke until people got over being shocked. It was the same with driving. Uncle had given her a car for a wedding present, when it was supposed no woman would ever drive alone outside the city limits. Arland had come down here by herself, and little by little she'd drive farther and farther until everyone took women's driving themselves all over the country as a matter of course. Arland has the outward air of fragility and inner daring of our grandmother, who would never sit even on the gallery without a veil over her face to protect her complexion, but who could shoot off a snake's head with her pistol. As a girl Arland had ridden and driven dangerous horses. Uncle never had much use for sissy women.

"The water looks so lonesome, as if nothing had ever been on it or ever would be except an occasional canoe paddled by an Indian." She pointed to a half-submerged wreck of a little boat near the bank.

70

"It's quiet here, but not calm. That's a place crying out for murder. You could tuck a corpse in there and never find it."

"Buzzards would."

"I know what you mean, Jane. There's a sort of force to this place. It's made for sultry revenges and large, violent emotions."

"You've been brought up in the school of literature where people's feelings are saturated with nature, where nature takes a hand in the muddling and general confusion of the characters' lives—young love flourishing in spring and blossoms, storms appropriately accompanying the despair of turgid souls, and a sinister setting before you can bump anybody off in real comfort."

She laughed. "But this place does suit you in a way, Jane. It gives you something to get your teeth into. Jane, you are happy, aren't you? I am." The pale falling light brought out the gold in her hair and eyes and deepened the dark bloom of her skin. Her face had a look of joy, deep and secret and still.

I picked up a little shell and threw it in the general direction of the submerged boat. "I don't have all the accessories you have— enough money, an adoring family, and a knack for getting the most out of every day and every hour. I get mad at details—the possum grabbing my best hen, Mr. Jeff being such a pest, and Tillie not understanding what she's told, but——" I thought over what she'd asked me. It was one of those times I felt close to her. I suppose she's the only person I've ever felt really close to, at home with. Not Kitty, never Mark, except maybe for one moment—much as I loved them both. With Arland it's a natural intimacy, born of the same blood, the same associations. There was at times a strong physical resemblance between us, and at times deep inside us there was a strong feeling of being united, a memory of the same source. We understood each other sometimes with a casual word, though our tastes were different and our essential natures unlike.

"It's worth it," I admitted. I looked at the riverbank rolling off like a curl of smoke and the dull river with a twist of current dragging through it. Not far out was a whirlpool. It was smooth in the center, radiating threads of force, dragging bits of logs and branches under, then shooting them out again. The river was rising. The spring flood was getting under way. Jagged logs and films of drift rocked up and down, lifted from the ground where they belonged, and were carried off. I watched the whirlpool and saw a twig-laden limb eddy to its center and go down and not reappear. Maybe it sank to the bottom. Maybe it was flung along beneath the surface to rise far downstream. Then I knew why I watched the whirlpool. Secretive, powerful, it was to me a symbol of sexual passion.

I felt a fiery sense of confidence in myself. Loving Mark gave me strength, an almost wicked power, like the whirlpool with its smooth surface and hungry undertow. I could draw everything to me, everything I wanted, and fling aside all the rest.

When I went back in the house, I knew Mark had come. Whenever he was in, he brought with him something of the outdoors. Dogs leaping, dogs sleeping, and muddy foot tracks; earth from the swamp and the river's edge. The fire blazed in the living room, but Mark wasn't there. The clock ticked, and the dog by the fire thumped his tail on the floor.

"You know you've no business in here, you muddy thing."

But the dog kept thumping, maybe realizing I wasn't going to drive him out this time. Not in my present frame of mind.

The clock ticked, letting the second fly, and there were sounds of footsteps and banging from the back of the house. Mark's footsteps. He was proabably looking for cold biscuits in the safe. The clock's ticking and the footsteps moving around wove into an irregular pattern of sounds.

In a minute Mark would come in here. But he didn't, so I went to find him. In the hall I met Mr. Jeff. He bowed gravely and so did I. This evening I wasn't cross with him. He went on to his own room. I wondered what he was thinking about and what he was feeling, if anything. I wondered why he wanted to lose all the sharpness of sensation in a fuzzy blur, or if, somewhere in that alcoholic labyrinth, there was a stage where everything became bright and clear and happy, and if he was always trying to reach that level and, after he had lost it, get back to it.

Mark was on the gallery, finishing off a cold biscuit filled with bacon. He'd left the safe doors open. The other night a coon had gotten in and spooned up a whole bowl of clabber, doing a neat and thorough job. I'd come out and found him and shooed him. Tonight I just closed the safe and didn't refer to the coon.

"Hi!" Mark greeted me.

"Where've you been?" I asked him.

He gave a vague account of his ramblings.

"Arland and I walked around for hours."

"Where is she?"

"Gone on home." I went up to him and put my hands on his shoulders, trying to feel his flesh and muscles and bones through the thickness of a wool shirt and a battered leather jacket. I could see his face plainly in the lamplight from the kitchen window.

He kissed me, then he said, "Don't you reckon we ought to brew up some kind of festivity for Arland while she's here?"

"Well——" I looked through the window at the grimy kitchen, the cracked walls lined with ancient saucepans and twisted tin spoons. Hettie called them "kitchin intentions," and that's all they were—just intentions. On a shelf in the safe was a plate heaped with a mound of stiffened grits and an icy horror of a fried egg: Mr. Jeff's breakfast. Another plate held his dinner—mustard greens congealed in grease, a chunk of cornbread, and a grisly slab of meat reposing under a coating of what Hettie called "raised gravy." When the larder was low, Hettie would say, "I reckon I'll jes' raise us some gravy," and a violent frizzling would ensue. Mr. Jeff would rouse himself at some ungodly hour to come and eat.

If we gave a party, Claire would come and sniff at everything, and Mr. Jeff would probably act up. But Mark was smiling at me, and I didn't want him to stop, so I said, "If you want to have a shindig——"

He was looking at me, his light eyes intent, and he seemed to be waiting for some answer beyond the matter of having a party.

"Let's give one. I'll ask Arland when she'd like to have it."

"But don't stir up a storm of work over it, Jane. Just give 'em plenty of that old kickapoo juice, and they won't care about anything else."

"All right." I let go my clutch of his shoulders and tightened my arms around his neck. The deficiencies of the house, the leaks and cracks and rat holes I'd grown to know so well, didn't matter. For a while all of it took back the strangeness, the sort of fascination I had felt the first time I had ever seen it. Mark kissed me again, a long, hard kiss—the kind I liked. It was warm in the circle of his arms, and the night around was cold and still, without a moon, without stars, but held the whole year curled up in it, the flowers and the fruits and the crops. And all the future.

Arland liked the idea of the party. "But don't go to a lot of trouble."

"Hettie says, 'Tell folks you don' mind takin' the trouble, but don't tell 'em they ain't bein' no trouble.' No, it'll be fun, and I want Uncle to come for a while, if he will."

He said he would. I particularly wanted to show Uncle I could get along in the life I'd chosen, and to show him that at least one of his female relations could navigate under her own steam and not stay perpetually draped around his neck. Now that he was old and not particularly well, it seemed to me high time he was getting spiritual and mental elbow room.

Mark kept casually asking everyone he met to come to our party. And they would not only come, but bring everybody they happened to meet—that's what always happened. But it didn't matter. Mark had provided ample quantities of whisky, and I'd done what I could with the house, and hung some Chinese lanterns on the gallery and on the branches of a tree out in front.

"It looks nice," Mark commented. "And so do you." We were standing on the steps, watching the cars coming down the hill. The lanterns bobbed, and a newish moon was hanging over the river. It made a reddish glow on the water.

Uncle came and seemed to enjoy himself. Mark had saved some really good whisky for him, and I'd pulled up the most comfortable chair by the fire, but Uncle wouldn't stay put; he roved around and entered into the spirit of the thing. After he left the party grew louder and wilder. Gertrude, in the back hall, was amusing herself by spitting olive seeds into a knothole in the floor, and the men were beginning to cluster in the kitchen, telling jokes, each worse than the last.

"I'm going to shoo them out of there," I told Arland. "It ruins the party when they go into a huddle like that."

"It's a lovely night. Tell Mark to get them out front and we can play King William was King James's son."

Everybody trooped out, too well oiled to feel the cold, and we all circled round and round, singing out the words with a thumping inflection, holding hands, all together, as though we were always a complete circle, united in all our hearts and feelings. Mr. Jeff came out on the gallery and watched us, glowering at our foolishness.

Arland was near me. She leaned over and whispered, "Why not ask him to come on out and join us?"

"He'll spoil things," I muttered back. "But if you want him, go ahead. It's your party."

"You ask him, Jane."

So I broke out of the circle and went up to him. He didn't seem to hear what I said, but he let me take his hand and lead him down, and he wove in and out with the rest of us, and even growled out the song, sounding like a dull buzz saw. I looked up; Mark had been watching me, smiling. When it was Arland's turn to choose, she chose Mr. Jeff. It was the first time in years, maybe ever, that anyone had chosen him as the one they loved the best, and, though he had to be helped up and down, I think that somewhere way back within himself, he was pleased.

When it was Mark's time to choose, I stopped singing to watch him. There he was, standing alone, and the rest of us were revolving around him. His light hair was ruffled, and his gray eyes looked particularly brilliant. He hesitated; he wasn't looking at any of us, but seemed to be looking at something in his own mind. Then he laughed and came over to me and took my hands.

We kissed each other, and the moving figures around us blurred and faded away, the bare, gnarled willow, hung with gay lanterns, seemed to be bursting into an exotic flowering, and the silly words of the childhood song changed to my ears and became twisted into a wild tribal chant.

Of course it was only a game, but still . . .

It was late when everybody left, still laughing and caterwauling.

"It was a good party," Mark yawned, coming in just as I'd finished plaiting my hair. "I'm glad you got Uncle Jeff into it. He didn't hurt anything."

"It went off fine," I agreed. "The coon got in the safe again and was going good on a bowl of tomatoes, but I didn't make any noise; I just left him to have himself a party too."

"And Uncle Jeff finished off the dregs of the hooch, so everybody's happy. What are you doing all horsed up this hour of the night?"

I'd put on the negligee and nightgown Arland had given me for my trousseau. Yellow chiffon set with lace and run with blue ribbons. My good things didn't stay in a state of pristine freshness very long down here, where a general dinginess prevailed, but I felt tonight called for my best efforts.

"I was waiting for you."

He put his arms around me. "I don't see why you're always grumbling about your hair." He kissed the top of my head. "It feels good

—so soft and silkified, like a baby's. And you look like a little girl playing lady in all that outfit."

"But I'm not a little girl."

"No, that's what's so . . . interesting." He put his hands on my breasts, then picked me up and carried me to the bed and began untying ribbons. "And if I tear all this flimsy-flamsy, you'll raise unshirted hell tomorrow——"

"But not tonight. Go ahead, you're doing all right." I couldn't help thinking he was almost too adept at getting a woman's clothes off her, but I wouldn't let myself think about those others.

"This is good," I whispered, clinging to him. "Even better than the night on the hill—though that was good too."

"As an initial performance, startlingly good."

"You were half afraid of me then."

"You were an innocent and well-brought-up virgin. Put yourself in my place."

"I don't want to," I sighed. "I like my own better. Don't you think I have good bed manners?"

"Supreme."

I liked being a woman, and having so many nerves, all of them highly charged. And I liked having those secret ones deep inside wake and throb up in my brain and down in my heart and all through my body. And Mark had chosen me, the one he loved the best. Just a game, but I could make it real. I would hold him so close, twine myself around him, absorb him entirely—until there wouldn't be a thought or a heartbeat that wasn't tangled up with me.

I wanted him to feel carried away, as I was—like something tossed and shaken in a whirlpool's dark spinning. And after this we would never find ourselves back in the usual groove of living, but in some remote place. And that's what he would like—to find us flung, panting and exhausted and satiated, in some strange place we had never known before—that he would never be able to reach again except with me.

There are no undiscovered places any more. Long before all the places were found, all the sensations and emotions were known and sounded—sometime, somewhere. But there are a few places, just as there are some feelings, that have such strength and wildness and take so much daring that only a few people can ever find them.

⒔ Chapter Six

"You had a good party," Gertrude commended me, and it went down in local history as a good party. Jim Ledyard had finished the night by careening on to Jackson, where he had a business engagement the next day. I suppose he sang as he traveled. Anyway, all three hundred pounds of him, twirling an empty bottle over his head and shouting King William was King James' son, burst into the hotel dining room at eight-thirty, where a bunch of sober people were munching sedately on their breakfast.

With us, Mark and myself, everything went well. It was as though the aftermath of the party—those hours of love-making—had really taken me to a different level of living. I felt lazy and contented—the only time in my whole life I had ever felt contented—and instead of scouring and prodding others to scour and hustle and bustle, I let everything alone and mooned about and wandered around outdoors.

Then one night when Tim and Arland were still at home, we all went to a party at Mistletoe Grove. The party happened to follow on the heels of a trying day. In the morning Mr. Jeff made me mad—so mad I threw a plate at him. Then I went to Miss Martha's, to get my new dress to wear. There she was in her poky room, turning over patterns with all the brooding gloom of a gypsy queen about to turn up the fatal card. I didn't like the way she'd made the dress, and her general gloom irritated me—woke me from my calm. I felt I'd better get back to Wishmore and work at changing it, or I'd wake up to find myself old and dull and hopeless.

That night, getting ready, I became more dissatisfied with the dress, and worked myself into a grumbling mood. A sharp longing to compete seized me.

"I'm sorry, Jane," Mark said when I was grumbling. "I know you don't have much—not the things you ought to have. But you've sure acted like a thunderstorm all day."

77

He, too, was somber and silent that night, but he couldn't know how I felt, because possessions meant nothing to him. He never wanted stocks or bonds or land. He never noticed what he ate or cared what he wore. He didn't even have a favorite gun. He liked wide, unintimate things, like the swamp and the river, and nobody could ever own those or, to my way of thinking, feel very cozy with them. I said that to Arland, and she said, yes, those and the sky. She has something of the same sort of abstraction. I believe if you gave her a book and a fire to read by in winter, and a tree to read under in summer, she'd let the world wag by.

Mistletoe Grove is a queer old house. That night suited it. The moonlight came and went. The clouds weren't those light, scuddy ones that make the earth look gray and the moon small and white. They were black and piled and plushy, with torn silver fringes. A strong wind harried them across the sky. When the moon was free its light was thick and rich and the shadows were intense. Not that Mistletoe Grove needs a moon or a night. Even in the most matter-of-fact daylight it's dreamy and strange. The house is huge, octagon-shaped, story after story. Only the basement is finished. The Civil War stopped the building. Hollow tiers of rafters are enclosed by a dome. Arched windows, little balconies with pairs of columns go all around, and owls and squirrels and bats and things scitter and scamper in and out. The niches planned for marble statues are empty. The graceful staircase leads up to nothingness. Arland says it reminds her of in Xanadu did Kubla Khan.

A tunnel of low, winding road, with banks on each side and moss-dripping trees tangling overhead, at last gives way to an open circle; and there is the house, looming at you. Just before we reached the open space, I caught a glimpse of a wild plum in full bloom, a spread web shining against the black of the other trees. The petals flew in the wind. The queer perfume of the thing reached out to me, tang of wild honey, savor of spring rampant, carelessly flinging away its flowers. It promised; it teased; it made me feel I don't know what—as if life was hurrying by and the very essence of it must be snatched before it was whirled away and blown on the wind.

I turned to Mark, but he wasn't looking at me. I wondered what he was thinking and feeling and started to ask him, but we were already there. The lighted windows showed in the basement, and the bulk of the house piled up black above them. The moving crowd inside made shadows against the yellowed oblongs. A little orchestra pounded and squeaked away cheerfully, and Gerald Ladd met us at the door, pleasant as ever.

He lived here alone, the last of a big family. The others had died or moved away. The ones who'd moved away had done well, and Jerry might have, too, if he'd gone in time, but he'd stayed and I suppose the weight of that empty house over his head was too much for him. Everybody liked him, and other drinkers gravitated out to keep him company. Mark had often found Mr. Jeff here, snugly holed in. Lots of times strangers, if they liked their liquor, found their way out. Heaven knows how; it's a most devious road—and dropped out of sight. There was that man from Birmingham. They say he hadn't touched a drop in twenty years and had joined the Temperance League; but something in the atmosphere of the town must have done something to him, because he either wandered into a saloon and met Jerry, or met Jerry and wandered into a saloon in his company. They had a few, then drifted off together. The man from Birmingham disappeared. After a while his wife and family were sending frantic telegrams. Finally somebody remembered seeing him with Jerry, and, sure enough, there he was at Mistletoe Grove.

Jerry led me in. When I asked him how he was, he said, "Fine, just fine," then dropped his voice to a confidential tone. "Except for those little men. I declare, Janey honey, I've had to keep running them off. They've been cutting down all the trees. Look at 'em——" He gestured toward the moony, moss-hung branches. "There, there— you see?" He almost conjured up for my eyes a horde of little never-never creatures.

Jerry loved to have parties, and Gertrude, at that time dictator of all celebrations, had fixed up this one. The first person I heard was Tim. He was back from Washington, and his voice carried above all other sounds. He flung his arms around me and kissed me. "Here's little Janey, my favorite cousin." You'd have thought I was the one person in the world he was longing to see. He had a knack of making everyone feel that way. You knew better, but you felt pleased.

I always fell for it. Besides, he was attractive, with his high color and his laugh and his alive brown eyes and his gift for apt speech. He gave off such exuberant, optimistic life. He kept an arm around me while he went on hailing everybody affectionately, talking politics and telling jokes to a group gathered around him. He could always gather a group. Mark stood to one side, not listening. When I got away from Tim I said, "You're mighty offhand with him these days."

Mark's light gray eyes darkened. "We don't hit it off so well any more."

"What did you fall out about?"

"Nothing much." I knew Mark wouldn't tell me. He added, "Tim's phony as a seven-dollar bill."

"You're just jealous of him."

"Jealous? What do you mean?"

"Of his success."

Mark laughed. "Oh, his success. We might as well leave it at that." I knew I hadn't hit on the truth. What did Mark care about getting ahead in the world?—with his queer ideas, not like other people's. . . . He made me so mad, never telling me anything. I left him and went to look for Arland. She was in one of the bedrooms taking off her coat. She had on a coppery-gold dress, and a chain of amber beads twisted around her throat. They were light and smooth and pale, and echoed the gleams in her hair.

"Aren't these old mirrors ghostly? Make you see yourself the way you'll look when you're old." The faded image slipped easily away, leaving her as she was, her face young and smooth and the candlelight starting the gold in her hair to match the deep luster in her dress.

I wondered what was the matter between Tim and Mark, what had happened to change their old friendship. It would make things awkward when we were all together. Arland had everything, and Tim was a success. Women measure their success by the quality of the man they love. But fate hadn't set a trap for me by making me love Mark. He wouldn't be Tim's sort of success, but he had his own quality. Anyhow, I didn't believe in fate. I slipped my arm through Arland's and we went out together.

That party was a sort of milestone. It was the first time I'd seen women like Claire and Bess Barrett get tight. The new era had begun. That night, too, I saw Alec again after a long time. He was Michael's brother, Mark's first cousin, and of course I'd always known him just as I had Mark. He'd been in the war, too, then had stayed away from home, working on a newspaper in Chicago. He seemed very worldly and attractive, and I was glad when he came over and began to talk to me. He's tall—taller than Mark, and less solid in bone. His eyes and hair are dark, and he has a long, well-cut, thinnish—but not too thin—mouth in a long, thin, brownish face.

"So you and Mark are married! Somehow, I never expected him to plant cotton or himself."

"Why not?" Our marriage had been sudden and had surprised people, and I always felt a challenge when they began to talk about Mark and matrimony. "Don't you think Michael's marriage a lot more startling?"

"Lord, no. Have this drink. Powerful combination—corn and coke. Don't know how everybody around here stands as much of it as they do; can't be much to the theory whisky is bad for you. Michael saw a pretty face and immediately fell in love. He's the marrying kind. Any pretty girl would have done, and he'd make a good husband for any woman not too exacting. It's his destiny to marry and plant cotton." He smiled at me. "I'm not questioning Mark's taste at all, you understand, but I've always thought of him as a rolling stone. Never thought he'd come back to the groove he'd left."

"Where else would he go? I should think all of you would have been fed up with the war."

"I was. To the teeth. Though I never got any farther than Paris and had some pretty good times. They'll seem better and better as the years go along. But he couldn't have had much fun. He did a lot of real fighting. Some men seem to be made for war. When they find out how good they are at it, I suppose ordinary life is too tame for 'em."

That was exactly what I'd told Mark myself, but I felt a bitter resentment against war and all masculine junketings. "Tim's supposed to be our local hero."

Alec glanced over at Tim surrounded by his adoring coterie. "So I understand. . . . Knows how to make the most of it too. People take you at your own valuation; might as well set it high."

"He's getting places."

"Sure, sure. He's got all he needs to charm the masses. And a perfect instinct for getting at the really important people who can help him to a goodly share of the juicy jujubes growing on the upper branches. Perfect sense of timing: he knows just when to plug for an issue and when to let it go. Some people have a knack for keeping their finger on the public pulse. Then he has all the glow of a man perfectly satisfied with himself and so with the rest of the world.

People eat that up." Alec refilled his glass and brought some sandwiches. "You know when they told me Mark had married Jane Elliston, I couldn't quite place you. I thought of you as an infant, which of course you still are. More ice? How do you get along, tackling Wishmore and its mortgage and Cousin Jeff thrown in?"

"It's exactly what I didn't want—to get buried in one of these old places around here. Now look at me. And there's Arland, who'd like nothing better than to cocoon herself in layers of moss at Holly Trees. Yet she gets to go to Washington and be in the swim of things."

"Would you like that?"

"Well, I used to want to go away to a city and do some kind of interesting work and make a lot of money and meet exciting people."

"A lot of money doing what?"

"I don't know just what."

"But you chose Wishmore."

"I chose Mark. Wishmore and Mr. Jeff were dumped in my lap."

"Beginning to be sorry?"

"Of course not. Mr. Jeff's a botheration, as Tillie puts it, but I've grown fond of Wishmore. Not fond, exactly, but I suppose you'd say ambitious for it. I'm not going to leave things lay the way everybody else does around here. I've got lots of schemes. I can't work on them all at once, but give me time. I'm young yet!"

Mark came over to talk to Alec, and the talk soon veered to politics. From there it would go to hunting, so I went to fix my hair. It was a perfect torment to me, fine and hard to curl. What a gulf used to separate the straight-haired from the curly-haired! I used to pray for curls. When people lament the passing of the good old days, I always think of the mosquitoes, and the plight of girls with straight hair.

I took the wrong turning and found myself in a room where there were no lights. I was fumbling my way to the next, where a lamp was shining, when I heard Gertrude and Claire talking behind the half-open door. Their backs were turned. Gert's red hair was ruffled up, and her shoulder strap was slipping down.

She'd been young when she'd married Alec and Michael's father. He had money, and her family thought it was a good marriage. He was a nice man, but poky, and I think she felt more or less suppressed during his lifetime. He soon died, though. Then she ran through the money he'd left her. The boys were fond of her and helped her, but she was always broke. It didn't bother her; she enjoyed life. She was crazy about horses and parties and men and whisky. Now she was free, and public opinion didn't make her hide her tastes any more. People liked her—particularly men. She was the frank Good Sport just coming into fashion.

Claire was modern, too, in a different way. She was the everything-is-just-too-futile type. She had style and some beauty, but there was something sharp and brittle about her good looks. How different they both were from the portraits looking down from the smoky walls— like another race of creatures! But if the women in hoop skirts had crystallized into their past, cut off from us, Claire and Gertrude were set and framed in the twenties. I didn't know that then. I envied them with all my heart and longed to be accepted as their equal. I didn't know a day would come when they would be out of fashion, too—set back into the past.

That night, though, they were sure of themselves and their place in the sun. Gertrude was the center of all gaiety, and Claire's popularity and brilliance had been dinned into me all my life.

"I don't know why he married her," I heard Claire say, and I listened shamelessly. "She doesn't belong to our crowd. Arland dragged her in to all the wedding parties." Your crowd was important. Members of a "crowd" fought like wildcats among themselves, but banded together against outsiders.

"She's not bad-looking." Gertrude bent over and poured herself another drink. "She's colorless, though. I don't see why he took to her." I resolved then and there not to be a pale shadow of Arland but to refurbish my own looks. Colorless!

"I don't believe he's in love with her," Gertrude finished.

"I don't either—not a bit. Guess he was lonesome. It's a pity; Mark's got something."

I felt on fire all over. When I could move I scuttled off like a terrified rat who's eaten a meal of strong poison. I hated both those females and longed to get even with them. I tried to tell myself it didn't matter what they said, but it did, because they had forced me to face what I already knew and had never admitted to myself.

Of course they didn't know anything about Mark and me, and how much we wanted each other. Then I thought of how he'd asked me to marry him. He hadn't said he loved me so much he couldn't do without me. He had never said he loved me. He'd married me because he thought he owed it to me after what had happened, because he'd blamed himself for letting me be so reckless, and because he knew how much I loved him.

I wanted to go find him and make him say he loved me, but I was afraid. He'd just say I was a fool to listen to those tight owls: they rip everybody up the back; forget it. Cheer up. To hell with it!

It wouldn't be enough. He must never find out I knew he didn't love me. He must go on thinking I was too young and inexperienced to know the difference between what he gave me and what he could give. I'd fight for him until I had all of him. He wanted me, anyhow, and I was his wife. I wanted him and I was going to have him. We would have children, his and mine. We would have our life together. I was going to mold it the way I wanted it.

I left the house and went out by a side door. The moon was shining, and I pressed close to the wall, in the shadow. In the room near me I could look in the window and see Alec and Arland sitting on a sofa, talking. Nobody else was in there. Beyond, in the other two bigger rooms, the dancers were whirling around—a swirl of colors moving to an up-and-down seesaw tune. I could see the dim, odd-shaped room where Alec and Arland were sitting. The sofa had loops and scrolls on its back, and gleams of light slid along the worn gold frame of the pier-table mirror. There was a ripple of amber in the drink Alec was holding. Candle flames wove threads of brightness in Arland's hair and woke a deep sheen in the stuff of her dress—gold too. A study in dimness and dulled golds.

I caught some of their talk. They were discussing Mr. Dasheel. Arland's face looked small and ivory-colored and her eyes dark, and she kept fingering her beads as they slipped and clicked on her neck. I wasn't paying much attention, but I noticed her hands, and I had the feeling Mr. Dasheel's name somehow made her nervous.

Then someone came in and asked Arland to dance, and she and Alec left the room. Outside, where I was, the black-purple and poured-out silver shifted and steadied. Figures wandered from light to shadow, lost, like ghosts. They were drifting off to the parked cars, looking for whisky or for a place to do a little petting.

Some of the shadows kept changing, but some kept a constant dark. Two people were coming toward the house. I watched them idly, resenting them. A man and a woman. Shadow blotted them, then the moonlight bleached them. They paused in an angle of the wall.

I couldn't see them plainly, but I could make out her light dress and see the darkness of his sleeve as he put his arm around her. They clung together and kissed, his head bent, their bodies so close they seemed one. I bit my lips and my heart burned, envying their evident enjoyment of what they were doing. Then somewhere near somebody opened a door, and a ray of light caught them like a pointing finger. I knew now why they had held my eyes. It was Mark kissing Claire. His mouth, his body. The light briefly showed his yellow hair and her green dress. She ducked her head and he swung her into the shadow.

I started to lunge forward, but somebody caught and held me. "Now what are you going to do?" said Alec. "Whistling curses between your teeth!"

"Hit her—hit 'em both!" Tears of fury stung my eyes, and I felt a rumbling pain in my stomach the way you do when you are mad or frightened. I tried to break away, but Alec held me tight.

"No, you don't. Keep your shirt on. Go out there and raise a scene? It will just make you look like a little goose."

He was right, but I longed to vent my anger. Alec drew my arm under his. "You really are in a rage, aren't you? Sailing forth to lambast the guilty pair. Born and brought up to be a lady too. And so primitive. But it's refreshing to find someone so frankly red of tooth and claw. Don't you know husbands and wives should have their freedom and nourish their individuality these days?"

"Let me go, Alec."

"Not until you're calmer. I'm afraid you won't have one of these amicable divorces."

"Or any other kind."

"You will have some sort of upheaval unless you take these little episodes in your stride. There's nothing to a kiss at a party. Forget it and come neck with me, then you'll be even."

Alec couldn't understand what the episode meant to me. Maybe Mark didn't love me, but he wanted me; now he'd showed me he could want other women too . . . I was just one among many. It left me with no weapons.

Alec lifted my chin and kissed me, but I didn't respond.

"You can do better than that," he reproved me. "Such a fiery temper generally means a corresponding ardor along other, more agreeable lines. Try again." So I did, and he said, "That's better, but not as good as you could do if you put your mind on it. Sometime when you get your mind off Mark, we'll have to go in for this in a big way."

When we went in the house I found Mark and marched up to him and told him I wanted to go home. He looked surprised, but he went. When we were on our way he said, "Where'd you go off to?"

"I was outside—kissing Alec."

He didn't seem at all jealous. He laughed. "That was fast work."

"You were out necking that damned Claire."

"Oh . . . didn't expect you to find that out."

I leaned over and bit his hand as hard as I could. His flesh was tough and sparse, but my teeth were sharp, and I felt a tiger's own relish when I tasted his blood in my mouth. He didn't move his fingers; he kept the car at the same rate of speed. He didn't say a word either all the rest of the way home.

As Alec said, it was all very unimportant, but it never does me any good to realize that when I'm upset, or to know that other people are much worse off than I am, or to contemplate serene, natural aspects and meditate that the sun will rise and the stars keep steady on their courses.

Again I caught the perfume of the wild plum in flower, taunting me. But they were only flowers, fragile and soon blown away. There would be lots of plums, though, and I would make jam. I was Mark's wife, in his house, and in the fall I would gather plums and the last, teasing flowers would be long gone. He would go off far into the swamp after ducks and geese. But he would come back to sit at his own table and eat the ducks and the geese with wild plum jelly. I would win.

We went back to Wishmore. Mr. Jeff was snoring on the horsehair sofa. Mark put a blanket over him. I stalked on. The house and the people in it and the night outside, with the wind booming in the swamp, struck at me with an innate hostility. But I would fight back.

Mark followed me into our room, lighting another lamp. When I was ready for bed he came and stood beside me, fingering the lace on the collar of the robe I had put on. It had been pretty, but was in a decidedly posthoneymoon stage, like us. I'd fried bacon in it and made coffee in it, and it was frazzled out, without allure.

"Perk up, kid."

I turned my head, and a large hot tear plopped on his hand, the one I'd bitten. "I didn't know you felt so down in the mouth about it, Jane. Women! Such a to-do over things that don't matter. But pull in your horns. Have I beaten you because you were out kissing Alec?"

"That was different. That was revenge." I still would have preferred to pull Claire's hair clean out of her scalp. "You don't love her, do you?"

"Who? Claire? Just because I got tightish at a party?"

Claire wasn't important to him; I could realize that. But, then, neither was I. Who was? I stood there looking into the mirror. Colorless! That's what they had said. Anger had given a greenish tone to my skin. A smooth, indefinite kind of face—not memorable. But it wasn't going to stay that way. With skill and determination I intended to acquire more than nature had bestowed on me.

"Stop sulking, baby." Mark turned me around and held me tight. I yielded to his kisses, but I reached up and twisted the two plaits of my hair around his neck and pulled them hard around his throat.

"Smooth, shiny hair—could be lethal."

That night there was a great deal of passion in my love-making, and no inhibitions, but not much tenderness either. I scratched and snarled and bit. Like a wild animal that has once tasted blood and found out its sting and savor. I had always been told love changed bad people into good, and made good ones into angels of light—such was its power, but the school of thought in which I was reared ignored the basic earthiness of everything. Arland's pretty beads came out of a dead and stinking whale, like perfume's base. Jewels are dull lumps dug out of the ground. Love is not always exalting, as I was finding out. It was dragging me down into all sorts of evil feelings, ugly and hard.

I had a queer sort of dream. I was following Mark through the swamp. He looked as he usually did. The swamp, though, was somehow different. You know how fuzzy a dream is around the edges. He moved along steadily, but I pushed and strained to keep him in sight. Then he stopped, and a woman came to meet him. He went and took her in his arms, as he had held Claire. The same pose, the same gestures. I could see him plainly, but I never saw her face at all.

ᴥ§ Chapter Seven

How well I remember that year, from the night of the party to the time Kitty was born. Mark worked hard during the hot summer, but it was worth it because the crop was good, and I had high hopes. You always gamble on that perfect year when you'll have a bouncing crop and soaring prices. Something's always wrong, though, about that picture: either droughts or high water or no one to work it or no crop or no price.

Then I found I was going to have a baby. So was Joyce. She grumbled about the inconveniences of producing one and spent a lot of time on the sofa, eating too much and doing her nails. I used to go and rout her out and make her walk. I didn't have time to flop and I was glad over the baby. Here was somebody I could love, somebody who would be mine as Mark never would be. Maybe I would love him less, and he would love me more.

Arland began sending lavish baby dresses, and I felt myself superior to her. She wanted children and didn't seem to be having any.

We had a shock during the winter. Uncle was taken suddenly ill, and died a few days later. The day of the funeral was cold—the coldest day we'd had in several winters. The north wind whipped through Wishmore's cracks and crannies. Sharp granules of sleet had fallen heavily enough to cover the surface of the road and powder the dead fields. Icicles tasseled ice-coated branches. Smoke purled up from cabin chimneys, while the hands were cocooning themselves from the cold. Tracks of claws showed under the evergreens where the birds were trying to find shelter, their feathers puffed out. The hedge of thorn trees was bent over by the weight of ice. In a glitter of spikes last year's nests were defined, the crisscross twigs rigid as wires. The lifeless, silent land was bound together by the river's thick loops. The water, bitter in its cold dark, rolled without luster against the startling definition of its banks.

I don't believe anybody but Mark could have taken the car up the hill that day. We made it, and were on the road, slippery enough but better than the hill, and past Rosemont. The pines around the gate were black, the house invisible.

"I wish your aunt Kate had died instead of Uncle."

"You oughtn't to wish anybody dead. Poor Arland. I guess everybody who looked to your uncle will turn to her now."

"There's Tim."

"He's not like your uncle."

"All of you are so busy being sorry for Arland you don't think of me. I'll miss Uncle too."

Arland looked like a shadow, her face thinned out, her dense black clothes draining her of color. The house was crowded and so was the church. Uncle was gone, and much of the savor and flavor of old times had gone with him. He remembered the war. He'd struggled out of the ruin that had swallowed up the Ellistons and their kind, but he had clung to all the old standards and old ideas—honor and doing right and helping your family. It must have been a weight, pulling all those burdens. I looked across at Tim, his handsome florid face troubled. I knew what Mark meant. If Tim had to scrap certain principles to get ahead, overboard they'd go.

Mark was looking at Arland, his face dark and set. The gleam from the candles showed the scar. I wondered what he'd felt when he was wounded, trying to bring his plane back. He'd brought it back too. If he'd had a little less skill, a little less luck—— I wondered what he'd felt later, lying in the hospital such a long time. He'd never told me. I knew from the way he was looking at Arland how sorry he was for her and how much he could feel. It was that full depth of feeling —in joy, in sorrow, in love—that I wanted to catch and hold for myself alone. I put my hand in his and grasped his fingers tight until he turned and looked at me. I wanted his complete attention.

"Feel bad?" he whispered. I shook my head, but every now and then he turned and looked at me.

All the aunts, dependent so long on Uncle's help and judgment, turned to Tim for advice and comfort. "Arland's keeping everything just the way her father had it," Aunt Em told me one day. She had come, sad and brooding, to stay with me. Arland had followed Tim back to Washington as soon as she could leave, and Holly Trees, once so full of life, was shuttered and closed, with only Bedelia to take care of it.

While Aunt Em was still there, Mark came in from the fields and joined us. He said he'd been doctoring a sick mule, that the river was entirely too high for his liking, and it was time Ben was leaving his cabin on the tip of the point.

"Tim is a tower of strength," Aunt Em murmured. "Such a splendid young man. He'll attend to everything for Arland and for us, too, in spite of all his own affairs. I wouldn't be surprised if he became one of our really great men one of these days." Mark was listening, rolling a long, limp cigarette, and there was that mocking look on his face.

Spring came early and it grew warm too soon. There was no sharp clarity in the air, but a soft pervading moisture. Down here threads of water tangled around the roots of the willows, joined in the swamp, and gleamed slyly on the edges of the fields. The threads became ribbons, and the ribbons met and became one. The baby was almost due. Mark had begged me to go stay with Aunt Em, but I had too much to do at Wishmore. The river had never been known to come into the house, but Mr. Jeff was not taking any chances. He had jug after jug of white lightning parked in the attic, ready for anything.

The house had been prudently set far back, almost against the hill. I looked out at the ocher-colored water, quite deep now. It looked harmless enough, until you noticed the fret of current. From the top of the hill the flood showed itself. Louisiana and all the point, too, was under water. Levees had broken across the river—one crevasse after another, but our levee was only a breakwater anyhow, and here the river rose unimpeded, without obvious drama.

"How are we going to make a crop?"

"Replant—that's always the very devil."

"Do you realize that means more work and expense?" I felt naggish.

"Sure. But what else can we do?"

"How're we going to live?"

"Borrow. We have before."

"We're in deep now, and we'll have a child to support."

"It won't do you any good to fret yourself sick over it . . . we'll worry along somewhichway." He said he had to go see if everybody was off the point safely. "Scared to stay here? I won't be long."

I shook my head and watched him row off until he was blotted out of sight, as if he'd plunged into the trough of a roll of green waves.

The trees in the fullness of their moist shining rippled in a warm wind. They did not toss and sway when the wind struck them, but their tops rounded and curled forward, supple and full of sheen, like foamless ocean ridges. The motion made me dizzy. Lew took me in the skiff to one of the cabins. An old man had died, and the family were in a state. They couldn't bury him here—the water was too deep, so they had to move out with all their things and lug the corpse with them. I watched the whole regatta start for the hill, complete with litter of pigs, then I went back to our house. A gust of wind sailed the mop and broom from a corner of the gallery and spun a pail onto the bricks below. The water wasn't at the back of the house, only in front. It lapped at the bottom step. Not long after it had covered the bottom step. It wouldn't get in the house, though, but it looked so sly, creeping up.

A flowerpot fell and broke, and I called for Hettie to come move the ferns in. One of Mr. Jeff's fishermen friends was talking in the kitchen, where Hettie had fixed him some grits and grease. This old man had dug holes all over the place, looking for money presumably buried by Spaniards or pirates or Lennerds just before the Yankees came. Mr. Jeff was confident all Wishmore was a mine of buried treasure, and he was always cheering on the diggers.

On account of my interesting state Hettie wouldn't let me touch any of the plants. Not even to water them. "Die as sho as you born. My sister done hoed her a fiel' of melon when she was in yo' fix, an' dey done wizzled up like they'd bin scalt."

Clouds began to gather in layers, and a few heavy raindrops fell. Then the sun came out again, and I went to look at the garden, still unflooded, since it was behind the house. I hated the weather: dense warmth and false blue sky and that insistent wind. Tornado weather. My garden was full of bloom. Fresh-torn petals whirled. Perfume from the flowers was heavy, like a funeral. It made me sickish. The garden would die if the flood came in. It left the land fertile, but the touch of the river was poison to all existing plants. The roses were pale and hung their heads; they'd fade soon. Thorns and stems were pliable, as if the moisture everywhere had weakened their fiber. It was a year of blights and insect pests. Webs curled young leaves. Bugs chewed buds, making round holes with stained edges. A thunderclap and a very definite pain drove me into the house.

The house was dark from the darkening sky. This was a fix. A storm was coming, the baby was coming, and Mark was nowhere around.

The thunder crackled again. The darkness in the sky was sudden and intense, coming from the clouds banking in the southwest. Against their purple the trees' green was crude and fresh, like the color a child uses to paint with. It made the earth seem strangely naïve and helpless.

Why didn't Mark come in from that damned swamp! I could picture him dead, sodden, face down, with a tree blown on him and water flowing over him and his mouth filled with mud and ooze.

I wondered what on earth to do, caught down here with the river and the coming storm and the baby on the way. Just then he came in, and a flash of lightning, sharp and blue, flung a peculiar light on his face. Thunder rattled the windows, and the house shuddered lower in the slippery earth.

"What's the matter?"

"It's the baby——"

"You better get out of here right away. I think the car can make it to the hill; it's not that deep yet right in front."

"I can't go. I'm afraid of the storm." The restless, flickering lightning was all over the sky now, and the worst of the clouds, in the worst possible direction, held all the livid look of a windstorm. One spring my own father and mother had been killed in a tornado. A few years ago a colored child was missing after one. They found the body caught in a tree, with buzzards circling around.

"Jane, we'd better make a start."

I wasn't afraid of anything but storms, but I had a deadly terror of them. "Let's wait until it's over. Babies take a long time, particularly the first ones." My face twisted.

"How do you know? This one mightn't."

"I'm scared."

"We have to go. I'll tell you why. After a downpour the water around the house will be so deep we won't be able to get the car through."

"Well, go park the thing on the hill a little way, then I can get to it by skiff."

He shook his head. "That won't do. You know that road—it's bad enough now. A tree or something might fall across it, then what? Come on, let's get going." He didn't point out to me that it was my fault, that I should have stayed at Aunt Em's.

The water sloshed on the bottom step. Mark put me in the car. The wheels churned in the deepening water, but moved at last. I looked at the flooded land and the isolated house. The rose vine on the front gallery had been covered with bright pink flowers. The wind was frilling their petals all over the water to the front gate. The road was lost, but we sloshed and wavered through it until we reached the slippery hill.

We had just started up when the storm was on us with a roar. The trees over our heads were bending and curling. "You can't make it," I gasped.

"Just watch me." The car slipped sidewise. I thought the back wheel was going over the edge, but little by little we pulled up the steep road. We were about halfway up when I saw the big pine sag downward just in front of us. There was a particularly violent crash of thunder just then, but I could hear the crackling and splintering in the branches. I would have jammed on the brakes, but Mark pushed off the gas, and we shot ahead. Just behind us the tree hurtled itself across the road, the big branches sprawling.

"Our only chance," Mark said. "I knew when it fell it would fall downward. The only thing to do was to get ahead of the damn thing."

At last we were in town and at the hospital. I'd had a God's plenty of nature by the time Kitty got herself born.

Kitty was tiny, scowling, wrinkled, and lobster-colored. I had wanted a boy, another Mark. He himself had no preference. "She'll fill out. Just now she looks old as the hills. Cynical too. What you so down on the world for, sugar?"

"I wish she was as pretty as little Steve. He's a beauty." Joyce had had her baby a week before I had mine.

"She's got the right number of toes and ears and things, and a good fire-siren squall."

I held her, already fiercely doing battle for the little beastie. "You'll show 'em, Kit, won't you? You're going to be beautiful and fascinating and have glorious clothes and a gorgeous time and a wonderful life."

"I guess you're not the bland, maternal type," Mark said. "You're out for bigger and better chunks of prey for the cub."

I enjoyed my stay in the hospital. Everybody came to see me and everybody brought me presents. Arland sent me lots of things and wrote me every day. I'd written that I was supposed to have had an easy time with Kitty, but was not going to be lyrical over the process. It might be nature's way, but I could think up some a lot better.

She wrote back she'd laughed over my account of Joyce moping from sofa to sofa, then having the whole hospital in an uproar. "She won't have 'em like tadpoles, the way her mother did. Did you ever read that story—I think by Zola—about the woman who had fifteen and became more and more beautiful after each one, until after the fifteenth she was absolutely dazzling? I wonder why he's supposed to be a realist. Anyway, I wish I had Steve or Kitty or, preferably, both. I'd love to be Kit's godmother. Of course you're naming her for your mother. Aunt Kit was so sweet."

Aunt Ada brought the family christening robe, and Aunt Em brought me the silver cup and spoon my mother'd had. Her name had been Christine, not Katherine.

We went back home to Wishmore. As we drew up I remarked it looked like a haunted house. I felt a sort of chill, there in the hot sunset. The water had come to the house, though not in it. The pink rose on the front gallery was dead. A pair of mockingbirds always nested there. They wouldn't come any more. Their old nest hung abandoned in the withered, rustling leaves. It was like a bad omen.

Instead of flickering with cotton's live dark green as it ought, the ground had begun to sprout with coarse-leaved, strong-fibered weeds. Their upstart rankness perverted the rich soil. Most of the hands had straggled back, bringing their mules, their frazzle-feathered chickens, their pigs, their pickaninnies, and their lean yellow dogs, but some of the cabins stood empty, marked by the flood.

"Where's everybody?"

"Some of them have drifted off," Mark said. "Tired of it down here. One or two families have lit out for Chicago. CooshFoot went, but he came back. He told me they went straight from the train to his cousin's house. They had a fine dinner, and afterward they went for a walk. He got lost—couldn't find his way back to the house. So he got somebody to tell him the way to the station, took the next train, and came back home."

"Didn't he tell them anything?"

"Not a mumblin' word. Believe he's written to 'em since."

The flood had flung the season out of focus. Nothing was natural or in its right place. I groaned. "What a lot of work!"

"Jane, we don't have to stay."

"Where'd we go? Light out like CooshFoot and get lost and come back?"

"We could go most anywhere. I'd do better—I know it. I could find a job. Take up flying again, maybe. Some air line might hire me."

"Do you want to?"

"I always have. This is no place for me. I'll never amount to shucks down here. I love the swamp and the river, but I don't want to plant. No talent for it. I guess you wonder what makes me think I'd be worth a hill of beans at anything else. But I have a feeling I would ——"

"Leave like this? Be failures? Admit the damned river's beaten us? Defeated by inanimate things, people adrift from their moorings? No, Mark. I don't want to. One hard year won't get us down. We can make a go of it. Make a go of Wishmore. Pay off the mortgage. Buy some more land somewhere—maybe go in for something besides just cotton."

Kitty stirred in my arms, opened her eyes and then her toothless mouth, and let out a long la-la of rage and self-will and hunger. Mark took her. "All right, old gal. Chow for you." He gave a sigh.

"Let's start over again someplace else."

"No, I won't let Wishmore go. Don't ask me."

His face darkened, but he didn't say any more. He began to unpack the car, and we went in with our brand-new child into the hollow, echoing house, heavy with dusk.

I worked, scouring and scrubbing and hauling things down from the attic and putting them back in place. All through the hot days I worked, but I grew so sharp of tongue and short of temper Mark and Mr. Jeff tried to keep out of my way. Mark was working hard too. He wasn't in the house much; when he was, he was quiet. Mr. Jeff went about, restless and uneasy, or roved far in search of whisky. He no longer felt acclimated to his own peculiar sort of existence. He didn't eat much and, when he did, he went scrattling around for his food at the oddest hours.

At first Kitty didn't thrive. She was skinny and fretful, even though I went by all the latest books. Then one day Mark came in with a smooth-faced girl. "Lilly says she'd like to nurse the baby." She was Ben's daughter from down on the point. She didn't know a thing about making a formula or sterilizing a bottle, but she soon caught on, and she had a magic touch with Kitty. The little devil grew fat and placid, too, as if she imbibed a soothing blandness from Lilly's touch and voice.

People didn't come to Wishmore often. Mark said I wasn't very cordial to them when they did. Then one hot day, when the sun was a glare of incandescence on the yellow land, I had a caller.

The first was Joyce, who announced she was going to spend the day, and hauled herself out of the brand-new car Michael had given her for producing Stephen. She'd left him at home. She ensconced herself on the couch and watched me while I worked. Her conversation was not exhilarating: she talked about her short hair. I'd cut mine, so she cut hers. She talked about her new clothes while she munched on chocolates she had brought to me. I said it was too hot for chocolate. I told her she would get fat. But she remained obstinately slim and fresh and pink, with a vaguely wistful look. Melting to the beholder, unless they knew her.

She talked about Gertrude and Bess Barrett, who had taken her up and admitted her to their inner circle of friends. She talked about "poor Momma" because Poppa stayed away from home so much.

"Go see her, Jane."

"You ought to go more often yourself, instead of running around so much." Rita had gone, the children were growing up and scattering like a flock of birds. I knew I would go and get a good cook for her, help her clean the house, and urge Mrs. D. into a dark, plain dress she would loathe, but I doubted if it would bring Poppa to heel this late in the day, and said so.

Fortunately Joyce was going to Bess Barrett's cocktail party, so she took herself off to dress and preen.

Later, after sunset, when I was sitting at the back of the house, Gertrude came down. She had done well by the cocktails. Her large hat was askew, her gloves were wadded in one hand, and a bead bag dangled from one finger. She was one of those women who look best in sport things, but her dress was a wildly flowered chiffon—and a frizz of red hair was falling in one eye. She flung herself into a low chair, saying "damn" when her flesh-colored stocking sprang a run.

She hailed Mark, who came sauntering around to the corner of the house. He and I were not on the best of terms at the moment. In fact, we weren't speaking. We'd had a fight about Mr. Jeff. Mark had accused me of being mean to him, and I'd said he ought to be in an institution. Anyway, I didn't want Kitty brought up in the house with him.

"It would kill him. He likes to rove. It won't hurt Kit; he's nice to children."

I said I was fed up to the teeth with having to be sorry for all these people who simply caved in and didn't stir their stumps to do any better, the town's working with them.

"You're a hardhearted little devil."

"Why not? Who wastes any sympathy on me? I'm fed up with living with him."

"But half this place belongs to him; he has a right here."

"All the same, he ought to be in an institution."

"That's out. It would kill him in short order."

"Why not? What use is he?"

"You know I warned you about him before we were married."

"I was a perfect fool and only eighteen!"

"Meaning you'd know better now. Guess you would."

I knew he wouldn't forget what I'd said.

I hadn't seen him for the rest of the day until now. He asked Gertrude if she'd like a little nip. She'd nipped too much already, but he fixed a drink for her and one for himself, and sat on the gallery railing, saying nothing, just listening to us.

Lilly came out with a scowling Kitty. Gertrude made suitable sounds to and about her, and Lilly took her off. "She's picking up," Mark said. "When she was born she was the spitting image of old Judge Twombly on his ninetieth birthday. Now Steve was always a likely lad."

"You know, Miss Jessie came to see me in the hospital, and do you know what she asked me?—if Miss Kate liked having Kitty named for her! She knows perfectly well the child's named for my mother."

Gertrude went on to an account of Miss Jessie finding the gate off the Haydons' cemetery lot and getting it hauled off in a dray. Then she told us about Claire's engagement. "She was showing everybody her ring today."

"It's high time she landed her fish." She'd been visiting her sister. "She's been sent to hook one often enough. Is this the rich one Cousin Olive had her eye on?"

"I think so. This one has money—so they say."

"Of course. Sure to. He's a fine, wonderful boy and comes of lovely cultured people. I bet the wedding'll be as soon as Cousin Olive can rustle up eight or twelve bridesmaids. Another wedding present!"

The mention of Claire's engagement didn't seem to faze Mark. He'd finished his drink and was whittling on a piece of cedar, carving some sort of little image. "Got to put in a few licks of work. I'll bring out the whisky for you, Gertrude. You'll want more. How about letting me ride up the hill with you when you go?" He got off the railing, leaving the little figure he'd carved.

Gertrude said sure. He came back with the bottle and fixed her another drink, then left us. Gertrude watched him. "I could fall for Mark myself. Of course Tim's the great Dream Boy, but somehow Mark's more my dish. Arland's certainly absorbed in Tim. No wonder. Bess says when she was up in the Delta they were talking a lot about politics and thought Tim was really headed for big things. Bess has a new car a block long."

"Sam must have a good practice."

"Not that good. That was guilty conscience. Bess got wind he'd been running around with Ludie Daniels while she was gone—taking her joy riding. She said she wouldn't put her foot in the car after that woman had been in it. So Sam had to get a new one."

"Was Sam?"

"Wouldn't be surprised. She seems to have them all by the ears." Gertrude flung off her hat and lolled back in her chair. She rolled her blue eyes at me. "Nobody can hold a candle to her for looks. Ask Mark if he didn't think so at one time." She was very tight. "The girls in his crowd used to have a fit because he ran around with her."

Of course they would herd together—the "nice" girls against the dangerous outsider. Except Arland—and she, as usual, would keep her thoughts to herself.

"She gives the impression of never having been an innocent virgin. But I tell you, Jane, I believe the cause of her downfall was going to too many revival meetings. I remember once when there was a big one on. Brother What's-his-name was certainly stirring up the devil. There was a big crowd every evening in the tent. No wonder, the way he ranted about sin and sex. Even if you weren't curious on those topics you would be after he got through. Old man Daniels was always there, and Ludie too. That night she looked like she was drinking it all in but thinking a damn sight more of the pleasures of this world than hell and brimstone in the next. She came out with the others, fanning herself with a big hat, and her eyes looked big and shining. Mark was waiting for her, and they went off together. The way she looked at him! I was sort of jealous of them—they were so young and good-looking. I wondered where they went and what they did!" She laughed. "There's a story now she's running around with some man, and he's married."

"Sam?"

"No, Sam's just a side dish. This is someone else. But he's plenty smart or plenty careful, because nobody can get a line on who it is." She pulled herself out of her chair and stood, a little unsteady, studying me, but I didn't say anything. She offered me a cigarette and I took it. I puffed inexpertly; the smoke or something made me sickish. I walked with her to the car, and Mark came up to go with her. He could drive her up the hill, which was just as well, though at the moment I didn't care whether she slipped off the edge or not.

"Don't wait supper for me, Jane, or wait up."

"What's going to keep you that long?"

"Got things to attend to."

"How are you going to get back if you don't take the car?"

"Put my foots in the road."

I watched them drive off, and went back to the house. Lilly had already put Kit to bed, and was singing her to sleep. The books said not to, but it seemed to work. I fixed supper. Mr. Jeff came in and gave me a deep bow and retired to the ell. He was only a ghost, but there was Kitty. She was no ghost. She was new and a tyrant as babies are, but she was asleep now in her own dim curled-up world.

I ate some figs with cream on them, but they tasted slimy. I cleared the table. Next day I found I'd put a plate of cold biscuits into the refrigerator and left the fresh milk in the safe by mistake.

The house was all quiet. I went out on the gallery. The thermometer was over ninety, and mosquitoes sang and bit. There was the smell of the river and the rank smell of decayed vegetation. I loved Wishmore, but tonight it didn't love me. It kept proclaiming it didn't want to be pruned and planted and owned. The river, the knotted snarl of growth forever pushing forward, the very earth of it, formed by the river, was of the wild, and to the wild kept returning, damn it! It roused in me a stubborn persistence to conquer it. It had won out and left its stamp on everybody else who'd tried to wrassle with it, but this time I'd win.

The spread of the point looked empty in the moonlight. The tangle of the trees made a web woven together. A haze hung over the sky, and the moon looked as if it would never wax or wane or move from a fixed point. It didn't look round or solid, but thin, burned-out by long-ago fire, reduced to one dimension. There were no shadows and no radiance, only a pale and ashy lifting of the dark. Poets praised it, but it showed itself for what it was—a worn-out infertile thing, and the landscape reflected back the unmitigated heat of its lighted surface, its wanness and sense of death.

This was the earth: marred by flood, sizzled by sun, but still the earth. Alive, ready to grow, drawing richness from the slime of the mud and the glare of the summer. Dig deep enough and you'd come again to its hot core—core of fire, a reminder that it, too, had once been part of the dazzle of a star.

Kitty piped up, and I went in and changed and fed her. She guzzled and burped and grumbled and gurgled down to sleep again. She was here because once Mark and I had been together in the most complete physical togetherness, but at the moment she was conceived I hadn't been thinking of her in concrete terms. I had wanted Mark, and he had wanted to make love. I don't pretend to understand men—it's unlucky for me I've never wanted anybody but Mark. Why is faithfulness supposed to be a virtue? It's just a nuisance. If I had been attracted to a lot of other people and attractive to them, we would both have been happier. I watched Kitty's little puckered face smooth out as she slept deeper. She wasn't just Mark and me joined together; she was already herself. As she grew she thrust us apart instead of uniting us.

I went out on the gallery. I wanted Mark, and he didn't come. He had been treating me with a sort of detached kindness lately when we weren't at swords' points over something. Unfortunately, the angrier he made me, the more I wanted him. Where the hell was he? And with whom? Gertrude's accurately planted darts quivered. Did Gertrude think Mark was the man? Was he Ludie's real interest? She had hinted as much. I knew from the way that woman had looked at him he was the one—the one of her real choice, as he was mine. They'd had an affair once; what I didn't know was whether, tired of me, he had gone back to her.

If only he and I could have kept on as we had begun—go off together again as we had once—into the heart of the dark burning night. Up there on the hill, where the stars sent a vague powdery luster on the river and the plumed density of the trees offered us shelter for those long hard kisses, and the dry faintly scented pine needles were a bed for our bodies locked and mingled. Then it had been a passion sufficient to itself. Now the love I gave him wasn't free and unencumbered and never would be again.

We had a child to provide for and Mr. Jeff to snarl over, and the place, and a mortgage dangling around our necks. I didn't really want to go back to freedom. I wanted to plan ahead, be secure. I wanted marriage and children, the snugness of a firelit circle. But he didn't. He wanted to prowl outside, along jungle byways. Maybe he was tired of me and marriage and was prowling now.

But the recurring fever of wanting him was as strong as it had been at first. It was late now, and still he didn't come. As my rage against him grew, so did my desire to have him. My heart beat hard and thick, my head was swimming, and my pulses were thrumming. "The weeping Pleiades wester, and I lie down alone." Only the Pleiades weren't on hand, of course, since it was summer, and I certainly did not intend to lie down alone. Not if I could help it.

I couldn't stand my thoughts and imaginings any more, so I called Hettie to come stay with the baby, and I got in the old jalopy and tore up the hill and into town.

I drove past Rosemont and along the road until I reached town and Main Street, hot and dull and empty. I didn't see Mark. Then I turned into the street where Ludie lived. I parked the car in the deep shadows and, keeping well in the dark myself, I walked a little way until I was right across from Ludie's house. I'd come here once before. Then I'd sworn I'd get Mark away from her. I had, but I wondered if I'd kept him away from her.

Her room was dark. There wasn't a light in the house. Her mother was asleep. Ludie was gone to meet some man. Maybe Sam Barrett, maybe Mark.

I wondered how they could meet without everyone knowing it, but people did. There were places. One I knew about. A colored woman owned the house and rented rooms. It was a dull, prim-looking place, just like all the rest of the block, only neater, and it had a high fence around it. There were others. For what the Negroes called "quick service." And suppose you met someone you knew? They wouldn't tell, being in the same boat. But rumors get around, because I knew of the house, and my knowledge of the illicit was limited.

I wondered fleetingly what the colored woman herself thought of her customers. Nothing, maybe, being used to human nature and glad of the money. Perhaps, though, behind her blandness lurked a certain cynicism.

Mark wouldn't mind going there if he wanted to see Ludie badly enough. I knew perfectly well how you can be carried out of what is supposed to be your own atmosphere into an alien one, and you don't care.

My imagination was too clear. I could see Ludie looking around the empty street, scudding past the light, sidling through the gate, knocking, being shown the room where he waited. He would get up smiling, crushing out his cigarette, and his shadow would dance on the wall. The door would close quietly behind them. I could see the room I'd never been in, and would certainly never be in. There would probably be crepe-paper roses on the mantelpiece and a clock. Of course a clock. And a brass bedstead. The woman would have bought that with pride when trade was brisk, which it always would be—no doubt discarding the "reb bed" that would have been there. Which bed would have found itself in the junk shop, then would have been picked up by somebody with a nose for antiques, and by now would be passed off as having belonged to their great-grandfather, accompanied by appropriate legends of Aaron Burr and Andrew Jackson having slept in it. The present brass bed would have a bright purplish-pink bedspread, I was sure.

I tried to stop conjuring up nightmares for myself, but I couldn't stop. I could just see him go to her, and take her in his arms. Maybe he'd waited, feverish and impatient, and would say, "I thought you'd never get here." But he wouldn't, because he'd have been sure she would come. Just as she would be sure he would wait. She'd say something, casual enough, and it wouldn't matter, because she'd be pulling her clingy dress over her head and flinging it aside. She'd sit on the edge of a chair and kick off those high-heeled fancy shoes she always wore and unroll her flesh-colored stockings from below her knees. She always rolled her stockings. No girdles or bras for her. She didn't mind advertising the gifts of nature. I suppose a lot of modesty is vanity anyway. I've often wondered why the less well-endowed Victorian females bothered with those neat pads on their bosoms. After all, they were no use in the clinches. Victorian men must have been let in for a lot of disappointments.

And she'd strew her scant but gaudy underpinnings all over the room . . . he'd go to her and draw her to him, his hand hard and brown on her bare white shoulders, and the rings of her hair would fall across his arm. He'd light a cigarette and put it in her mouth, watching her. Then he'd take it out and put it in the ash tray with his. Her face would be turned to his, her hair spreading out on the pillow with a ripple and gleam running through its dark, and her black eyes half closed with their wicked shine glinting, a shine like dark water reflecting a surface gloss, and her mouth half parted. I had never seen her mouth when it was not thick with lipstick. That would be long gone now, but he would be past noticing or caring. Her face and body would gleam up at him, and they would never bother to turn out the light. Then the shadow of his face so close would darken hers. The cigarettes would burn on, forgotten, hers with lipstick around the edge. And the smoke from them would waver up and mingle.

That's what I thought about, alone in the dark. Nobody passed me. No one came and went from her house. The street light shone on its blankness. The moon flickered on the dark window. A few leaves, already dry, sifted down from the tree overhead. A car rocketed by, packed with young boys and girls coming from a dance. I heard their laughter and the tune of some fool song.

I went back to the car and drove down to Wishmore. Mark hadn't come. I sent Hettie back to her cabin and waited again. Maybe the aunts were right—the aunts and all their ilk—when they thought nobody ought to feel as I did. Long ago the morning star, shaking with its burning, set in the hot-colored, sullen sky, had shone in my eyes like a warning. What I was feeling was all wrong, not because it was sex, but because I was caught and wrung in the grip of the cruel Venus whose other face is hate and who longs to wound and maim and kill.

The dogs began to bark, and I heard Mark whistling as he came sauntering down the hill toward the house. The sight of me sitting there startled him. "What you waiting up for? Anything wrong with Kit?"

"No, I'm waiting for you. Where on earth have you been all this time?"

"I told you not to wait up. Had to see that man about the timber. I told you that." While he talked he was patting the old hound.

"Not till this late you didn't."

"Ran into Sam and a couple of other fellows."

"Sam'll have a sweet time convincing Bess if he's out this late. He's been running around with Ludie Daniels."

He laughed. "Gertrude must have been dishing out the dirt." He lit a match and looked at me over the flame before he blew it out. His face was thinner than it had been, with shadows in the hollows below his eyes.

"That nasty, vile, stinking little polecat! They ought to tar and feather her and run her out of town."

"Oh, shut up, Jane. You sound so damn vicious!"

I wanted to accuse him, tell him all I'd imagined, and beg him to tell me the truth. I was afraid. Afraid to show myself as I really was. Afraid of the absolute contempt he'd feel for me if he hadn't been with Ludie, afraid of his lies if he had. Or maybe he wouldn't even lie. He might say, "All right—what of it?" What would I do then? I wouldn't leave him. I couldn't kill him. And there wouldn't be any other solution.

"What were you doing all these hours?"

"I told you. Had a few drinks. Rolled the bones awhile."

"Stop shooting craps. You know we can't afford it."

"I don't. Just tonight. Got to keep my hand in. Won."

"Well, stop it."

"For God's sake, shut up telling me what to do and what not to do! I'm fed up with it. Shut up and go to bed."

"Don't you tell me to shut up——" My hand was thrust out to slap him as hard as I could, but he was too quick for me. He caught my wrist. "No you don't."

His fingers around my wrist made me weak all over.

"Mark, you make me like this. It's all your fault. I got simply wild, waiting, not knowing where you were. You make me so damn mad——"

He knew very well what I wanted, but he let go my wrist and moved away from me. "Hell, I've got to be up before the crack of day to ride out and look at that timber. You act like you need sleep yourself. Here." He pushed a roll of bills in my hand and went into the house.

I stood there, winding my fingers in the worn dirty money. I hated him. Damn him, damn him, damn him!

∽§ Chapter Eight

Something happened to me then, and I never really got over it. It left a lingering scar. I was silent and sulky. Mark and I didn't make up until one fall night when I was changing Kit's bed and he came and took her out of my arms. "Wet as a rat—regular fountain of youth." He tucked Kit in her fresh bed and put his arm around me. "You're colder than frogs. You ought to put something on when you go padding around at night." I was not an alluring object. I had on an old, faded nightgown, my eyes were sleep-bleared, and my mouth was full of safety pins. Shivering, we went back to bed, and Mark blew out the lamp. The stars glittered in. Nearby an owl hooted, and I sat up.

"What's the matter?" Mark asked.

"Owl. After the chickens."

"Forget the cares of the place for a while." He pulled me down. "I'll shoot the damn thing tomorrow. You're skinny—nothing but skin and bones."

"You're always telling me about my defects."

"You're crazy. I don't. Just telling you not to wear yourself to a nub." He touched my lips. "Mouth still full of safety pins?"

It wasn't, and he kissed me, and I couldn't help kissing him back. For a while I thought everything would be all right, the way it had been at first. But it wasn't. I heard Mark fumbling around for his pack of cigarettes. He lit a match.

"You'll set the house on fire. Smoking in bed all the time."

"Not much loss." A shutter was banging, and in the walls rats were playing football with pecans. You could hear them scurrying, and the rattle of the nuts.

"It's all we've got."

He gave a groan. "Don't let's get started on our troubles this time of night."

I sighed and he asked, "What's the matter?"

"Nothing. Only you don't escape very long, do you? It's fine while it lasts, but then you're right back where you started."

"I guess you aren't supposed to use it as an escape. Of course, a hell of a lot of people do. But it doesn't work out so well in the long run. It's supposed to be part of a whole, and the rest ought to be right too."

"And you mean the rest isn't. With us."

"Is it? We ought to make it be. We've got Kit now."

I lay awake, resenting him. It was his fault things weren't right. The owl hooted, nearer, a threat in its harsh cry.

That winter Ludie Daniels married and left town. "To a doctor," Gertrude told me. "Supposed to be well off. But there's something not quite right about him. Bet he does illegal operations." Anyway, she was gone. Her mother went out West to live with one of the married sons, and the narrow brown house passed into other hands.

I didn't say a word to Mark, or he to me. The harm she'd done seemed to linger. I knew Bess Barrett and Sam were always wrangling, and they had been very happy before that summer Bess was away, when Sam had buzzed here and there with Ludie. Mark and I had our ups and downs too. We couldn't seem to get back to the time that once had been.

Some power of attraction drew Ludie back. She had not been gone more than a year when suddenly she was in our midst again. A backwash from the wave of night clubs and speak-easies hit us. Speak-easies were mushrooming everywhere. The most luxurious one was the Owl's Nest. It had a bar and a gambling room and a wide dance floor. Here Ludie had ensconced herself. People said she had part interest in it, but everybody wondered who had set her up. Either she had taken his money when she left her husband, or the money of someone else. She herself had become mysterious. She seldom appeared on Main Street, but all the town had taken to going out to the Owl's Nest to drink and dance and gamble. Sometimes Ludie did not show herself at all, then again she would appear. People told me she was more beautiful than ever and wore beautiful clothes. She would display herself briefly on the dance floor, or hover for a few minutes over the gambling table, then retreat to her own rooms in the back.

It was a logical unfolding of the saga of Ludie. From the narrow brown house with its nasal holier-than-thou atmosphere and the revival tent meetings, she had progressed to the shining lights and clicking dice of the Owl's Nest. Keeping as it did a surface conforming to the letter of the law, all kinds of radiations spun out from that place. There were tourists cabins. Well, why not? It was on the highway going north. But the cabins, set in neat little grass plots, were more for illicit loves than for travelers. Brawls began on the dance floor. They were quickly subdued and finished outside, and the dancing went on. At the tables around the dance floor waiters slipped money out of hands and put whisky in them. Everybody knew you could buy it there. Couples slipped out to the cars and necked, and husbands and wives found them out. A dozen marital difficulties sprang from some episode starting out at the Owl's Nest. Sleek cars parked briefly. Hard-faced men went in, stayed awhile, went off again, up toward Memphis, down in the direction of New Orleans. Bootleggers. Big-time bootleggers. Well, you had to buy whisky somewhere. Ludie, seen or unseen, was the center of it all. Like some strange flower, she had burst out of the hard dry soil of her environment to bloom in this spurious glitter.

❧ Chapter Nine

Tim knew people: their weaknesses, their hopes, what they wanted, and just how they intended to go about getting it. He had a genius for getting in with the right, the important, people. I've seen others play that game, too, but not so well as he did it. He was smart enough to disguise what he was doing by being the soul of geniality to people who weren't important at all. I know now how clever he was. He was aware that some seemingly obscure individual might at some later day become important, and he let no field lie fallow.

Of course he had a driving ambition, but he hid it. He carried out his most careful plans in an offhand way, with an air of impulse, as if he just dashed headlong into things on the spur of the moment.

His family and mine were not pleased when Tim, first running for Congress, accepted the help of Mr. Dasheel. He was a large, bland person with influence in the north of the state and a great deal of power in the counties around us, where he had a lot of property. Uncle said Dasheel had mixed himself up in some shady company, and the company had "mulcted"—Uncle's word—the widow and the orphan out of their money by their tricky manipulation of stocks and shares. Tim claimed Dasheel had been an innocent victim, and had lost a lot in it himself.

The deal—whatever it was—faded in people's minds, and when Tim won his race, Dasheel was at Uncle's house that night, the night of the celebration party. His influence had certainly helped Tim win. What favor Tim did for him up in Washington I don't know. I didn't see Dasheel again until after Uncle's death.

Then, afterward, Dasheel would drop in for dinner at Holly Trees when he was in town. He didn't look as though he'd ever lost a lot of money. He wore the most immaculate and beautiful white suits and smoked expensive cigars. When Tim ran again, though, Dasheel didn't appear, nor was there any public mention of his support and backing. Yet they must still have been friends, because the section of the state where he had most influence voted heavily for Tim.

Mark said Tim played in his usual luck, because when the tumult of the Klan was at its height he was already in office, and in our state it had passed its zenith before he came up for re-election. "He walks on eggs better than any man I ever saw."

There was never any violence in our town, but old friends stopped speaking to each other, and someone asked the bishop just *what* was under the cathedral. The bishop said the furnace. The idea got about that arms and ammunition were stored in the basement against the day the Pope would set sail for these shores and take over. Some of the older people were confused over the thing. I went with Aunt Em to see Cousin Medora, who lived in an old house in the middle of the woods and would have been perfectly helpless without her colored people. Roaring into her ear trumpet, I asked her if she'd had any trouble keeping her hands on the place. Our hands were getting frightened and wanted to make tracks for Chicago, but stayed because they knew Mark would take care of them. "He ain't gonna let nobody meddle with his folks," CooshFoot said. "They come down heah in dey sheets, and he run 'em clean off with dat gun he done brung home from de wah."

Cousin Medora said she didn't see why the Klan had to ride again. There were very few Yankees around, anyway, and those had been assimilated.

The Klan annoyed me because I didn't want the darker race upset. We were always needing cotton pickers and cooks and gardeners and washwomen and nurses, and I saw no reason to encourage them to go and perform those tasks elsewhere. I was always for keeping them happy.

"How do you suppose Tim stands on it?" I wondered.

"He's in a pretty ticklish spot," Mark said. "Lots of big shots up there are dead against it, and lots of pretty important people in this state. But a lot of voters are in it. Maybe he joins a parade every now and then here at home and discards his sheets on the outskirts of Washington. I wouldn't put it past him to run with the hares and hunt with the hounds."

"Why don't you like him any more? You used to be such friends."

Mark gave no satisfactory answer. He said Tim was just a smooth, gleaming hunk of façade.

"He's smart."

"Plenty," Mark admitted. "Watch him wangle himself out of this one."

And he did. Some of his enemies—and he didn't have many then —accused him of belonging. I don't think he ever out and out denied it in a public statement; he let the accusation slide. As far as I remember, his only public reference to it was during a speech when he said taking justice into secret hands led to abuses. The Klan had died down then, and he was speaking in an anti-Klan county.

The buoyancy of the opulent twenties suited Tim. He rode the glowing wave. The good years, the fine fat kine of the dream, were at hand. We felt it in town; we even felt it at Wishmore. New cars glittered on Main Street. Pickaninnies began to wear bright rust-colored shoes. Cotton was going up. Plant it, harvest it, pack it in thick bales. There's something sumptuous about a big fine bale of cotton showing its humpy side through its sacking and straining at its metal bands. Like the good old days before the Civil War, and the good old days before the boll weevil, and the good old days during World War I—we were all justified in plowing and planting and sweating and hoeing and picking and hanging on by the skin of our teeth through flood and drought and insect swarms and glutted markets, because here were the good times again. Hold on long enough and cotton will make your fortune. It's bound to happen, or so we all dream. You might wind up in the poorhouse while you wait for the good times to come back again, like an inexact and fleeting comet, but hold on.

In those days Tim could speak with fervid optimism and feel and make us feel his confidence. He could promise riches and happiness and peace and world trade and better roads and better schools and we could all believe. He decided to run for the Senate in the next election. He wanted a chance at the important committees, the real decisions, the real power. Prominent people in his party were beginning to watch him and talk about him.

The whole family were in a fever over his plans and his hopes. I felt I had a part in Tim. Hadn't I gone with Arland that first election to hang posters on trees and interview voters? It gave me a stake in his future. One day when he and Arland were in town, I went to the house. It was hot and the windows were open. There was a big new car drawn up near the front gallery, and from inside I heard voices. Tim's I recognized, not the other, until Mr. Dasheel came out of the front door just as I went up the steps. He looked at me, clawed off his hat, and hurried by without stopping to speak. Tim stood in the door and watched him go.

I believe that was the very day Tim and Dasheel came to the parting of the ways. I can't be sure. Tim didn't say anything to me about it. His preoccupied expression smoothed itself out and he invited me in and offered me a drink, and talked just as usual. I didn't want a drink, but he did, and swallowed it down fast, as if he needed it. I went on upstairs to find Arland, leaving him there, and what he thought about I don't know, but I wondered later.

Now about twenty miles below town the hills fall away to a swamp. It belongs to the river rambling through it. When the Mississippi is high, the swamp's river overflows and laps all over the low ground. Creeks join the river, and the land itself is lost, wrinkled with their grooves and spilled over with their waters. No one owns it, shadow clings to it, the sun falling off from the coarse growth. All the country round, even beyond the swamp itself, is lonesome. In places the county line wavers on first one side of the swamp's river, then another, and the state line breaks in here and there to wander, too, until all the boundaries are uncertain and usually lost in layers of flood. Sometimes when you cross the bridges on the highway a snarl of water is rushing by, almost to the bridge itself, and you feel its threat.

The swamp made itself useful for moonshiners. They could hide their stills and make their whisky in peace. There weren't enough officers of the law to invade the swamp and stalk its shadows and fall in its bogs. And besides, there were conflicting county and state lines. Little by little all the rackets of prohibition got under way. There was too much money to be had in the brewing and sale of whisky, and the swamp changed. For a while nobody seemed to notice it when the old-fashioned type of moonshiners gave way to more highly organized competition. The rivers and creeks still overflowed, the willows still dropped deep veils. Just as the rivers and streams netted the soggy ground, denizens from the real underworld of the big cities began to creep in and set up their own kingdoms and keep up their own wars with each other. Slowly a sense of ugly doings—a sense of murder—began to seep out. Trucks appeared on the highway and disappeared from it. Strangers once in a while showed their faces briefly in some of the little towns beyond the swamp, and vanished again. Sometimes the young men in the towns, idle loiterers with nothing to do and an itch for money, followed them off.

For a while nobody was very much interested. If the swamp was the hide-out for people who found other places too hot to hold them, as long as they stayed there and preyed on each other the public hardly knew or cared.

Then a Chinaman slid into the office of a lawyer practicing in a small town tucked off in an out-of-the-way county. He wanted a man sued. He wanted his money back. He'd hired the man to kill the murderer of his brother. The hired killer had agreed to do the job, and had sent the Chinaman a package. In the package was a finger, a human finger. Proof. The killer was worthy of his hire. He said it was the finger of the man who had murdered the Chinaman's brother, and the Chinaman was content. But he happened to see the murderer of his brother driving by along the highway, still alive. The killer had not done the job, and the Chinaman wanted his money back. The lawyer must bring suit, so he could get his money back.

The vagaries of the river's current played their part too. One day a respectable fisherman was out at the river's edge, and the Mississippi washed a dead body against his boat: a murdered man, dumped in the swamp's river, borne into the Mississippi, pulled down by the current and spewed out again, dead, bloated, riddled with shots. He had not been supposed to reappear or tell tales dead men are supposed to keep secret. But the corpse told a good deal. The corpse, when alive, had been badly wanted for a holdup—an armed robbery in a Texas town. He had fled here to the swamp. In the swamp he'd pitted himself against person or persons already in possession, or they had felt he would.

After that the story of other murders came to our ears. There were sporadic efforts on the part of law and order to get into the swamp and clean the place up, but the killings went on.

"Looks like somebody's in on it," Mark said one day to Sam Barrett; they'd been hunting and had come in. Over their drinks they were talking about the dead man found in the river. "Looks like there must be."

"Might, at that. But it's no easy place to tackle. Not enough men to do it!"

It was not long after that Tim broke with Dasheel for good and all. They hadn't been agreeing. A bill came up before the House. Tim was its ardent supporter; Dasheel was against it, or vice versa. Dasheel withdrew his votes and his influence and backed Tim's opponent. Tim could do the best he might without him. It was all calm, with no name calling. They were both quiet about the break. The aunts said Tim was putting dignity back into political life at last . . . I wanted to know when it had been in. The founding fathers had called each other everything under the sun.

Mark mused about it. "I don't get it. He throws Dasheel over; says, 'I don't want you any more.' And there's an election before too long. Now why——"

"Maybe Dasheel threw him over because he wouldn't back down about the bill."

"Don't think so. Tim's strong—stronger than Dasheel now. Not like him to make a clean break. Tim likes to rise above the folks he formerly needed but keep 'em in his entourage and throw a few sops to 'em. He's damned smart at it."

"Well, if Tim wanted to break it off, I guess he thought it would look bad to do it after election. So he got it over with before."

"But why the outright break? Dasheel's taking it lying down too. Not a yip."

"Maybe he doesn't know anything against Tim to yip about."

"Sure he does. Plenty of odds and ends he could gather up and trot out. Guess Tim knows yet a plenty more on Dasheel, though. Therefore the mutual silence."

The affairs of Tim and Dasheel sank into silence, and for a while affairs connected with the swamp sank into a simmering quiet, too, until the day when a highway patrolman saw a long black car careening around the curves of the highway, going south. He tried to stop it. Instead, the men in the car shot the patrolman dead, but not before he had managed to wound one of the men.

It was a lonely stretch of road and dark was coming on, and it was nearly an hour before the patrolman's body was found. The car had disappeared. It wasn't seen in Baton Rouge or New Orleans. The men in it were the ones who'd held up a bank in a Louisiana town, and had crossed the river and were headed south.

The patrolman was a nice boy with a wife and young baby, and the people of his own town were wild with fury and excitement. At last enough raging deputized citizens and local and state police gath-

113

ered together to invade the swamp and clean it up. Whatever influence had been used to keep things quiet couldn't hush this up. They found plenty, including a house on stilts full of medical supplies. They had brought the wounded man from the car to it. The rest of that particular group had cleared out, but the whole pattern was plain enough: where the whisky was made, how it was sold, and where the protection was coming from.

Dasheel was the man keeping things quiet, and getting paid for it. A lot of others were involved too. Of course, Dasheel had never intended to get in it so deep. At first it had been easy enough to wink at a little whisky making and take a cut on the profits for the closed eye. It hadn't stayed simple and easy. There was too much money to be had. Too many undesirable characters smelled it out and wanted to be in on the game. Too many shifty-eyed gentlemen, wanted for a little holdup somewhere or an unexplained death, winged their way to such a safe refuge. It had grown more and more complicated and more and more dangerous. Dasheel didn't know how to get out. He might have wormed his way out of the mess if it hadn't been for the bad luck of the patrolman getting killed.

What keeps all of us breathless and sleepless was whether or not Tim's name would ever be connected with it all. I was sure Arland must be frantic, and I was frantic for her, but when she came home in the midst of the excitement, she showed not a trace of any kind of fear, either by what she said or what she didn't say, or the way she looked.

There was plenty of evidence against Dasheel: whom he'd met, when money had changed hands. There was no evidence at all against Tim. At Dasheel's trial Tim's name was hardly mentioned. None of the witnesses had ever laid eyes on him, or had any dealings with him. There was no record, written or spoken, that he'd ever put his hands on any money in connection with that or anything else.

"Of course Tim wouldn't be mixed up in such a mess," I said to Mark, when it was over and we could draw a free breath.

"Not exactly mixed up, but he must have had an inkling of what was going on; he must have done a little discreet soft pedaling now and then. Of course he was too smart to get in deep on anything as dangerous as that. He saw pretty well when it was all getting too hot to handle, and was like a cat on hot bricks until he rowed a pretty good distance from a ship he knew was sure to sink."

"Maybe he didn't know a thing about it."

"Maybe. But if he'd been absolutely innocent—completely ignorant of everything—why would he have cut loose from Dasheel at all? He wouldn't have known he had to. The way I figure it, he said to Dasheel, 'Let me skidaddle while the skidaddling is good, and neither of us will spill any beans about anything.' " He added, "As you know, this is for private consumption only. I'm perfectly ready to fight a duel for Tim any day—in public. Noble character, much too fine and too noble ever to dream his old friend could ever stoop, etc."

Naturally Tim's opponents tried to cash in on it. You never heard so many speeches beginning, "The finger of suspicion" and "The finger of suspicion inevitably points." There was no real meaty savor in any of their finger pointings. There was no evidence. Nothing they could prove. I read dull column after dull column—Tim was lucky in having opponents of a surpassing dullness, rich only in clichés—to see if any of them would size things up the way Mark had, but none of them hit on his arguments.

A good many people might have had a few sneaking doubts about Tim, but they either smothered them or forgot them. I even heard some people say that if Tim did have faint inklings, he couldn't have told on Dasheel.

The patrolman, poor boy, was long buried. His widow married again. The secret house in the swamp rotted. Floods lapped it, worried it, and eventually carried it to the Mississippi. After its seethings and eruptions the swamp sank back to its usual somnolence.

Tim's confident voice rang out, telling his hearers to come and be part of the nation and the modern world, to believe in themselves and their future, and to plunge into the opulent stream of the golden present. Planters loaded with mortgages and share croppers in their eroded hills listened to him and went to the polls and voted for him. The candidate running against him, a colorless soul, lagged far behind. Before midnight, on election night, we all knew Tim had won. Mark said his speeches had the flavor of a high-school pageant—"calling the turn on the Indians, the French, the coming of the Spaniards —once he even lugged in De Soto standing on the banks of the Mississippi—and all the Civil War heroes. He could have said the whole damn thing in one sentence: 'Let's get in the chips, boys.' "

Dasheel went to jail. Tim went to the Senate.

৺§ Chapter Ten

Tim and Arland came home for Christmas, the Christmas of '28, and all the family gathered for dinner at Holly Trees, following old custom. Unfortunately, on Christmas morning Mark and I had one of our disagreements. It was, as usual, about the place. He was saying land was a burden.

"The matter with us is we haven't got enough land, Mark. If we had another place on this side—— I'd like one near Newstead—that creek bottom's good—and maybe one in Louisiana. Then we could branch out, have cattle and timber and sheep and maybe turkeys——"

"And possums and coons and owls and polecats and a bear or so ——" Mark was sketching a plane and only half listening to me.

"Oh, shut up." I looked at the drawing. "It has queer wings——"

"That's a Lennerd invention. Fly faster."

"I want land. I'm afraid of stocks. Tim's doubled Arland's money on the market, but I wouldn't fool with it even if I had the cash. Gertrude showed me hers. They're just pieces of paper to me."

"Didn't know she ever bought anything but whisky."

"She's got some shares of something. They've got pictures of a woman in a nightgown with a wreath lopsided on her hair. Somehow land looks more substantial."

"Taxes are substantial. I'd like a good job." Mark flung down his pencil. "If I'm ever going to strike out, now's the time."

"Don't be a fool. Now's the time to hold on. We've had some good years. We'll have better." We'd lowered the mortgage, and looked forward to putting some improvements on the place. We even had a telephone and two cars. "Throw away all our work! Never heard of such a ridiculous idea!" Besides, some day Miss Kate might die, and I wanted to be on hand when she did. I wondered if she was secretly married to Mr. Charlie. It might make a difference. Of course she could will him everything. But he wouldn't live forever. Miss Constance would give it back to the Lennerd heirs.

116

"That's the trouble with you, Jane. You think it's crazy because you want to stay here. What about me? Why do we have to do your way instead of mine?"

"Because mine's practical and yours isn't."

"You've never let me try it."

"I tell you once and for all, Mark Lennerd, I'm not going out on any wild goose chase of yours."

"Why the hell shouldn't I have a chance at what I want? Tell me that!"

"You don't know what you want. If you did, you'd never have come back. You'd have known when you came back from the war."

"If I once got going I might find out. This way I never will."

"For the Lord's sake, shut up about your blasted career, Mark. Knuckle down to what's on hand. You're ruining Christmas."

He muttered that I ruined plenty of his days, and went off to dress for dinner. I'd made him mad, but he'd come around. Later he'd realize I'd been right. Later on, when he was older, and not so restless, he'd be glad I'd kept him here where he belonged. We'd do all right with Wishmore, and spend our old age on top of the hill at Rosemont, and be happy, and he would admit I was right all the time.

He came out ready to go to Arland's. On the way we talked to Kitty but not to each other, and collected the aunts one by one as we went along. "It's nice to see the tree shining out of the window where it belongs," Aunt Ada said. "It's sad, all these big houses meant for big families and high living, with just a stray old maid rattling around inside, living on toast and tea."

"Rosemont's sad."

"Pitiful. And Katie was such a beautiful girl. Presented at court too. Shut up there for all these years. And black up there. Pitch-black."

Arland met us at the door, wearing a pale soft-colored dress and looking younger than she had since Uncle's death. That, and afterward, when she was worried over Tim's career and the struggle with the election, had kept her pale and strained and thin. She seemed happier now. Her hair and eyes had their luster again and her skin its brown-rose tints.

The house was warm with fires and bright with candles; there was a truly glorious smell of Bedelia's cooking, fuming out of the big kitchen and teasing us, mingled with scents of wine and flowers and evergreens. The tree, sweeping to the ground in symmetrical tiers and tapering to a fine point, was lit by little wax candles. Arland scorned the easier and safer electric lights. We'd had little wax candles as children, and Arland's trees would always blaze and twinkle with them.

All kinds of people milled through the house these days: rich sportsmen down for the hunting, businessmen, politicians, reporters, and various others who wanted to cultivate Tim, or ones he wanted to cultivate. What would Aunt Margaret think of Dasheel, or of Tim for having known him? A man mixed up with holdups and rumrunning. Rackets. In her day the word "racket" meant the noise children made. The house itself, though, always looked just the same. The draperies hanging in exact folds, the curly-footed étagères bearing an assortment of figurines, china boxes, and various fragile dodads were arranged in just the order Aunt Margaret had placed them. And the old easy, semifeudal life, maintained first by Uncle's sense, and then by Tim's up-and-comin' shrewdness, could still go on, whether Arland was at home or in Washington.

Whole droves of Negro families—they had cabins out beyond the vegetable garden—still considered themselves as belonging to the place. They supplied generation after generation of cooks and maids and gardeners and milkmen. They were always around, sweeping the walks, raking the leaves, crowding the kitchen, picking pecans or figs, and being liberally rewarded. They toted what they pleased, and Arland supplied them with medicines and loans, got them out of jail, and brought their pigs to sleek maturity by the liberality of the garbage they took from the house.

Today batches of Sophie's and Bedelia's children, dressed in their best, popped up from every bush and shrub, shouting, "Christmas gif'!" In a few days, loaded with presents, we'd go out to Newstead and have a Christmas tree out there for the plantation people.

When we went in the house, Sophie's youngest was sitting under the tree, her bright round eyes peering out at us, a shiny toy in her hand and her mouth stuffed with candy.

Arland asked where Mr. Jeff was. We hadn't been able to find him, and supposed he was in jail. Arland said she'd save his dinner. "Alec's here. Isn't that nice?"

It was, and just as she spoke, he came out of the library to meet us and be welcomed. We all went into the room for our drinks. Kitty

118

and Stephen whirled around the tree, and the candlelight shone in their eyes. Joyce and Michael were there, and Mark and Alec began to talk together about Alec's last trip to Europe.

Arland had borrowed Stephen for Christmas Eve. Imagine parting with your child on Christmas Eve! But Steve would rather be with Arland anyway.

Aunt Tee sighed a little because her sons weren't with her. She made a good deal of to-do over them, but I think she enjoyed her freedom, her calls, her friends, and her lending library. The aunts read all the latest thrillers and all the most shocking modern books, then murmured, "So terribly frank. So needless."

Alec admired Kitty. "Tee must teach her to flirt," I said. "She taught Arland, but not me."

Mark heard, and looked at me and grinned. Alec looked at me, too, and gave me a meaning sort of smile, as though he knew just what Mark meant. He couldn't quite.

"Flirting wouldn't interest Jane," Mark said, and went on talking to Alec.

"That's right," Aunt Tee commented. "Jane, you must take your aunt Margaret's place. Arland's away too much, and really, Arland, your mother would think you were too tolerant."

"I'm sure I don't know what Margaret would say these days." Aunt Em sighed.

"You-all got a little out of hand once." Arland poured more cocktails for everybody. The aunts didn't realize it, but they adored cocktails. "Over Mrs. Ames."

I didn't remember her, but the others did. "Very tall," Aunt Em said. "Really too tall for a woman."

"But stylish, Em."

"Almost too stylish." Aunt Ada was "sensible" in her clothes, always lagging behind the fashions.

"Wonderful hats," Arland mused. "Like Easter egg baskets. The men called her a fine figure of a woman."

"Padded?" Mark dropped what he was saying to Alec to listen.

"Probably, but the rumor got around she wore tights under her clothes instead of the regulation number of petticoats."

"How did you know, Arland?" Alec was charmed by Mrs. Ames.
"We didn't."

"But if she didn't stalk out in 'em, what was the difference?"

"She gave a slinky effect—very slinky," Aunt Ada said.

"Anyway, Mamma decided not to call. And one by one the rest of you sneaked off and did call. And Mrs. Ames gave a party; nobody talked of anything else for weeks before or after."

"The White Rose Ball she called it, after a book somebody in her family wrote—*The White Rose of Columbia*."

"A Tale. By a lady," Arland said. "We had it."

"Such a sweet little story," Aunt Tee murmured.

Alec groaned. "How did women pore through all the trash they did?"

"Of course you know all about it, you wretched Tee. You got invited to the party, and Mamma didn't."

"I didn't go, Arland. You know I never go anywhere."

"I went," Aunt Ada admitted. "The house was filled with white roses, big ones, and Mrs. Ames wore white satin and diamonds in all that piled-up fair hair, and there was a course supper with a caterer from New Orleans."

"No wonder it rankled with Mamma. She pretended she didn't care, but she felt pretty grim about it, you could tell."

We were laughing about it when Tim came in, beaming, his arms laden with gay packages. Presents for everybody. He kissed us all, told us about his long-distance call, and seemed really delighted to have us gathered around him again.

In his looks and ways he reminded me of those vivid young Southerners—the aunts always called them cavaliers, thereby endowing them in my mind with an aura of fine lace and dash—who rode off to fight for the Lost Cause.

Tim, though, was of the present. He told Arland he'd talked to the man he wanted to find and it was all arranged, everything was fine. Some plan, some deal. An inside piece of information, the inside track on a big deal, a little advice on an important undertaking—publicity, or profit, or both.

He would keep on rising in the world, and Arland would rise with him. I couldn't help envying her.

He was talking to the aunts about his parents, how they always spent Christmas in the country with his grandmother, and how he missed having them with him. "But can't break up the old tradition." He always paid lip service to old traditions. I wondered how many he'd stepped on.

120

We went in to a dinner of full panoply. I sat next to Alec. I asked him about his trip, and he said he wanted to go to Russia next. Everybody started arguing with him. None of us had ever been there or knew anything about it. I had surreptitiously read the works of Ouida, and had only vague ideas of princes with vast possessions and bags of turquoises to fling about with nonchalance. What Alec was saying sounded dreary. If I couldn't be Catherine the Great and have Potemkin and the crown jewels, it didn't interest me. "Anyhow, it's awfully far away."

"Nothing is," Mark said. "Air age."

"Wonderful age," Tim gloried. His eyes shone with the joy he felt in his own living.

Arland said it was a hard age: look at poison gas and tanks. "Like horrible bugs grown into monsters to crawl and crush, as if things not human had taken over to grind us all up."

Mark said all ages were hard, and there was nothing intrinsically evil in bolts and nuts. "You drew a picture once of Front de Boeuf's castle. Romantic-looking ruin, drooling with ivy, and a moon in the offing. But the real thing was on the grisly side. They poured molten lead when provoked. It's people, not machines, you mind."

Arland said we ought to stop being barbarians and really care what happened to people. It was high time we were changing ourselves.

"Stop talking war and weapons," Tim put in. "There won't be any more. But I must say the last one had its moments. Paris——" His eyes gleamed. "In the spring of 1918 you learned how to make the most of your time, I tell you!" Tim could always get the best out of life. He would have savored those brief, sparkling days and nights: a leave in Paris, on the horizon the boom of guns; in the city a surge of zestful adventure crammed into hours. I looked at Mark, seeing him with that French girl he had loved. She had shared a part of his life that I never could. He would like the danger, the sense of the shortness of time. . . .

Tim began to talk about the future. We would have bigger and better cars. We needed good roads, and he was going to see that we had them all over the state. Cars, radios—everybody would be part of the world. Women who'd drudged all their lives would have electricity and machines to do the heavy work. They'd stay young and be happy.

I ate the last of my charlotte russe. I had asked Bedelia for the recipe, but I know that smiling, fat fiend had left out something Mine didn't taste like hers. Before we left the table Tim made us drink a toast: "To next Christmas, and the next, and all of us gathered here."

Arland called the jail. They had just let Mr. Jeff out. She came and sat down near Alec and me. We began to discuss people's looks. "Kit has Mark's coloring," Arland said, "but it gives an entirely different effect on her." She had Mark's light luminous eyes and ash-blond hair, but a fair silvery skin instead of his dark one. "Kit looks cool, and he doesn't. Authors who say you can tell the hero is a noble character by his upright bearing and firm chin are so tedious and silly, but you can tell something about Mark from his looks, can't you? His eyes and hair are so light, but he just doesn't have a blond temperament. You can tell he's quick, and hot-natured. It shows through." Mark was talking to Michael about building a boat and getting mad about it, telling Michael he was wrong.

Alec wanted to know what she meant by a blond temperament, anyway. They were arguing about it when Tim came over and took the chair next to mine and asked me about Wishmore. He listened to my plans and the story of my struggles with much more attention than Mark ever gave me on that subject. "You're a wonder, Janey. You've had a time, but you're going to get the good of it."

I told him how Mark wanted to leave Wishmore and how I insisted on staying. "You're perfectly right. I don't doubt Mark's ability for a minute. But hold on where you are. You're ambitious; you've got land sense, cotton-growing sense, I bet. Look at the quality of your cotton. I wish we had that place!" Everybody said Tim had doubled the value of all Arland's money. Maybe he had inside tips; maybe he just had the knack of success with everything. "Another thing, Jane." He lowered his voice. "Property around here may be worth a lot some day. I've been talking to geologists and oilmen; they think there might very well be oil around, and I believe it."

"Why don't they come here, then?"

"They will, someday. I believe in it. I do. Stick around, and hang onto your land."

I began to bask in the delicious glow he conjured up. I wished, not to be married to Tim, but that Mark had some of his qualities while still remaining Mark.

Mr. Jeff appeared, gave us all a haughty wave of his hand, like a monarch none too pleased with his subjects, and marched into the dining room to eat his dinner. The group in the library broke up, the aunts went off to their separate dozings, and all of the rest of us went to first one house and then another. Throngs of people joined and dissolved and met again until after dark.

Just about dusk there was a blast from the fire siren and the clang and tear of shiny red fire engines coursing full tilt down Main Street. Athwart the largest was Mr. Jeff. As the great flaming thing tore past us, we had a glimpse of him, on his head his hat, dilapidated but painted silver, with two holes cut in it as though he were a rabbit and needed apertures for his ears to come through.

We crowded into the car and raced full tilt after the engines. The alarm came from the hotel, but by the time we had parked and joined the milling excitement the fire was out. Miss Jessie, it seems, had meddled with the Christmas tree until she had set it and the mezzanine afire. When we drove off we saw her lilting down the street, conscious of a deed well done. A strange concoction was on her head, a bulging reticule dangled from one hand, and she was wearing her well-known coat, the one the moths had nipped so freely. Around each mothhole she had worked embroidery, using the holes as part of the design. Off she sailed, magnificently serene and smiling, the wind playing with the folds of the coat. Like Byron, she enjoyed conspicuous solitude.

That night Joyce and Michael had their party. I didn't like her new curtains. She'd consulted Bess instead of me, and they were not right for the room. Nor did I like her new dress. I loved mine. I had paid too much for it, but I loved it. How could I ever have? Why did women ever let themselves be stuffed into those long-waisted short-skirted sacks? I had short hair now, and a new permanent, and used lipstick. Arland was in gray, and she had a big ostrich feather fan, like curls of smoke.

When we got there Tim was the center of a group, everybody hanging on his words. Arland was in a corner, near the fire, shading her face with her plumy fan, listening to some man. She had a look of withdrawal from the throng about Tim.

Alec danced with me a lot, and later in the evening drew me into a cozy nook to talk to me. "I heard you talking to Tim. You seem to be one of his admirers."

"Aren't you?"

"When I'm with him. He tells you what you want to hear. Bet that Dasheel business scared him plenty. It scared me. I was so afraid he hadn't thoroughly disentangled himself in time. But he had; he's smart. Most of the criticism has died down by now. But to get back to our muttons. You're going all out for that place of yours these days. I can understand Mark's argument. The time to dump a plantation is when you can. Let him dump it, and you dump him."

"You're crazy!"

"Perfectly sane." He smiled. "You two don't really suit each other. Break away while you're young. Remake your life."

"You're just used to a lot of sophisticated people who're always swapping wives and husbands. Besides——"

He raised his eyebrows. "Oh! You still have that yen for him. Thought you'd be over it by now. But you're a tenacious little beast."

"Just what do you think I ought to do with myself?"

"Marry me."

I laughed. "You—with one foot on land, one foot on sea."

"Seriously, Jane. I'm sorry you're still yenning for Mark. You're the only woman I ever thought I'd want to marry. For the life of me I don't know why——"

"You ramble on like that because you know you're safe."

"Try me out some day."

"You'd be off like a bat out of hell."

"It's no use arguing at this stage of the game. But try me out." He looked as though he really meant what he was saying too.

"I'm hanging on. You aren't the marrying kind, anyhow."

"Much more so than Mark. I rove only from habit, not nature. You led him to the improvised altar, but can you make him drink steadily of matrimonial waters?"

"Why not? What's wrong with him?"

"Not a damn thing. Only he's an adventurer at heart and likes freedom. Now I want to settle down."

I said Mark was just an escapist like everybody else around here —just didn't want to buck up against strenuous reality.

Alec shook his head. "He's the essence of the untamed male. There are still a few around, though they are getting scarcer."

"You mean he trifles on me?"

"I didn't mean that. Though I think it's very likely. Don't narrow your eyes at me like you're about to spring. He needs a quiet all-right-

I'll-wait-until-your-return sort of woman. You're both too dominating by a damn sight."

"Tim's dominant. A go-getter. I don't think Mark is. He's a dreamer."

"So was stout Cortez. And a few others of that ilk. How do you-all get along, anyway?"

"We have our ups and downs. I don't get along with anybody. Except Arland."

"Bet you don't. Yet somehow I think you'd be good for my soul, hard little brute that you are. Maybe not soul——"

"You don't sound much like my idea of an ardent boy friend."

"That's because your ear is attuned to the 'Honey chile you sho is booful' line of sweet nothings."

"Powerful little flattery has been poured on me. But your nothings are sour as green persimmons."

"That's the modern touch. The thing now is self-analysis and soul probings. Doesn't work with you. Don't believe you have a soul. I'm sure you have no nuances. You're all in black and white."

"Then aren't you barking up the wrong tree?"

"By all the laws of logic I ought to be hovering around Arland, trying to detach her from Tim. She's exactly the sort of woman I most admire: the way she dresses—so simply you aren't dazzled, but you gradually realize it's the very height of art, only a very knowing woman could suit her clothes to herself so perfectly. And she's so beautiful, the most really beautiful woman I know. That little short cat's nose, and that off-gold coloring. Sometimes she's all line; you only see how graceful she is and what delicate bones she has; sometimes she's all color—gold hair and eyes and skin."

"She and I are supposed to be alike."

He studied me. "You are, very. In some ways."

"Maybe that's what keeping you here."

He shook his head. "The likeness comes and goes. The differences are plain. She's a complex person. You aren't. Maybe that's why I don't hover. She might see through me and not let me see through her. I pride myself on understanding women. I couldn't stand for any of them pulling wool over my eyes, and she's perfectly capable of pulling it."

"She's feminine and old-fashioned. I'm not very."

"She has a feminine manner. She's been taught that. But not a female way of looking at things."

"She's got intuition."

"Women claim that as their special quality. Why the hell should they? It's a mixture of natural understanding and applied experience. Here, don't you want a drink?" He looked at my full glass. "You haven't even swallowed that."

"Gertrude's had plenty; look at her." She wavered about in a backless twinkly dress, and her hair was down over one eye. "She said her dress was wonderful—trimmed with seegrums. I told her it would be, before the evening was over. And it is." Everybody had on sequin-trimmed dresses except Arland. Claire's—she was here on a visit—was an all-beaded tube, backless, and her backbone stuck out. "Looks like a particularly bony, scaly fish," I'd pointed out to Mark. Claire was full of herself and the way she entertained in the city and the big football games she went to and how much she made at bridge. She had a habit of turning her hats upside down so we could see the swanky labels.

"Gertrude'll get in a fight with somebody before morning; she always does when she's this tight."

Alec went to fill my plate and agreed she probably would. The dining room was right across from our cozy alcove. People were beginning to drift toward the table, where the candles burned and the poinsettia centerpiece I'd fixed for Joyce that morning flared like a group of meteors.

The ham had a fine glaze, and I knew the fruitcake was loaded with richness, whisky, and nightmares. Louise was bringing in hot biscuits, and her eldest son followed, bearing scalloped oysters. There were dishes of watermelon pickles on the table and, flanking the turkey, a long platter of tomatoes stuffed with shrimp.

Alec came back with two well-filled plates. "Don't you ever get tight, Jane?"

"No, and don't intend to."

"Makes you feel good."

"A mint julep sneaked up on me once. Made my jaw stiff and tingly. That's all."

"I'm pleasantly tight now. You didn't go far enough. Don't you think I'm good company? Anyhow, I feel scintillating, courtly, irresistible; life's rose-hued, and I'm ready for anything. You ought to try it. Escape from your dutiful workaday world and all its problems."

"But your problems just sit and wait for you. You can't get away unless you drink like Mr. Jeff or Jerry Ladd, and they escape the good things as well as the bad. Look at Mr. Jeff. It doesn't make him happy; he moans and groans and howls to himself by the hour!"

"Poor old critter."

"Poor critter is me. He's ruined his own life, hasn't he? Everybody around here is just too damned tolerant. That's what's the matter with the whole place! But I took Mr. Jeff on and I'll just have to 'endue' him, as Tillie says. But don't 'poor thing' him to me!"

"The tolerance you gripe about, though, gives this town its atmosphere. It's a relief to sink back in it and not have to keep up with the Joneses."

"We just keep on giving parties when our phone and lights are cut off. Just be amiable and have enough ancestors who spurred their steeds and flashed their swords and you could murder a slew of aunts before breakfast and get away with it. Say, 'I had to get rid of the aunts,' and people would say, 'Oh, did you?' and take it in their stride. Look at Mr. Jeff; he pops in and out of jail, and we shake our heads, but I put up with him, and Arland keeps his dinner hot, and who thinks anything about it? Not even my strait-laced family! Who pretend to be easily shocked."

"But it's nice. Someday I'm coming back here and just relax. It'll suit me to a 'T'. But I'm kind of scared to. I know I will just sink into lassitude and not accomplish one damn thing."

He took my plate. "You wolfed down all that food already? Want a refill?" I said I didn't, and he sat down again.

"I wish I knew all your faults," I told him, "so I could analyze them the way you do mine."

"Leave me hang around, cutie, and you'll learn 'em."

I eyed Gertrude across the room. "I tell you one thing: I don't have to fuddle myself up with a lot of whisky and illusions! I can face things—look 'em in the eye. All these people who have to be good and tight before they can make love! It shows how little nerve and feeling they really have! I can make love—and plenty—cold sober. Catch me blurring up life's best sensations!"

"You've got something there. I guess that's why I want to marry you, if we're really getting down to brass tacks. Come on, let's dance."

We did, and after a while Tim cut in. He was a wonderful dancer, and I loved whirling around with him. When the music stopped he expertly landed us right under the mistletoe. "We're kissing kin anyway." It wasn't exactly a cousinly kiss, though I must say I liked it. It didn't mean anything. He was just having himself a glorious time, enjoying the food and the drinks and the holiday spirit and the people. Enjoying, too, his own power to charm everybody.

On the other side of the room Arland and Mark had stopped dancing and were talking by a window. The glass behind them took on a thin ghost image of them both, colored but transparent, with a spatter of reflected lights over their heads.

She was talking to him, and he was listening, frowning and intent on what she had to say. I wondered idly what they were talking about.

It was getting late and somebody suggested we all go on to the Owl's Nest and see what was going on out there. There was bustling and scurrying, and altercations about who was going in which car, and who was too drunk to drive, then a piling into cars and the flash of headlights. In the house the candles were guttering out and fires turning dull. Cigarettes piled up and overflowed from ash trays; empty and half full glasses were everywhere. In the kitchen the servants had finished their feasting and were toting off the drumsticks. Joyce was already on her way. I moved a wet glass from a mahogany table top, muttering to Mark how much she was like her mother.

"If that gal had a little more sense, she'd be a moron." He grinned.

Arland announced she was tired and would go home. "Tim can run me back, then join you out there."

We tried to persuade her to come along, but she just shook her head, repeated she was tired, and said to me, "You know I hate places like that anyway. Bore me to death." She and Tim went out, Tim calling over his shoulder, "See you all later."

Mark watched them go. He was frowning and blowing smoke through his nose like a dragon. "What's the matter?" I asked. He gave a little jump, the way people do when they don't know they're being looked at.

"Not a thing. Let's get going."

I had never been to the Owl's Nest, having a certain aversion to the spot where Ludie queened it, but I was curious too. I had heard so many tales about it, about the money won and lost, the strange and unknown characters who tore up in big cars and went off again, and the wild goings on in the supposed tourist cabins out behind the main building.

Alec chose to go in our car with us. It was a soft, warm night with drizzling rain, starting then stopping, from low, rolling clouds. Before we reached the Owl's Nest its lights made a rosy glow in the lowering sky, like something on fire. Then we rounded the curve and there it was, bright and spuriously citified, set on the highway and in the midst of the stretched-out fields of the open countryside. It was a jumble of parked cars outside, and inside a deafening jazz orchestra made a pell-mell of brazen brayings.

"Why, Mark, it's the place we stopped at on our first date ages ago, remember? Only big now, and all changed up."

He said it was "on a boom now," and remarked to Alec you could get pretty fair whisky here. You could also get other things, they said.

The other time, small and squalid as the place had been, there had been a magic to it in my eyes. My mood had made it vivid, a mysterious and fascinating spot, the like of which was ne'er on land or sea. Now it had no charm. It was only a hot spot, of none too savory repute, and Ludie made mischief and money here.

If only Mark and I could get back to the feeling we'd had then! I reached for his hand, but he seemed intent only on parking the car in a suitable spot, and paid no attention to me.

We pushed our way in the howling mob, working through masses of people to the table Tim had engaged, and found our own crowd again. Bottles came out of pockets, and scurrying waiters brought ice and sodas and cokes. Colored bulbs and Christmas decorations were strung across the ceilings. It was the sort of place that stales and cheapens every idea it seizes, even Christmas. The colored lights made the people jostling on the floor look awful. I loathe Christmas effects in the wrong places.

Everybody in town seemed to be here, and lots of people I didn't know. Most of our table got up to struggle to the fearful sounds coming from the band. Some of the worst emerged from the saxophone in the hand and mouth of a pimply youth with slicked-down hair. Then a meretricious blonde in a few beads yowled something about her man through a loud-speaker to great applause. Tim came in, hailing everybody and being hailed by them and making a royal progress through the room to our table.

129

Alec said it must be awful to have to know and be known by such reams of people. Then he stopped what he was saying and looked at the moving mass on the floor with great interest. He asked me, "Who's the knockout? Right over there in the spotlight." I turned and looked too. The spot cut the blur of the other lights and focused on her in clear white rays. It shone on other people, too, but you didn't notice them, only her. There she was in a short swathed glitter of rose-and-gold brocade, her back bare, bracelets moving and twinkling on her arms, and on her feet gold slippers with rhinestone heels. "Ludie Daniels."

He'd heard of her, and I gave him a résumé of her history. I also told him about the rumor that some unknown had set her up in state out here.

"You mean somebody in town?"

"So they say, but nobody can get a line on who it is."

Bess Barrett nudged me. "Do you see who I see?" She looked a little pale, as though the sight of Ludie scared her, bringing back painful memories. It seemed to me Ludie was more formidable now than she had been. The music stopped on a screaming discord, and my eyes followed her progress. She was turned toward me now. Her black hair had a lacquered sheen, her skin was white and rose. She turned to her partner and laughed about something. Drawn together by the push of people, she and Mark were getting closer, closer until they saw each other. She nodded and waved to him; he smiled and spoke and went on, but she paused where she stood and watched him. On her face was a look quite different from the synthetic smiles and automatic flickering of eyes and lashes she gave every man. It flashed over her face for just a minute, caught by the hard white glare, but I recognized it and knew it for what it was—avidity and hunger. He was the one she wanted, and she hadn't let go. Tucked in the flash of bracelet on her wrist, a long bright-rose chiffon handkerchief dangled, and her long red talons, startlingly red and shiny, clawed into the thin stuff. Then the crowd surged through a little space and I didn't see her.

I danced with Michael. He made a few remarks about farming, and said sitting up late at these parties was killing him. I didn't really hear him. Alec cut in, but I wasn't really interested in him any more. I tried to keep my eye on Ludie. She stood out in a crowd. Once she was near, looking up at her partner, a big man, very well dressed.

I didn't know him. I could smell her perfume and see the thickness of the lipstick on her mouth. The lights overhead shone in her eyes, turning them ruddy. Her dress was expensive, and its glow and gleam suited her, showing off the lines of her body, still perfect, and bringing out the vividness of her face. She looked prosperous. She must have collected a big chunk of money from the vanished husband, or else it was true somebody was keeping her in affluence. In her clothes, in her assurance, she might almost have been *femme du monde* at first glance. Then you caught the overtones of the half-world where she lived and reigned.

The gambling here was probably crooked; the liquor covertly bought and sold was illegal; the cabins were not only for travelers, but on the surface everything was smooth. Scandals were veiled, people who began fights were gently eased out, and gamblers who lost a lot of money held their peace.

"Jane," Alec said, "you're asleep on your feet. I told you you were too sober. A spot like this demands your being well oiled or you don't enjoy it. Let's go out to the car and do a little necking."

I wasn't interested. I'd been in fine fettle with Alec paying so much attention to me. Now my glow of feeling had chilled. Mark was still at the table, laughing with Bess Barrett and building houses out of match folders. "Have I lost ground?" Alec asked. "You kissed me before. Thought you'd do better this time. How come?" Ludie had disappeared into the gambling room, and Mark had looked up. He watched her go until the glitter of her gold and rose was out of sight. Suspicion clawed at me. He'd seemed gay, in high good humor all evening, and he'd wanted to come here.

"Come on, Jane," Alec urged, but I shook my head.

"Why don't I make some headway with you, gal?"

I said of course he did.

"No, I don't get to first base. Never mind, a time will come; then you'll find me handy, maybe."

"If that time comes, I probably won't find you at all."

When Alec and I came back to the table Mark made a bolt for the gambling room. I tried to keep him from going. "Don't you dare go in there and gamble."

"Hell, I'm not. Pipe down." But off he went; I couldn't stop him. In a few minutes I sent Alec after him. "I'm tired; I want to go home."

Tim came up. "You-all pushing off? My luck's running so well I hate to leave. Want to come watch?"

I shook my head and advised him not to stay and lose his shirt. He laughed. "Can't lose tonight. Luck's going my way."

On the way to the car Alec told me he was leaving town the next day.

"Aren't you ever going to settle down?"

He smiled and kissed my hand very nicely. "When you're ready to take me up on my offer."

We took him back to Michael's and started for home, Mark whistling "Jingle Bells." Beyond the town, on our road, the black pines sighed, and the little cabins cuddled in the folds of the slopes. I kept thinking of Ludie. She was dangerous, sitting out there, offering excitement to all the restless.

"I wish Tim hadn't stayed. He'll probably end by losing plenty."

Mark made no answer, then he said, "Tim doesn't take care of Arland's property any more. She told me that tonight. She said he was so busy she didn't want to bother him with Newstead and the stuff in town, so she was running things herself."

"I think that's foolish. He made a lot of money for her."

"Maybe she didn't approve of all his ways of making it."

"You always have it in for Tim. He doesn't do anything other people don't do, only he's more successful."

"Had his finger in a lot of pies."

We were passing Rosemont. I sighed. "That's my pie. How do you suppose your aunt Kate passed Christmas?"

No doubt the solitary horseman, my cousin Charlie Selwyn, had gone there and then had ridden away, going back to another large, aged mansion buried in trees and silence.

"Listen, Mark, if Mr. Selwyn dies first, what's to keep us from getting your aunt Kate's money?"

"Dunno. Lennerds live long as parrots."

Josiah had first come here, but Ephraim had made most of the money. He had been a grand gentleman, living his long life with vigor and joy.

"Aunt Ada says there's a portrait of Josiah and Ephraim, too, and they're just gorgeous. When I get Rosemont I'll show 'em off."

Mark chuckled. "You sure indulge in some pipe dreams. Old Horace is there, too: pretty nice old cuss. Talented."

"He laid out the gardens, didn't he? I bet it's a wilderness in there now." My mind was busy restoring the gardens and cleaning and mending all those gods and goddesses Horace had brought back from Italy. They stood in the long alley of oaks leading up to the house. I had always wanted to see them. "Can't you just see him scribbling verses to ladies and building summerhouses and sketching ruined temples?"

Mr. Horace had been buried in the little cedar-veiled cemetery on the bluff near Rosemont. Part of it had crumbled away in a landslide, and Horace's bones and his tombstone, with a long list of all his virtues, had fallen in with the spilling earth. These cavings were always gashing out big chunks of the bluff. But he'd chosen his garden more wisely than his resting place. Wishmore Point protected Rosemont from being undermined.

Horace's garden was an elaborate pattern imposed on the wild land. Beyond its roses and formal box hedges the pines sprang and the briers tangled, and the river cut its great curve to eat at the foundations of the bluffs. Horace had bravely ignored the sad and savage shape of nature. The river had gathered up his poor bones, and the secret springs of change had sapped at the world he knew until it had all crashed down. But the ghost of his garden was still there, fighting time and neglect. It was waiting. It was waiting for me.

"There must be enough left to restore the gardens just as they were," I said. "And Horace's ghost will be pleased. Arland says she's sure he haunts the garden."

"Probably," Mark agreed. "You know, Alec thinks of himself as modern, but I bet he's a lot like old Horace."

"Alec doesn't amble along garden paths and build pavilions."

"No, that's the sort of thing a cultivated man of artistic tastes did in Horace's day. Alec does the modern counterpart of it. Different sort of thing, but same kind of person." He laughed. "I can imagine Alec living Horace's sort of life and having a pretty good time doing it."

"Don't you like Alec?" I wished Mark had shown a little jealousy.

"Like him fine. I don't see any harm in a man's enjoying life and not working too hard if he doesn't have to. Alec thinks and reads and knocks around; he knows how to use a lot of spare time. Great Uncle Ned started out sort of like Horace, but got sidetracked into being a hero. Seems he knew a lot about strategy. Just as well he got killed before he had to come back here."

"But he was just twenty-one! And there was that girl in Virginia in love with him."

"What would have been left for him? He'd have had to hustle and he didn't know how."

"Any sort of life's better than being dead."

"I don't know . . . he'd have been dead now anyway."

"You can't like war, Mark."

"Filthy business. Make brutes out of people who would otherwise be pretty decent. Makes nuts out of lots of 'em too. I guess they'd go nuts anyway, though. It's like a crevasse. You know how a crevasse leaves the soil where it goes through all sandy and rank, unfit for use for years. Lots of weeds spring up. That's what it does to the mental atmosphere. And all the damn lies! But all the same, I did pretty well at it and, unlike Tim, I don't seem to do so well in the piping times of peace."

"You've had some bad luck."

"It's not that, Jane."

I knew we were on the brink of another set-to as we'd had that morning. "Everybody's prosperous now. By next year even you won't be restless any more. Everybody else is getting rich, why shouldn't we? If we could ever get a little rich, we could branch out. Money makes money."

"Money—that's all anybody thinks about any more. To hell with it."

"You won't feel that way when you get some. Let's just do the best we can——"

"Oh, damn! Don't let's start arguing." The car skidded, and Mark twisted it back in the road again. I wished aloud for more gravel and told Mark for heaven's sake to get after the local politicos again.

"You let everything slide," I accused him. He didn't answer, and all the stormy atmosphere of the morning clouded over us again.

"I suppose," Mark said, "you'd like me to take Tim as a model."

"Well, he's a success in his career, and everybody's crazy about him. He gives Arland everything she wants and a wonderful——"

"Everybody's crazy about him," Mark echoed. "You think she is?"

"Of course! Why not?"

"I just wonder." But he didn't enlarge on it. He began to whistle again. We'd soon be home, where the fires would be out, and the house cold, and the Christmas tree dark. Kitty would be asleep, well tucked in, and Lilly asleep on the day bed beside her, her mouth open, showing a pride of gold teeth. Lilly had had perfectly good strong white ones pulled out to put them in at the price of all her wages.

"Mark, I'm sorry I was cross," and I put my head on his shoulder. We were going downhill now. The rain had stopped, but there was a mass of clouds on the horizon. They dressed themselves into towers, flaunting a useless decorative effect above the flat, sodden landscape. In their depths lightning flickered and faded and flickered again, lending them a wild and secret magic.

As I fell asleep my mind was still a jumble of Mark and Ludie and Alec. The telephone woke me. We'd had it put in the house the winter Kitty was sick, and I started up with the same sort of uneasy tension as when, worried about her and listening for her cry, I'd slept only in snatches.

Mark went to answer it. "Bet it's the Purple Dog." That was a colored juke joint, and they were always getting the number mixed with ours. But it wasn't, and I got up to listen because Mark was so quiet. He listened, then he said, "I'll come right away. But don't worry, Arland, he's right around somewhere." He came away from the phone and began flinging on his clothes. "Tim hasn't come home."

"Maybe he lost his money and is trying to win it back." I looked at the clock. Six-fifteen, but still dark. "Or he may have stopped and had something to eat."

"He might. But not at the hotel coffee room. She called there. He hadn't been in, and he left the Owl's Nest at half past four."

That would have given him time to eat and get home. Mark was usually so casual, but he was serious and upset about this, and I began to be uneasy. "I'll make coffee."

"Haven't time." He started off, calling back, "Listen, Jane, get Michael and tell him to meet me at the corner of Elm and Main. I'll phone you as soon as I find out about things." He slammed the door. He was worried. I wondered why he was so concerned. I phoned Michael; he came awake slowly and finally grasped what I was saying.

"What you reckon Tim's done with himself?" he began, then broke off, as if fear had seeped in him too. "I'd better get going."

I built up the fire, dressed, made coffee and drank it, telling myself Tim would be back at home before Mark could get up the hill. All the same I was restless. The dark lightened, and mists rolled up from the fields and curled and billowed on the surface of the river. It was still cloudy, but the wind had changed. I moved from window to window. I decided to get out the other car and go to Arland's, and was halfway to the door when the phone rang. As soon as I heard Mark's voice, I knew everything was wrong. "Come on in here right away."

I couldn't ask him any questions, but he gathered breath and told me. "We found him. On the old Edlinton Road. He'd missed the bridge."

"Killed?"

Mark answered yes and hung up. I couldn't take it in. Tim—— Somehow I never thought he could die. It was impossible. I burst into tears, and tears were still streaming down my face when I reached Holly Trees. The sun had come out, and shadows danced on the driveway. The sharp leaves of the hollies glistened, and the two big camellias by the steps were in fullest bloom. The windows were hung with red-ribboned wreaths. The tinsel on the Christmas tree glistened. I went in to find Arland. How could they ever tell her!

The road where they'd found Tim was winding and full of curves. It cut from the highway over to our road in a wandering, roundabout way. It was slick from the rains, and there was a sharp curve leading directly to the bridge. Tim's car had missed the bridge and had plunged down the bank. It was a heavy, powerful car and was not much damaged but Tim was dead. Killed instantly, they said and hoped.

❧ Chapter Eleven

One fall evening, nearly a year after Tim's death, I went to spend the night with Arland, lugging Kitty along. Aunt Ada, who lived with Arland now, had gone out of town on one of her innumerable church conferences. "Arland says she doesn't need anybody," I said to Mark, while I put a fresh dress over Kitty's head. "But I don't like her shut up there with just Bedelia."

Kit was eying her reflection with solemn satisfaction. Clothes loomed large in her life, and this dress, a present from Arland, was her favorite.

When we were near Holly Trees I said, "You don't come here much, Mark. I bet it hurts Arland's feelings."

"Did she ever say so?"

"Not a word, but she must notice you don't come like other people do."

He said he thought maybe she wanted to be to herself some, but he didn't want to hurt her feelings.

"She oughtn't to be left alone. It's time she stopped shutting herself up and brooding."

"Does she?"

"She's cheerful enough, but she just stays home. Not doing much of anything." Arland and her sufferings were the subject of much of the aunts' conversation. "Of course her heart is broken," they agreed in chorus. "But she ought to try to rally."

"This place never strikes me as cheerless," Mark commented as we reached the house. Lights shone from the windows, Bedelia was singing in the kitchen, and Stephen was making a noise all over the place. He met us at the door and said he was staying for supper. He was tall for his age, with reddish hair and quick dark blue eyes, and pink under his tan cheeks.

In the way he talked and thought he seemed much more the child of Arland than the production of Michael and Joyce. I didn't see how Joyce endured having her son fonder of another woman than he was of his own mother, but she didn't seem to mind. It left her with more freedom to bat around wasting time. Joyce was an emotional slug.

Arland came to meet us and told Mark to stay to supper too. "Bedelia's made chocolate mousse and hot rolls."

Mark hesitated, then, maybe mindful of what I'd been telling him, thanked her and said he would. I must say the house didn't seem dreary, and the library was bright with long-stemmed red lilies. Michael came to get Steve and was easily persuaded to stay too. Joyce, it seemed, was still racketing around with the girls. She spent most of her time with Bess Barrett and Gertrude now. Never mind, someday I'd bring them all to heel.

"They've gone to eat spaghetti at——" Michael swallowed and turned red. I knew where they were. Out at the Owl's Nest. Arland had, of course, never been there since Tim was killed. As a matter of fact, she hadn't been there that night either. I hadn't gone there since, but Gertrude's crowd had formed quite a habit of running out and eating and drinking and gambling, rather enjoying the fruity reputation of the place.

"Why do you-all go out there and help Madam Ludie get rich?" I asked Bess once. She'd tightened her mouth. "Thought we'd better help her make money. If she gets enough with her gambling and her little love nests—because everybody says that's what they are—maybe she'll let husbands alone."

I never mentioned Ludie to Mark, but I was conscious of her ensconced out there, like a sleek sort of tropic spider in the center of a web, stretching out shiny filaments.

"What made you think of looking for Tim on that road?" I'd asked Mark.

"Everybody was looking on all the roads."

"But you went out there and found him."

"He'd been out in that direction. It was natural to look for him around there." That particular road was familiar to Mark. It was the one we'd driven over the first time we went riding together, that night I always remembered.

"He was probably tight."

"Probably," Mark agreed. "Damned dangerous spot."

We went in to supper. There were candles on the table and a bowl of yellow roses. I envied Arland her china and silver, and I noticed Kitty taking in all the details. She's always loved pretty things and luxurious surroundings and had already begun to be critical of Wishmore. In some ways Kit reminds me of Aunt Em, and Aunt Em adored her, because she was quiet and kept clean and was conventional. Of course Kit's conventions are modern, the standards of her own time and her own set of friends.

I complained because my yellow roses hung their heads. "And I work like a dog, Arland, and you never do."

"I let my things go peacefully into leafage. Your swamp soil changes everything. I never saw such sweet peas—fat, scarlet and purple and flamboyant——"

"Maybe swamp soil gives Jane her flamboyant ideas too," Mark said.

"I don't think they're half as wild as some of yours."

We left the table. The children were out in the hall, making wigwams out of Arland's good sheets, and Michael and Mark began to talk about the stock market. I'd been busy fall house cleaning and had paid no attention to the news. I now wanted to know what had happened. "Stock market broke. Bankers are throwing themselves out of windows."

"Why didn't they know it was going to happen?" I demanded. "Aren't they supposed to know everything?" I glanced at the paper. There seemed to be plenty of reassuring statements from the highest sources. Anyway, I didn't have any stocks, and Arland had sold all hers and all the ones Tim had left her. She'd bought some little houses and offices and was remodeling them because she didn't want them torn down for filling stations. It was fun, and it gave her something to do, but I thought it rather a foolish way to spend money. No return on the investment.

Arland said she thought she would sell her cotton.

"Aren't you going to wait for it to go up again?" I asked.

"Suppose it doesn't," Mark said. "Nobody thought the market would break."

I suddenly thought of Tim. He wouldn't have liked this. It was not in his scheme of things. Mark leaned forward to light Arland's cigarette. "It's a funny point of view. Hurtling yourself out of a window twenty stories high just because you've lost a lot of money.

Look how long I've lived without ever having any, and without the slightest impulse to leap over the bluff."

I said I wouldn't jump, I'd try to make it back.

Arland was sitting under the portrait of Doña Ana. She hung over the fireplace, and I've always wanted her, but she went to Uncle because he was the eldest, and then to Arland. I'll get a set of Chadwick-nosed gentlemen and proper whaleboned ladies. Doña Ana, in her oval frame, was fragile and languid, her shoulders and arms smoothly emerging from a vaporous film of a high-waisted dress in the fashion of Josephine and Pauline. A pale rose had a faint luster in her hair, and the frail pattern of a mantilla drifted over a tall comb. Everybody says Arland looks so much like her—the same small features and rather dark skin and gold-brown hair and eyes. So do I, almost, but I looked less like Arland than I used to, and was too modern to look like the picture at all. I have to admit Arland's resemblance in the pose of the head, possibly cultivated, the same lurking dimple, fortunately inherited, the same sort of smile, beginning in the eyes, a sort of secret amusement she and Doña Ana do not share with the rest of the world. Arland's named for her; at least, she's named for our grandmother, Anne Arland, who was named for her.

She used to love to think up remarkable tales about Doña Ana. At times, in our imagination, she was a Castilian heiress who eluded her duenna and the convent walls and eloped with the handsome governor to the new world. At other times she was the child of pirates, who rescued the governor from their clutches and their cutlasses. But as far as any authentic story is concerned, Ana, as an ancestress, is a total and complete dud.

She was not scalped by Indians, nor did she warn the settlement of an impeding massacre and thereby effect their rescue. She didn't die young, and she didn't live long enough to be heroic and full of derring-do between sixty-one and sixty-five. She didn't fall in with Burr's conspiracy, and there's no old family legend to the effect she fell madly in love with him. Audubon did not give her dancing lessons. She didn't entertain Andrew Jackson after the battle of New Orleans; nor did he, or Henry Clay, or Seargent S. Prentiss, or Sam Houston, or General Grant sleep in any of her beds, as far as we know. However, her portrait conjures up a pleasant haze of duels, coaches, and old waltzes—all the well-publicized aura of the Good Old Days.

You can have the Good Old Days. Let others expatiate on palatial steamboats and happy darkies and the gracious customs of plantation life. They forget the dust, the malaria, the flies, and the cholera. Everybody forgets the cholera, and did it rampage in these parts!—and the yellow fever and tyrannical fathers and heavy husbands and how many children women had and how many babies died.

I strongly disapproved of Arland sitting here at Holly Trees in a welter of old pictures and traditions and gewgaws.

Michael was talking about the cotton on that place of his that ran to the left of Newstead and Dewberry Landing called Miss Kate's Bottom. "My cotton's pretty fair, but you ought to see Aunt Kate's."

"I wish I had that place," I sighed. When and if we ever got a sniff of the Lennerd property I fully intended to make a play for it. "It's such good level land."

"We used to go there on picnics," Arland said. "There's a grove of cottonwoods just beyond the old house. They sounded like taffeta petticoats swishing. The house is in ruins and the garden all choked, but when we went there, there were lots of narcissus and daffodils, and those soft, silky, fuzzy little roses still bloomed year after year." Arland was easily diverted from what to do with this year's crop to the picnics of the past.

I said I didn't know Lennerds lived there, and Michael said, oh, sure, one of his and Mark's great-uncles.

"He was killed in the war." Arland always knew the ramifications of everybody's family history. "And his wife died leaving lots of little children, and they went to live at Rosemont with their uncle. One of the boys was a great friend of Great Uncle Louis. He was lame and he wasn't very happy, rather shoved about among the others."

Michael and Mark said Uncle Josh was a tough old egg, and told Arland to go on. Michael folded his hands over his expanding middle to listen.

"George used to go see Uncle Louis, and Louis would hear his cane tap, tapping up the steps, nearer and nearer, until he reached the door. Then he told Louis how he planned to run away from home and never come back. But it was a secret—nobody must know. And he did go, and Louis never said a word. Every now and then Louis would get a letter from him, but he never wrote to anybody else, and nobody knew where he was or what he was doing. Then he was found dead on a railroad track, outside some Northern city. He'd been murdered. It was mysterious; no one knew who killed him or why, and they never did find out. Maybe they didn't try hard enough.

"Louis thought about it a lot, and one night he dreamed he heard George coming up the stairs, just as he used to do. He heard his stick going tap, tap, and knocking on the door, and George came in and sat down on the bed and began to talk. 'I'm going to tell you all that happened, because you are my true friend. I'm going to tell you why I was killed and who did it.' And he held up his cane. 'I was killed with this.' Uncle Louis said he woke up with a cold sweat pouring off of him, and the rain was falling in the gutter tap, tap, tap."

I can't tell the story the way Arland did, or catch the cadences of her voice the way it sounded in the quiet room, but we all fell into its mood, with its mystery and sadness, an individual tragedy set in the melancholy of the South after its lost war.

Mark gave a long sigh and got up and mixed drinks. "There's a kind of fate about the damned Lennerds."

"Sure is," Michael grumbled, a tribute to Arland's powers, because he was a happy and placid soul. I wondered if I'd bring bad luck on my head by yearning for their inheritance. I try not to be superstitious —it's all foolishness—but Southerners absorb superstition young.

"They've managed to prosper pretty consistently," I pointed out. Mark shook his head. "Not in their souls. They've got a sort of fever in their souls." He and Arland embarked on a discussion of heredity and environment, while Michael sipped his drink and listened.

In the hall Kitty and Steve were stretched out on the floor looking at a big book full of colored plates of Indian chiefs. Sound of body, clear of eye and brain, they looked secure in their happy childhood, free of all vague ghosts. I thought of future Lennerds instead of past ones. It would be a good thing for Kitty and Steve to marry. The Delmans—— Well, I didn't object to the Delman strain. The Lennerds unmingled with something else might go cobwebby, and then the Lennerd property, instead of being dispersed, would be joined again: great hunks of good land, all in the same family, gathered up, set in order. Something might well come of it.

Michael called Stephen, and Mark got up too. He said he must be off. He had business to attend to before he went back to the house.

"What business?" I demanded.

"This and that." Kitty had come to stand between us, watching us with her large grave eyes, and I couldn't be too insistent. Mark would tell me only what he pleased anyway. A knife edge of hostility slid over me, and the consciousness of how attractive he looked standing there, his eyes like Kitty's in their shape, but gray, brilliant in his dark face. I wanted to go to him and say, "Take me with you—anywhere," but I couldn't. I had to watch him leave, with the slightest of good nights, when I wanted a long kiss. I wondered what he would do with his brief freedom; it seemed to be precious to him.

I turned to Arland. Her eyes looked dark—dark and sad, and I felt sorry for her. Mark was gone only a little way, and I was missing him. Tim was gone for always. Her face was sad, full of emotion beaten back, veiled, set to passive endurance. We went on upstairs. I had the room that had been Aunt Margaret's. Kit went to sleep in the little bed, but I pottered about restlessly, trying different kinds of cream on my face. It was a pretty room, frilly and becushioned. I don't understand people—they're so contradictory. Aunt Margaret was so strait-laced, yet she had such frivolous possessions. Who would expect such a rigid Scotch family to have such a passion for things so Italian and opulent? The house was full of mosaic-topped tables and madonnas and scenes of Venice. You could tell Aunt Margaret's things from the Elliston things at a glance. A plain table with straight legs was Elliston; a tiered, convoluted, bemirrored étagère came from Aunt Margaret.

I felt restless and sleepless. Arland's light was still on, so I went in. She'd taken off her black dress—black always shadowed her—and put on a yellow robe afloat with wide yellowish lace. She was plaiting her hair for the night, and the folds of lace fell away from her arms, and the folds of sleek silk curled on the floor. The color and luster brought back her own luminousness. She saw me in the mirror. "Let's go see if there's more mousse." On our way downstairs Arland paused on the landing. "That bird's been singing like this, night after night." It was a soft night, starry, scented with sweet olive's second blooming. A mockingbird was singing and flying from bush to tree, and back, as he sang. He sounded like a wren, and like a cardinal, and like a jaybird, and like a young chicken. He'd finished with this year's nestlings. He no longer had to find twigs and strings and guard the finished home and feed his brood and scold cats and owls and snakes and humans. The young ones could fend for themselves now. He'd shed his old feathers and had new ones. His song was not the springtime courtship to lure a mate; it was for himself, his own satisfaction, his joy in the night and his world as he found it. Right now. He sang like a catbird, then gave a note pure and lovely, unfamiliar to me. I asked Arland what bird it was.

"I don't know, but I've heard it sometimes in the deep woods; it always makes me want to get up and follow—I don't know where. It's so elusive."

We went on into the pantry and settled ourselves to heaped-up saucers under the swinging light. It was half past one in the morning.

"Arland, I've been thinking about you. I know it takes time to get over the sort of shock you've had. But you mustn't sit in this house in seclusion always. Doing nothing. Oh, I wish Hettie could cook like Bedelia!"

"We might as well finish it." She gave me another helping. I thought she hadn't heard me, but she had. "What do you think I ought to do, Jane? I've seen a lot of people today. A man about the gin, and half a dozen of the Newstead hands. One of them had a cousin in jail. Another one's wife had left him; he wanted her back at least until the busy season's over. Old Franklin wants a car—you know how it goes. Then the architect from New Orleans is here to talk to me about those buildings. And Tim's family are coming in from the country tomorrow." The poor things were so crushed by Tim's death they never went anywhere except to come here and talk about Tim.

"That's not what I mean. I mean you ought to take up an active life —the way you used to live. I know it won't be the same, but you mustn't vegetate forever."

"I didn't like the hurly-burly. I got into it all to help Tim. Now I can choose, and I prefer to vegetate right here."

"I don't blame you for being completely beaten down by what happened. But sooner or later you must pick yourself up. Remake your life. Someday you'll marry again."

She smiled and shook her head. "I don't intend to."

"Oh, I know it'll never be like Tim——"

"I hope to God it wouldn't be!" Her tone and the darkness of her eyes startled me, so I didn't take in her words right away. Then I swallowed a large blob of cold mousse the wrong way and choked. A flash of anger lit and changed her face with its dark burning. "You make me feel like such an awful hypocrite I can't stand it! I just have to speak out to somebody! You see, Jane, it was a dreadful shock. His being killed like that. I wasn't brokenhearted, though. I was brokenhearted over Tim a long time ago. So it wasn't the way you think, and the way his family thinks, and the way everybody thinks!"

Arland telling me this with her own voice. Some other person was speaking out of her mouth, a person with her features but whose real face I didn't know.

"For a long time I hadn't loved Tim at all." Her voice was low and calm, and the anger had faded from her face, but I was still dazed. "I didn't love him; I couldn't. You never guessed?" When I shook my head, she went on: "I suppose you didn't. You saw him as everybody saw him. I hid it, since I'd decided to stay with him. I didn't want anybody to know, not even you. He's dead, and it's no use going into all this. But all of you—your attitude—has made me feel so false, such a liar somehow."

"But Tim—— He was so attractive, such a success. You loved him so much."

"I know I did. Too much. And too long."

I kept seeing Tim, and hearing him, and Arland looking at him so rapt and enchanted. She couldn't mean what she was saying now.

"You'll have to tell me, since you've begun. I think I'm crazy, or else you are. You didn't love Tim. I can't take it in. It was all so perfect, so wonderful—the way other people aren't." I felt winded, as though I'd been running. "It knocks the props right from under me."

"It's long, and it's tangled with so many things. You know how I felt about Tim when I married him. And afterward too. He used to be full of talk about how decent people ought to try to govern the country. I drank it all in. I thought he was full of grand ideals and ideas. Of course when he got in with Dasheel, it was something of a blow. That's the first time it dawned on me he wasn't always going to act the way he talked. It was politically expedient, but I didn't want him to be expedient. We argued about it by the hour. Dasheel could be useful, so Tim used him. After all, at that time nobody knew anything definite against the man. So I tried to swallow him. Tim took the line he had to get started somehow, and had to use the material available, and that Dasheel was a fine fellow, just misunderstood now and then by his enemies. Later, of course, when that awful business came up——"

"Did Tim know what was going on?"

"I don't know. By that time Tim didn't tell me everything, the way he had once. He wanted me to help him but never to criticize him."

"Did you ever suspect Tim knew?"

"I didn't know what to think. Tim was awfully upset. We went through a bad time, I can tell you. And we had to pretend to each other and everyone else everything was wonderful."

"And yet"—I looked back over it all, trying to remember how it had been; it was strange how the details of it were already buried and blurred—"Tim couldn't have known. Something would have come out, somebody would have told. Dasheel would have."

"That's what I kept telling myself. But there's another explanation. Dasheel might very well have thought it would go easier with him if Tim didn't get involved, if he stayed out entirely, won his election, kept on getting ahead. Then of course he could use more influence to help Dasheel himself."

"Did Tim help him?"

"Yes, I think he tried to. He pulled various strings to make things easier for him. I told myself he was doing it for old friendship's sake, which was natural enough. And yet I couldn't help wondering if he was doing it because he was afraid not to. My mind kept churning and churning it all over. Long after it was over. I suppose I was always afraid it wasn't over. Well, it's over now. In a final, finished way. I don't want to think of it again or ever talk about it any more."

"You kept up appearances. I don't see how you did it."

"Because I had to. But in private I was critical. At least, in the days when I still had hopes. You know how Tim loved to be adored and admired. He couldn't stand criticism. From me, least of anybody. So he began looking around for someone who'd think he was perfect. He soon found her."

"You mean he had an affair?"

"Affairs. When I found out about the first one I was out of my mind with misery. We hadn't been married so very long; I wasn't prepared. She was a silly little thing, but sweet and pretty. He told her he was going to get a divorce, but of course it was the last thing on earth he wanted. She was a perfectly insignificant girl in his eyes. She made him preen himself—wafted all the incense I had stopped wafting, and I think he cared about her for a while. But by the time I found out about it, she'd become insistent, and he was sick of her. He was brutal about it too. I would have given him a divorce if he'd wanted one."

"Why should you have? Hell, I wouldn't!"

"If someone doesn't care for me, I don't want him! I'd much rather let him go."

146

"A divorce would have hurt him too. You could have had a nice, sizzling, juicy revenge."

"I never could see what good revenge did anybody. The last thing I wanted was to hurt him or spoil his chances in any way. We'd have just all been wretched, particularly his poor family. And I was fond of him. He said let's forgive and forget and start all over, and I was willing to—perfectly willing. I just couldn't. It's the way I'm made. I'd loved him a lot. I didn't see why some of it wasn't left, but it had gone."

"Maybe you were lucky it did go."

"Maybe. No—no, I wasn't. I didn't like the blankness. And all the pretense it was there when it wasn't. But the next time he had a love affair flourishing I didn't care. I didn't suffer at all. Nobody suffered. I didn't. He didn't. She didn't. She was a hard, glittering, important person. It was just vanity for both of them and soon died down. She liked him, and he liked her importance. He didn't know I ever caught onto it, and I never said a word. After that episode I handled him much better. I suppose because I didn't love him any more and didn't expect too much from him any more. I could look at him objectively, and cut my coat according to my cloth.

"I thought we could rock along pretty well. The essence of feeling had gone, but the surface was smooth enough, and he was pleasant company. After he'd finished with Dasheel and weathered all that and had won his election, we both felt he might really do something worth while. Then there was another woman. When I found out about her I was scared. It had been going on a long time, off and on. It worried me. I was afraid it might all break out into an open scandal. He was afraid too. I think he wanted to drop her but didn't know how."

"At any moment the fat might drop in the fire and start sizzling. Go on."

But she wouldn't. "It's no use talking about it any more; it's over and done with."

I longed for her to tell me more, but she wouldn't answer my questions. "Poor Tim. He's dead now, and it's no use raking it all up. I shouldn't have told anyone, even you. Though I know you'll never open your mouth to anybody. Don't even tell Mark."

I promised I'd never breathe a word.

"I feel free of the whole complicated coil, so I had to relax in front of somebody. And I can't with anyone but you." She drew a deep breath. "You see, it isn't a nice storybook story. The 'lived happily ever after' the aunts expected."

Arland had stepped down from her pedestal with a vengeance. She hadn't idolized and adored and been idolized and adored to the exclusion of all else. She was no longer wrapped in a bright and somber cloak of love and tragedy and romantic heartbreak, complete with an enshrined memory. She had come down among us struggling, milling females in our ceaseless war for men. Only she had refused to keep on fighting. She had detached herself. "But you kept on letting people think he was perfectly wonderful and you adored him."

"It's mostly on account of his family. You know how his parents are. They worshiped him. Now they worship the idea of him. How could I ever tell them I stopped loving him, and why? Besides, what harm can it do for people to keep on admiring him? Somebody might even think, 'There was Tim, headed for great things,' and go and accomplish something."

"But it would rile me so! I'd go ahead and burst out with the truth."

"I bet you wouldn't. I'm vain, you know. I'd rather they'd go ahead and think it was a perfect marriage. Can't you see why?"

I could. "If you go on long enough, you might believe in it yourself."

"I'd like to, but I won't."

"Mark once said he wondered if you loved Tim any more." He'd said it the very night Tim was killed. She flushed. "He won't open his mouth," I reassured her.

"I know he won't. I noticed he didn't like Tim the way he used to when they were boys. What happened?"

"I don't know. I asked him. He wouldn't tell me. You ask him. He might tell you."

"No, I won't ask him."

"How did you find out about Tim and those other women?"

"The girl herself gave things away the first time. She kept telephoning the house and writing to him. Poor child. So naïve about it all. As though Tim would give up anything for an obscure little secretary. When she grew desperate she didn't try to hide it. She wanted me to know, so there would be a divorce and she could marry him. I found out about the second through gossip. Tim didn't mind. He wanted me kept in the dark, but he didn't object to other people commenting on it. There was a certain panache to that one."

I knew just what she meant. Tim liked the effect of plumes waving in the breezes.

"And the other. He got worried and dropped hints. He needed help. I suspected. I had no proof until after his death. Then I knew. Poor Tim, for all his charm and shrewdness, he wasn't ever quite grown-up."

"You catch onto people. I don't. I thought I knew you—inside and out, but I didn't."

I remembered what Alec had said about her. "Alec thought you were good at pulling wool over people's eyes."

"I had to. It wasn't from choice."

"I didn't know you. Or Tim. Or Mark."

I knew every word she'd told me was true. It was the real picture of Tim: scheming, quick to use people, careless of their feelings, faithless. But the Tim I remembered kept materializing before my eyes, his dark eyes beaming confidence and joy. He had come to tell me he was everything I had once thought he was. I saw him as a boy, waving to everybody as he flashed by on that wild, shiny chestnut mare of his. Dolphin, her name was. How she leaped and pirouetted, and how perfectly he managed her. I saw him older, on Arland's gallery, his eyes gleaming as he played the mandolin and sang "The Spanish Cavalier." I was outside the charmed circle, outside, and he was its center. Outside, in brooding adolescence, but while he sang and I watched from a distance in the drowsy garden, I felt it wouldn't be long before some door opened to me and I would find myself in the middle of some enchanted happiness all my own.

Arland, too, was thinking of what had been. "Jane, do you remember that day we walked by the river? So pleased with our life, and so much in love! I've never forgotten it. It was the last time I was really happy. After that things began to happen to me."

I remembered very well. Then I had been confident of my own power, sure of myself and life too. Arland was detached now. I was still entangled in the struggle and the striving.

"We were fatuous little beasts." Lapping up primitive sex and feeling so satisfied. All snuggled down in our marriage beds, which turned out not to be made of roses. With a sort of pang I remembered how Arland had looked when she'd said how happy she was. She was still young. She had been a pretty girl; now she was a woman with more than just beauty, full of subtleties and changes, but too shadowed by what had happened to her, and too secret and guarded. That early morning look of youth untarnished was gone for good.

"Any woman who thinks Love Is All is a gump. And we were." I cast my mind over the women we knew, and few indeed were the ones who lived as though love were their whole existence. They found men necessary to take them out, throw sops to their vanity, marry them, support them, father their children, and make out income tax blanks. I didn't consider the virgins, young or old, placid or sour. But the others. Aunt Tee had been a successful flirt and a successful wife and mother, but she had been a most successful and cheerful widow too, in spite of the incense puffed at the shrine of the Departed. Claire wanted marriage, complete with a dozen of everything, except children, and an apartment at a good address. Gertrude has been called man-crazy, but to her one man is about as good as another. They were tangled in her mind and her feelings with the steaks and the whisky they laid on her table, and the parties they whooped up.

All these women seemed to me luckier and wiser than Arland had been and than I now was. "We were entirely too intense, Arland. Put out too much. It's a mistake." But I couldn't help it. I still couldn't help it. What I felt was something older and stronger and darker than what is known as romance. Known and worshiped and feared long ago.

"It still was worth it," Arland said. "For a while I was happy. I'll just keep on loving Tim for that, and forget all the rest."

Bruised and shaken, Arland had picked herself up and dusted herself off. She was free from the bru-ha-ha moiling around me and my kind. She was on her way to some ivory tower of her own. She would climb in and pull up the drawbridge, and smile down on me. Owning herself. At last. Until, in time, she loved somebody else.

"In a way I feel a lot sorrier for you than I did before. In another way, a lot less. I suppose I begrudge you your freedom. I'm still being buffeted." I pondered over ivory towers, but couldn't see myself in one. It wouldn't suit me. Give me the tumult and the shouting. Arland said she felt blank, and I didn't want to be blank.

Tonight, when Mark had gone, I had a sort of seething burning inside, destructive as a coil of flaming lava. It was better to be alive, though, than dead. If the fire ever left, it would be a hard mass—

black, with jagged edges. I was afraid of what might be buried in it and what might grow out of it.

"What's the matter, Jane?"

"Just the way things are. Mark and I didn't hit it off. I snap, and he snarls back. I guess I make noises like a wife." Most women tended to get tangled in daily cares and yap about them. Look at Mary Shelley, born to be a rebel, with rebellion pumped into her, ending up by wanting a good pew in the Church of England.

Mark didn't love me. He was drawing away from me more and more. I wanted to tell Arland I was afraid, with Ludie sitting out there setting traps for the restless, the ones who wanted to get out of bounds. He used to want her. Maybe he wanted to go back to lawless pleasures, lawless as he was. She still wanted him. I'd seen it, and recognized what I saw. I couldn't tell Arland. It was something she wouldn't understand. She'd scorn such a tenacious passion. She hated cruelty. I couldn't show her the clawings of a tenacious passion, how cruel it was to me, and how cruel it made me.

So I kept still, and the moment to tell all passed by. The unshaded pantry light glared down on us. Our faces were naked from too little make-up and too much revealed emotion. The last of the chocolate mousse was a dull thin puddle in the bottom of the dish. A design of fat, satiated cupids skittered around the dish's edge. A clock, not a grandfather's clock, but our grandfather's clock, struck four, hissing between each stroke. Arland was looking at me, a strange look. At least it seemed so, because after her revelations she no longer seemed the same person. Her powers of concealment frightened me. The mockingbird was still singing. Free from his mate, free from his duties. Not thinking of past summer or coming winter. Joy under his smoky feathers, under his small bones. Joy inside himself for himself. The full, varied notes poured into the night, and all the quiet brimmed with his joy. Free and glad to be free. Was freedom so delicious, so delightful, so blissful? I didn't know. Somehow I felt I would never know.

Somewhere there was someone Mark wanted more than he wanted me. He wanted me less; it followed he wanted someone else more. I felt it. I knew it. The way an astronomer knows there must be another planet. He doesn't know where it is or what it is like. But it is there. It has to be there. Because the planet he has on hand—the one he sees and knows—veers, pulls, deflects from its charted course by the pull and the power of the unknown star.

❧ Chapter Twelve

By now I suppose most people have forgotten the depression, we've had many worse shocks since. Even I might have forgotten, but it was tangled up with my personal life. If times hadn't been hard, maybe things would have turned out differently for me. What remains vivid to me now is the emotional part—what happened to me during the worst of it and maybe because of it.

We were stuck down there at Wishmore, getting poorer and poorer, and Mark and I began to hate each other. Before times got so bad either Mark or I, or both of us together, would have had a chance to make something of our life with each other.

I was brought up to think of marriage as a static state. You grew up, fell in love, got married. Of course you didn't go about it the way I had done, but I always preferred to forget that. Never mind, you got married, and then you were happy. It was like some sort of mixture you stirred up and put together and put aside, and it was supposed to mold itself like Jello. Nobody told me how easily it unmolds and unjells in the heat of conflict.

Mark had liked me well enough in a way, for a while, but he even stopped liking me. If he had ever felt for me the way I felt about him, even at first, I would have remembered and been grateful and put up with whatever came after. I kept waiting for him to feel it, but instead he closed in on himself, shutting me out, showing me less and less of what was in his heart and in his mind. Arland had put up with Tim because once he had loved her and made her happy. It hadn't lasted too long, but at least it had been. I demanded a great deal more than that from Mark, but I really didn't have that much.

To get along we needed a life padded with ease and comfort, full of interests apart from each other, but we didn't have it. We had a lot of hard work, the sort of work Mark didn't like, and as things got worse it all seemed so fruitless. Or if we'd felt and thought alike about our common problems that might have drawn us together, but we didn't.

We were always in opposition about how to run the place and how to bring up Kitty.

Mark thought I encouraged Kitty's vanity too much, awoke in her too much competitive spirit against other children, and aided and abetted her love of fine clothes and the right people. Mark said I was making her material minded and too conventional.

Born as Kitty was in such a primitive spot, where nature is as raw as raw, she behaves as though she'd seen the light of day in a penthouse. She loathes all active sports except dancing, and is afraid of all kinds of animals, both wild and domestic. She has none of Arland's love of scenery and seasons, or my intense preoccupation with the land: clearing it, pruning it, fighting it, forcing it to give me back crops and fruits and flowers against its ready impulse to burst into briers; or Mark's love for plunging deep into untamed and untrammeled spaces. Kitty loves civilization and social life, with all its codes and comforts, conventions and restraints.

Mark and I even disagreed about abstract ideas if we ever fell into a discussion. My raw nerves kept striking sparks from his, also raw and plenty fiery. I lost my temper more often than he did when I began to rampage about things that went wrong, and nearly everything did. He would stalk out, or shut up tight, or else answer back in the mocking way I detested, not so much in words as in his tone and the expression of his eyes, full of before-the-storm lights.

This sort of thing might have gone on and on when a certain night came. The night when everything happened at once: the climax, in a way, of my life and the lives of a good many other people too. Everything led up to that night and wound away from it and was always entangled with its happenings. I've often wondered what would have become of all of us if things hadn't boiled into that sudden upheaval. If it was a stroke of fate, or if the same sort of thing would have happened, only more slowly and in a different way.

It was a quiet September evening just like any other evening for the last two or three weeks, effectively hiding what it had in store for us. The sun lit up the brown rows in the fields and the stretches of sedge beyond them, then went down behind the swamp. Carts creaked up the hill loaded with cotton nobody seemed to want to buy, and then dark came, with lots of stars shining steadily and owls hooting at each other.

After Kitty was asleep Mark and I were going over the plantation books. Mr. Jeff had wandered in and collapsed on the sofa in the hall. His snorted-out snores rasped all over the house. A rat was gnawing behind the bookcase. He'd be well in before day at that rate—a vigorous brute of a rat, with an eye toward some snuggery for cold weather.

"The hands have been feeding me hard-luck stories all day," Mark said. "Poor devils, it isn't their fault they haven't made anything this year."

"I wish they'd stop yowling. We're in a worse fix than they are. We aren't going to make anything either, and we'll have to carry them. At least they don't have all the responsibility the way we do."

I believe Mark thought I was pretty hardboiled about the tenants. I'm not really. I've never turned my tenants off in hard times, or taken advantage of them in any way. I've let them stay put, and doctored them and fed them and given them presents and let them walk off with the pecans, but their attitude of mind annoys me so much I always find myself scolding them and lecturing them. The hands at Wishmore were a simple, improvident lot, their mental processes not too far removed from the lore of their ancestral jungles. When they had any money they promptly squandered it on lots of food and corn likker they didn't need, or expensive and useless gewgaws from plausible merchants, and all my talk and all my explanations showing them how they were being cheated moved them not at all. When times were good Hettie had bought a breakfast set—some light wood upholstered in imitation red leather. She paid and she paid, and when she couldn't pay any more, the store sent down and hauled away the breakfast set. At least they would have, but I caught them halfway up the hill and raised such unshirted hell the driver turned around and brought the furniture back. I made Hettie look and find her tattered receipts, and saw she had already paid three fourths of the atrocious price. Then I went to the store where she had bought the stuff and gave the specious owner a piece of my mind. Hettie paid the rest out of her wages, on the dollar-down dollar-forever plan.

"Why'd you buy it in the first place, you blithering old idiot, when what you needed was a good, plain stove?"

Hettie answered nothing at all, but she adored that furniture. Arland, when I told her about it, said she knew how Hettie felt. She'd once gone to buy a plain navy blue dress to travel in, and come home with a pale pink mousseline de soie.

"You'll set your house on fire with that old stove," I roared at her. "Then you won't have anything!"

She only poked out her mouth.

"If you ever go near that man again, I swear I'll skin you alive," I promised her. Did she stop going there? Certainly not. The next time she wagged down Franklin Street that self-same merchant spotted her and lured her in to her further undoing, and mine. They were all like that down here at Wishmore. Didn't I find that old Lew had borrowed money to meet the payments on his rattle-trap third-hand car—borrowed at 20 per cent interest? Mark threatened that person with jail, and he backtracked, and Lew went on tinkering with his precious car, wiping it and polishing it and spending money on parts for it, struggling up the hill in it, getting drunk in it and almost wrecking it.

I was always feeling sorry for the tenants, but they drove me mad. All my life I'd heard people say complacently how well they understood Negroes and how simple they found the whole thing when you did understand them, and of course all Southerners do know them inside and out. I have never understood them. I frankly can't ferret out their mental processes at all, and I know perfectly well they are hiding everything they possibly can from me about their real meanings and intentions.

Of course Aunt Em and others like her contend that the tenants on the plantations and the colored people in town find the South exactly to their taste and are all happy as larks there. She is as good as she can be to old Albertha. She is, as she says, a Lady, and ladies are always good to Those Beneath Them. The Ellistons always treated their slaves well. No doubt they did, but I sometimes wonder how those upright and God-fearing Christians could ever reconcile themselves to slavery in the first place.

Of course Aunt Em is used to those rows of shacks spreading out on the edge of town in all directions, and she is unaware of some of the peculiar workings of the law when some colored man gets into difficulties with a white person. Her attitude annoys me. Nothing annoys me more except that other attitude—people who've never had to run a cotton plantation thinking that the landlord, poor harassed beast, lives in the lap of luxury battening on the tenants. Maybe some batten. I never have.

We worked Wishmore on shares. "It was a mistake in the first place ever to try to run it that way," I said to Mark now when we were discussing our plight. "It's the worst system in the world."

Michael didn't try to furnish his tenants. He let them get what they needed from the stores, then when they got into debt it was up to the stores to carry them until next year when, it was hoped, they'd do better and be able to pay. It had been Mark's idea to furnish the Wishmore hands himself. He thought he could buy for them better and cheaper than they could for themselves, but the way it worked out we had to carry them. They were deep in debt to us, and we were deep in debt to the stores and to the bank.

Usually, after the cotton was picked, our hands foraged around and found jobs for themselves during the winter. The women cooked in town or took in washing. The men hired themselves out, gardening or driving trucks or hauling drays. Now jobs weren't easy to find. Nobody wanted to take on more help, and some of our more ambitious people who'd gone to Chicago or Detroit in the boom years were coming back, not knowing what else to do with themselves.

This was what was facing us right now, and the mournfulness of the tenants got on my nerves, principally because I knew it was up to us to take care of them, and I didn't see how in the world we were going to do it.

"You know what a low standard of living they have anyway," Mark said, "and if it gets any lower, it's going to be mighty grubby."

"They won't starve down here, and that's something." They had meal and sweet potatoes and plenty of firewood, but that didn't solve the problem of shoes for the children and warmer clothes for winter, and nearly all the cabins needed repairs. I thought of poor old Jeb, sick for two years now, and in winter so bent and crippled with his rheumatism, shut up with a swarm of children and cats and dogs and a none too amiable daughter-in-law. He needed lots of warm blankets and expensive medicines. The cabin had only ill-fitting shutters to keep out the wind, no windowpanes. When the shutters were closed it was pitch-dark inside, except for the firelight, and always full of noise and smoke and drafts.

"Let's look over everything, Mark, and see what we can do."

We opened the books and worked on them for a while, then Mark pushed the heap of bills aside, all in a snarl.

"Don't do that, Mark. I'll never get them all straightened out right."

"What's the use of mulling over them anyway? We can't begin to pay 'em. I wonder if in all the world somewhere I couldn't find some sort of place for myself. Where I could use the sort of knowledge I have and make something out of myself. Lord knows this isn't it!"

That's what he'd always wanted, or thought he wanted—a place far away, a million miles from Wishmore, and probably from me, where he thought he could achieve some sort of fabulous success.

"Don't be so dreamy and impractical all the time! Your head's always busy with some never-never land! You'd better occupy yourself with what's here and now."

"I have, and you see how it works out. We're in the red. Look how the mortgage has grown. Where do we go from here?"

"You guess we can get another loan for next year's crop?"

"Not if anybody's got a ray of gumption. We haven't even paid the interest on the mortgage."

"How're we going to run things, then?"

"Damned if I know!" Mark lit a cigarette, and the match made a scratching sound, grating on my nerves.

"We can let the mortgage ride for a while," I meditated, "but we've got to get enough to meet the interest and make a crop."

"They won't take the place; they've got too many defunct plantations on their hands now. Wish they would, then that would be that."

"Don't talk like a blithering fool, Mark. What would we do if we lost Wishmore?"

"At least we'd be free." Free—that's what he wanted. To have no binding ties.

He added, "Other people are in just our fix, plenty of them."

"Not as deep as we are. They haven't had as much bad luck. Besides, most people—Michael, for instance—manage things better than you do, Mark. You've never put your heart into running this place. You know you haven't!"

"What the hell have I done or not done? I've stayed down here because you wanted to, when I damned well knew we should have gotten out when the getting was good. I'm not going to take the blame for the mess we're in."

"You don't want to shoulder responsibility; you never have. Now look here, Mark, you've got to do something, and do it now. I don't care where you get money, or how, but get it! If you were worth shucks, you would——"

He didn't say another word, but his face changed and became taut with fury. I was afraid of him when he gave me that look of distilled hate. Before I could speak he was out of the room and gone. I heard the car door slam, and the headlights wheeled across the room as he turned the car and went tearing up the hill. I was holding a pencil in my hand. I bit down on the top of it so hard it broke, and pieces of lead and wood were sharp in my mouth. I almost choked before I could spit it out. After a while I opened the books again, but the rows and lines of figures twisted before my eyes. Dead numbers. All the years of work added up to nothing gained, everything threatened. All the years with Mark added up to the same thing. We hadn't gained anything except Kitty. She was everything, of course, but still we should have something to show for our relations with each other besides this constant tension driving us farther and farther apart.

There was a sort of analogy between my feeling for this place and my feeling for Mark. Wishmore baffled me, kept defeating me until I grew so angry I hated it, yet I loved it too. When I looked out over its acres it kept telling me, "I will reward you if you find out how to handle me." I resented it, but I wanted it, every bit of its damp rich earth brought here by the river, every piece of its tangled moss-draped swamp, the very shape of its long slanted curve pushing into the Mississippi. It owned me, but someday I would own it if only I could find an answer to all the problems it posed.

I loved and wanted and hated and resented Mark in much the same way. He baffled me too; he made me furious, but he attracted me too much. Someday I would find a solution to my troubles with him, then I would own him and he wouldn't own me.

I had to find him before his anger hardened into an unbreakable mold and tell him I hadn't meant what I said. All my mistakes with him were like stones added to a wall. We didn't wipe out our past quarrels and start all over again . . . we started where we left off, with the high shadow of past disagreements between us.

Tonight, when I'd spoken to him the way I had, I'd lost faith in him. I was thinking he was like all the other people around here—like Mr. Jeff and Miss Kate and Aunt Em, simply taking what fate chose to hand out, utterly unable to ride life or shape it for himself.

When I'd first met Mark I had thought he had superior ability—a sort of greatness. Maybe because I was in love and steeped in the peculiar illusions love wraps around itself. Yet even now he, like Wishmore, was what I wanted. "Learn how to deal with me, and I'll reward you," he still promised me, without giving me any clues as to how to deal with him.

After a while, I decided I would try to go and find Mark and tell him I was sorry I had said all that. I had a feeling that if I didn't go now and straighten out our quarrel, things would be finished for us. There was something in his expression—— He wouldn't take much more, though I didn't see what he could do about it.

I hauled out the other car. We had two, both old, and both relics of more prosperous times. It moved slowly; it wheezed out for new parts, but I got it going and lunged up the hill along the narrow winding road. Clouds of dust were acrid in my nostrils and gritty between my teeth. I passed Rosemont, deep in the dark, and wondered what Miss Kate was up to. She'd be shut up there all alone tonight, since Mr. Charlie Selwyn had been sick for two weeks now. "Low sick," one of the hands had told me. I wondered what it must be like to live perpetually in a world so shut off from other people's daily living. Did Miss Kate and Miss Kate's temper ever lunge out after Mr. Charlie? Did he lunge back? He was always so polite, so charming to everyone; yet she was the only person he cared for, if he still cared for her. Perhaps she reined her tongue and her temper for him, or maybe, like me, because she loved him he made her madder than anybody, and she didn't. I wondered if those two were tired of each other and clung together only because they were old now and didn't have anybody else, or if their feeling lasted and lasted. Thinking of Miss Kate sent a thrill of warning through me. I was quarrelsome, and Mark showed he was tired to death of it. The lonely silence behind Rosemont's closed gate held a shadowy threat.

I went on into town and cruised up and down the streets, looking for Mark. The whole town looked withered and tired and drab and down-at-heel. Some of the stores on Main Street were untenanted. There weren't many people in sight, only a few loiterers draped on the corners and huddled on the bank steps. They didn't seem to have any particular place to go and nothing on earth to do with their time. Their inertness reflected the spirit of the whole place—a sort of waiting to be taken out of the doldrums, with no effort made to get themselves out by their own exertions.

When I wanted advice I usually found myself at Arland's, but I didn't want to tell her all I'd said tonight—she'd certainly blame me— so I didn't turn into her always open gate. Soon I found myself almost automatically taking the highway leading to the roadhouse Ludie Daniels kept. Of course Mark wouldn't be there, unless he was trying to make money by gambling. I told myself if there had been anything between Mark and Ludie since I'd married him, it must be over by now, over long ago. Arland had convinced me of that, or had she? I couldn't remember actually accusing Mark of carrying on with Ludie, not in so many words. Maybe I was afraid actually to accuse him, but when I mentioned her there was something strange in his manner—a shade of guilt, a shadow of mockery, as if he didn't really care what I thought. Something I couldn't quite define, springing out of a basic indifference to me. But he hadn't been indifferent tonight when he'd gone tearing away; he'd hated me.

Colored lights winked in the dark. Ludie's place. Its glitter had faded, too, when you saw it close up, though from a distance it still had an air of promise, the promise of pleasure. The tourist cabins, nests of so many succulent rumors and blazing scandals, looked deserted. I don't suppose they were all empty, though. Sin marches on. I slowly circled the main building. The lights were still on, and the doors and windows wide open. The orchestra was there, a dwindled little band. They weren't playing at the moment. A few couples looking profoundly bored, were at the tables, and a few people were in the gambling room. They were all white-faced and slit-eyed under the hard lights. You could easily recognize Mark in a group, and I would have seen him if he had been at the gambling tables.

It was deep relief not to see him, an easing of tension. Everything seemed simpler and more real, and I vowed to myself it was the last time I'd go prowling around in the night on his trail, spurred on by my crazy imagination. When I saw him again I'd make offers of peace, and we'd both stay at home and work things out some way. I had let the ghost of Ludie ride me entirely too long.

Just as I had almost completed the circle around the house, my heart gave a sideslip and began a spiraling, wheeling-down sensation, like a machine broken loose and out of control. Parked in the shadow of a tree was Mark's car. It was unmistakable, and under my own headlights the license plate jumped at me and the numbers on it went jangling through my brain. I slammed on the accelerator and kept going, whamming across the highway without looking. I didn't care if anything hit me and smashed me or not. Nothing did, and I tore back through town.

I had been right all along, and my rightness was killing me. I had driven him to Ludie; he'd gone straight to her. I might have known it.

In my heart of hearts I'd always known it. Just a few days ago I'd passed her on the street, dressed to a fare-ye-well, wafting heavy perfume that reminded me of China trees in flower on a hot sticky day, a red hat on her head, long earrings in her ears, beautiful still. Her hot thick black eyes had raked me with a sidelong look, her thick painted lips had curved. Maybe she had known Mark would soon come back. Maybe she was exulting over me because he had never stopped going to her. He was there, with her, in one of those secluded dens of hers. He'd lied and lied and lied—lived a lie.

I wondered how he'd worked it all this time. Then I thought of the side road. It cut from the highway near Ludie's place and wound through to the upper river road we had to use to get to Wishmore. It was lonely: hardly anyone ever used it. That was where Tim had been killed, on the sharp curve. His car had leaped the bridge. Because it reminded me of his death I always avoided it, but it would be easy for Mark to slip along its turnings; he'd hardly ever see anyone. So safe and short and easy. Just made for him to go to her. Was it my fault things had never been right between us? It was his fault, and hers!

I was through town, the houses thinned out, and the road turned between high banks. Beyond privet hedges dim lights from Negro cabins blinked out. The road curved sharply, the banks fell away to the long slopes toward the river and the ravines on the other side. Then I came to the place where a big chunk of land had fallen in during last winter's rains. It had looked as solid as any other place, but secret springs must have gnawed at it for years until the undermined soil had given away and gone tumbling into the river, making a great gash in the bluffs.

There I stopped the car and there I sat, I don't know why, except that I didn't want to go back to Wishmore. It held none of the security of home any more. I don't know how long I stayed there; time had no meaning at all. The cave-in had opened up the view, and you could see the lazy curve of the Mississippi for a long way. There was something cruel in the unregarding calm of the warm and lovely night. It gave me nothing at all of its peace; it only seemed to tell me people ought to be happy in it and certainly weren't.

The memory of every angry scene with Mark became more intense. There had always been a shadowy third person egging us on. When had he started going back to her? How often did he go? I thought of the other time I'd followed him, thinking he was with her. He'd denied it. No, he hadn't denied it, because I hadn't accused him. Now I'd accuse him and he couldn't deny it. If he only could! If he only would! It was too late. I'd never believe him now.

I suppose Aunt Em and people like her would say I got my just deserts—that I should never have married him the way I did. Yet it had seemed to me the only way I could get him, and I had to have him. And it had been worth it, even without contentment. It hadn't been like a marriage in some ways, but like a tangled-up love affair. Moments like those quivering days known as weather breeders, poised on the brink, ready to spill over into storm. Sun too bright and too hot, sky too blue, every object defined, touched with sheen and glitter not its own and clouds of blistering brilliance gathering to spread and get dark and crack wide open with lightning.

At last I started the car again and went on. There was nowhere for me to go except to Wishmore. I would have to let myself into the house, with Kitty asleep, and Hettie snoring in the chair, and the dead lump of Mr. Jeff on the sofa. I would go in and wait for Mark to come back from Ludie.

If only I had the strength to meet him when he came as though nothing had happened; to say I was sorry I'd told him he wasn't worth a damn; to smile and pretend, and let everything go on as before, only knowing instead of suspecting. That's what Arland had done, and that's what she would tell me to do. But she had been lucky. After the first affair she hadn't loved Tim any more. He was not the person she had thought he was, and finding it out killed her feeling. I was unlucky. Mark was the person I'd thought he was all along, and I still cared. I couldn't let go. Since I couldn't let go, it would be better to keep my mouth shut. Let him go on making a fool out of me, and then what would happen? Maybe some night like this I'd follow him out there and kill them both.

I didn't even realize I was passing Rosemont when a scream, then another, then the crack of shots tore the quiet night wide open. It startled me so the car almost sprang out of my control and leaped into the ravine. At first I thought I must have gone completely crazy and had screamed out without knowing it, and that the shots were the echoes of my wild brain. I slammed on the brakes, and after the car had stopped there was another scream and another shot. It was real, and the last scream had sounded strangled, cut off, smothered and extinguished by the shot. It was a human voice made inhuman by the very depths of terror. I knew it had come from Rosemont, and I knew Miss Kate was up there all by herself. And now not alone.

I don't know how many screams and shots there were. I only know they ended, and the night took up its silence. Only the crickets kept up their whirring. The road was empty, and the shadows didn't move. I had a violent impulse to go to Wishmore as fast as I could and call the police from there. Yet if I did, it would be too late to be any help at all to that old woman. Somehow I was sure I couldn't be any help by now anyway, but I couldn't simply ride off. I would have to go up there, have to try to do something. My clothes and skin and hair were drenched with the sweat of stark fear. For a minute I couldn't think at all. I knew I couldn't bring myself to go up to that dark house alone; then I remembered the cabin huddled at the foot of the next slope, just beyond Rosemont's tall fence. Clenching my hands on the wheel, I made it there. It seemed hours before I reached it, but it couldn't have taken more than a minute.

The cabin, scrunched close to the ground, like a cowering little thing, was closed and shuttered, but light came stealing from a knot-hole. They'd heard the screams and the shots too—they must have. I beat on the door, yelling, "Let me in, let me in," but there was no answer. "Open the door; it's Miss Jane." At last the door creaked open a little, and a man's head peered out, his breath whistling from between his lips. It was Andy Sack. I'd known him for years, but at the moment I couldn't even remember his name.

"What's gon' on, Miss Jane? In de name ob God, wha's done happened?"

"I don't know. I was passing by. Come on, we've got to get up there and find out." My courage had come back. The only telephone anywhere near was at Rosemont, and I had to get to it, and to Miss Kate.

"I'm scairt to, Miss Jane." Andy opened the door wider. A woman was crouched on the bed, her dark face gray. A child looked out from behind her, a little bright-eyed, frightened animal.

"You've got to come. Miss Kate's up there all alone. We've got to see what's happened."

"Lawd Gawd," the woman moaned. "Pore Miss Kate, wha' they done to her?" She rocked back and forth. Andy turned, and I thought for a minute he was going to shut the door again, but he only went to get his gun from the wall, and then he was ready to come along.

" 'Tain't no use to carry on," he said to his wife. "Usses got to go up there like Miss Jane says." After he'd closed the door behind us I heard the woman scuttle across the room and ram the bolt. I wished myself back in there with her, in some safe enclosed place all lighted up.

The soft earth and gravel skidded under my wheels as I turned the car. The heavy growth of bushes and trees along Rosemont's fence were black. They would show green again in the morning when the sun shone on them, yet when I was passing them I thought they must have shot out of the ground with black stems and black leaves springing from black roots.

The big gate was closed but not locked. Afterward I wondered what I would have done if it had been locked. I could have climbed the fence, but I didn't know if I could have nerved myself and Andy to walk up the drive to the house. The gate was rusty, so few people ever came or went through it. Andy opened it, and the grinding of the hinges sent ripples all up and down my spine. He crawled in the car again, looking all around, then huddled down beside me. I wouldn't let him get in the back. I made him sit right up with me, with his gun. I drove on through.

"I reckon it's a good thing for me you done come along, Miss Jane. They might-a got to thinkin' I'd been up there doin' no good."

"They wouldn't—everybody knows you."

"Mebbe they wouldn't, but mebbe they would-a—can't never tell." I knew what he meant. No wonder colored people never wanted to see anything or hear anything or tell anything. They were afraid of being enmeshed in circumstances.

"Andy, what exactly did you hear?"

"Shots, an' 'er awful hollerin'. She hollered out."

"Miss Kate?"

"Yes'm. I knowed it was her what was yellin'. Then more shots, then she hollered again." Neither of us could remember whether the screams or the shots had come first. Andy gave a deep sigh.

"Ain't never knowed nuthin could-a scairt me so awful bad."

The night had completely taken back its peace. Nothing had happened, nothing could. Yet the sound of the screams and the shots was still too real, still hung too heavy in the air for me even to try to forget them. I had heard so many descriptions of Rosemont: a visitor coming here in 1845 had given a minute account of the house and the garden and its contents; old Mrs. Lennerd had written how it looked between 1860 and '65; Aunt Emily had told me about a dance given in 1900. In the last few years no one had seen the house and the grounds except Mr. Charlie, and he didn't say what it was like now. So when I found myself within its gates for the first time I had a sense of being in a place I'd seen in a dream and feeling a shock at finding it real. I had heard so often of the row of statues under the live oaks along the drive. Now they came out under the headlights and stepped back again with a malign life of their own. The house burst suddenly from a mass of trees blotting out a block of stars. Black, closed, silent, it mocked the screams still ringing in my ears.

We got out of the car, hating to leave its shelter, and the boards of the gallery crackled under our feet. I tried the locked front door and then the long shuttered windows on either side of it. I was shaking, but my head was clear. Too clear. I've never forgotten any least detail, except how long it all took. Time is unclear. The gallery went all the way around the house, and we went along it, looking behind us at each step we took. A door was open at the side, and a light from it cut the dark with its narrow band. It showed the patterned shadow of a bit of wrought-iron railing and the worn floor boards and a few dark sticky drops on the gallery floor. There were side steps leading from the gallery to the grass of the upper terrace, and where the light touched it the grass was long and dry. The light didn't reach far. I was glad it didn't. I didn't want to see too much.

Andy stopped, and so did I; then I whispered to him to come on, we couldn't stay there. We carefully sidestepped the dark drops and looked in the open door. I knew we made a target for anyone beyond the gallery, and I wanted to move fast, but for a moment I couldn't move an inch. We were seeing what was Miss Kate's study. A tall lamp burned on the desk, and beyond its glow the room took on duskiness. It did not seem much disturbed, except that the chair by the desk was overturned. There was an open bottle of ink on the desk, and an open book was right under the lamp.

We hurried in, and I shut and locked the door. The long window next to the door was open too. I ran to it and snatched the dusty curtains together. "Here, Andy, stand and put your gun through the curtains. If you hear anything, shoot. Watch, and if you hear or see anything at all, just shoot. I must find the phone."

I supposed I had braced myself to see Miss Kate lying here dead or dying, and the very emptiness of the room was a shock in itself. It frightened me more not to know what had happened than to find out.

I looked around wildly for the telephone. Thank God, it was right here on the desk, before my eyes. I might have had to grope and stumble through the infinite black of the house looking for it. I snatched it up, steadying it against my body. The operator sounded sleepy when she first answered, but she woke up when I told her to send the sheriff and everybody she could get hold of out to Rosemont. Then I locked the door leading to the rest of the house. Somebody might be waiting there, watching us. My knees felt like pieces of boiled spaghetti, and I slumped down on the sofa against the wall. My foot skidded. I'd stepped on a drop of blood. It made me so sick at my stomach I thought I was going to throw up, but I didn't. When I could bring myself to look down at my shoe, I saw there was no visible mark on it, though I had on white sports shoes. But when I looked closely at the floor I saw two or three dark sticky spots, one a little wider and smeared where I had stepped.

Blood on the floor in here, and blood on the gallery . . . more than in here, and more, maybe much more, through the grass and bushes outside. Maybe Miss Kate had run outside. No, she wouldn't have done that. If she could have moved, she would have run farther into the house, it seemed to me. Because of the blood I began to be sure she must be outside, but I did not dare go searching beyond the walls of this room. I could only wait for the sheriff to come.

I tried to call Miss Kate's name, but I couldn't utter a sound. My throat was squeezed tight and dry. There was no sight or sound of anybody, except Andy, obediently training his wavering gun out of the window and whispering, "Lawdamighty Gawd have mercy" all the time. He'd never used his gun for more than anything but killing rabbits and partridges. I wondered if he could force himself to use it on whatever shape might come looming at us.

I was sure it didn't matter whether I called Miss Kate or not. Call her long, call her loud—she would never answer now. While I waited with Andy in the stifling heat of the closed room, I forced myself to my feet and tried to take in every detail of what had probably happened. The overturned chair had a split back, and a scrap of white cloth was caught in the jagged edge of the break. It was a piece of

Miss Kate's shirtwaist, one of those shirtwaists of the early 1900s she had always worn like a sort of uniform, as though she belonged entirely to the ranks of the past and would not admit the present.

The phone had evidently not been touched, except by my own hands. I thought of calling Mark; he could get here quicker than people from town. Then I remembered he wouldn't be there—he was with Ludie. And I felt all hot and wild and not afraid any more. I felt like a murderer—not someone in fear of one—because I wanted to kill.

Then all of a sudden I could almost see Miss Kate's hands clutching wildly for the phone, clawing the air before my eyes. If she had been sitting in front of her desk—if she had, she could have reached the phone, unless her hands had been torn away by violence.

The pile of papers on her desk was not much scattered. The open page showed rows of numbers, and the pen was lying slantwise across it. The point had jabbed itself in the paper, leaving a line of ink. She must have been sitting here with her back to the door, going over her accounts, just as I had been doing down at Wishmore earlier in the evening. She must have sat here night after night, year after year, in perfect safety. Then came this night, and she wasn't safe any more. Someone must have watched her from the bushes of the upper terrace, someone who had crept up out of the dark tangle nearer and nearer the house, until he or she or it could choose the exact moment. Then whoever or whatever it was had climbed the railing, avoiding the path of light.

Then I noticed the desk drawer. It was half open. I went nearer and looked at it without touching it. The keys dangled in it, and right in front was Miss Kate's revolver. Maybe she had heard an unusual sound in the stillness and had unlocked the desk drawer to get her revolver. But the watcher had been too quick. I could see her outstretched hand, ringed and wrinkled and small, could see a shadow leap and seize her and jerk her hand away from everything that might have saved her—the phone and the pistol. Then she had screamed—the scream must have come first, and whoever had attacked her had shot, bungling it, letting her cry out again until the shots had mastered the sound of her voice. She'd fought for her life, she would fight, just as I would have done, but whoever had grabbed her had pulled her away, dragging her out of the room and down the side steps. God knows where or with what aggravations of brutality! I wished I didn't seem to see it all with so much vividness. The only thing I couldn't see was the killer—who or why.

Why could be guessed at. Everybody always said Miss Kate kept lots of money hidden in the house. Now, when the banks were so shaky, people said she'd drawn everything out of them and stowed all the cash she had somewhere in Rosemont. Maybe it wasn't true, but it sounded true—in character. Whoever had attacked her hadn't had time to look for the money. Those screams must have unnerved even somebody used to killing. Then Andy and I had come, and our coming would have upset any plans for a thorough search of the house. Was it someone she had never seen before or, worse still, someone she knew and recognized?

She was small and thin like me, but she had struggled hard to keep on living. The night was perfectly still, and she had a carrying voice. "I used to love to hear Katie sing," Aunt Em had often said. "She had a lovely voice, so well trained. She had the best European teachers."

It struck me how strange it was for me to be here where Miss Kate had never asked me and where I had always longed to come. How strange for me to be here now, like this. The big rooms stretched on all sides of me, crammed with furniture and treasures I had yearned to see and to touch and to own. The masses of silver, thick with tarnish, never used; the cabinets full of china, dust dimmed; and the bookcase full of books. Open them and their painted pictures would bloom again. But the house, like the princess in the fairy story, once so magic to me, had turned into a monstrous shape in my hands.

When death had come here before it had been the decent cessation of life. Now it was like the death in the jungle and the swamp; not for people, not for houses, but all raw, watching, and pouncing, and the shrieks of the victim in the clutches of the thing that watched and pounced. And I was afraid, not only of what had happened, but of death itself. I think it was the first time I was ever conscious of it, or realized it would come and get me too. I didn't know how or when or where, but it would come.

Miss Kate had once been young and beautiful and rich. She'd had a European education and had driven along behind high-stepping horses. She'd queened it in Paris salons and come back with stacks of Paris clothes, and young men had wanted to marry her. How high she'd held her head, with plumes wavering and shaking in her black hair. How could she possibly imagine what was going to happen to her on a September night in the year 1932?

I suppose she couldn't imagine being dead, just as now I couldn't. There was her pistol, glimmering at me from the half-open drawer. Almost to her hand, but not quite.

I thought of Tim, hurtling off the ledge, and I thought of the side road, and the side road made me think of Mark, adding the sickness of my own feelings to the sickness of being here in this room. I was afraid of everything, within myself and outside too.

I almost grabbed the phone at that minute and tried to call Mark; then I didn't. A dim-colored moth was fluttering around the lamp. Automatically I brushed it aside. I was too late. It fell back on the open page, writhed and crumpled up.

My mind turned to the thought of the money that might be here. Maybe the murderer or murderers had just thought there was money here, or maybe they had known it. People were desperate for money these days. I was desperate myself.

If it was here, who knew it? If she had drawn out big sums from her account, the bank would know. But if she'd drawn it out little by little for the last few years, the bank wouldn't know whether she still had it or had spent it. Unless whoever had killed her had seen money lying about on her desk, for instance, and grabbed it, there would have been no time to make a search for it.

I didn't think it would be lying about like that; she would have been careful. I wondered who would inherit this house and her plantations and her money, the stocks and bonds and cash that helped make up the Lennerd fortune. How all of us, except Mark, had cherished the breath and aura of the Lennerd fortune! Would Michael and Mark and Alec get it, or would it all go to Mr. Charlie?

I hadn't thought much about it lately; it was all so out of my reach. But was it so out of my reach now? Of course it was awful for me to think about it now, at this moment, but I needed it more than the others. Why should Mr. Charlie have it all? People said he was well off anyway. Michael was better off than I was, and Alec always seemed to get along. But if I had money, I wouldn't fight with Mark so much. If I had money, I wouldn't lose Wishmore.

If Miss Kate kept money in this house, where would she keep it? In this room, where she worked. This very room was the most likely place. In the desk—— Well, I couldn't look, with Andy standing right there. There was nothing but the pistol in the half-open drawer. Suddenly I decided I would look in the desk, quick, before anyone came, and they would be here soon. I said to Andy, "I'm going to look in the desk and see if there's any clue. But don't say anything about it." He only muttered, "Yes'm." He wasn't paying any attention to me; all he wanted was to get out of here.

There were four desk drawers besides the half-open middle one. They had handles. I tried one gingerly. It wasn't locked, and it slid open easily, but it was entirely empty. I closed it and wiped the handle with my sodden handkerchief. The one below it was empty too. The others were full of papers. I didn't dare start rummaging through them, but, as they were unlocked, I didn't think she'd keep any big sum there.

I looked at every piece of furniture in the room before I really noticed the smallish table by the wall. To anybody else's eye it was just a drop-leaf table in abominable condition, but not to my eyes. There was one exactly like it down at Wishmore; they were evidently a pair. The one at Wishmore must have come from here, or the one here had come from Wishmore. One day years ago when I was doing fall house cleaning and trying to polish the table, I had discovered the trick. If you touched it a certain way the whole top turned around and there was a little hidden drawer beneath it. I used to keep my locket and my bracelet there safely out of reach, and I had never even told Mark about it.

I felt sure that if there was money in this house and in this room, it would be in the table. Blood money, all grisly and crawling. But I only wanted to see if it was there. I didn't want to touch it. If you could touch it—take it—you could do anything. You set yourself apart from your own kind—from Mark, Arland, all your family, and all your traditions. You became one of those people who will do anything for money, and because you will are no longer quite human.

I knew all this, but I couldn't take my eyes off the dim outlines of the table against the wall. Tonight had hardened and changed me. I was no longer the same person I had been at sunset, at eight o'clock. The quarrel with Mark, then seeing his car parked at Ludie's, and Miss Kate's screams, coming up here and sitting in this room and thinking—— I could never go back and be what I was. Some heavy evil had soaked through my pores. I hated Mark and Ludie so. I wanted to do them in, get revenge, kill, strike. I wanted the money. I was aligned with the murderer, out in the dark places, cut off from my civilized world and from civilized people, and I didn't think I could ever get back into it or to them any more.

Be decent; don't think of the money; put it out of your mind. Look for it if you get a chance, and if it's there, take it if you damn well can. Take it, and if you have enough guts, you can get away with it, and nobody will ever know.

The siren on the police car whined from around the curve. "Here they come." They'd be careening up the drive; they'd all be here in a minute or so. There was no time to spare for hesitations. I spoke to Andy while still watching the window. "Here's a candle. Light it and go around to the front."

"Miss Jane, I'm scairt to. If you was to come too——"

"Nothing to be scared of. The police are here; you're perfectly safe. Hurry, do what I say. Go on and do what I say, and close the door behind you; they're coming." I was so nervous, so afraid he'd think I was up to something. He took the candle, but he still hesitated.

"Andy, if I ever get rich, I'm going to build you the finest house you ever saw. You've been a lot of help tonight. Now go on."

He went. The door was shut and so was the window. There was a minute, not more. A minute to make a move or to refrain from moving. I went to the table, and I forced my hands to steadiness. I pressed, and the top swung around. There was the little drawer, and in it were two heavy, unmarked brown envelopes. I grabbed them and tore them open. There was the money, wads of it. I stuffed it all down the front of my dress. The envelopes were too stiff, so there was nothing to do but put them back where they came from and hope to God no one would know they were there. I whirled the tabletop around into place and wiped it off. I was just in time too. Feet were coming; voices were raised. I pushed the wad further down my bra, ran to the door, and flung myself on the sheriff.

"God in heaven, Jane," he kept repeating. He was a cousin of mine, Bob Hammon, a pleasant and easygoing sort of man, used to sitting in his office with his feet on the desk, swapping jokes with the taxpayers. I knew he'd find all this stupefying, and I was not afraid of him much; he couldn't possibly guess what I'd done. "My God, girl." He kept patting my shoulder.

They were all crowding in with guns and flashlights, regular police-men and suddenly summoned citizens, now deputies. They all asked questions; they all talked at me and each other, confused and out of their depth. They wanted to know where Miss Kate was, and when I said I had no idea they mostly scattered, taking up the search, through the house, out on the grounds. This sort of thing had never happened around here before, and nobody knew exactly how to deal with it.

I suddenly felt charged with a hot, clear alertness—a sense of my own strength; I could manage anything now. I'd stolen, and I'd tell any necessary lie without a qualm, and maybe when I saw Mark again I would kill him. But I wouldn't show any of that. I'd pretend I was about to collapse with fear.

One of the deputies pointed to Andy. "What's he doing here?" I told him how I had gone and brought him back with me. "He's been with me the whole time."

Bob gave Andy a vague look, not much interested in him. "Andy's all right. Known him since I was knee-high. Now, Jane——"

He asked me what I had touched, to try to remember exactly. I did remember exactly. The money down my dress shifted against my skin. It was a thick lump weighting me down. I told him I'd only touched the phone and the door and the curtains and the other door, and I kept my eyes away from the table.

They began to notice all the things I had noticed, but I didn't offer a word, only answered their questions.

"You did just right," one of the deputies muttered. "You sure kept your head; you sure must have been scared to death coming up here." I didn't want them to think I was too brave or too clearheaded. I didn't answer, just leaned back and closed my eyes.

"You're all in, Jane. Here, Luke. Drive her home in her own car. Someone can follow you and bring you back. She can answer questions tomorrow. I've got to stay here and direct the search. First thing, we've got to find Miss Kate. Jane, did you see anything or hear any-body?"

I shook my head.

"What makes you sure somebody killed her?"

I told him about the shots and the screams, and how she didn't scream any more; they had already noticed the spots on the floor. They'd trampled on them when they all came surging in, but I don't suppose it mattered much. I must have turned bright green, because Bob said, "You get out of here before you collapse. Where's Mark?" I only stared at him. "Why didn't you phone him? She's his aunt!"

"I guess I just didn't think." I suppose it seemed queer, my not calling my own husband. He could have come right up the hill and been here much sooner than the police from town, and I felt I hadn't made the right answer. I should have said he wasn't home. I had a sense of traps and snares being set all around me; I mustn't begin to flounder.

I was glad now I hadn't tried to reach Mark. Suppose he had answered and had come? Then I never would have found a way to take the money. I had become tangled up in Miss Kate's murder through no fault of my own. I'd come up here from a sense of duty, to help her. Since I couldn't, I'd helped myself. Maybe all along something in my subconscious mind had told me to handle it alone; that there was something in the situation I could use.

My blank face and blank voice showed none of this to Bob Hammon. "I reckon you couldn't think of everything, scared as you were." So my mistake passed unnoticed. He asked, "What's your number?" I told him and, as I went out of the room, I could hear Bob talking over the phone, telling Mark what had happened. So Mark was back at Wishmore.

I got in my car and Luke drove. Somebody got in another car to follow us, and we left Rosemont. Lights were moving all over the house and all over the place. Men were calling to each other, and more cars were coming up the drive as the news spread. It was news to shake the town with a bang out of its drowsy apathy.

We turned down the road toward Wishmore. Luke Preeley kept muttering that this beat everything he'd ever heard tell of, and he had heard a God's plenty in this town. "Lotta queer doin's always goin' on, most of 'em among what is known as our best folks. Looks like the higher they hold their heads the queerer they act—but never nuthin' like this. Pore ole lady. I wish to Godalmighty I was shut of it all! Can't make head or tail of it. Reckon it had to do with money, most likely—somebody thinking she had a lotta money." He gave a deep sigh. "Reckon that Andy could have skittled back to his house and holed in before you got there?"

"Not a chance in the world. Don't you-all go barking up that tree. He couldn't possibly have had anything to do with any of it."

"No, I reckon that won't wash. But somebody must have done her in." He had no particular wish to get Andy into trouble, but it would have simplified matters for them all if they could have found a culprit close at hand.

When we drove up Mark was outside waiting for us, pacing around restlessly, his pistol in his hand. "You all right, Jane?" He opened the door and helped me out, asking Luke questions. "Have they found her yet?"

"Still lookin' when I left."

I began to feel dizzy and strange, and I didn't hear very plainly what else he asked Luke, or what Luke answered.

"I'll be up as soon as I can," Mark said, and Luke got in the car which had followed us, and drove off.

Mark led me into the house. "Poor kid, it must have been one hell of an experience from what Bob was telling me." His voice sounded far away, as though it had come out of the past, when there was nothing to separate us from each other. It made me feel queerer than ever. Everything wavered before my eyes. Then I found myself in a chair in the living room, and Mark was standing in front of me, pouring whisky into a thick glass. "Drink this, it'll make you feel better."

"Now it seems so unreal. I never saw her but once, and when I got up there I didn't see her at all."

"I know. Like it never happened. That's what I felt when Bob was telling me. Drink your whisky, Jane. Help you snap out of it."

I drank it. It was fiery and strong and made my throat tingle, but it cleared my head. The room, and Mark's face, focused.

"That better?"

I nodded. Now everything was plain. The lamp shone with a steady light. There were the account books just where I had left them. Everything in the room was just as it had been—even the rat was still cutting away behind the bookcase; yet it was all different. That, too, made for a feeling of strangeness—the sameness and yet the difference. How could I come back here and find it all just as I had left it, when nothing in myself or in my life could ever be as it was?

"Awful thing. You had guts to go up there. If I go on now, will you be afraid to stay here with just Hettie?"

Of course it was awful, but he had never loved his aunt Kate, and he wasn't pretending to now.

"No, I'm not scared." I'd never be afraid of anything any more.

"You'd better have another drink." He poured some more out, but I didn't take it. I put it down on the table. Mark was watching me. The way the light fell, there was a band of shadow across his forehead and under his eyes, and the rest of his face was illumined by the lamp. I don't think I've ever seen his face in more exact detail: the sun-browned skin grooved by the scar, the blunt nose and full, clear-cut mouth. I'd always loved his mouth—and his kisses, rare of late. His hand, brown and hard and hot with life, was over my own chilly one.

I caught a glimpse of my own face in the mirror, gray, framed by draggling hair, like nothing so much as an old mop. I longed to fling myself against him, to have his arms go around me and feel the warmth and pressure of his body against my own. Not to speak, not to accuse, but simply to fling myself against him, yielding to the feeling I had for him. It was as easy as that. He would hold me and comfort me and forget we'd parted with a lot of hard words, and maybe he could change me back into what I had been. But I was afraid. I hesitated because he was watching me, and his eyes, in the band of shadow, were so direct and bright and intense, that I began to think of the money again. I felt he could see right through my clothes to where the wad of money was lying against my skin. If I flung myself against him, he might feel its thickness under my light dress, between my breasts. Now I don't believe he would have, but I was upset, and I was afraid, because if he ever knew—if he ever even guessed—he'd never be willing to touch my body again.

I was so damned conscious of what I had done, that the money seemed to be digging its roots down through my flesh and through my bones. I hesitated and the moment passed—the right moment, because Mark asked, "Jane, how in the name of God did you happen to be along there, going along that road at that time anyway?"

That was the fatal question. A thousand times since, I've wished he hadn't said those words right then. It flung me right back into my hatred for him. I could see his car parked under the willow tree at Ludie's. I could see him, shut up with her, her head flung back, his mouth pressed against hers, giving her what belonged to me.

"Because I was following you." There was a brass bowl of those orange Cosmos on the table. The faint scent came to me; their bold color flared in the lamplight. I had always loved them, bright like stars among the autumn leaves; yet ever since that minute I've never been able to endure the sight of the things.

Mark took his hand from mine and straightened up. His face tensed. "I didn't see you. Where did you see me?"

"I saw your car parked out at Ludie Daniels' roadhouse, where I knew you'd be, damn you! No wonder you didn't see me! You were curled up with her somewhere! Now try to lie out of this one!"

The scar on his cheek looked leaden and shiny, and his eyes narrowed a little, but he didn't lose his calm. He never did.

"I wasn't there for the reason you think. I can explain later. Right now I want to get up yonder, and you'll just have to take my word for it."

"Take your word—— Oh, stop your damned lying. You've lied and lied——"

"Shut up, Jane. You don't know what you're talking about."

"Don't I? You've lived a lie for years and years. Everything about you is a damned dirty lie, and I hate your guts."

"I guess you're right, Jane. It's not a bit of use my trying to tell you anything. You don't believe me and you don't believe in me." He didn't sound angry, only tired. Tired to death of listening to me and looking at me and enduring me. It was that boredom of his that turned me so wild.

"Believe you! How in God's name can I believe you when you go sneak off to hole up with Ludie Daniels!" Fury shook me so hard all my muscles twitched, knotted, and quivered. "I stay down here and slave and sweat year after year, and wear old clothes and lead one dog's life. Do you help? Not you! Trail off in the swamp and lope back, pretending you're trying to do something, when you don't! Why, all this time you're probably taking every damned red cent you can lay your filthy paws on to pay that damned whore! What do you care about me, or Kitty either? All you want is to get off and go to sleep with that painted piece of tallow. I know you—you and that vile bitch. I know all about you. You think I'm going to take it, don't you? I'm not! Do you hear that? I'm damned if I will! You've made a fool of me for the last time—you low, vile, stinking, rotten——"

The echo of my own voice sounded hoarse, coming from somewhere besides from in me, and all words were inadequate. What I was feeling yelled for stronger weapons than any words. All those newspaper stories of people who killed their wives and lovers and husbands.

They sounded unreal when you read about them. "She killed him because she loved him." "Everything went black." They weren't unreal; I was right there with them. Awful people, people you didn't know. I knew them. I was one of them. It didn't seem unnatural to hate and to kill. Violence had become the normal thing for me.

There was his pistol lying on the table. I had a blinding impulse to pick it up and pump the bullets—all the bullets—right through him. I stretched out my shaking hand for it; my fingers were tensed and clawed to grab it, but he reached out and took it first and put it in his pocket. I couldn't stay my hand though. The pistol was out of reach. The only thing left was the half-full glass of whisky. I picked it up and threw it right in his face. He didn't move. He only wiped his wet face with his hand.

"Hell, I'm fed up with all this," he said under his breath. At the door he turned around and said, "So long," and went on out.

The room was perfectly quiet except for the clock ticking and my own breathing. One of the orange flowers in the bowl let its petals fall; one, and then another, then a shower of them.

I really had wanted to kill him. I'd meant to. The part of me ready to kill suddenly crumpled up and fell away, like a garment you pull off and step out of. As soon as I could make my feet move I ran out, but I hadn't started soon enough. "Mark, come back!" I called. The car was already moving. It went bumping down the rough track. The taillight winked at me, then disappeared in the dark as the car rounded the first curve of the hill.

✑§ Chapter Thirteen

They found Miss Kate's bullet-ridden body in a tangle of honey-suckle vines behind the broken-down summerhouse on the second terrace. Bob Hammon told me when he came down to see me the morning after the murder. He was wretched. "It's all the damnedest thing! Why did something like this have to happen just after I got myself elected?" He mopped his forehead and his heavy neck. It was a hot gummy day, but if it had been zero weather, he would still have sweated freely over his predicament. "All the time and money I spent getting into office! Sure wish some of those blatherskites that ran against me was standing in my shoes now!" He gave a groan. "You never saw such a hubbub. Whole town on its ear, and bunches of reporters springing up from everywhere, taking pictures and asking questions and scribbling."

I hadn't been to bed. I'd bathed and dressed and hustled Kitty off to school. I wasn't even interested in poor Miss Kate just then. I wanted to be alone to think things out. "Did Mark come up there?" Mark had not come back to the house, and I was trying to find out what Bob Hammon knew about him.

"Yeah, he came. He helped find her. Of course I know he never had anything to do with her, and didn't care too much about her, but I tell you it was no pretty sight when we did find her lying there. Mark said he'd passed earlier in the evening, and everything looked just as usual."

I wondered just when he had come back to Wishmore. Probably during that time when I was sitting by myself on the bluff. I had forgotten how time had jumbled itself, because everything else was so clear to me.

"Where did Mark say he'd been?"

"With Michael." Bob did not seem in the least interested in Mark's whereabouts now, or what he had done with his time the night before. I was afraid to ask too many questions. I didn't want people to ever know he had been with Ludie, or to know I knew it. Of course Michael would back Mark up, or perhaps Michael thought Mark had gone straight home. Maybe Mark had told Bob Hammon he had been with Ludie. All of them had probably put in a little time with Ludie, or else wished they had. They had no doubt just leered and thought he was a lucky dog, and kept their mouths shut. Or maybe Mark hadn't told them anything.

Anyhow, neither then nor later, with all the people who were suspected, and still are suspected, did anyone ever seem to think Mark had anything to do with his aunt's death. I'm sure a good many of my fellow citizens vaguely think in their heart of hearts that I had a hand in her murder, but not Mark. For once mass opinion hit on the essence of the truth. Mark couldn't have done it. His absolute indifference to his aunt Kate and her possessions was too well known.

"Tell me again, Jane, everything you know."

Sick of it all, I went through the whole story. Not the whole. I had my own secret. Somehow the real murderer and I seemed to be on one side, and the rest of the world on the other.

"Pore old lady, she sure landed me in one hell of a fix. The way we figure it, somebody began to think long and hard about the money she was supposed to keep in the house. They sneaked up on her and she hollered out, and they pumped bullets in her. That's what it all adds up to. But a funny thing—we searched the house and found every damn thing in the world but money. Where is it? The bank says she's been drawing out her account for two years now. Hasn't much cash in her checking account, though she used to have a lot. Maybe she spent what she took out, but it doesn't seem likely. The question is—where is it?"

I forced myself to look him straight in the eye. I didn't know exactly what to say, and remembered I'd read somewhere how guilty people always say too much, so I said nothing.

"Or else," Bob went on, his face puckered with worry, "somebody made it look that way. Maybe somebody who knew Mr. Charlie was sick and wouldn't be going over there as per usual. He's been in bed two weeks now, weak as a cat too. Reckon the shock'll kill him? Folks always said she was sure to leave everything she had to him. Maybe she intended to, but we didn't find a sign of a will or anything like that. I guess her heirs'll inherit."

For once in my life I felt absolutely indifferent about Rosemont and the land. I felt so blank and drained I didn't care if everything went to Mr. Charlie or not. I felt too tired and numb to feel sorry for Miss Kate or myself.

"You look bad, Jane. No wonder. Well, I guess nobody ever really expects to fade out of the picture—not like she did, anyhow. Gosh, it was awful. But you've heard enough about it. You know old Mr. Durly and Miss Faust? They had some kind of set-to with Miss Kate because their animals kept getting over in her place. I went over to see what kind of account they gave of their evening. You ever been there? Must-a been a grand old house once, but I thought it'd fall in on me before I could ever get out of it. They've got newspapers piled up to the ceiling, and goats and chickens wandering in and out— mostly in—and strips of goat meat, all rat-chewed, dingle-dangling in strips from a lotta rusty bedsprings——" He looked up.

Mr. Jeff was standing in the doorway giving us dark looks. He'd heard the news that morning, and his face looked shrunken over its bones. He felt the news of Miss Kate's death more than he wanted to admit. "Shut up like that all by herself——" he muttered. "She was the prettiest girl——" He stumbled off, and Bob stared after him.

"Reckon he feels it. Lives in a world of his own, though. If I could only get a break in this case! By the way, how did you happen to be riding along there that time of night?"

It seemed to me a vague suspicion had come into his voice. I could easily reconstruct how people's thoughts might go when they found out there was no will. They might think I knew that fact, and they knew I must need money. I could have shot and killed her, and bribed Andy to drag her into the bushes. Of course it was fantastic, but the real truth was probably just as extraordinary.

Only most people wouldn't think I had the coolness and villainy to carry out such a thing. If they ever had an inkling I'd taken her money, they'd certainly think I'd killed her for it. I'd done a dangerous thing; I had to keep my head.

"I was coming home from Arland's," I answered calmly. Hettie used to say " 'Tain't no trouble to tell a lie." It isn't. I would have died rather than let Bob Hammon know I had been following Mark and had found him with Ludie. If anybody had ever guessed what had happened between us because of that woman—— Bob Hammon was far too preoccupied with his own troubles to pay much attention to me. My lie sounded plausible enough.

180

"Get me some whisky, Jane, like a good girl."

"Mr. Jeff's is rank poison. I'll get you some of Mark's."

"Mark told me he had to go on a trip. Where's he going?"

"You mean he's left town?"

"Said he was going to. Tell the truth, I wasn't paying much attention to him. I thought sure you'd know where he was off to." So he had gone out of town. It was ominous for me. Maybe if Bob thought there was something peculiar in his going at just this moment, he would make Mark come back.

"He signed a statement and said he'd drop me a line in case I wanted to get in touch with him. I don't suppose I'll need him though. He doesn't know anything." Nothing had aroused the least suspicion in Bob's mind. I think he guessed Mark and I had parted on bad terms, but he was too absorbed to be interested in that angle now. He had no idea of making Mark come back. "Said he had business to attend to. Let me get on back there and see what's going on."

After he had gone one of the colored boys came and pounded on the door. "Mr. Mark done told me ter give you this." He thrust a piece of white paper at me. It looked very white and stark in his long black fingers. "Where'd you see Mr. Mark?"

"Las' night. He stopped der car goin' up der hill and handed me this."

I took it and leaned against the post of the gallery to read it. The boy went off, whistling. The paper, inside, had been torn from one of Kitty's school tablets and thrust into a used envelope. Pinned to the note was a check for a thousand dollars, signed by Michael. I read what Mark had written. "I asked Michael for this loan and hope it'll help. Use it and I'll pay it back as soon as am able. It isn't any use for us to try to get along any more. Not only last night, but everything. I guess you realize it too. We just can't make it. I'm going away and I'm not coming back. You and Kit can have everything of mine. I don't know what it'll be, or where I'll be, but I'll let Sam know and he can forward whatever papers I'll have to sign. Take care of Kit." That was all. I took the piece of paper and went in my room and locked the door. There by the bed was the table—the twin of the one at Rosemont. I had taken the money and put it in there. Now I whirled the top around, and took the money and looked at it; then I counted it. I had taken seven thousand dollars. I put

Michael's check with it. I whirled the top back into place again. It was right and fitting that the table, like the one at Rosemont, should keep the secret of the money as the one at Rosemont had done before. It was strange how the table would have kept its secret from everyone but me. I did not put Mark's note away, or read it again. I remembered every word he had written. I tore the paper into small pieces and put it in the big ash tray beside the bed. It had been the ash tray Mark always used. That was his side of the bed. I lit a match and burned the scraps, and the flame not only crumpled the paper and ate it up, it was eating me up too with a reaching fire. I felt myself withering as it crept along my nerves and ate into my heart and soul. The paper turned into wavering ash, and there I stood; there I had to stand and put up with it. If only I had killed him when I had the chance!

I unlocked the door and left the room. It looked just as it always did, shabby, but orderly and used. There was the crack on the ceiling and my things and Mark's on the bureau. The sun came in in the usual spot. It held its secrets. No one would know how Mark and I had lived here and what had happened between us. No one would know the money they were searching for was in this table by my bed. No one would know the words Mark had written to me.

The house was quiet. The whole of Wishmore, house and cabins, fields and swamps and river, was soaked in haze and silence. Kitty was at school. Uncle Jeff had drifted off. Mark had gone. The house was suddenly drained of living. I went to the phone and called Arland. When she answered me, I asked her to come down right away. She said she would. After I stopped talking to her, I sat and waited until I heard her car, then her footsteps.

"Jane, I'd have come sooner, but I thought you were busy with Bob Hammon, or maybe trying to rest."

"What have you heard?" I was no longer interested in Miss Kate, but I wanted to know what people were saying. She had heard all sorts of rumors. Somebody told her I had seen the murderer; someone else told her I'd found Miss Kate's body. Maybe someone else had even insinuated I had had a hand in an elaborate plot to do way with Miss Kate. If anyone had told her that, Arland would never say so to me. I told her what had really happened—at least the part I knew.

"It was brave of you to go up there."

"I pretty well had to. I couldn't hear the shots and the screams and not try to do something." I knew I had to make myself out to be a noble being, while in my heart I was twinging with a sense of mortal guilt. There was the roll of money lying in the secret hiding place in the table. On the top of the table was a brass candlestick and a heavy ash tray and an old hymnal.

"Still, it must have taken a lot of courage to go up there."

"You would have, Arland."

"I suppose so. I hope so. Poor Miss Kate. She'd never done anything to deserve having this happen to her." Arland was the only one of us who took the time to really feel for Miss Kate. The rest of us were too absorbed in our own thoughts and our own affairs to think much about the victim.

"Arland, say I was at your house all evening." I watched her to see her reaction, and as I looked at her closely, she, too, seemed different from her usual self, as though all the turmoil of last night had in some way gathered her into its moving tangle and was twisting her up in its coils. Her eyes had a deep, far-off burning; her cheeks were flushed with sudden color, like the stain of some wild bright poisonous berry. Her quiet, veiled charm had flared into a tensed, hectic beauty. Her lips parted with her quickened breathing. "My house?" She looked away from me to light a cigarette, and I saw her hand shaking. She answered me in her usual voice, though. "All right. Just tell me exactly what you want me to say, so we can both have the same story."

"I didn't kill her."

"Jane, what in the world makes you say that—to me?"

"I don't suppose you think I did——"

"Don't talk like that!"

"Don't you know some people are going to think so? And say so? I passed there; I went up there; and, since there's no will, they'll see I stood to gain by her death."

"Nonsense, Jane, you're just wrought up."

"I am, but all the same, don't you think it's funny my wanting you to say I was with you?"

"You have a reason, but you don't have to tell me what it is. You don't have to tell me anything you don't want to. I was at home from half past eight on, so it's all right. What time was it when you heard her?"

"I don't know. Midnight, maybe. Or later, or sooner. I've lost track of time. I told Bob I was on my way home from your house. I did go right through town, so it sounds all right. The truth is, Mark and I had a regular knockdown and drag out——"

Arland watched me. There were dark circles under her eyes, making their brilliance haggard, and smoke drifted over her face in a pale weaving feather, then thinned and stretched into the room.

"You don't seem a bit surprised."

"I'm beyond surprises." There was something sad in her voice, an echo of my own misery, but my own held me, so I was unaware and uninterested in anything anybody else might be feeling.

"I suppose you saw we were headed for it. Anyway, we had a fight and he went off, and I was so upset I got in my car and just rode and rode for hours." My fury against him woke again and soaked up the blankness that had stupefied me. I was all alive with it again, and everything was damnably sharp and clear. I understood then how people go out and drink themselves and drug themselves un- conscious in search of escape. Drugs, drink, death itself—anything to get away from their own selves. I couldn't go and hurl myself in the river. There was Kitty. The other remedies weren't strong enough. You'd wake up and be with yourself again, chained to it. The only thing was to fight your way through. Where was the end, though? This lurching, sideways wheeling my heart was doing couldn't go on. Maybe it would until my heart finally stopped.

I wanted to fling myself on Arland for comfort, and tell her every- thing: how I knew Mark had been with Ludie, and all we'd said to each other when I accused him. But she would blame me, for my lack of dignity, and my violence. She didn't make scenes. Besides, pride burned me up. I couldn't tell her. One thing I would keep to myself forever, how Ludie Daniels had beaten me in the long contest— winner at last.

"Mark's left me."

Arland offered me not a word. Her lips quivered, her eyes, so large and dark, burned with their own secret flame. She was lost in some feeling of her own, not willing or not able to give me anything I needed.

"He's not coming back, Arland."

She didn't say, as I had thought she would, "He'll come back." I wouldn't have believed her, but I wanted her to say it even though I knew better. She accepted it, and her acceptance gave it a reality I had not completely felt before. Now there was no hope.

184

"You seem to have expected it, Arland. I suppose from what I've told you and what you've seen it was plain enough to you we were headed for the rocks. Now it's a slam-bang smash. You don't even seem sorry."

"You know I'm sorry for you, Jane." She spoke almost in a whisper. She didn't say anything else. She drew a long, shuddering breath, then she got up and went away. I watched her go. The sunlight touched her loosened hair and waked it to gold, and intensified the fiery flush of color in her face. The sun wrapped all around her as she moved away; then she got in the car, and its shadow took her, and I couldn't see her plainly any more. Then she, too, was gone away from me.

No one who has not lived through it can imagine the excitement over Miss Kate's murder. Bob Hammon questioned Miss Faust and Mr. Durly. The police had found a lantern in their woods, and thought that somebody must have been watching the gate while somebody else went up to the house and killed Miss Kate. Whoever had watched had seen my headlights coming around the curve and had run toward the Durly place, dropping the light in the woods.

Gertrude found out Mark had left. She came in once at dinnertime and saw his vacant place. "Where's he really gone?" she wanted to know.

"Mark and I have separated. I guess you might as well know." They might as well all know now, while they were absorbed in Miss Kate's murder. Let the greater excitement swallow the less. "He never was domestic. But isn't it just like him to leave now when he's got something to stay for? Instead of Mr. Charlie's getting the property, the Lennerds will! I hope I get a teeny-weeny slice of something. Oh, I mustn't talk like that. I sound like a buzzard. But of course none of us really knew her. It was terrible, but it doesn't automatically make us love her."

There was no use to try to avoid the carloads of reporters who found their way down to Wishmore. At any other time I would have enjoyed the newspaper stories and the pictures of myself flung all over the country. I had always wanted to be in the limelight. Now I didn't like it. My own bitterness of heart kept me from being interested in anything. Besides, there was something a little sinister in all the notoriety. I could imagine people all over the country saying to themselves, "She's certainly mixed up in it somewhere."

All the family skeletons clanged through the papers for months.

There were pictures and pictures of Rosemont, from all angles: the front view, the side view, and of course the ruined summerhouse. It was a graceful, lightly built thing, made for a flirtation on a summer evening. Its collapsed arches, choked and bound with vines, the thought of Miss Kate's blood-soaked body found there, gave a bitter contrast to what had been and what now was. It epitomized all the decay and ruin and tragedy heaped up in these old Southern houses.

"Murder Stalks Palatial Ante-Bellum Home."

There were pictures of Mr. Charlie, and his house, and his out-house, and his horse. "Southern Romance Defies Time."

There were pictures of the Durly house, too, the tottering columns, the goats, and the pond. All its secrets were torn open and exposed.

I looked a long time at the pictures of Miss Kate, taken when she was young and beautiful, dressed in the satin and jewels and feathers for her court presentation. Her big dark eyes smiled at me. What happened to you? I asked her. What had turned her in on herself? She had come back to Rosemont; maybe the very air of that lonely place had corroded her. These old places seemed to have that effect on the people who lived in them year after year. It frightened me; it had always frightened me, and it made me resolve to fight the weight of past things and work my way into the future.

The mystery deepened. There was no evidence against Mr. Durly and Miss Faust, so Bob had to let them go back to their goats and their woods and their house. They had had a bitter fight with Miss Kate, their goats had trespassed on her property, and their lantern had been found, matching one in their house. It was too slight.

I became uneasy. It might not be too hard to build up some sort of evidence against me. I caught the atmosphere from Aunt Em's be-moanings. "How I wish you'd never heard her; it did no good for her, and it's terrible for you—mixed up in this! I wish they'd find who really did it."

Bob Hammon and his deputies and his bloodhounds were harried by the newspapers and the taxpayers. I was glad when he at last unearthed what everybody seemed to think was a likely suspect. A colored man, a stranger, had been seen lurking around Rosemont early on the evening of the murder. He had come from Chicago, driven back here by the depression, and he had a criminal record.

It was proved he had been staying in one of the tumble-down shacks on the edge of the ravine where the town frayed out to the river road. It would have been easy for him to have crossed the ravines and sneak up to Rosemont that night. It would have been easy, but did he? He had become frightened and left town before the police found out about him, but the dogs had lolled their tongues and gone baying straight across the ravine to the dump where this Dave Lammy had been living with a poor half-witted creature named Dumpy Bailey. They arrested her when they found the man's clothes in her house and his gun hidden under her mattress. She was too stupid to have gotten rid of it, or maybe she didn't know anything about it, as she claimed. Several bullets had been fired, and they matched the bullets found in Miss Kate's body.

Bob, and his deputies, some panting volunteers, and the dogs crammed themselves into cars and tore through the flats of Louisiana and on up into Arkansas, looking for Dave Lammy. The papers carried streaming headlines about the progress of the chase.

They caught up with him in a small town in Arkansas, but he resisted arrest, as the phrase goes, and the local police fired and killed him. With his death the truth, the whole truth, and nothing but the truth, vanished in a perpetual fog.

Now nobody would ever really know whether Dave Lammy had shot her himself or had had accomplices, or whether he had been the accomplice of someone else, or had been hired to kill Miss Kate.

Some people said it was mighty damned convenient for Somebody to have damning evidence out of the way. They didn't believe he had gone up there and killed Miss Kate unless Somebody had put him up to it. They could never settle in their minds who the Somebody was, or quite bring themselves to connect this shadowy, murderous someone with the people walking around in their midst. Others thought it was all completely logical. Dave Lammy had known Miss Kate kept money in the house; he'd gone up there to steal it; she had screamed and fought; and, in a panic, he had pumped bullets into her and dragged her out. To this day, I don't really know what did happen at Rosemont. I've thought and thought and suspected everyone in turn, then decided it must be Dave Lammy who killed her. All simple. Then again, I'd start believing in some dark skillful plot.

There was really no one to bring to trial but poor Dumpy. The courthouse grounds swarmed. Only the bloodhounds, resting after their endeavors, were curled up asleep under the shade of the magnolias. Everyone else milled and pushed and craned their necks, and on the assembled faces was painted such hungry curiosity, such avidity for sensation, I was afraid. I was a witness, and there was the crowd, waiting for some carcass to be thrown to it to appease its appetite.

Everybody I knew was there, as well as masses of people from other towns and from the country, drawn here to drink in every detail of the melodrama of Miss Kate Lennerd's life and death. There was every sort of sensation provided. The courtroom was so packed I thought people would begin to crawl up the walls like flies. There was a reek of spittoons and stale cigar smoke and the unwashed among the horde. Outside, it was a mild fall day, the leaves falling slowly, crumpled and brown, taking on a sheen from the sun.

I saw Alec for the first time since he had come back for the trial and the settlement of his great-aunt's estate. I had been too taken up with my own feelings and my own problems to think about him. He was looking at me, and he smiled. I wanted to put on a good performance on the witness stand for his benefit. Then I forgot him because I saw Ludie Daniels, standing far back in the room. A vivid green outfit showed off her too well-known curves, and all the men around her were covertly aware of her. I was thinking how happy I would be if somebody had pumped her body full of bullets and left her huddled up, blotted out in a rank mass of vines. Then nobody would want her any more. Then, too, I would probably be on trial for my life. Mark was gone from me, but now he was gone from her too.

I saw Arland, too, and, as on the day after the murder, she was unlike herself. She had grown thinner, and she had on a deep red dress. I never remembered her wearing red before, and it startled me. I wondered why she never had; the color was somehow wonderful on her, but it changed her, giving her beauty an intensity and ardor.

I took my place beside her, and when I went to take the witness stand she pressed my fingers, but I didn't need her help now. My basic indifference to anything and everything but Mark's desertion gave me courage to face them all. Maybe some of these people did think I had killed Miss Kate. The knowledge of the money I had stolen when she was lying there dead, with her blood seeping out of her veins and soaking into the ground, made me feel guilty, but I had been living with my guilt, and I no longer cared. I faced down the judge and the lawyers and the crowd. I faced down myself. I had done what I had done, and it was too late to be sorry. I knew very well if I had it all to do over again, I would have whirled the top of the table and taken the wad of bills.

My testimony was clear, and no questions rattled me. I'd been to see my cousin, Mrs. Laidlaw, and I was going home. No, I had no idea what time it was. I heard shots and screams. I knew they came from Rosemont. I knew something awful had happened. I was terrified, but I went and got Andy Sack and we went to the house, and so on. Afterward, Andy corroborated every word I said. They must have known I couldn't have killed her. The screams had hardly stopped before I was knocking at Andy's door. Unless they thought I was lying and Andy was backing me up. They could look at me and tell I didn't have the physical strength to drag her into the bushes. Yet of course Andy could have done that. To this good day when people, gathering in little groups, start reminiscing, telling all the old tales, I wonder what they say about me when they go over the story of Miss Kate's murder.

"When did you last see Miss Kate alive?" one of the lawyers asked me. I said I didn't remember. I'd never spoken a word to her in my life. They also asked if I had an idea of how she intended to leave her property, and I said I didn't know. We had all thought she intended to leave it to Mr. Charlie. I'd never really expected to get my hands on anything of the Lennerds' until after his death. His sister, Miss Constance, was the soul of honor. She would never have kept Lennerd money. We had hoped to get it back from her. Now I was an heir, long before I had any right to expect it. Yet I couldn't feel any joy. I told myself I must be glad, must enjoy it, because now it was all I had to think about.

They were talking now about the cash Miss Kate had drawn from the bank. I folded my hands, in their new gloves, in the lap of my new suit, and I lowered my eyes in the shadow of my new hat. Then I raised my eyes and looked calmly into the faces of the crowd. How well did I know about the money! Behind the locked doors I had counted the notes. Now I realized I was quite safe. Mr. Wallace from the bank told how Miss Kate had drawn out her account, gradually, in small sums, ever since 1930. She had kept only enough to cash a few checks for the plantations.

She had drawn out a good deal more than the seven thousand I had found, but she had paid out some of it. There was testimony to

189

the effect that no large sum had been found in the house. No large sum had been found on Dave Lammy either. He might have hidden it or disposed of it in some way. It was part of the mystery. I could have cleared up that angle, and maybe, somewhere, there is somebody who could have cleared up the rest. If so, they are as wary, and as lucky, as I was about my own share in the whole grisly set of circumstances.

They kept questioning poor Dumpy Bailey about the money, but she was completely incoherent. She was a light woman, with most of her teeth missing, and light grayish eyes, unable to focus on anything.

It was never clear who she had helped, and why, yet they sent her up for a long stretch in the pentitentiary. She was the victim of the whole snarl; yet I don't think she was entirely innocent, except that she was half-witted and hardly responsible. I felt sorry for her, but there was no way I could help her. Maybe if I had told about taking the money it would have helped her a little, but not much. After all, they had to give up asking her about it, and she must have been at Rosemont that night. She admitted she'd stood by the gate watching the road, holding the lantern. "An' der gate swole up and st—retch out. Den hit done swunk up no bigger'n my fis', den hit done SWOLE up agin." Bob Hammon never primed that statement. You could see how the gate must have looked to her, changing shape to her clouded brain and clouded eyes as the lantern swung back and forth in a shaking hand.

Then it was over, and we were all struggling out of the courtroom. Photographers flashed their lights, and reporters came up with note-books: reporters tall and short, fat and thin, some beaming, some with cynical quirks to their mouths, some from little town papers of one or two sheets, some from thick city papers.

Gertrude finished what she was saying to one of them and worked her way to me, her hat pushed back, and her eyes glazed with ex-citement. "How does it feel to be famous, Jane? And I guess you'll be rich too." She got along swimmingly with the press. They gave her drinks, and she told them everything she knew about everybody.

I saw Miss Jessie Bryerson sailing toward me, but suddenly Alec was beside me, and we ducked out of her way before she could reach us. "You were fine, Jane," he said. "But then I knew you would be. Nothing fazes you, my magnolia blossom. Didn't everybody turn out, though? Look at Mr. Durly. He's had his whiskers shaved for the first time since Arland's wedding. He looks positively spry.

And Miss Faust has got on sure enough clothes. She always looks as though she just wrapped dried corn shucks around herself, or anything she found handy in the field after the crops were in. Even your cousin Charlie is up and at 'em. When we were all braced for him to collapse from the shock."

Mr. Charlie spoke to us with his usual aptness and dignity, and went on.

"I'll be damned!" Alec looked after him. "He's riding off in a car. Never saw him in a car before in all my days. Where's his horse?"

I told Alec he was being entirely too flippant for the occasion. "Maybe so. But I don't see why I should pretend much grief. Are you going to? She was too shut away and mysterious ever to seem real to me. She'd grown into a legend while she was still technically alive. Though it was horrible enough. But so queer it goes off into a sort of fantasy. Not quite real either."

Miss Jessie caught up with us, and I couldn't evade her, though I knew exactly how the wedding guests felt when the Ancient Mariner buttonholed them.

"Dear Jane," she purred, "you were quite marvelous. It must have taken unusual courage to go up there. Anybody who has that much daring could have—— And you told your story so well—to the last detail. They could not entangle you once—not once."

When we escaped again Alec laughed. "How gently but how completely she's implanted the idea that you had motive, opportunity, cunning, and the necessary bravado!"

Alec saw me to Arland's car. She hadn't come yet. "Where's Mark?"

"He's picked up his foot and gone."

"Have you any idea where?"

"No, the ends of the earth, for all he's told me."

"You look very stylish, Jane. But you don't look well. Is he coming back?"

"I don't think so."

"Perk up. I'm back. I'm going to settle down here and not budge. When I leave town I always miss something, so I'm just going to stay. How are you taking his going? You look rather as though you'd had some wakeful nights."

"It's not pleasant to have your husband walk out on you."

"They do it every day. I wouldn't let it give me an inferiority complex. You'll get over it. And I'm here to console you, ready to be a settled citizen. Seriously, Jane, you'll let me try my hand at consoling you, won't you?"

"The gods arrive?"

"I wouldn't put it quite so strongly. But it'll be pleasant having your company while we wrangle over our gains."

"Don't let's give it all to the lawyers. Sam's firm is hanging around drooling."

"Aren't we all? Except Mark. But if you'll look kindly on me, you'll find me quite biddable. Be seeing you, my dove."

Sam Barrett came down to see me. He settled himself in Mark's chair, though Mark cared no more for one chair than he did for another. Mark's dog came and sniffed him, and went off . . . he wasn't the one the dog missed. Sam had heard from Mark, and I asked to see the letter. It was from a town out West, and from the little he said of himself Mark was doing stunt flying here and there around the country, going from place to place.

Mark was giving everything he had—Wishmore and whatever he might inherit from his aunt Kate—to me, with the provision I'd leave everything I had from him to Kitty after my death.

"He needn't have thought that up, Sam. Kitty's my child!"

"You're young. He might have thought you'd marry again and have more children."

Sam couldn't know how queer it seemed to me—the idea I would have children who were not also the children of Mark. I didn't want any other man's child. Only his.

Mark also asked me to look after Mr. Jeff.

"He takes himself off, and leaves me holding the bag!"

Sam grinned. "Left something in the bag besides Mr. Jeff though! I kinda envy him, Jane—never giving a tinker's damn about any of the Lennerd stuff. If I was in his shoes, my mouth would be watering for it."

"He's dumped Mr. Jeff on my lap, and I suppose I'll have to take care of him. I can't just drop him. I don't shirk my responsibilities."

"Why don't you get a divorce, Jane? It's pretty clear he's not coming back. I could fix it all up for you——"

"No, no indeed!" Free Mark, so he could marry any little tramp he picked up? I certainly would not!

When I was lying awake at night, hour after hour, I tried to turn my mind to what I would do with my share of the Lennerd inheritance. I used to think about money and call up pictures of brilliant gardens in bloom and big parties and myself looking beautiful in furs and velvets. I used to think of the Lennerd plantations, of neat cabins in orderly rows, and fine, fat corn, and the cotton gin humming. Now the thought of it all took on no life. Money was dead, limp greenish stuff; land was blank, dull, profitless.

The heirs gathered for the settlement of the estate. We all faced one another, faintly tense before we began to talk, but after the first silence was broken we were at ease together.

"I don't have any interest in Rosemont," Michael said, when urged to tell what he wanted. "But it would be mighty convenient to have the plantation next to my own land."

We all agreed it would be, and decided to give it to him. There were plantations in Louisiana. Alec got two of them. He sighed, and I asked him if he didn't think it was fair. "Perfectly fair, but it means a hell of a lot of work to ride over 'em. I can see the hours and hours I'll spend knee-deep in gumbo mud, and I know I'll have to get over there and nurse levees in high-water time."

There was another place in Louisiana, called Beulah Land. It was below Dead Man's Bend—a swampy, soggy, boggy place, but my mind played with its possibilities as I remembered the wonderful growth of timber down there. Miss Kate had always planted part of it. The cotton was superb if there was a dry year; in a wet year there was none. It was no place for people to live. Why not move the tenants, and let it all grow up in timber?

"The inheritance taxes are going to kill us." Michael wrinkled his face over the papers. "We have to pay them right off too." We thought over that awhile, then went back to dividing up the property. I wanted Dewberry Landing, and said so. "And the house." The others all looked at me as if they were seeing someone they couldn't quite understand, someone different from themselves. At the moment I didn't want Rosemont. Miss Kate's study rose before me with a staggering impact of detail. But I remembered how I had wanted it, and there was Kitty. Aunt Em was always urging me to bring her up to be a True Southern Gentlewoman—a state which seemed to me to be without many advantages. Kitty would hardly remember anything of what had happened at Rosemont, and when she grew up it would be the right setting for her if she had money. She might very well be glad to live in it. The story of Miss Kate would have faded out by then, and the house would have another aura. I would not let myself be afraid of Miss Kate.

Michael's plain, good face flushed. "You can sure have it, for all of me."

"Me too." Gertrude was with us. She'd had, and spent, her share of the Lennerd possessions, but Michael and Alex thought that as their stepmother she was due for a little something. Her expectations had led her to celebrate by taking a few drinks of whisky. She was not sober, but she was in an agreeable mood. "I don't know why anyone wants it—so somber and shadowy. Ugh! Think what you'll hear at night!" She eased her fat feet out of her shoes. "However, you're welcome to it as far as I'm concerned. I hope you'll let me take tourists through it. Miss Kate never would, and now of course they are simply wild to go there. I suppose since you're such a good housekeeper you'll wipe up the bloodstains. Too bad; it makes it like Darnley at Holyrood. But do remember just where they were."

Alec said he didn't think the bloodstains would make it very livable. Joyce was rearranging her hairdo. She was wearing it in a new way. Newspaper references to her beauty had made her oblivious to everything else. She slipped a light shining curl over her finger. "I wouldn't be caught dead in it."

The rest of us cringed a little, but she remained unaware of the too extreme aptness of her remark. "You hit the nail on the head," Alec murmured. "That's what we all feel, except Jane. And she's a toughy."

So Rosemont was mine. Fortunately for me, the estate was settled before these old houses and their contents became so desirable and so sought after, or Joyce, awaking at last, might have given me trouble. Since then she has often bewailed her lack of foresight. At the time, though, she saw only a melancholy house, much too big, shadowed with moss-draped trees, and the inside stuffed with masses of uncomfortable furniture, and no doubt ridden by a ghost more potent than the bland and amiable spirit of old Mr. Horace.

"Do you mind, Alec?"

"You crave it, Jane; you take it. I want to see what you're going to do with it."

Rosemont was mine and Dewberry Landing was mine and Beulah Land was mine, and Wishmore was mine—except for the mortgage.

Everything was peacefully settled, and we all parted with one another on good terms.

"It's an achievement," Alec said. "It's the first time the Lennerd property has ever changed hands without prolonged lawsuits."

"Sam will have a fit, poor thing. He thinks we're all cooped up here wrangling and that he will be able to extract some very toothsome plums out of the broil."

"It's no time to waste anything on lawyers," Michael pointed out. "Just what are we supposed to run all this on? Air? There's plenty of land, but we'll have to sell some timber to pay taxes, and a lot of the cabins need repairs. There's a big crop this year, but who wants to pay anything for cotton? I guess none of you-all have much cash to spare——"

I knew he didn't. He was a good soul not to ask outright for the money Mark had borrowed from him. I had cashed the check, and wouldn't it look strange if I offered to pay it back at this moment? I decided not to say anything. I needed it.

"But Miss Kate had lots of stocks and bonds and things. There must be plenty," I said.

The two men exchanged looks. "Had is right," Alec said. "Take a good look. Here they are—everything out of her bank box. G. and I. Railroad. First mortgages, four per cent, due 1934. These have gone ——"

"Gone!" I felt perfectly blank. I knew nothing about stocks and bonds. I should have realized how they had depreciated along with everything else, but the idea of the Lennerd opulence was so firmly planted in my mind I couldn't believe him.

Gertrude gulped, "How do you mean, gone?" She saw the picture and name on the stack of bonds. "Oh, that's what I have my stock in —five shares!"

"Had, my dear, had. The road is in receivership. Folded. Defunct. It's not going to pay."

"You mean I won't get my money back?"

"If the capitalist system should creak on to the year 2000, you might get five cents on the dollar, but don't expect your assets in this particular railroad to tide you over the present crisis, sugar."

"My God!" she moaned. "Five shares! Everybody said invest, invest. I did, and look what happened! How many pints of whisky would that buy? Oh, why didn't I drink it all up when I had the chance!"

"I know what you are suffering," Alec told her. "I took a plunge in this myself, and felt very prudent and conservative and saving. What you spent in the boom you enjoyed, and what you saved you haven't got. You know, Miss Kate was by no means as smart as we all thought. We all had the idea she was sitting up at Rosemont using her seclusion to preserve the 'Lennerd fortune.' I don't know why we thought she was wiser than anybody else in the country. She wasn't. Her stocks and bonds are just as deflated as everybody's. She turned out to be just like all the rest of us. Just land poor."

"You mean there's no money?" I still couldn't quite grasp all Alec was saying.

"There's no ready cash. All unready."

Joyce didn't understand any of it, and Gertrude, fortified by the glow her drinks had given her, could let a gentle haze blur her minor losses. Michael took the blow stolidly. His land was at least unmortgaged, and he was a good farmer. Alec probably still had enough to live on. He had been working on a newspaper in New York these past few years, but he had told me he didn't see much future in it; he was tired of it, and had decided to come back home and see what he could do with plantations. I had told him it was the wrong time, but he'd answered it was the wrong time for every sort of enterprise, and he had to begin taking care of his land sometime.

"You take it calmly—all this worthless stuff we're saddled with," I said.

"I've known it ever since Michael and I went in the bank box. And there's nothing to do except hang onto it and hope it'll come back someday." I was shocked into a void. My hands and knees shook and my head felt light. Now, when I needed it most to bolster me within and without, and to cushion other blows, the Lennerd fortune had dissolved like a pile of sunset clouds. It was no use to sit and dream of it any more.

"What about her jewelry?" I asked.

"Here it is. It was in the bank too." He produced a series of small faded boxes and opened them one by one. The different-colored stones in gold settings rippled out, light in bright confusion. Alec took the pieces out: earrings, brooches, bracelets. "Here are the pearls." They were in a box by themselves. He held them up. It was a necklace, double strands, each pearl round and smooth, collecting all the glow in the room and blending it to its own muted, permeating gleam.

"Let me see it." I took it from Alec and let it slide through my fingers. It wound itself against my hand, and I hated to put it down, though its soft light was ghostly. She had worn these pearls when she was young and beautiful, admired and adored.

"Let's sell the jewelry," Michael suggested.

"We won't get near what it's worth now," I pointed out.

"We need money for the taxes."

"We could sell some timber. It's a pity to sell the jewelry. We could divide it, and then each one of us sell it if we wanted to."

Gertrude said she'd sell her share of it, and Joyce didn't at that time admire old-fashioned jewelry.

"Here's a ring." Alec brought out a wad of tissue paper and unwrapped it. The fire of diamonds shot out at us, and the deep Gulf Stream blue of the big sapphire in the middle. "This wasn't in the bank," Alec said. "It was on Aunt Kate's finger."

He put it down on the table and nobody picked it up.

I asked why did he suppose the murderer hadn't snatched it off her hand.

"Maybe he thought it would be too incriminating."

"He couldn't get it off if he'd tried." Michael's round, reddish face grayed with the memory of the dead hand, and the ring, probably bloodstained. "It's small—it had to be cut off her finger."

I reached over and picked it up. I felt squeamish about touching it, but I beat down the flutterings in my stomach. If I let myself act that way about Miss Kate's things, I'd never have any peace of mind. I handled it and saw where the gold had been cut.

"They ought to have let it alone," Alec muttered. "Let's sell it. Nobody'll want it."

I closed my hand over it. "I do."

The others didn't say anything for a minute, then Alec said, "All right, take it." Then he changed the subject. "We've got to talk about the taxes, since everything else is settled."

We did, and when we were through, I sighed, "Here I am, settled with that house, a most enormous white elephant, and a lot of plantations like a herd of brown elephants."

Alec laughed. "Let's see you ride the lot of 'em, Jane."

"If you've got too much on your shoulders, I'll try to take Dewberry Landing," Michael offered.

"What with?"

"I reckon I could scrape around and scare up a down payment." If Michael could talk about down payments, he didn't really need the thousand dollars Mark had borrowed from him. I needed it worse. Arland had come to me and offered to lend me money, but I'd told her I'd had plenty from Miss Kate. I'd go and tell her exactly how things were, and accept her offer. She could lend me a thousand too.

I thought of Dewberry Landing. It was good rich land in the creek bottom. The fields were level, and the cottonwoods sang like rippling water on the bank of the silent river. The creek might, and undoubtedly would, overflow; cotton might keep going down, and the crops sometimes fail—it was the nature of crops. But land was land. Look at those stocks and things—just pieces of paper. You couldn't watch the people up North who had charge of those companies, but you could put your feet on your own land, and watch it, and know what was happening to it; you could at least plant sweet potatoes in it, and go dig them up and eat them.

All those years ago young Josiah Lennerd had come down here to take possession of the tract of wild acres a grateful government had given him. He had been an officer in the Navy, and he had been one of the volunteers who had offered to sink the frigate *Philadelphia* in the pirate's harbor during the Tripolitan war. For that he had received a land grant. His picture was hanging in Rosemont still, and the Lennerds had hung onto his land. Through war, through reconstruction they'd clutched it. Through good times and bad. The Ellistons had once had land too—across the river, all the way to Arkansas, but they had lost it. Nothing was left of the Ellistons but an old house and a few females. Their name had been a power in this town, but soon it would be no more than a dying echo. They didn't know how to hold onto their land, and they had too few and too female children. The Lennerds were more ruthless and more fertile. Spiritually, I welded myself to them. I knew how they felt, and I'd hang on too. I'd make any sacrifice, go barefoot, live on cornbread, before I'd let an inch of it get away from me. Hold on, weld it together, build it up. Maybe some day Kitty and Stephen would marry, and their property would be joined together.

"No, I'll keep it," I told Michael. "I'll keep what's mine."

Alec gave me a long look. "I thought you'd say that," he murmured.

I was also keeping what was not mine. Seven thousand dollars. What could I do at this stage of the game but keep it? It was not fair to the others, but when I'd taken it I didn't know it was the only money. I'd thought there was plenty. Now I did know, but it was impossible to give it back. I couldn't confess I had taken it. When I had lunged for it I had been driven by my own burning need. I hadn't quite realized I was depriving the others. I still had a burning need, and it was too late to give it back. Too late to feel remorse. I smothered my pangs of conscience and, what was so awful, they were so damn easy to smother.

❧ Chapter Fourteen

One afternoon I went up by myself to look at Rosemont. I had the keys, but I had put off going there. This time I took my nerves in hand, and climbed straight up the hill. If you took the path and didn't mind steepness, it wasn't a long walk at all.

As I climbed, the soil grew lighter and drier. The mockingbirds flew from the flat land up the hill, back and forth, but the red-winged blackbirds never left the swamp. The pines wouldn't grow at Wishmore, but they steepled the hill and its crest. My feet slipped on the pine needles; their scent in the sun brought back the night years ago when Mark and I had been together. He had given me those long intense kisses, and I had watched the star shining in the water with all its sparkling, and the pond had taken on an immense life beyond itself. The pond was still there, cupped in the hollow, small and shallow now. A pair of white geese careened on it. There had been ducks too—decoys. But the other night I'd heard the wild ducks flying over. The decoys had heard the far-off crying and had gone to join the band. Imperfectly tamed, like Mark, the voices and instincts of the wild had been too much for them.

I looked down at Wishmore, where Mark and I had lived and made love and quarreled and had a child together. For the time being the swamp had paused in the ferocity of its growth, and in the distance the trees were delicately penciled, pale and restrained in their outline.

Smoke was rising from cabin chimneys, fanning out against the pale sky. The river drew a long silvered curve, and a velvet-textured shadow hung over Wishmore Point, falsifying reality.

There was no truth to the landscape's dreamy peace. No truth to the unsubstantial strokes of the willows, lightly suspended between earth and sky. All those trees had deep-seeking roots, foraging into the heavy soil, matted all around with undergrowth, thickening into tangles, bursting with spiked thorns. The river was not shining, but mud-laden—snarled with whirlpools, greedy and treacherous; and the cabins, so cozy and secure-looking, were hot in summer and cold in winter. The hands, living within these rickety walls, had their hates and fights and loves and illnesses, the eternal struggle with the crops, present poverty, vague hopes of next year—and fears of it too, since the future might be worse than the present.

As I looked, a sunny mist held it all, and all of it seemed to melt away, recede, telling me my life there was finished. I turned my back to it and went around to Rosemont's gate, opened it and went in. I had imagined coming here with Mark, not alone. We would walk here together, through the avenue of oaks. Beneath the shifts of light and shade the statues would lose their frozen attitudes until they were no longer lost images in an alien world, but changed to gods and goddesses again, breathing old harmonies, offering all their gifts to us. But I was alone, and they were dead, and hostile in their deadness, their blank eyes empty. The shadowed road turned, and the house was in front of me. There it stood, overlooking the river, dominating the ravines around it. Its treasures of furniture and silver and china, its box-hedged gardens—all of it cut out of the untamed landscape and enclosed against it, a dream set in the wilderness, relic of an ideal. I didn't want a relic; I wanted a setting for living and loving. It was only the setting for death. Death of its own time, death by violence. Death had stricken its sort of life, and the life within it.

I unlocked the front door, and its chill stole over me. I went from room to room. Spider webs wound over the flutings of the chandeliers, and dust filmed the mirrors. I opened the top of a table traced with mother-of-pearl fishermen catching mother-of-pearl fish. Inside was a set of chessmen—ivory, intricately carved. With my footsteps sounding after me as though an invisible self kept following me, I went through the house to Miss Kate's study and opened the side door, letting the sunlight in with me. Dust motes set up their dancing. It was all in order now, the desk drawer closed and no sign of what had happened here except the broken chair propped against the wall. I thought of the money I'd stolen. Dulled, lifeless bills, yet with a suggestion of having had a part in lots of different lives. Some of the notes were crisp still, some frayed and browned. Some smelled of tobacco—reluctantly pulled out of dingy pockets. One twenty-dollar bill still held traces of some cloying perfume. Who had paid them out, and what had been exchanged for them before they found their way to the table drawer, then to my hand? All of them were soaked with the sound of Miss Kate's hopeless screams. I wouldn't let myself think about it. Miss Kate was gone, and I was here. I went on through the house, upstairs and down.

What luscious harvests had built and furnished this house; what loaded wharves and freighted ships, taking cotton to all the world, had made the Lennerds able to stock these cabinets full of china, all painted with birds and flowers, with all that array of silver, twisted with tendrils and garlands, and enabled them to drink the best wine out of thin ruby-colored glasses from Venice and Bohemia. Now it was all smeared with time and disuse, and cotton had no empire.

Miss Kate had been an illusion. Because she was mysterious I had endowed her with qualities larger than life. She'd only been a tired old woman without direction or purpose, without friends or youth, making no effort, not even succeeding in holding onto wealth. The house had loomed in my eyes larger than anything real. I had dreamed of it as the background to the life I wanted to live in it. Now that I no longer had the life to put in it, it shrank.

I had pictured fires leaping in these empty grates, and the mirrors showing Mark's face and mine, close together. In one of these vast beds we would lie in each other's arms.

Since he had gone away from me the house showed itself empty and silent, challenging me to change it, fill it, give it again what a house needs to breathe. I left the shuttered rooms and went out again. Miss Kate herself began to whisper to me: "I had more than you and, little by little, I lost it all—beauty, charm, money. What have you to keep fate from doing you in, taking everything away, even life itself? You will come up here and shut yourself in, and who will love you? Your child will grow up and leave you, and someday you will be a strange, lonely old woman sitting in a moldy old house, and then death will come and it will all be over."

It was one of those times for me when life seems to come to a halt. I couldn't see any way ahead. "Midway through the journey of life I found myself in a dark wood, having lost the right way."

I sat down on the front steps and began to cry, my face in my hands. The tears kept slipping through my wet fingers. I hardly heard footsteps on the gravel road, but I looked up and there was Alec. My dusty hands had dirtied my face, my hair was tangled, and some of the grime of the house had transferred itself to my clothes.

"Why these tears going plop?" He sat down beside me and patted my shoulder.

"Mark's gone. And I don't know what to do or where to turn."

"I'm here, turn to me." He smiled. "You look about Kitty's age, too young to have so much weight on your shoulders." He took out a nice clean handkerchief and gave it to me.

"Nothing's the way I thought it would be, Alec, and I'm afraid——"

"Of what?"

"Of myself—and everything. Of coming up here to live and getting queer and strange—like her. Kitty'll grow up and go away, and I'll be alone, and what am I going to do with myself?"

"Let's grow older and more damn peculiar and more foul-tempered together. But I get what you mean. I must say this place is rather too moss-draped and slithery-shadowy at this hour."

I shivered. The chill of the house had bitten into my bones and seemed to have penetrated all the air. There seemed no way to escape from the state I was in. Then I realized I must start looking for some way out . . . like an animal in a trap. It bites off the caught paw and leaves it behind and gets out and keeps going. I had to keep going. The house had turned into a strange shape writhing in my grip. But the rest of the story goes like this: keep your hold on the monster, once a magic princess, through one dreadful shape after another. Keep your hold, and if you don't let go, you will find you have the princess again, yours forever. Maybe it's the same with life itself. Hang on. If I tried, I could certainly make the house into a princess again.

I sat up and dried my eyes and blew my nose on Alec's handkerchief. "I'm not going to let it get me. Mark's gone. If he won't come back, he can go and be damned, and break his damned neck. We don't have the money we thought we would, but I'm not going to let that beat me either! I'm not Miss Kate, I'm me. I'm not a fossil. This isn't the past, it's now. It's no use following a senseless pattern, and I'm going to have enough guts to break out and make a new one. My way. This is my house and my life and I'm going to wangle it the way I want!"

"Now you're the old absurd Jane—the way I like you. But just how are you going to manage all this?"

"I've thought and thought. I'm going to leave Wishmore and bring Kit and Mr. Jeff up here. Also seven maids with seven mops to clean this house and open all the windows and light all the fires and shine all the silver and haul out most of the china and polish the mirrors and invite everybody here and give big parties. I'm going to keep on planting Wishmore, of course, and the best part of Dewberry. But I'm going to put some cattle out there too. I'm going to move every last tenant out of that Louisiana bog and scatter them on the other places and let the timber grow over there."

"Just how are you going to tackle all this with things as they are? Sounds rather grandiose—like the Seven Cities of Cibola."

"I'll tackle some which way. Things aren't going to be like this always. Everybody says this part of the country has no future. Why not? I'll show 'em. The whole country hasn't gone to the dogs, and neither has this part of it—not forever. It's ridiculous."

"You sound just like Tim. You know the governor and his staff are coming here next month to dedicate the auditorium to him. He worked to get it, so I suppose they should. And poor old Mr. Laidlaw is bringing out some sort of biography about him. Seems like the wrong time. He was so optimistic. Optimism sounds extinct and dodoesque."

"I don't see why. And Tim was smart. You have to grant that."

"Yes, but he had a good stretch of years. He wouldn't know what to do now any more than any of the rest of us. He couldn't have been that smart."

"Maybe he was. Maybe he would know. There are people who know how to use any set of conditions. And I intend to be one of them, Alec. Just watch me. I was in the dumps, but I'm going to work out of things. Do you suppose there's any truth in the idea of there being oil around here?"

"They say there's a pot of gold at the end of the rainbow."

"But the oil companies have come here. They wouldn't bother to come and tie rags around if there wasn't some chance it was here."

"Well, they haven't looked over this stretch of country before. They're just wildcatting, you know. I wouldn't put much hope in the fact they're prowling around."

"But they did bring in that gas well over in Louisiana. That's a sign of something."

"They think now it's just a gas pocket. They drilled north of it and south of it and east of it, and got absolutely nothing but dry holes. You know that, Jane."

"But every time I get around any of the plantations there are new rags tied on bushes, and they've got men going around seismograph-ing."

"They do that lots of times. They'll poke around, then give up and go off, and that will be that. You'll never hear of them again. Rags or no rags."

"I remember that Christmas day, just before Tim was killed. He told me he thought there was oil around here."

"Part of his nature. He saw untold wealth everywhere."

"He'd studied geology; he knew a lot about the formation of the soil and things like that."

"He knew a lot about dishing up to people exactly what they wanted to hear. People still worship him. Jane, didn't you think it was strange he was killed at just that place, on just that road?"

"I did rather wonder why he was there. He must have been pretty tight."

"Why that road?" Alec persisted. "It was queer."

I twisted his handkerchief in my fingers. That road. Ruined forever for me now. First by Tim's death. Then by my idea of Mark going along it, on his way to Ludie. "I'm not counting on Tim's ideas. Or on anyone's but my own."

"When did you think out all that stuff, Jane?"

I'd had plenty of time in my sleepless hours, but I must not mope any more. I'd be practical and work hard on what I owned.

"Jane, since you seem to know what to do, and I sure don't, why not add my land to yours? Why not get a divorce? It's time the Lennerds were welding themselves together. Get a divorce and marry me. Such a comfortable feudal arrangement."

I started to say, "I don't love you." Then I didn't. I'd always been honest, until lately. Where did it get me? I told people what I really thought, and they mostly disliked me. I showed Mark how much I loved him, and gave him everything I was. He got tired of all of me. Maybe if he had never known me as I really was, he wouldn't have been tired. Now I was a deserted wife for all the world to see and scorn. A woman who wanted and loved and wasn't wanted or loved in return. Women weren't made to be honest. Bitterness had eaten at Arland, too, but it was something to have kept the world from knowing. She had shed an aura of successful, if tragic, romance around herself even if the nights were long and lonely.

I could play a part if I set myself to do it. It would be hard, but I would learn. I had already learned too much about myself. I must hide what I knew from other people. The night of Miss Kate's murder had changed me. Part of me was killed too. Burned out. I'd stolen. I could keep a secret now, and I intended to profit by it. Now I knew the trick of keeping other secrets if necessary. I'd be as sweet as pie to other people and use them if I could.

I could use Alec. The more property I could control, the more I could jiggle things around. I saw that. If I married him, everyone would see I wasn't so forlorn a creature after all. It would build up a façade for my crumbled pride. I would have a refuge.

Alec saw my hesitations and struggles. He was very astute, and my new self, just coming into being, didn't sit easily on me yet. He put his hand under my chin and tipped up my face. "What goes on?" He smiled. "You think you'll never get over Mark, but you think you might try me all the same, don't you?"

"I'll get over him. You can love more than once."

"Sure. But you don't know it yet. It doesn't sound like you. Where'd you read it? Only you don't read——"

"You aren't in love with me, are you?" I wanted him to say he was, but he didn't.

"I dunno. Maybe a little. The biological attraction of a lazy and—I flatter myself—complicated nature for a simple and ferocious jungle beastie."

I made up my mind the jungle beastie was going to take on a civilized glaze behind which it could crouch at ease. Beginning now.

"Anyway, I think it would be interesting to marry you, Jane. Sorta fun. Get away from the notion love and marriage are one and the same. Nonsensical notion. People always used to marry for land and castles. Then the lord of the castle went off to harry a neighbor or do a little light or heavy crusading, and a troubadour strolled over and strummed under the castle walls, and the lady, finding existence boring, let him in. And they cooked up love and went on strumming about it. I don't care about the plantations, sugar. You can run 'em any fool way, but I think we ought to get along pretty well. Come on, it's getting late. Let's hie hence from this elegant but extremely ghoulish spot."

We started off, and I looked back at the house. Blank, lightless windows and tall columns were all fading in the chill and bluish twilight, like something quavering and settling under fold after fold of deepening water.

"You can't live here all by yourself with Kit and Mr. Jeff. You aren't too imaginative, but you'd go batty as all get out. Anyway"—he steered me from a fallen root, and his hand was warm and comforting —"I don't make love so badly, and that's what you want, isn't it?"

I didn't answer, and he went on. "How did you get so sexy? You didn't get it from ideas on life and love currently afloat, because you don't follow trends of thought. It sure to God wasn't the way you were brought up. I guess the Anglo Saxon race when exposed to this climate and this setting just soaks up an exotic flavor."

He turned and kissed me there in the shadow, with the cold statues watching us. He knew how to kiss, but his mouth wasn't the mouth I wanted. I didn't draw away, though. I kissed him with all the skill, if not all the ardor, I knew. He seemed satisfied. Alec has always thought he understands me perfectly. He knew I was passionate, but he couldn't understand how all my passion was for one person. Maybe it's just as well. I wonder how other women are. I only know I am unlucky. Oh, well, they say all cats are gray at night. But not for me. Besides, I don't want a cat. I want a tiger.

Divorces are easy to get in Mississippi. Mark signed papers, sending them from some address in Central America. Michael had a letter from him, and told me Mark had gotten some sort of job down there flying for a rickety two-by-four airline. It didn't sound profitable, just dangerous.

I told Alec I'd marry him in the spring. Aunt Em and all the other aunts registered shock. There'd never been a divorce in the family. "There ought to have been, then. You can't tell me, with all the females in the family tree, some of 'em didn't have husband trouble."

Aunt Em said they preferred to Endure All in Dignified Silence. Certainly they'd never taken Another Mate.

"Even when left high and dry?" But I decided I wanted to range the family on my side, so I experimented with new tactics. I sighed, and told them how lonesome I was, and how much I needed someone to lean on, and by sighs and a few tears and innuendoes I made Mark out a brute, let Aunt Em feel she was perfectly right in objecting to him in the first place, and ended by reconciling them to the situation.

I didn't see much of the aunts—I was too busy. Alec and I drove down to the Louisiana place. The trees were wonderful, the hands in the last stages of poverty, eking out a miserable sort of life in dilapidated cabins.

"They're glad to get out of there," I told Michael when he and Alec and I were discussing things one evening at Arland's.

"It's a funny way to do a plantation," Michael said. "The cotton's fine when it makes, but it does get bogged out most every year."

"I don't need all these people if I'm not going to make a crop——"

"You can hardly turn them off, Jane. They won't have anywhere to go," Arland interrupted.

"I'm not. I'm just shifting 'em around and giving them much better places to live." I didn't believe in turning off tenants. Besides, when you needed them you couldn't find them. I didn't explain my second reason to Arland. Let her think I was kindhearted. "The government has to move the levee back; it's caving badly right there. They'll have to pay for the land they use. I'm arguing with them now, and I'm certainly going to put their feet to the fire."

The place, called Beulah Land, perhaps because of its extreme remoteness, since it was not Paradise by any stretch of the fancy, had no mortgage on it when I inherited it, but I clapped one on it. Alec and Michael thought I was reckless, but I'd lived with a mortgage a long time, and I knew the bank didn't want to foreclose just then. What cash I had I used warily—a little here, a little there, and made it go a long way. I bought a good strain of cattle for Dewberry Landing, and one of the hands I moved over there knew a good deal about how to raise them. I put some money on Rosemont, too, and made ready to move in. Gertrude's tourists were rather a nuisance, wandering about when I was working there, but when Gertrude said how eager they all were to see it, I had an idea. "Charge them twice as much as you do, and divide with me. You'll end by making more than you do now, because I'll fix up the house with the money I get, then twice as many people will want to come." I was being very pleasant to Gertrude these days; she had her uses.

"I doubt if people will pay all that——" But she was willing to try my way, and it worked.

Once, when she brought a gaping throng, I was so preoccupied and tired I wanted to turn them all away, but I told myself this was a business enterprise, so I tore off the apron I had on, threw aside the dust rag, hid the broom, and put on my best manners.

I was well repaid. Among the group was a lanky boy from Texas. He only stared and murmured "Gee." I went and talked to him, and asked him questions. He was jobless, just drifting around the country, but I found out he'd worked on a cattle ranch. I told him about Dewberry Landing and my plans. "There's an old house there," I said on the spur of the moment. "You want to go there and live and help me?" It turned out he would. He did, and Wiz Durman became one of my best investments.

There was a reporter there, too, that morning. Gertrude was telling him all about Miss Kate and her life and her death. He drank it in, and turned to me. "You're brave to come live here."

I thought out my answer before I spoke. "I feel I owe it to poor Aunt Kate. She loved this house . . . . I don't want it to go to rack and ruin. I want it to be a sort of monument to her."

Gertrude was so astounded she had to go to the car and get a little swig. "Did Miss Kate love it?" she said to me later. "She didn't act like it, and she surely didn't love you, or any of us. Why the song and dance? You wanted this house, you've got it."

"It was such a tragedy, Gertrude. I realize now we were all wrong; we should have done more for her. And now the only thing we can do is to bring this place to life, wipe out all the unpleasantness. I tell you that night affected me more than any of you realize——"

"It sure must have." But she was impressed. "I can see you've changed." When columns came out in the newspapers headed, "Niece Makes Old Home Shrine to Memory of Murdered Aunt," Gertrude didn't jeer at me all over town as much as I expected her to do. Alec said the article was corny, corny, corny, but a lot of people read it and came to town just for the purpose of going through Rosemont.

Having so many fish to fry kept me from seeing much of Arland that fall and winter. She said she wasn't well, and she didn't look it. She stayed home most of the time. She admitted to me she had lost a good deal of money herself, but it didn't seem to worry her. "I'll pay you back as soon as I can," I told her. I had gone to her and borrowed.

"Don't bother about that for a minute, Jane," she reassured me. "I know how much you need it. Keep it. You'll put it to good use. I believe in your schemes."

She was the only one who did. I went one evening to see Aunt Em, who had been complaining of my neglecting her. The old house looked shabby. The camellias on the front lawn were swathed in aged quilts to protect them from the cold. Aunt Em was upstairs, huddled in front of the fire, hobnobbing over weak tea with Cousin Olive and

Aunt Ada, and complaining of the weather. Like most Southerners, she considered a cold snap a personal affront.

The ladies' conversation could be easily guessed. It always went into reverse. Cousin Olive brought the late gossip, then they reverted to the old scandals. I must say they are still meaty. Aunt Em refuses to consider the present. It is always Too Unpleasant. Of course she never saw the past as it really was either. She never saw our ancestors as a lot of hard-riding, hard-drinking pioneers who were almost bound to get ahead in a land of endless opportunity. She sees a batch of flawless creatures, practically royal, living the life of Riley in a place that never was on land or sea. She had even traced the Ellistons clean back to the Plantagenets.

Cousin Olive said, "Well, Jane, how are you coming along?" and asked a good many questions. Aunt Em murmured she didn't see where I got so many Radical Notions. Any sort of change left them horror-struck, and by the time I had spent half an hour with Aunt Ada's pious hopes for my future happiness with Alec, and Cousin Olive's pourings of cold water, and Aunt Em's sighs, I felt as cheerful as though I had been closeted with Poe's raven.

I was in a particularly restless fit that day. I had been hurrying here and there, and was in the throes of moving out of Wishmore. Everyone there had been bemoaning their lot. Mr. Jeff didn't want to go live at Rosemont, and Hettie's relatives had pumped her full of stories of the "hants" awaiting her on top of the hill.

My dutiful visit to Aunt Em increased my tension, but I took good care not to be snappish. Alec had been very tactful with them, and the aunts had become fond of him but, as I left the room, I heard Cousin Olive say, "I never thought Jane would get two husbands!"

I went then to see Arland, as I wanted to ask her to come with Alec and myself when we went to be married. She was the only person we did want. As soon as I went through the gate, I felt somewhat soothed. And as I reached the door and saw the firelight shining out in the dusk, the look of secure and established peace seeped into me. This house was an unchanging oasis in the whirl of things; just going there made me less feverish.

Kitty came to the door to meet me and announced she was going to spend the night. She led me into the library, where Arland was. She had been reading to Kitty and Steve. There were bowls of fresh violets around the room, and honey jonquils in the tall vase Arland always used for them. A tea party was in progress, with jam-spread biscuits and a plate of Bedelia's thickly iced chocolate cake. The fire fluttered up the chimney in great waves of flame, and the lamp was lit—the one with the big intaglio globe. I had always loved it as a child. When the light was off it was a vague nothing, but when the light was on a whole scene showed up—a lighthouse sending out its rays, and a little island set in a gentle ripple of waves, and a pert-sailed ship dancing toward some happy sheltered port.

The glow of the fire touched Steve's red-brown head and Kitty's fair plaits, and woke a rich autumn gold in Arland's hair. It bathed all their faces in warm rose, and made glints on the gold-and-scarlet binding of the book Arland held.

"I like those names in that story," Stephen sighed. "Balsoura and Samarkand——"

"They were wonderful cities," Arland told him, "with golden minarets and porcelain walls, all glazed with beautiful designs, and streams running through the streets—clear green water full of gold and silver fish."

They had once been real, not just fairy-story cities, and Genghis Khan had besieged them one by one and laid them flat. I wondered why they hadn't all stood together and saved themselves.

While Arland talked to me, the children took the book and stretched out in front of the fire and looked at the bright pictures. They looked in the fire and the cities rose before them, with their gardens and mother-of-pearl palaces, lost so long ago in the burning sand.

I told Arland my plans for marrying Alec, and what I would wear. While I talked I, too, looked in the fire and thought of lost things. Arland begged me to stay to supper, but those three seemed so happy and complete without me. I needed them, but they didn't need me. Somehow I felt I spoiled the charm of the circle by breaking into it with my cares and my projects, so I didn't stay.

I went on back to Wishmore. The house was black and cold and empty. I lit the lamps and the fires, for the last time. I tried to eat, but I couldn't swallow the thick cold bread, and the icy lumps of butter stuck in the roof of my mouth. So I washed the dishes and put everything away, and started again with the back-breaking job of packing the books. A fat old volume fell, and as it fell, it dropped open. I glanced at the page before me. It was yellowed and spotted with age, and gnawed at by silver fish, and covered with fine print. Years ago someone had pressed a rose there. The dry veined petals still clung to the paper, spread out transparent, and the words showed through, as if they had burned themselves into the rose, shriveling up its life. I read,

> Alas! Our young affections run to waste
> Or water but the desert; whence arise
> But weeds of dark luxuriance, tares of haste . . .
> Flowers whose wild odors breathe but agonies . . .

⌐§ Chapter Fifteen

In that time, just after Mark left me, I went through a curious division of living. I moved and spoke and carried on each day's activities—busied myself with a hundred projects—and it all seemed to be carried on by someone different from the secret self struggling below the surface. While I was living under the outer layer of existence, I began to wonder about other people—if only a little bit of them stuck out like an iceberg, while the other three fourths was hidden.

You couldn't feel that about someone like Aunt Em. All of her was in plain sight—all neat and tidy. Not Joyce. With her you were always expecting some ray of thought to light up her rather wistful eyes, or some expression of feeling to come from those smooth and blandly smiling lips. Then you stopped expecting it and knew it wasn't going to. Not Gertrude. She was completely adjusted to the passing moment and whatever it might bring. She had thoughts; they came spinning out from the curly convolutions of an imaginative but fuzzy brain. She had feelings; they effervesced in speech. In five minutes she told you all about herself. In ten, all about everybody else.

But Mark—how little of himself he had ever shown me! All the time his thoughts had been forming, his resolutions taking shape, until the whole mass of them struck me.

Arland too. She had always hidden most of herself. I began to understand her better. Something of what I was suffering she had also suffered with Tim. He had loved her in his way, but it wasn't her way. He had never actually wanted to leave her, but he had left her in spirit long before he had been killed. The person she had loved had disintegrated before her eyes. All the time he was killing her feeling for him, she had gone on smiling and talking and giving parties and going to them and bolstering him up in the eyes of the world.

At last she was free; she had stopped caring. It was her nature to stop caring, to let go; but at first it must have hurt. I knew now it must have taken more than passivity to build up a contented life after what had happened to her.

She was not really happy now—not with the happiness of someone whose life is full and who has everything she wants, but she had learned to put her own self aside, as if it was of no real importance to her any more. She had learned to lavish herself on other people. That was her great charm. You could go to her at practically any hour of the day or night and she would put aside whatever she was doing and immediately be free, ready to be absorbed in whatever woes and confidences and hopes you had to tell her. You could always be sure of her sympathy—sometimes hardly spoken, just inferred, and always tactfully offered. When she did talk about her own thoughts and feelings, those infrequent moods had a peculiar fascination, a value like a plant, secret and closed, putting forth its flowers only rarely.

That was why I felt outraged somehow, that day when she had come to Wishmore—the day after Miss Kate's murder, because she had seemed so preoccupied with some problem of her own.

"What was the matter with you?" I asked her. "You weren't a bit like yourself."

"I was excited."

"You weren't any help to me."

"I know I wasn't. You know there are times when nobody can help you." And she seemed to withdraw again into that secret core of her living she never allowed anyone to penetrate. She was right, of course. You have to save yourself; no one can save you, just as no one can wreck you.

I wasn't capable, though, of making her transition of growing outward toward the hopes and joys and miseries of other people, making them mine, and so escaping.

The trouble with women like me is that there is no real substitute for love or the pleasures of love. Maybe if I had been mellow with past happiness or had acquired wisdom, I could have written it off as experience and so found some peace of mind. But I was neither mellow nor wise, so I filled my days with work and my head with plans.

I determined to change my whole way of living and all the circumstances of my life. I struggled to change my looks and my manners.

It made a good line of defense, but it was a second line, proving I had been beaten back from the first and most important position.

I'm not a good Christian, and one reason is because I can't seem to accept Christianity's major premise, that it's good for you to suffer. I know some people become Beautiful Characters, and some produce sonnets. I didn't do either. It didn't help my soul to be miserable; it hardened it.

That tiresome story about the little Spartan boy who let the horrid little fox chew on his vitals until he fell dead without a single "ouch" is my most unfavorite of all the odious moral tales cluttering my childhood. I don't think it's brave to refrain from crying out when you're hurt. Scream, struggle, fight back. So when my own phantom fox took up its abode in me and bit and tore and looked at me with its ghost fox-fire eyes shining out in the empty dark, I battled with the beast.

Kitty and Mr. Jeff and I, the reluctant Hettie and her niece Tillie, full of gloomy ideas about what would happen to us, moved into Rosemont. A few weeks later Alec and I were married. We went on a short honeymoon to New Orleans. Alec impressed me. He knew how to order meals and where to go and what to say on all occasions. Physically, we got along very well. It was much better being in his arms than to feel no one wanted me at all.

I enjoyed my honeymoon more than I had expected, but on the ride back from New Orleans we both fell silent, thinking about all the problems waiting for us. It was the gloomy spring of 1933, when the banks had all closed their doors. I had no money in them anyway, but the town looked blank and sad and in a cold driving rain, and the road to Rosemont, dark under the wet and sighing pines had a melancholy wildness.

On an evening like this the big house would gather its army of icy shadows to meet us. We turned into the drive and the atmosphere of Rosemont enveloped us, but when the house came into view Alec and I both shouted "Look!" at the same time.

The shutters were opened, and firelight shone from every room. When we reached the door, Arland and Steve and Kitty were there to meet us, the children jumping up and down. Kitty had already attached herself to Alec with the easy affection Aunt Em always showed for people who put her at her ease.

Arland had lighted all the lamps she could find and had filled vases full of flowers. Michael was mixing old-fashioneds, and Joyce was ensconced in the most comfortable chair available. Gertrude soon rode up in her tinny little car, and we drank and had a hot supper.

Bedelia had baked an enormous cake in our honor, and there was a sound of chatter and cheerfulness in the kitchen.

"She came with you?" I asked Arland. None of the colored people had wanted to visit Tillie and Hettie in Rosemont's kitchen, or even in their own little house in the yard; "hants" troubled their minds. But at last Arland had prevailed on Bedelia to call, and her beaming bulk was a good omen. She had great prestige, and the others would follow her example.

Our first evening at Rosemont was gay enough. By mutual consent nobody talked of hard times and collapsed banks, or the misery of the late freeze, which had come out of some grim Northern place and fallen unmercifully on the silly fruit trees, all in full bloom.

The gay mood didn't last through the following weeks. One raw, blustery day, I prodded Alec into going over to his own place, Tooka Point. He went, saying he wished nobody had ever bought Louisiana; it was a mistake—and he knew he'd get stuck. I told him he simply had to go and see about the new drainage ditch. He went, but since he was not back by the middle of the afternoon, I was sure he was stuck. Alec was not one to contemplate his sodden acres or his ditch with such rapt interest all those hours.

I was busy in the library, adding and subtracting, wondering how much I dared allow on one plantation at the expense of the others. I longed to paint the house, but the land came first. I'd made that mistake when I'd gone down to Wishmore—I'd put my money on the house. Mark had been a fool to let me. I knew better now. Get the plantations going, then tackle the house.

Besides cleaning and polishing, the only concession I made to my nerves was to put away the marble busts on the bookcases, and to keep Miss Kate's study locked. Used as I was to marble busts on bookcases, their glimmer in the twilight was apt to give me little frizzles along my backbone. I had never gone back to the study since I had been living in the house. Now I thought of the two long stiff brown envelopes I'd left in the table's secret hiding place. They had been too thick and crackling to stuff down my dress. I thought I'd better get them and destroy them. I crossed the freezing hall, unlocked the study door, found the envelopes and came back. Someday when I had the money I was going to build a downstairs bathroom and turn the study into a dressing room, full of frilled taffeta and clear bright colors and flowering wallpaper.

The envelopes had just turned to ashes and gone flaking and fluttering up the chimney when I heard Gertrude calling me. She came on in. I mixed her a drink and brewed some coffee for myself, and we huddled close to the fire. It was inadequate for this huge room. We'd just settled ourselves when another car drove up, and Arland and Helen Ledyard came running up the steps, just ahead of another downpour of rain.

"What possessed you-all to come forth on a day like this?" I demanded. Then I realized how I sounded, and hurried on to tell them how glad I was to see them. "It makes it much less dismal to have company."

Arland, shedding her coat, looked around. "It already seems much more cheerful than it did."

Helen agreed with her. Helen was a sensible woman, who mostly stayed at home taking care of her husband and children, but she was good at all kinds of tiresome worth-while jobs other people didn't want to tackle.

"I hope you will cheer it up, Jane," Gertrude said. "And not shut it up. People are wild to see it, you know, and you can at least pick up a little change if you let 'em."

"I do let 'em, but the change I pick up is rather a drop in a bucket. A place like this eats up money."

"I know." Gertrude, usually so exuberant, seemed somewhat gloomy. "I haven't had any lights or phone for a month."

This was a common state of affairs with her, and hadn't kept her from giving a large party last night. Alec and I hadn't gone, and neither had Arland. To disperse her gloom, Arland asked her if it had been a good party.

"Fine! We cooked steaks over the fire. Bob passed out and crushed all my lilies along the front path. But he's picked himself up by now, and I guess the lilies will in time."

"How are the New York cousins?" They were the ostensible reasons for the feast, but I think Gertrude would have had it anyway.

"All right. Sort of party proud. You know. 'We went to so and so's and met so and so.' We aren't like that; we just get together and have a good time."

"Someday I'm going to have lots of parties," I promised. "Right now I'm wondering how I'm going to pay taxes, or how anybody is."

"That's one reason Helen and I came today; we want to ask you to put this house on tour. Aunt Em's too. Then maybe it'll help with your taxes. That's what we all hope, anyway."

Of course I'd heard about the Pilgrimage, and knew about the plans being made, but I had been so preoccupied with my own affairs I hadn't paid a great deal of attention to any of it. The idea had been first thought out and suggested by a friend of Arland's, and it had all the wildness and risk of any really original proposition. That is, all the die-hard jog trotters would moan that it would never, never work. Of course they said that about my schemes too, and maybe they would be proved right, but I intended to try.

Now I turned this Pilgrimage project in my mind, and decided it had a certain brilliance, and I wished I'd thought it up myself.

In town, and just out of town, were quite a number of houses built before 1860. Natchez had not been in Sherman's path, and after the fall of Vicksburg it had had no military importance, so it had escaped most of the ravaging and destruction. The old places were nearly all shabby and neglected like Rosemont. They looked lonely and sad, but they still had a reflection of past opulence, and here they were. The plan was to invite the public, people from all over the country— all over the world—to come and make a tour of them. An aura of Southern life and Southern hospitality in the ample days was to be re-created as much as possible. The owners of the houses were to receive in costume—resurrected out of trunks, or copied from Godey prints.

I knew Arland had been writing letters all winter to everyone she'd ever known or heard of. Maybe nobody would come. But anyway we could wait and see what happened. And if I hadn't thought up the whole thing, at least I could get in on it and work on it.

"I've been racking my brains to think of some way of making real money out of the house. Of course put it on tour. And the Elliston house too."

"We couldn't broach the subject to Miss Kate," Helen said, "but with you owning it, it's different."

"Entirely. I'm all for it. Aunt Em will hem and haw, but she'll come around. Put Arland to work on her."

"I have. She says she wouldn't know what to do or what to tell people. I told her just to pretend she was giving a party——"

"—in the year 1850. These older people just don't want to be routed out of their lazy stick-in-the-mud existence. But you know the aunts, Arland. Just tell Aunt Em to comport herself like a true Elliston,

218

and I'll attend to all the practical part. Once get her into the swing of Grandma's hoops and that rotten old lace jacket she cherishes, and she'll cotton to it. We won't be able to get her out of her regalia."

"There's a lot of opposition," Gertrude pointed out. "Plenty of people say it isn't going to be any real help, just a lot of trouble."

"There's always opposition to anything new. We can buck it. Only I wish this place wasn't so shabby. I'd like it to be the way it was meant to be—magnificent."

Rosemont's garden was a sort of ghost now. The camellias and sweet olive had grown into trees, and the azaleas had spread wide and tangled together, but the grassy spaces were rough and weedy, the box unkempt, the paths almost lost, the fountains broken, and the summerhouse haunted. I had done the best I could with the house and the garden, but the whole place had been neglected for years, and it didn't lend itself to freshening up with a little paint and a few yards of cretonne. It needed landscape gardeners, not old Lew pottering around with a hoe and doing a little sporadic raking and weeding.

"The houses are shabby mostly. But here we have these houses and hardly anyone ever sees them, and I think people would enjoy seeing them. They'll have to use their imaginations, and be able to visualize how it all was. We want to make a kind of picture of the past——"

"Like a story book." I smiled.

"Yes. But there was so much to it that was worth having, and there's still something left. It ought to be brought back."

Alec came in after dusk, at last, ungummed from the tenacious mud of Tooka Point. He sat in our midst, mixing highballs and listening to us, and flinging in a suggestion now and then.

"Jane, I see you're getting into this up to your neck. Gal—with all your other undertakings! But you always thought you could lick your weight in wildcats!" But, rather to my surprise, he seemed to think the whole thing might very well work out successfully.

"Whatever you do, don't do it gingerly. Present it all with a grand air and a fine flourish. Psychologically I think it's pretty sound. People are all in a muddle. They might be ready to dream themselves into cloud castles—do a little escaping from the grim present and get back into romantic times when everything was lovely."

After the others had left I sat prodding the fire, and looking around the room, trying to see how it would look through other people's eyes. It seemed to me oppressive on this gloomy day. Pictures and furniture and mirrors were caught in a web of shadows. It held too many inanimate objects and too much past. It gave a richness, like a coagulation of leaves in the swamp, disintegrating, giving out an unhealthy atmosphere. I had to fight the house, just as I had to fight the land. Rule it, not let it rule me.

The whole town was morbid. It seemed to have no future, just memories. A highly specialized civilization had developed here, on the wild landscape. Nothing was left but its traditions and these old houses, gleaming out with a pale phosphorescence.

The portraits of the gorgeous Lennerds looked out at me, safe in their frames, set in their beglamored past. Ephraim, his eyes shining with the joy of living, and young Josiah, with his mouth so like Mark's, and Ned with his beautiful melancholy face and dark eyes.

It struck me that in their lives they hadn't been safe either. Ephraim hadn't known, when he had changed from indigo to cotton planting, and then had experimented with a new kind of cotton, how successful he would become. Josiah hadn't known he would ever come back alive from his expedition to sink the frigate in the pirates' harbor. And Ned had not come back from the war.

What other people had done I could do too. Or at least I could try.

All the people who prided themselves on their practical sense laughed at us. "It's just so much froth," the businessmen said, when Arland and I went to ask about advertising and getting the city hall for our tableaux. We had decided to give balls, with scenes of life as it used to be lived in the Old South. The city hall would lose its utilitarian aspect when we were through hanging moss and magnolias all over the walls and festooning the stage with crepe-paper azaleas. We would have tableaux, and a ballet, and afterward general dancing.

The mayor thought it was all foolishness, but he liked Arland, and had a natural indulgence for the silliness of womankind. "Do you think you ladies will need traffic cops and guides along the roads for just a trickle of cars?" he asked, but he gave us everything we asked for.

"Do you think it's ridiculous?" I asked Alec.

"Not exactly—a little pathetic. Here we are, trembling on the brink, yet we posture around in costume and make little pictures of life as it used to be in the golden days."

"It won't be pathetic if we make money. Since the past seems to be all we have on hand at the moment, why not exploit it? Play it up for all it's worth? Someday we might have a future. And I intend to be ready for it."

Miss Kate's murder had faded from the papers. I wrote to the reporters I had met and asked them to do some more stories. While we sent out circulars and pored over Godey prints and arranged scenes for the tableaux, I also had to cope with taxes and repairs and tenants' woes, spring planting and all the problems of Beulah Land, Wishmore, Dewberry Landing, and Rosemont in the year 1933.

People came to our Pilgrimage; it was a success. Some came from curiosity, to sniff the atmosphere of these old houses, so long sequestered, thrown open at last. Some came because they wanted to travel and couldn't afford Europe or Palm Beach. Some came because they genuinely loved beautiful things. Simple souls came, rich people came, painters and writers and architects came. I learned to tell with one lightning glance who was important, even if they didn't look it. Sometimes a well-dressed woman, descending from an opulent car, was worth only the entrance fee, while some seedy creature, lurking in front of some faded picture in a dim corner, mattered tremendously and could give us prestige by his or her presence.

I learned to whisk the intelligentsia away from Joyce and lead them to Arland; I learned to keep still when I found myself with some expert on architecture or china or pictures, and let myself go with the ignorant. I really didn't know much about antiques, but I learned. Sometimes by reading, but mostly by listening to the people who came and did know.

The businessmen liked the money the tourists spent in hotels and cafés, and the young girls liked to dress up and show themselves off, and the old ladies enjoyed the familiar atmosphere of their own memories.

Aunt Em's light old bones and fine faded skin fell naturally into lace jacket and lilac taffeta hoop skirts. Her opposition once beaten down, as I knew it would be, she was glad to dream herself back where she belonged, to re-enter her never-never land for two weeks out of the year. Tirelessly she received the crowd, telling family anecdotes, showing old miniatures, bringing out old wax dolls and faded letters from Henry Clay and Jefferson Davis.

While she was rummaging in the family archives, she came across a signed picture of Admiral Farragut.

Her hand shook. "Jane," she whispered, "how on earth do you suppose this got here among our things?"

"Do you suppose an Elliston backslid when the going got tough?" I suggested slyly.

"Jane, how can you insinuate such a thing! When you had two grandfathers and eight great-uncles in Confederate uniform!"

We hid Admiral Farragut and never mentioned him again.

Our old house was shabby but genuine, not only in architecture, but in atmosphere. "She's the real thing," tourists admired. They also thought Joyce, in pale pink and flower-wreathed ringlets, was a perfect reincarnation of the traditional Southern belle, unaware her father had kept a saloon in Ohio.

It was a success; then it was over. "Until next year," I yawned, when the last tour had ended and the last ball had been given and the guests I had entertained had taken themselves off. I had rented out some of the spare bedrooms to tourists. I don't think they slept very well, but they couldn't resist coming here. Then they would be able to go home and tell all their friends they had actually stayed at Rosemont.

We gave a good many parties, and Gertrude was a wonderful help at that. Her little house was always bursting with festivity. Arland entertained, too, on a grander scale. She wrote to everyone prominent she had ever known, inviting them to come to our tour. A great many on her list did come, and I was determined that they should not only tour but be shown delightful Southern Hospitality.

"Alone at last." Alec mixed himself another drink. "Have they all gone? Then let me relax from being a gracious host, and growl awhile. Jane, when are we ever going to have any sort of life to ourselves?"

"It'll be less hectic when things shake down."

"When are they going to do that?"

"Someday, if we work at them now."

"I feel harried. We scrimp and save and almost starve ourselves here at home to put on a show, then we work ourselves to rags over the plantations——"

"What else can we do? If we don't we'll lose them."

"I know. But I wish we could take it easier—just live a little."

"I don't want to live in a measly way. I'm tired of that. I want to live in a grand way, and to do that we have to have money. If we're ever going to get it, we've got to root for it. How're you coming along with Tooka Point?"

"So-so; crop's in the ground."

"It was such a shame to have to sell off so much timber at such a low price. But still, you had to plant. Tell me all about everything in detail." So we discussed Tooka Point.

"Anyhow, we have a diversity," I meditated aloud. "There's Beulah Land, practically jungle, and Tooka—good old Louisiana, with its advantages and disadvantages—and Wishmore, sort of semiswamp. Really, it's the worst of the lot, the most vulnerable to the river. I don't see how I ever expected to get anywhere with just that. Rich as rich, but too many counts against it, year in and year out. Now Dewberry—that's the pick of the bunch. Cattle ought to do well there, and fruit trees, and pecans. Rosemont's too full of ravines; land keeps sliding, except the hill."

"Rosemont's for panache, not practicality."

"I wish they'd find oil spouting everywhere! Even if they'd found gas over there near Tooka——"

"Do you still have oil ideas?" Alec looked at my locket, compressed waist, and sweeping skirts. "Absurd getup, but becoming."

"It must be. The girls say they get lots of new beaus when they're dressed up in hoop skirts." I sat down, with care. You have to, in such a rig, or the hoop will leap up in front. It also entangled itself when you tried to drive a car. From the next room, where there was a long mirror, my reflection showed itself—hardly me, this woman with hair parted in the middle and ringlets falling on either side of her face. I was much better-looking than I used to be. As Alec had once pointed out to me, I had the sort of face and figure you can remake into almost any model you choose—if you're clever about it. My fine lightish-brown hair was curled and touched with rinses to brighten it. My natural slightness and my darkish skin were advantages these days. People had begun to envy my angles and my sun tan. I'd learned to use lipstick and paint and eyeshadow to the best advantage, and someday, when I could afford it, people would gasp at my clothes. They were going to be wonderful, and rather on the daring side. Just now I couldn't think of spending on clothes; I'd begrudged the price of all of these yards of silk for my costume.

"A female in crinoline, dreaming not of sentiment but of oil," Alec said. "Something your grandmother never heard of."

"I can't help dreaming. They did find that gas in Louisiana."

My costume was authentic in every detail, copied most exactly, but a wild, and so-called "modern" restlessness pounded beneath the tight-boned corsage. Some of those others, now dead and gone, might have been restless too.

"They don't find it any more. You know they drilled near Tooka Point and found not a damn thing."

"The companies are still hanging around here, and as long as they are I'm not giving up all hope. We can't live on hopes, though. I've got a little scheme——"

Alec groaned. "Not another one!"

"This is a risk—a big risk, but I think it's worth trying. You know the price of cotton——"

"I ought to—don't hear anything else but."

"Well, the President says he's going to get it up to ten cents a pound. You know that speech he made——"

"Presidents have to make speeches."

"I'm taking the line it's going up."

"It's a cheering thought."

"I'm going out and buy it up."

"Speculate? That is a gamble. You'd better watch out."

"I'm not going to fool with the market. I mean I'm going out and buy up people's crops—as much as I can of what they haven't sold, and I'm going to put it in a warehouse and hang on until it does go up."

Alec began to point out all the drawbacks. I'd have to pay for storing it, and it might be a long time before the price went up, and if it went down instead of up——

"I've thought it all out; I know all that; I've been over all that in my mind already."

Alec grumbled and muttered, but finally said to go and do what I damned pleased. Then he asked, "How are you going to pay for it?"

I knew I had to guard my face and my words. His question made me nervous. I shouldn't have told him anything.

"You know, Jane, I was wondering the other day how you've managed to do as much as you've already done."

"How do you mean?"

"You know what I mean—improvements here, and improvements there, and now you're going to buy up cotton."

"You know I borrowed from Michael and from Arland too. Then I've put mortgages on the places that didn't have any." I was getting thoroughly frightened.

"I know, but you sure are managing to stretch it beyond all reason. How do you do it?"

"The government's bought a whole lot of willow from Beulah Land. The check's just come. They've got to sink a whole lot of mats down there to keep the river from caving more, and the willows are thick, and I sold a lot of that stretch——" It was all perfectly true, but if Alec asked more and more exacting questions, I didn't know how I was going to answer. What if he asked, How much did they pay? How much do you intend to spend on the cotton? I would find myself in a fix, and he must never corner me to such a point that he would begin to suspect I had money from some mysterious source. What mysterious source?

"Oh, I'd forgotten that," he said. "But still, I don't see how you can buy all that cotton. However, maybe it's just as well. It's one wild gamble, sure enough." Fortunately, he dropped the subject. Fortunately, he was Alec, and would have been bored if he had to look through columns of figures. He gave a mighty yawn and got up. "You're not the early Victorian ideal, my lamb, but you do look rather Jane Eyre-ish at this moment. Come, give me a kiss."

I gave him several, with great fervor, because I was so grateful his mind had veered from practical calculations. He kept his arm around me. "Let's go up. This business of living in the past and the present and the future is getting me addled."

We went up together. The past was dead and the present was hard. I had to live in the future to keep going. On the whole, Alec and I were getting along very well. We didn't have the scenes that had embittered my life with Mark. Alec listened to my plans, and if he found fault with them, always gave in with a tolerant good humor, like tonight. I enjoyed his company, and I was certainly glad I didn't have to go and sleep in that enormous canopied four-poster in solitude. I was glad I had married him. He helped me with my clothes, improved my tastes, told me all sorts of things I needed to know, and directed me in my search for tact and smoothness—necessary now when I had to deal with so many and such a varied assortment of people. Not only deal with them, but get the better of them.

I could never manage all the changes I was making in myself without him. Yet somehow our marriage lacked something—central heating, I suppose. I was glad I'd married him, but was he glad he'd married me? He had already begun to express certain doubts about the course our life together was taking, and he'd certainly veered toward a dangerous subject—how I had so much money to manipulate as I chose. He'd forget all about it, though, I told myself. As to his doubts about us, I'd try to please him and make him content. When I had time to get around to it, I was really going to work on our marriage and make a dazzling success of it. Like Rosemont, there were fires here and there, but also large chilly areas. Someday I'd do something about them. Not right now. Now I had to make money.

When I went out to buy the cotton I didn't take Alec with me. I didn't want him checking up on me. I didn't tell him how much I bought either. I went over in Louisiana, and where anybody had their last year's crop and wanted to get rid of it, I bought it. I drove out beyond Dewberry Landing. Everybody wanted to get cotton off their hands, at almost any price. Everybody except me.

There were some small farms beyond Dewberry, where the people made sometimes as little as two bales. Most of them had held their cotton, hoping it would go up. It had gone on down. Now they were desperate. I wanted to shout to them, "If you've held this long, hold a little longer." But if I was wrong, they'd blame me. And if I was right, why shouldn't I gain from it? So I bought and bought, with the money I'd taken from Miss Kate's table.

There was a colored man who had a little farm across the creek from Dewberry. He had two sick children, and had had to sell his mule to buy food and medicine for the children. He'd worked hard to make those eight bales of cotton. He was glad to sell it to me.

"You want the money now, or you want to wait awhile and see what happens?"

He looked away and his face quivered. I knew what he was thinking—all that back-breaking work, through the long hot days with the sun beating down. But he had to have the money now. He had to have a mule, so he could start all over again, the same dreary round of

226

work. So I handed him the money, and stored the eight bales along with all the others in the warehouse.

What I was doing was dangerous. I could lose everything; but the sense of danger and daring eased the pressure of the restlessness inside myself; when I was taking wild chances I somehow felt happier. In some strange way the suspenses and tensions I created for myself soothed me.

I held on, and finally sold the cotton I'd bought for four and five cents a pound at the price of fourteen cents a pound! It made me. That's how I laid the foundation of a new Lennerd fortune, not in the beglamored past, but in the dank spring of the worst year of the depression.

The day after I'd sold, I drove to the little farm on the other side of the creek. The little house on its rise looked more rickety than ever, the clothes flapping on the line had more patches on them, and when the old man came out, he moved more slowly than before. Another season of work and worry had added more lines to his face and a more pronounced stoop to his back.

We talked a little, and he answered my questions about his place and his children. "You wanted me to sell that cotton I bought from you, didn't you?"

"Yes'm." He looked puzzled.

"Well, I didn't. I held onto it. Here's your money." And I paid him for his eight bales at the price I'd sold it. I didn't wait for his thanks, but drove off, leaving him standing there stupefied by the only stroke of really good fortune he'd ever had. Ever since, he's always thought of me as a sort of messenger of de Lawd—the only person who has ever thought of me in that light.

After I had won my gamble on the cotton buying, Alec gave in to all my schemes with meekness. Through the next few years we kept on fighting for our land. The fact we had so much of it helped. If one crop failed, the others were good. Then the depression began to lift. The worst of it was over—this cycle of the worst, anyway.

The oil was a terrible disappointment to me. If only we could strike oil, we would be safe from all depressions, but we didn't strike it. One company drilled at Pine Ridge, and found a dry hole. Another drilled on the county line—dry hole. A third company drilled near Woodville—nothing. Nobody was interested in leasing land any more, for any price. Then, one by one, the oil companies pulled out, with their crews and their monstrous-looking gear. I couldn't quite give up, though. Maybe they were wrong, and I was right. Tim had said the structure of the land showed the existence of oil.

However, there was nothing to do at the moment but redouble my efforts on what I was sure of—the land itself. Dewberry became the apple of my eye. The crops on the level land did well, the cotton clean and shining in the bolls. The orchard flowered and bore fruit. The cattle grew sleek. The hands stayed put and didn't drift off, though they seemed to stab each other with more frequency than on any other spot I owned. The best workers always seemed to get into the most trouble, and Alec and I were always getting them out of jail.

The Pilgrimage had grown into a big organization now. The whole town flung itself into the spirit of it, and the crowds, instead of dwindling, grew bigger and bigger year after year. We made so much money the home owners were able to repair their houses, and we even took an old run-down house in the middle of town and restored it. We also had the idea of buying another big house in the middle of town and turning it into a tearoom and renting out the ballroom for entertainments. We needed more room. The town was always, at all seasons, full of visitors.

Then something happened. Just an incident, but it changed everything for me. It was a year after the oil companies had pulled out, one spring day when Rosemont was on tour and full of people. A cameraman had just taken my picture, standing in the front door, and was going off to take a technicolor film of Kitty and some of the other girls in the garden. My picture, and Kitty's, and the other hostesses' appeared now in nearly every magazine. The houses, inside and out, and particularly this house, were known all over the country. Rosemont's façade, its oak drive, and its stairway had become familiar even to people who had never seen it.

At that moment Mr. Jeff had chosen to stroll out from his room and wander through the crowd, his shirttails out, his face scowling, and his hat askew on his head. I looked around for Arland. She always managed him better than I did and could possibly persuade him back into his corral. I saw her coming up one of the garden walks. Over her head were some flowering peach trees, in full bloom, and the wind was shaking their translucent petals, scattering them in drifts.

The same breeze was blowing Arland's hair back from her face in shiny spirals, and her arms were full of pale trembling sprays, and her skirts whirled and swayed. An angry bee, all whirring velvet, circled over her head, then buried himself in a flower. Arland was with some man, talking and laughing. They left the path and came across the grass, and the wild violets seemed to be springing up under her footsteps. Though not because of him—he was dry and lank, not at all a poetical-looking creature.

"Here's someone I want you to meet, Jane," she said when she was close to me, and introduced Mr. Dennis. I smiled and shook hands with him.

"Arland darling, do go and see if you can get poor Uncle Jeff to gently fade off; he strikes a jarring note——"

She laughed. "I'll try, but why not let him wander? The skeleton's out of the cupboard now."

The governor and his wife and party were due in half an hour. I turned to Mr. Dennis and asked him into the house, wondering why Arland thought it necessary for me to meet him. He had a long face and narrow, shrewd eyes. "Thank you, but I'd rather wander around outside. I'm more interested in the land than the house."

"I'm always more interested in land——" I wondered why he was.

"I was here once before, with one of the oil companies."

"Oh! And do you think they are going to come back?"

"Not at any time soon. They all say they don't think it's worth the gamble." He saw I was disappointed, and his eyes twinkled. "But you know, the way I look at it, this country around here has a mighty interesting structure. If I were in their shoes, I'd certainly take a chance on it."

"Come on, if you want to wander around, I'll go with you, governor or no governor." We went past the garden and out to the edge of the hill and looked down on Wishmore.

"Mrs. Laidlaw tells me you own a lot of land around here. Well, all I can say—and of course it's just my own opinion—if I were you, I'd hang onto it mighty tight."

"You mean you don't think they've settled the oil question once and for all?"

"I can't tell you anything positive. I'm just one man. They think one way, I think another. It just looks to me as though this land has possibilities: take it for what it's worth. I might be wrong. It's a gambling game."

"Would you buy more land if you were I?"

"If I had money lying idle, reckon I'd take a chance on it. But you know it is just a chance."

I talked to him until I had to hurry back to the house to greet the governor, and all the rest of the day I thought about what Mr. Dennis had said.

That night, after all the guests had left, Arland and Gertrude, Alec and Michael, Joyce and myself were sitting in the library having a few drinks in peace and quiet. The others were relaxing, but I was caught in a fever dream of leases and oil companies hurrying back, trailing down the roads with all their equipment. My thoughts were all out wildcatting.

"Jane." Alec stretched out his feet and twirled his glass in his hand. He was dressed as a beau of the sixties, and the costume suited his long length very well. "I behaved prettily, didn't I? But I could have killed you for not coming and rescuing me from that lush enthusiastic female who writes for something. Bet it's goo."

"It's publicity, though."

"Your expression was very bland, Alec," Arland smiled. "You must have charmed the lady."

"When she left she said I was her ideal of what a Southern Gentleman should be—charming, cultured, leisured!"

"We must have made a lot of money this year." I did some mental calculations.

"That's what's so funny," Alec muttered. "It's all so papier-mâché. Reminds me of Potemkin's little village. Look at the Negro slums on our side streets, and our eroded land, and the whole damn system of things, and we go peacocking around talking about ancestors and pier tables."

"You can't say Jane doesn't work at other things too," Arland defended me.

"Runs herself ragged. And of course the tours have taken the town out of its innocuous desuetude—not always so innocuous at that! To my mind, though, all the crowds and the bustle and paved roads are spoiling our flavor. You've made people patch up their houses and wave the branches of the family trees and hang moss all over the filling stations. You're making it all over to some pattern of your own, Jane. Soon we'll have to start keeping up with the Joneses."

"And high time." I'd just won the gold loving cup for being the citizen who had done most for the town. "We are going to have a factory. And I bet we wouldn't be getting it if it hadn't been for Pilgrimage, because the bigshot who has a lot of say-so about it came here, and liked it, and talked to some business people, and thinks it just the town for his factory. He'd never have heard of it, though, if it hadn't been advertised already. And it's time we were having some industries."

"The good roads help," Michael said. "It used to take a whole day to get out to the Vineses' place. Remember, Alec, when we used to go visit them? You and Mark and I?" They began to laugh about the time they had all made themselves chaps out of sheepskin and ridden horseback, and the skins, imperfectly cured, had stiffened on them, so they couldn't get down from the horses. "Mr. Vines used to dress up complete with hat and cane and go around asking his tenants and his neighbors for a 'dustin' of meal,' and once we found the girls nursing a sick calf in their bedroom. You wouldn't know it since these new people bought it and fixed it up and stuffed it full of furniture they've collected on Royal Street."

"I wouldn't know it, and I don't like it. Frankly, I think it stinks," Alec said.

"Well, it would have fallen in, Alec!" I had helped make these old houses the fashion. You used to be able to buy them for nothing, but now people were frantic to own one, redecorate it, put it on tour and get themselves in the limelight.

Certainly Rosemont no longer looked the same. I used the Pilgrimage money to fix it up. Of course I did not change any of its essentials, only restored it as nearly as possible to the grand mansion the Lennerds had built, and furnished, in 1838. I had, though, added lights and bathrooms. Miss Kate's study was now a powder room, and people had forgotten it had ever been the scene of her death. At my parties and Kitty's the women and girls gathered there to freshen their lipstick and chatter together, effectively drowning out the echoes of the past. The little table had been removed and done over, and now stood beside the big bed in my room. Its twin from Wishmore was on the other side of the bed. I kept nothing in them, and never opened them. I didn't want Alec to know they did open.

I was thoroughly proud of Rosemont. I enjoyed opening a highly glazed magazine and seeing pictures of all its familiar aspects show themselves to me; yet the house hardly seemed mine. I would catch glimpses of myself in its multitudes of mirrors—a restless twentieth-century female, painted and permanented, hurrying through the rooms. It was and it remained a period piece, grand and exacting, so exacting in its demands for the perfectly appropriate chair, picture, ornament, it gave no scope to anybody's individual taste.

"I must say I'm worried about our collection of queer characters," Arland sighed. "When the old ones die off, where are we going to get any more? The younger generation seems so normal!" She looked around a little uneasily, maybe feeling Miss Kate's ghost might be listening, though I had pretty well exorcised Miss Kate from the house by now. How could her spirit even recognize it?—filled as it nearly always was with flowers and people and noise and lights, my parties, Kitty's parties, gatherings for cocktails, gatherings for dinners, and new bathrooms.

"The generation growing up has too much contact with the outside world," Alec said. "They'll get the edges of their peculiarities rubbed off and be just like anybody in any other town."

I looked at Arland. Her dress didn't look like the costume; it looked just like her natural clothes. I had noticed before how she has a way of fitting into whatever background she's placed in at the moment. I've seen her in the woods, or visiting in a Negro cabin, and she's as much at ease as in her own home or in Rosemont's double parlors. Tonight her flowerlike skirts spread all around her, whispering. Roses and flying cupids were painted across the gauze and lace of her fan, fresh roses were caught in her hair and in the lace falling away from her shoulders. Candlelight fell over her in golden waves, and her lips and eyelids were lengthened in a smile. Joyce was more obviously pretty, but she couldn't create an atmosphere the way Arland did.

"Right now you look so much like Doña Ana," Alec told her. I had to admit she did: the same dark dreaming look, and the fine-spun meshes of lace falling from hair to shoulder, and the same deep subdued glow of coloring.

"Do you suppose women then were as lanquid and fragile as they looked?" Alec asked. "They never seemed to wear anything but India muslin and something called mull. Somebody—Josephine, I think—complained because her shoes split, and the shoemaker said, 'But, madam, you must have walked in them'. Jane, where do you get all those tales about Doña Ana?"

"I have to say something when people ask."

"Let her speak for herself," Arland said. "She suggests a whole era to me: Napoleon crowned at Notre Dame, and Thackeray's description of the battle of Waterloo, and old New Orleans, with its dust and pirates and yellow fever and Creole splendor."

Gertrude had been drinking quietly. "I wish I'd lived then or at least inherited myself a house from old times. My own little dump brings me no cash."

"You have your place, Gertrude," I pointed out. It was a small plantation, right next to Dewberry Landing. I'd had my eye on it for some time—it would be nice to round out Dewberry's acres. Besides, if Mr. Dennis should be right about the "interesting structure" of the land around here, now was certainly the time to get hold of it, buy it up, and buy up blocks of leases while they were cheap. Nobody was thinking about oil any more except myself. But if they ever got so much as a whiff of oil in the wind, they'd all sit tight and not sell or lease an inch of ground. Of course it was a wild, desperate gamble, but that's how big fortunes were made. Lucky breaks helped, but mostly it was daring. Things were much better for me now; the plantations were in good shape, but now was also the time for decision. I could be satisfied, or I could plunge out in the dark.

Arland pushed open the long window to the side gallery and stepped outside. The night brought in the perfume of sweet olive and fruit trees in flower. A reaching spray flung its cluster of pearl against the dark. There was a sheen on Arland's petal-blown skirts and the outline of her face, half turned away. She began to sing the waltz she'd used in her tableau, and the tone and color of her voice lifted the sentimental melody to romance, fragile and doomed.

Against my will Mark's face took shape, too vivid and too real. The solid walls couldn't keep him out. I wondered what he was doing at this moment—probably flying over the jungles and sharp crude peaks, solitary in the sky. When I had gone to Michael to pay back the money Mark had borrowed from him, Michael told me Mark had already paid it back, every cent. Maybe he had half starved himself to do it, or had risked his neck on impossible flights. Lately, though, Michael had heard from him, and had told me what bits of news the letters held. It seems as though the company—a rickety little two-by-four company—had a certain importance, because its planes were the only method of transport between some outlandish point and another, unless you rambled through feverish jungles for days and weeks and months. A larger company was trying to merge with them, and had offered Mark a position with a good salary if the merger went through. It seemed strange for Mark to do well in a financial way.

Suppose I had gone with him wherever he'd wanted to go! I wonder what would have happened. It would have been a strange roving life, full of hardship and out-of-the-way places and insecurity and adventure, but it might have been happy. It was too late now. He'd left me, flung me aside. By God, I'd show him what I could do! He couldn't leave me to molder. I'd show him! All of a sudden I made up my mind. I'd buy land and I'd buy leases, and later on, if and when the oil companies came back, I'd learn their game and beat them at it.

"Gertrude, you say you are muddled up? Wouldn't you have more freedom and more money if you sold your place?" Gertrude managed it in an extremely helter-skelter fashion. I knew I could make more out of it than she did. Michael had once offered to buy Dewberry, in good faith. Perhaps my faith wasn't quite so good. I didn't want Gertrude to have the slightest inkling of what Mr. Dennis had said. I felt I would be able to drive a pretty sharp bargain with her, too, since with her a pint in the hand was always worth two in the bush.

"Why don't you let Jane, or Michael, give you a steer from time to time," Alec suggested, "instead of selling outright?"

"Don't meddle, Alec." I spoke more sharply than I had intended. "Gertrude knows her own mind." I began to draw a picture of what her life would be like without any trammels, working her into a receptive state of mind. I'd make her an offer later. Alec and Michael were both sitting there listening, and they'd be sure to tell her I wasn't offering her enough for the place. When she was ready to leave she felt very mellow and quite enthusiastic about selling her property.

When the others had gone Alec poured himself another drink and stood watching me. "You're different from what you used to be, Jane. You used to be so real. That's what drew me to you, the way you came slam out with all your thoughts and feelings. Now you're sort of—well, phony."

I didn't get angry. "You mean all this Pilgrimage stuff? I can drop it if you like." I was all amiable, wifely meekness. When Alec got into his analyzing moods I humored him until he got out of them.

"Oh no, not that. Why should you drop it? You do it well. It's hard to explain what I do mean, but, for instance, why do you want Gert's

234

place? God knows not just to give her money and freedom, the way you told her."

"She doesn't like bothering with it and working over it, and she's ruining it. I could make something out of it. Things slip through her fingers; you know that! I need more acreage out there. I want to make Dewberry a really model place. A sort of example of what can be done around here. Build really good cabins and restore the church, and select the tenants carefully, and make them have gardens and fruit trees around every cabin, and put in a lot of up-to-date machinery."

Alec was always talking about improving the standard of living for the tenant farmer. Of course the other landlords in the neighborhood would be wild, because they couldn't afford all that, and I'd be able to lure off their best workers. But I could visualize articles and pictures: "Landowner Solves South's Economic Ills."

"It would be fine," Alec agreed, "but a little phony too. It would be a showplace, possible only to people like yourself who have a lot of land, and who can, if necessary, rob Peter to pay Paul. It's really window dressing, and certainly is no cure for the underlying system of things. However, it'll look nice, and I'm sure you'll make a go of it."

"It will be fine. Don't drink so much, Alec. When you drink a lot you're always moody and talk about systems and see through a glass darkly."

"I'm not moody. It's just that you never tell me your real reasons for anything any more. As for me, I'm fast slipping back into being a leisured, cultured gentleman of the Old School. I feel it creeping up on me day by day."

"You have your own property; you can do what you please with it."

"I can, but I don't. I go across the river and get on a horse and lumber over the fields, but everything I plan you say, 'That's fine, but why don't you do so and so; you could make this and that.' And I listen and do it your way. Your ideas usually do pan out better than mine. I suppose that's what I resent."

"You can 'gang your ain gait.'"

"Sure I could. But I'm lazy. I don't really want a lot of work and bother. You surround me with creature comforts, and I let them lap around me. I was afraid if I came back here to live, I'd just slip into pleasant idleness, and that's just what I've done. I'm worried about myself and I'm worried about you. You used to be a downright frank little beast. Now you're so damn polite. And full of all sorts of wiles and guiles."

"You think I'm not honest? Alec, how can you talk to me like that!"

"I didn't say that. You're saying it. But are you?"

I buried my face in my hands and seemed thoroughly dejected. I was a little uneasy.

"I'm sorry, Jane. I guess I put it a little strongly. Come on, you're worn out."

We went up the steps arm in arm, a devoted pair. Model marriage, model ante-bellum home "where the Old South still lives," model plantations. Now if I could just root up a few model oil wells!

Honest? Well, the money I'd snatched from the table had helped me come as far as I had come. It had undoubtedly tipped the balance, given me leeway, made the narrow margin between success and failure at the most critical time. Because of it I hadn't been swallowed up. I had been careful with it, too, putting it all back in the land and the house, so I was justified, wasn't I?

As for Gertrude's place, I might be entirely wrong about oil, so why should I pay too much? I was taking the risks, so why shouldn't I take the gains, if any? Arland told that tale about a certain planter digging up his friend's money as well as his own after the war. It wasn't a pretty trick, but that's how he'd saved his house and his land. I wasn't that bad. I'd just go ahead with my plans, only I'd hide them more carefully from Alec. I had had my teeth kicked down my throat. Who had cared? Who had helped? I had had to take it. Other people damn well could too.

My room gave a wide view and a glimpse of the river. It might be a quiet lake, but it wasn't. It gathered up all its tributaries and dragged them to the Gulf, and down there, 'way beyond, Mark was flying. Now I went without thinking about him for months at a time. Yet every now and then, like tonight, the old yearning stole over me and influenced me. It was less a longing for his actual presence than an agonizing sense of knowing I would have to leave this world without ever really having had what I most wanted out of it.

⤸ Chapter Sixteen

A year or so later the government carried out a project for straightening the river's channel by cutting through some of the points where the Mississippi made its longest curves. Wishmore was one of the designated spots. They intended to dredge right through the point. The river's main current would come pouring through. When the water rose at all, the whole place would be flooded deep, deep. No one lived in the house, but I hated to think of the water rising to the top of the steps, whirling through the front door, invading the very attic, closing over the roof. The river had never attained the house itself, not even in '27, when all the Louisiana levees collapsed one after another. Then the Mississippi pounded where it listed, from Missouri to New Orleans. But not in my house. Now it would. Where the water curled lazily around the end of the point would eventually become nothing but a lake, cut from the main current, getting more and more lethargic. That part of Wishmore would be nothing but an island. What could I do with a damn island? Also, as the main current drove through it would inevitably eat. Before, in spite of its vagaries, the river had been the benefactor of Wishmore. It had built the point, fathered its richness, added to the soil slowly but steadily. Every flood, when it retreated, left a deposit of silt—a gift to recompense for being so trying. You never had to fertilize Wishmore, or worry about its land tiring of growth. It was tireless, always refreshed, always renewed. When they cut through the point, the river would become the mortal enemy of the land. The current, always hungry, would gnaw chunks here, nibble bits there. At every rise the river would carry off with it large clots of Wishmore Plantation. There was no way on earth I could prevent it from doing so.

I had held on; I was paying up all the mortgage. The crops these last years had been fine. Now the river would wrest it from me.

"How I hate to lose it; how I hate to lose it!" I moaned. "My good land."

"It's not an only child." Alec smiled. "You are not left utterly bereft, you know. You have a bit of acreage."

I had bought Gertrude's place right near Dewberry, and now I was thankful to have it. Alec didn't think I had paid her enough for it. I pointed out the place was run-down and I had to spend a bit on improvements before I could make it profitable—and to please remember that when he thought I'd taken advantage of Gertrude.

"But Wishmore's my eldest child. And I worked so hard on it, and was just getting it where I had some satisfaction out of it."

"The government paid you. Paid you well too."

"They damned well better had! But I would rather have kept my place intact!"

"It's supposed to be a plan to help everybody."

I thought, "Damn the general good," but as I had set myself up as public-spirited, I had to keep my mouth shut. Once Alec had told me I was the kind of planter who'd cut his neighbor's levee to save his own land. It's a course of conduct which seems perfectly natural to me. Of course I would. But I knew better than to tell him so. Alec has such damn ethical fits. A lot of theorizing people do. They can afford ethics.

"I can keep cattle down there and plant a little corn for the pigs. Anything I plant'll be ruined if the water rises at all, and I'll have to haul the cattle out, across the cutoff. And sooner or later the river'll eat it all up."

"Oh, that'll take a hell of a long time. But why don't you sell part of the place and stop worrying with it?"

"Mercy, no. I'll just use what's left as best I can."

"Why do you always set yourself up to battle such clementary things as the river?" Alec demanded. "Or undertake such mythical projects as finding oil where nobody else thinks any exists?"

I had been buying leases steadily, with whatever spare money I could scrape together. Businessmen who guessed what was in my mind, and Sam Barrett, who handled the legal part of it all for me, thought I was a plumb fool. "It's taking bread out of my own mouth to say it, Jane, but I swear I think you're way out of your depth now. Of course we all admit you've done fine with your new-fangled notions about your land, but this is a horse of another color." A wild horse, a phantom horse, different from just manipulating land, yet part of the whole, since if oil was there, it was deep-locked in the earth, and you had to own or get your grip in some way on the earth above it to partake of it.

Maybe I was out of my depth, but I intended to take most of the money the government was paying for Wishmore and buy yet more leases. I told Alec so. He was indulgent. "The truth is, you just like to own a hell of a lot of land and fret and worry with it. It's a disease with you. Not that I think there's any harm in it. Go ahead with your fancy work if it makes you happy. It's a sort of endless pastime for you, like your Aunt Em's yards and yards and yards of crochet."

The game fascinated me, drew me on. The danger of it lured me, and its dangling, evasive promises fired me. It was true, too, I liked having land. Wild, scraggy, poor land to develop—rich fat land to prune. I was always making peregrinations to one plantation or another.

Attending commencement exercises at the school on Dewberry, crossing the river to be at the funeral of some old tenant on the Louisiana place, or going to all of them in turn to decorate Christmas trees for the children—all these social activities were apart from the actual business of managing the crops and the cattle and the cotton gin we owned.

Alec kissed me, patted my shoulder, and went off whistling and feeling superior. Before I set out for Wishmore, I went to see Andy Sacks. He had been sick and I'd sent the doctor to him, and I wanted to know what the doctor had said. Also I wanted him to take the medicines the doctor ordered instead of dosing himself with a little coal oil. I had kept my word to Andy, and built him a new cabin. It was set farther back from the road than the other, beyond a narrow lane of crepe myrtles, and was a stout, substantial little house with a screened gallery, the envy and admiration of all his friends and neighbors. His wife had already cut the screen so the cat could get in and out. I scolded her for it, and Andy had patched the place, but I knew she would do it again.

I'd finished my visit and was standing in the road, latching the little gate behind me, when I saw Miss Jessie Bryerson coming along. She had walked all the way from town, she said, and she was dusty but serene, her wide face flushed. People said when she was young she had looked like a rose. She was a faded full-blown ramshackle one now. I knew she was on her way to Rosemont, where she had a habit of appearing. I couldn't discourage her too much, though I didn't want her there. How could I when she'd walked all that way? "Dear Jane, what a nice little house you've built for Andy. Now he'll be perfectly satisfied. He'll never say a word——"

"About what, Miss Jessie?"

"Oh, about anything that ever went on—that dreadful, dreadful time."

I pointed out Andy had already said everything he had to say, and his testimony had been perfectly clear. Miss Jessie just kept smiling at me in her irritating way. I told her I had to go on business down to Wishmore, but she proceeded to go back with me to Rosemont.

She said she wouldn't stop me, she just wanted to sit in the garden awhile and think about the past when she and dear, dear Kate had been girls together. I left her among the roses and chrysanthemums. I suppose she did think about the time when she had been young and lovely, admired for her brains and her beauty; maybe she wondered why life had gone and left her shabby and old and strange and lonely.

I took the path down to Wishmore. This year's corn and cotton had been picked. The tenants had moved away, and I had settled them elsewhere. The birds called to each other. The dredge was busy chewing into the point. I could hear its rumblings. Except for the birds and the dredge there was silence. The house was shut, so were all the cabins—empty and shut, waiting to be torn down, deserted and blank in the sunlight. Swords of light crisscrossed on the surface of the river.

I walked as far as the church the hands had used, and the graveyard around it. They had named it the Evening Shadows Cemetery. There were markers on the graves, but the leaves had drifted thick, hiding the offerings of old bottles and crepe-paper wreaths. Soon the river would be spreading over them all. I smelled the earth, rich, faintly chilly, damp under the rotting leaves. I noticed the faint band, round and even, circling every tree trunk. It showed the depth the last flood had reached, drawing a mysterious ring of shadow around the cemetery. A shadow like a guarded secret, as if the empty peace of this place baffled everything living, seeking, questioning, and restless.

Then I turned away and went back to the house and sat down on the front steps in a patch of sunlight. First I had gone through the house, from room to room. Coming out, 1 locked the door behind me. I don't know why, since it was completely empty. Maybe I wanted to shut in what the walls echoed. Tomorrow the wreckers would come to tear it down. There would be no more walls or steps or windows or doors. I locked the door—I think the first time the door had ever been locked in all its history. Guns sounded out in the swamp where a group of men were hunting. Their sharp cracks were clear against the rumbling of the dredge. Soon the gunners would start for home, and it seemed Mark must come back with them, and we would go in the house together and light the lamps and the fires and shut out the night and the river and the swamp. Only I knew he would never come, no matter how long I waited.

That morning there had been a letter from him. It was not for me, but for Uncle Jeff. Mark's writing on the envelope, under a strange Chinese postmark. Uncle Jeff was dead to the world, and I was too curious and impatient to wait until he woke up. I'd steamed open the letter and read it. And read it again, until I knew every word he had written. Mark had gone to China. I might have known he would. It was like him to give up the place where he was doing well and go off out there where the fighting had begun. It was the fall when the China Incident broke on the world. I had not paid very much attention to the newspaper accounts. It had all seemed so far away. Now it didn't seem so far any more. I had never thought a war in China would affect my life, but ever since I'd read Mark's letter I had known my life was affected, drawn into it.

From the few letters and the presents he sent to Kitty from time to time, I'd tried to weave a background—something solid, where I could place him. I had studied maps and read books. I remembered the names of remote towns, and tried to construct them for myself, the streets and the sounds, and the color of the sunlight, and the people who moved there. What did he eat, where did he sleep—and with whom, what did he do with his spare time?

I followed his flight on the maps, tried to find out about the jungles or deserts he flew over, the climate of them, and what sort of people lived there—if any—and what kinds of animals, and what grew there, and whether there were storms to be encountered, and mountain peaks, all clouded, and, if he were wrecked what chance he'd have of getting out alive. So I had tried to project myself as best I could into countries and climates and among people not my own.

Now he was in China, and I would try to follow him into its vast far-off dangerous reaches. I knew nothing about it, but as I thought over what he had written, I had a sense of masses of people in wild flight, and perilous rivers, and the thickness of invading armies, and the light of burnings. I had an impression of stretches of yellowish dusty soil and over it a steely gray-blue sky, and a glint of steely sharpness—the wings of his plane.

Years ago we had gone on a picnic in Louisiana. At the picnic we met a retired major. He was a flier, too, and he and Mark knew each other. They had first met in France. At the picnic they'd talked together by the hour, reminiscing about the past, discussing the future. When they said good-by, they had agreed to keep in touch with each other. I knew Mark had had at least one letter. Maybe they had kept on writing all these years. I knew the major had now gone out to China, and was training volunteers to fly and fight for the Chinese, gathering the adventurous from every country.

Mark's letter didn't explain if the major had written to him, or if the idea had leaped at him of its own accord. It didn't matter. I knew he would have gone, urged or not. He'd scented war and danger and taken off to get in the thick of it. It was like him to drop everything, the place he'd made for himself, the semisecurity he'd achieved, for something more hazardous.

In his letter he didn't speak of me, except to say, "Please tell Jane to send me some more pictures of Kit." That was all. If I'd ever mattered, I did no longer. What place had I in his expanding horizon? I didn't matter any more than any other possession, and his ownerships were brief. I gloated over houses and furniture, land and crops. Alec had his favorite books. Kitty's things were of supreme importance to her; Arland at least kept what she had, but Mark cut straight through life, caring for no object. Free of them all. He had left this house almost empty-handed, as a plane might zoom through a cloud bank and let the clouds close and form again behind it.

From now on I would follow the war in China, learn the names of strange cities and rivers, try to understand what was behind the news dispatches, let my heart sink at retreats, plow through the war correspondents' reports of what was happening at Nanking. The people around me might be mostly unaware of it—it was so far away, but it would be near to me now. I wondered what would happen to Mark, how long he would stay, what adventures he would have, and how long he would survive.

It was getting late, and I got up. Mark had left Wishmore; now I was leaving it. I would never set foot in this house again. I had been spellbound when I first saw this place, on that hot summer's night. The surrounding dark had enfolded it, and the lamp's dull light had glowed with magic, and all real outlines had been obscure. It was strange how the same words and promises, even the same gestures, were supposed to cover relationships as different in their essence as my easygoing fondness for Alec and the stormy years Mark and I had spent here by the dark river. Anger and violence. . . . But we'd had love too. It had been shot with jealousy, and hate rippled through like lightning, and its symbol was the morning star shining in my window, flaring in a blazing sky.

This house had nothing to give me any more. Let it go. Let the Mississippi pour over Wishmore, taking it back from whence it came. The guns sounded nearer. The men were coming back. Mark was out hunting, too—a different kind of hunt.

In the August of 1939 I had a letter from my old friend, Mr. Dennis. He was in north Mississippi and he wrote how he had noticed the raw earth in a freshly cut bank along a railroad track. Then he noticed the same formation in another place, then another. He was, he said, sending a report to his company. It might be well, he hinted, to watch what might happen up there.

I could just see the raw clay bank in some lonely spot, with the brambles and trees growing on its crest, and in the distance a short train, with an old-fashioned engine poking along vaguely from one isolated spot to another. That red earth, so poor, producing poverty and spindly cotton, held the promise of bursting riches.

It was not long before all the newspapers told of drillers rushing to that area, and I read every scrap of news with wild excitement. That lonely country with its disheveled cabins and scrawny mules and old-fashioned plows became suddenly charged with twentieth-century activity: men and trucks and machines, drillers and speculators and lawyers.

They hit it. Oil at last! A proven field in Mississippi, and rippling excitement stirred and swelled in our own town. Strangers with stuffed brief cases appeared with magic speed in the hotel lobby. The roads began to shake with huge truckloads of oil machinery, the summer sun making the long steel pipes glisten. Then everybody and anybody who owned an inch of land was besieged. The oil companies wanted leases, and they wanted to buy royalties and they wanted to buy mineral rights. They came to Rosemont in droves. It was a ticklish business dealing with them, but I enjoyed the game. I learned to play it, learned not to be too eager to come to an agreement. I held out against them, and laughed at their first offers. Finally I leased some of Dewberry at a dollar an acre and a dollar renewal, on not too long a lease. I could afford to wait. I owned so much land and had bought so many leases I was in a strategic position. They had to come to me. I was slow in committing myself; I'd rather keep freedom of action on most of my property. They planned to drill all over the county. Before, they had gone only six thousand feet, to the Wilcox formation. Now they had machinery to pierce twice that depth. Besides, the world, teetering on the brink of war, would need oil—all they could get.

"How does it feel to be right?" Alec asked. I had come in to tell him I had signed the lease. He was in the library, hanging over the radio. I turned it off to talk, but just before I flipped the dial, I caught what the announcer was saying. It shocked me out of my exhilarated mood. I had been busy all year. Cotton was going up, Kitty was growing up, and the oil situation was hot as hot. The town had begun to bustle with new life. The Negroes were spending money, and the cafés were full of hard-eyed, hard-muscled drilling crews. The hotel lobby, where once Miss Jessie had sat in spendid solitude, was milling with oilmen and lawyers and speculators, day and night. Even at parties nobody talked of anything but oil and whether they would or wouldn't lease. The outside world, so long ignored, and ignoring, had seeped in, changing us. Now the outside world had come right here into this room. It was a beautiful room, giving a sense of depth and space, as though living could be unhurried and leisure important, here within its book-lined walls. The voice on the radio threatened it. Nothing was safe.

"Will they fight, Alec?"

"I'm afraid so. It's too late to stop now."

I groaned. "But maybe we won't get in." I thought of the China war, which Mark was already in. Anyway, he had still kept alive.

"Don't be too sure. We always have. Look at all those French and Indian wars. What were they but part of European struggles. Look at the War of 1812. Part of the Napoleonic Wars. And then we had all the advantages of the fact there was such a thing as distance. Now there isn't any."

Unfortunately I'd found out Alec was usually right about things like that. His ideas, delivered from the depths of an armchair, with a drink beside him and a cigarette coiling smoke from between his fingers, were sound.

It was in practical plans that he fell down. They sounded wonderful, but didn't pan out when put to work. He laughed about it himself. More and more he'd come to let me have my way about his property as well as my own. Lapped in the comfort and luxury of Rosemont, Alec could dilate by the hour on the effect of the freight rates on the economy of the South, the Negro problem, and the cotton market. He discoursed mightily on diversified crops and bettering the situation of the tenants, but I was the one who struggled through the intricacies of the government loans, saw that the planting was done, kept the cabins in repair, and sent the sick hands to the doctor. The people of the town had come to admire me, as they, too, began to want more and more the things I'd always wanted. I think my colored people admired me too. I worked for their good.

He was a perfect host, easy and effortless. He made himself delightful to the aunts, paying them that court so dear to old ladies, and he was never impatient, as I was, with Mr. Jeff's gyrations. As a landholder he distributed candy to the pickaninnies and joked and laughed with the older ones, and listened by the hour to their woes. To them, he was the source of all blessings. Even Kitty felt that way. Alec's perfectly chosen and perfectly timed presents meant more to her, I believe, than my long fight to give her the sort of background she wanted and I wanted for her.

I sat down and began tearing open my letters, glancing at them and putting them aside. Kitty was giving a big party tonight and I was in a hurry. I flipped the pages of a new magazine, and suddenly Mark looked at me. "Colonel Mark Lennerd of the Flying Tigers", his picture, and an account of his exploits. I read it, then showed it to Alec. "He's been there almost two years and he isn't dead yet."

"Coming along, isn't he? If he can stand the pace, and I guess he can, he'll get more and more famous. Doesn't look like he's changed much."

"He's got a lot of wrinkles."

Kitty came in while we were talking about him, and saw the picture. "Isn't that grand? Why, he's a hero! I'm so proud of him!"

Her admiration stung me. She wrote to him now and then. I had instructed her to describe the life we lived here at Rosemont. I'd wanted him to know I was a success, but he had never cared for things like that anyway. I had not been prepared for him to become one too. I resented this troublesome and troubled world now shrieking for men like Mark and finding them all too scarce. Now he was part of larger issues, more important than I could ever be, and more useful.

When Kitty had left the room, taking the magazine with her, Alec said, "Cheer up, Jane. I always told you Mark was made for war. You be satisfied with the arts of peace."

"When a war is on the arts of war seem more important. Anyway, it makes me damn mad for Kit to get up a sort of worship for him at this late date and think he's wonderful and boast about him. He shot off like a bat out of hell without giving her a thought! I feel as cross and snappish about it as one of the workers in the vineyard— one of the ones who struggled through the heat of the day, then found the latecomers got the same old penny. I never did see the justice of it!"

I went off to attend to Kitty's party. Arland came over to help me with the flowers. She had a touch with them I never could acquire. After they were all fixed we went on the gallery to have a coke. "How beautiful this place is, Jane. Think of all the other beautiful places in the world; so many of them will be destroyed and wrecked. It's sickening. I hope someone will always take good care of Rosemont; there might not be many lovely things left when all this is over. Of course the other war was terrible, but I was so young and foolish I was more excited than anything else. Now I know better. You can always stand up to anything, Jane, but I feel old and useless."

"We won't be in it," I said, but I heard a steady thudding, as if merging armies far way sent shuddering echoes over every inch of ground all over the world: it was just my own heartbeats I was hearing.

"Everything spiraling down and nobody able to stop it." Arland made a twisting motion with her hands. I could just see a plane streaking down the sky with Mark in it, but I was only looking at the mild and empty air above the stretch of lawn and the silky interwoven tints of the garden.

I asked Arland if she had seen Mark's picture and she said she

246

had, and we talked about him some. When she left, I walked part of the way to the gate with her and watched her as she went on to her car, parked outside the gate. The statues were rosy in the afterglow stealing through the dark leaves, and the light wove a web around Arland, deepening the gloss of her hair and the color of her dress and the warmth of her skin until she moved in the deeper shadows. Beyond the gate heavy trucks went grinding down the hill where they were taking oil rigging down to Wishmore. They had begun to drill down there, and all the town was watching and waiting for the results.

Rosemont was built for lavish decorative effect and, little by little, I had restored its old splendor and revived its original intention. I had sent samples of the upholstery and hangings to Lyons; they still had the old patterns and rewove the material for me. The double parlors were in pale ashes-of-roses brocade, and some of the little chairs were worked in petit point in faded pearly tones, doves and garlands. The draperies in the dining room are more vivid, and in the library, darker and deeper.

After twilight the candles were lit inside and the Chinese lantern lit outside, and all the doors and windows stood wide open. The orchestra came, then the crowd of boys and girls and a sprinkling of older people. The vastness of the rooms showed off the grace of the girls in their whirling dresses. Through the massed lights and flowers their faces sparkled again in the mirrors.

Nobody seeing the house tonight would dream it had ever been shuttered and darkened and isolated; nobody would think about the murderer who had once stalked through the flowering garden, where the lanterns swayed and clustered like Aladdin's jeweled fruit. Miss Kate's screams didn't echo any more. Even I seldom remembered them. Her pearls were around my neck. I don't really love them the way Arland loves hers—Uncle gave them to her on her sixteenth birthday—but mine are larger and more impressive. When people admire them I say, "Yes, they were Miss Kate's." At first they used to recoil a little. When I first wore them Aunt Em said, "Oh, Jane, how can you? They would make my Flesh Creep," or, "Pearls mean tears." But she is used to them now. They don't haunt me. I am too tough.

Kitty came down and Stephen was waiting for her at the bottom of the steps. He was not seeing his cousin and playmate, but a new

Kitty, almost a stranger, flinging a soft enchanting disguise over the Kitty he'd always known. She was poised and self-possessed. Perhaps almost too complete, too finished, for her age. She had none of the uncertainties and awkwardnesses prophesying change and evolution. She was happy tonight; she had always had a taste for grandeur and formality.

Arland came in. Sometimes her beauty seemed veiled and unemphasized, as though shadowed and suppressed by the restraints she put on herself. Not tonight. My thick skin and small features stood time pretty well. I had a little pucker between my eyes and was getting a line around my mouth—too much strenuous concentration. I looked younger than I was, but tonight Arland looked as though age would never touch her at all. She wore clusters of grapes in her hair and a sweeping violet dress, catching jeweled lights in the candles' glow.

"Those lengths of purple make me think of Tyrian dyes," Alec said, "and triremes drifting on wine-dark seas, and Homer's long-limbed women weaving webs of fine linen."

She went in to dance. All the young boys danced with me dutifully, but they danced with her because they wanted to.

Later in the evening I went upstairs to Kitty's room. The lights were off. I wondered why, and went to turn them on. Then I heard a rustle and saw the pale blur of a dress. Kitty was huddled by the window, crying. "What on earth's the matter, child?" Kitty, the belle of the party—of all parties!—crying up here in the dark.

"It's Steve," she gulped, "and that Emmy Barringer!"

Emmy was a redheaded nymph, and I had noticed Steve dancing with her. "She's vamped him, Mother. He's going to take her riding during intermission—she told me so!" She choked on a sob. "I've always loved him, and I thought he loved me. Now she'll get him!"

"One ride doesn't mean much; don't carry on over it. You have everything!"

Emmy was undoubtedly beautiful, but everybody said she drank too much and necked heavily.

"She's not a very nice girl, Kit."

"She's not nice at all!" Kitty sat up and wiped her eyes and turned on the lights. "Mother, there's something strange about that girl, and for her to rope Steve in—— I just can't stand it!"

"Maybe if you just dropped a hint about her——"

"Oh, Mother, he'd just think I was a cat. It would just make him all the more curious about her! You know that."

It was true enough. "But, Kitty, you can hold your own."

"With anyone else; not with her. I'm pretty enough, but she's just bursting with sex appeal. They fall for her; they can't seem to help themselves!"

I hated Emmy Barringer with a hatred I hadn't felt since I'd hated Ludie Daniels, and I knew exactly what Kitty meant. Ludie showed her age now; she was thick and fat, her pink-and-whiteness slapped on and caking off, her black eyes hard in puffs of flesh. She was just what I had foreseen she would be—not that it mattered any more to me what she was.

Maybe Emmy would grow old and ugly and of ill repute some day, but it didn't help Kitty now. By that time it might be too late.

Of course Kitty didn't know how deeply I shared her feelings. She thought of me as a highly practical, thoroughly respectable woman. It never dawned on her that I knew anything about passion, a passion darker and deeper than any she would ever feel. Even if I had told her, she still wouldn't have believed me. She saw me in such a different light. I had had no one to fight for me, but I would fight for her.

"Go wash your face and put on your make-up," I told her briskly. "And get down there to your guests and behave yourself. I'll see if I can't cook up something."

"Mother, do you think you can?" She had faith in my powers, but I had no idea what to do.

A little while later when I was telling all this to Arland, I saw Kitty on the dance floor, smiling and self-possessed again. Steve, though, was dancing with Emmy. He looked troubled, but fascinated.

"What can we do, Arland?"

"Not anything. Steve has sense; she won't take him far."

"No man has sense in a thing like this. She's an aristocratic and latter-day Ludie Daniels."

Arland was watching Emmy. "Ludie was of the earth—earthy. This girl's a modernized version. There's something off key about her, Jane. I can't quite place it. I believe she's neurotic."

As soon as Arland said that I knew it was so. Emmy laughed as she passed us. There was excitement in her laugh; she was highly charged, too keyed up, but she did give off an exciting quality. Her red lips writhed back from her little shiny teeth. I hated her so, her beauty seemed repulsive.

"I'll do something," I muttered. "Just watch me." Kitty was my child; I'd fight for her tooth and claw. They said Emmy liked to drink. I took up my station at the punch bowl. The punch was somewhat spiked, but not too much so for the young. Trays of highballs were being passed. While the servants were busy refilling the bowl, and nobody was looking, I half filled two empty cups with straight whisky, then filled them up to the top with the punch. So, when at the end of the dance Emmy came up to the table, I was ready for her. She drank what I gave her without a quiver. Then I offered her a second cup. "It's such a hot night." She hesitated a little, then drank it. The avid way she swallowed it showed me she had a taste for it. It was more than wanting to be gay at a party. I should not have encouraged her, but if she had the tendency, this one time wouldn't make any real difference. She'd either fight it or give in to it. Her afterhistory showed me I did perfectly right in trying to keep Steve away from her.

Her laugh grew louder, her startlingly bright eyes grew blank. I left the table, but in a few minutes she was back, holding out her cup for more.

Not long before intermission there was a small commotion. Emmy had passed out. I went over to her. Her face was blue-white, her lips curled back; she was as limp and grotesque as one of those lank boudoir dolls. Her sister Isabel hung over her, looking miserable. Steve came up and hovered around, asking if he could help. He didn't look fascinated any more, only worried. "She's so dead pale," he whispered. "She scares me." I knew he must be thanking his stars it hadn't happened when she was on his hands.

"Don't be upset, my dear," Alec said to poor Isabel. "We'll take her upstairs and fix her up, and later I'll drive her home myself. You stay down here and have a good time."

We put her on the bed in one of the rooms upstairs. "I'll leave one of the servants with her, and look in from time to time," I said.

"How in the world did she happen to get so drunk, Jane?" Alec asked. "Steve says she was at the punch table a lot, but none of the others are even tight. It's bad—such a young kid."

"She likes it, so I hear."

"Looks that way. You should have stopped her, Jane."

"My dear, how on earth could I watch them all?"

He admitted I couldn't. Arland didn't say a word about the incident, either then or later, but maybe she guessed something. And I am sure Kitty must have suspected. Emmy never opened her eyes until the dance was over. I didn't care what I had done when I saw Kitty dancing with Steve again. He drew her arm within his and they went out. They paused on the gallery a minute, talking. Kitty touched the orchids on her shoulder; he had given them to her. She looked up at him, then ran down the steps, catching up the foam of her dress. She stood there outlined, the slimness of her waist defined, her face tilted up, smiling. Steve followed her, taking her outstretched hand, and they moved off. Lantern glow fell on them, flinging rose and gold on her pale skirts and their laughing faces.

Alec joined me. "Come to the edge of the hill and let's look at Wishmore," I suggested.

We went through the back gate. Behind us the garden spread, landscaped, terraced, restored. The box was clipped, and the fountain played. Farther back the house streamed with light and music. As we went toward the edge of the slope, the throb of machinery down at Wishmore mingled with the dance tune, then dominated it, and at last quenched it altogether.

The river flowed through Wishmore Point now. They were drilling just beyond the cutoff. The tall webbed superstructure, pricked out with a thousand lights, reared against the swamp. The matted trees looked unreal in the glare, and the water jumped and quivered with brilliance. The machine age had invaded the primitive fastnesses of the point.

"Isn't it beautiful? Isn't it wonderful?" I sighed. "And they are going to drill out on Dewberry soon—on the piece I bought from Gertrude. They want to buy royalties. I'll sell some and I think I'll hang onto the rest. That way if we strike it, I'll have plenty, and if it's a dry hole——"

"You'll still have a good chunk of money."

"Thirty thousand dollars."

"If they hit it at Dewberry, are you going to give Gertrude any?" I laughed. "Why on earth should I?"

"No real reason; only you have a lot now, and she hasn't anything. She comes out the little end of the horn."

"Well, she sold it, and I bought it. If she hadn't sold it to me, somebody else would have bought it by now anyway, and you wouldn't feel any other buyer ought to share it with her, would you? I took the risks."

"Only, if she'd waited, she'd have had a better price. Jane, what really made you think there was oil around here?" He looked at me. "I know you had faith—everybody extols your vast faith—and you gambled, but there must have been some shred of something in your mind."

So I told him what Mr. Dennis had said. "I thought he seemed pretty smart, but of course he could have been wrong—dead wrong. And I might easily have been in the soup——"

"Instead of sitting pretty. That's true. You played to win, and you won. But you didn't tell anybody, did you?"

"Not a soul."

Alec gave a sort of sigh. He looked back at the house, then down at Wishmore. "It's a perfect reproduction of the good old days, isn't it? You've done it up brown. Flowers, candles, floating dresses, rich spiced food, pretty girls and fine young men and love-making. It could be '61, brink of the war and all. 'Rosemont, where the Old South still lives' "—he quoted our favorite Pilgrimage slogan. " 'And Wishmore, where the New South's being born.' "

·§ Chapter Seventeen

The progress of the well was a closely guarded secret, but I knew the tests were running high. Too many assorted people were trying to buy up too many mineral rights and royalties and leases all around. Some people parted with leases and property too soon and too cheaply; some would certainly hold out too long, passing up good offers in wild expectation of oil spouting from every pore of the earth where none would be. It was a tricky game. I sat and waited for Wishmore, like a hen on a nest.

One morning, before daybreak, we had the news. Wishmore had come in, and Alec and I were down the hill before sunup to share the excitement. The town went wild, and everybody streamed out to see the well. Gertrude gave a see-the-well picnic on the hillside. I was highly extolled for my faith in my section of the country, my town, my land, and myself. "It must be a supreme moment, Jane," Alec said to me.

"It's some comfort to know I won't be one of those genteely starving old ladies so plentiful around here in my youth."

The greatest change took place in the town between the time Wishmore well came in and Dewberry came in a year later. The dreamy isolation was gone—I hoped forever. Factories, big modernistic things, were sprouting their strange growth on the outskirts of town; buildings were changing hands, or being torn down to make way for bigger newer ones. The population doubled. You used to know everyone on the street; now you could walk for blocks without seeing a familiar face. I fitted into the new scheme of things much better than I had into the old.

Yet that summer night in 1941, the day the well at Dewberry came in, I was glad to shut the gates of Rosemont at last and hole in with just Alec and Arland. You couldn't really taste the sweet juices of triumph in the summer of 1941. No matter how often I cut off the radio, or how hard I tried to concentrate on my own affairs, I still had an uneasy sense that the tenure of all possessions was uncertain, and getting more so. It gave me something of the uncomfortable feeling I used to have when we felt it was going to be a big high-water year. You heard of heavy snows up North, and you heard the rain patter, patter, and you watched the drift and scud gather on the heavy river; then it rose and it rose and the levees kept breaking, and you didn't know what would happen next, or how deep the water would get.

I kept saying we wouldn't get in it. I said it firmly to the aunts that night before the good ladies were escorted home by Alec. Though they were completely unaware of that fact, they were all rather tight, because they had taken so many potations in honor of the well. But Aunt Ada would never connect her bursts of laughter, or Aunt Em her rather weepy fit, with the fact that they had imbibed a little lady-like punch and just a bit of liqueur after dinner, to say nothing of wine during dinner.

"Aren't the aunts funny?" I said to Arland. "They all disapproved of my marrying Mark, and then they carried on because I got a divorce and married Alec. You remember what they said about my coming here to live? Now you'd think they'd thought it all up themselves. You remember how they bucked against the idea of the first Pilgrimage? Now it's practically the center and mainstay of their lives. They scorned all my plans and nearly had a fit at my money-grubbing ways——"

" 'Chimerical' was the word." Arland smiled. "Yet they do rather lap up the results of your un-Ellistonlike activities."

"To hear them talk, you'd think they advised and counseled everything I've ever done. I suppose it's something to have shucked off the role of poor Jane."

I left Arland and Alec listening to the ten-o'clock news and went down to the second terrace. The radio's doleful voice made me nervous, and on this day and through this evening I wanted to regain a sense of elation. I sat down on a marble bench among the white flowers growing here. All the flowers on this terrace were white. I'd planted lilies in thick clumps, and they were in bloom now: spider lilies, and those white ones with wine-colored stripes, and butterfly lilies. They showed mothlike in the dark—fragile and tremulous in a light breeze, but they gave out a lush and heady perfume in the hot air.

The terrace was Arland's idea. She was a nighttime creature anyhow. Holly Trees and its inhabitants were always particularly alive in the smallest hours, the servants rambling from church or trailing back from their amusements, and Arland sitting up late, talking to her cronies, or else, when they were gone, reading, or fixing herself something to eat, or trying on clothes.

She had read a poem somewhere about pale flowers, and a purling fountain in the moonlight, and a white peacock dozing beside it, and thought it would be delicious for this spot. I'd built the fountain and it was trickling nicely, but I had not yet acquired the peacock. Now this second well had come in I might get one, though it would probably escape out of the back gate and do its drowsing on the hill and spoil the intended effect. I might also extend the garden to include the next slope, enlarge the pond in the hollow, and put a swan or so on it, in a poetic manner, though I was told swans are perfectly hateful in real life. I might and could do anything now. Also, I decided I would buy the finest fur coat I could find for Gertrude. That would please her and, I hoped, Alec too.

I sat looking toward the house, wishing I had gotten more brocade from France when I had been able to; now of course it was out of the question. Most of the contents of Rosemont had originally come from France and England. One of the tourists had told me the reason these houses were full of French and English stuff was that in the early days it was easier to ship it from Europe than to haul things from the North to the South. Anyway, the things in the house had doubled and tripled in value since I had acquired them; antiques were no longer a drug on the market.

Alec had turned off the radio, and I saw Arland go from the library to the front parlor and sit down at the piano. There was a vine festooned across the window, starred with that tiny, milky sort of jessamine. A silvery light fell across Arland's face from the shaded sconces. Music came slipping from her fingers. I vaguely recognized the waltz she was playing. It had been popular when we were girls. Against my will it made me feel nostalgic. It reminded me of long summer days, and Uncle sitting in his favorite shady corner of the gallery, and all the group gathered around the piano, singing and laughing. I hadn't been happy then. Now I wished I had enjoyed it all more; if I could go back, I would savor and cherish some of the things and some of the people I had taken so for granted. It was long gone: I couldn't get back to it or the world that went with it.

Uncle was dead, and Tim was dead, and Aunt Tee was dead, and Mark was a world away. The waltz wove on, spun-sugar music, of no real importance, yet given dignity by the dark and the thoughts it evoked. I had felt such wild yearnings on nights like this, summer nights full of promise. I had such visions of perfect happiness. Why had I muffed my chances at it? Because I had had a chance if I had just played my hand another way. I would have been happier and it would have been easier just to have followed Mark wherever he had wanted to go, and basked in his reflected glory instead of making my own success.

I couldn't help resenting the influence of his growing name. Stephen and his friends were making him into a sort of dream hero— the way we'd made Tim. Old Mr. Laidlaw's eulogistic biography of Tim had created a mild flutter of interest some years ago, but the old gentleman had died soon after, and this was a different world. Tim didn't belong to it, and people were forgetting all about him. Mark did belong to it, and he had come into his own. It annoyed me for Steve and Kitty and the whole town to idealize him the way they were doing. I had an eye for detecting in people whether or not they were going to amount to something; it was the only sort of intuition I did have—the same sort of sense that made me feel Mr. Dennis was right, that made me feel there was something special about wild young Jerry Radner. Now the whole world could see in Mark what I had seen when we had first met. I had lost my vision of what he was, and what he could be, and then I had lost him.

Arland said once that what men want is for a woman to sustain an image, so they can see themselves in her eyes. That's what she tried to do for Tim—I suppose that's why he had always loved her best. Only the picture she had held up to him of himself had been too much for him to meet, and he'd gotten tired of trying to. But if I had just held onto what I had first thought about Mark, he would have filled in the outline.

For a minute I thought I was back in the days when I was young and waiting for Mark. I heard footsteps and rustlings along the path, and it gave me almost a feeling he was coming toward me, out of the dark. But it was Stephen, holding back the bushes for Kitty to pass.

She came over to me and gave me one of her rare kisses. "Mother, we're engaged."

It was what she wanted, and what I had always wanted for her. They weren't too nearly related, and it would unite the Lennerd property, and they suited each other. But loneliness suddenly ached all through me. "You're both too young, child."

"Maybe in ordinary times," Steve said. "But I'm going to try for the Navy, and we'd rather get things settled between us before I go away."

This war, such a long distance off, was coming nearer and nearer. First Mark, then Steve. Kitty and Steve stayed talking to me awhile, then went to the house to tell Alec and Arland. Joyce was Steve's biological mother, but Arland had always been his real mother. Joyce was pleasant enough to him; her house was full of pictures of Steve as a baby, always taken with her. They were perfect mother-and-child pictures, but when he wanted someone to talk to, or needed sympathy, he always went to Arland. I remember the time someone ran over his puppy. He came storming in, holding the dead dog. Joyce was doing her nails. "Too bad, dear," she'd said, "but you can get another." I was groping for words to comfort him, but before I could speak, he was off. He went to Arland and stayed all day. She treated him as a grown person, and encouraged him to make his own decisions and use his own judgment.

He had been happy here, and had enjoyed his life. He was a good hunter and a patient fisherman. He loved these slopes and ravines. The sleepy soft winters brought him joy, and the hot summers other joys. He'd spent many before-daylight hours shivering in a duck blind, with the cold wind blowing from the river; and so many long hot days fishing from his boat; and so many summer nights, lying on the sand bar, feeling the warm breeze coming from the Gulf.

Steve doesn't talk much, but when I heard him discussing anything with Arland, or his intimate friends, I was surprised at how much he did know. He has helped his father with the plantation, and has read all Alec's books about modern economic problems, and sometimes they argued far into the night. But all those pacifist books and teaching that are supposed to have softened his generation didn't seem to have affected him very much. He didn't want to go away to fight, but if he had to, he would. And when he came back—if he came back, and I wouldn't allow myself to ever think he wouldn't—the place he had left would fit him again. Maybe not at first, but later.

The three of us went up to the house to tell Alec and Arland. Later, when Alec and I were in our own room, he said, "You've planned for this a long time, haven't you, Jane?"

"Almost ever since they were babies," I admitted.

"And, as usual, you succeeded."

I had made a new life for myself and, looking in the mirror, I knew I had almost made a new face for myself. I was better-looking now than I'd ever been. "But it ought to be a good marriage," I said.

"It ought. And, strangely enough, so is ours—though it got off to a rather forlorn start." He was smiling at me, and I got up and put my arms around his neck.

"You've had a lot to put up with, taking me on when you did." I gave him a kiss. "You're chary about saying it, but you must have loved me."

"I did. In my way. I still do. There have been times when I wanted to bash in your busy little brains, but I held my hand, too curious to see what you'd be up to next."

Somehow I felt that Alec knew all about me. Even about my taking the money. Or at least he must have guessed something near the truth. But he didn't say anything, and I was grateful to him. The money didn't matter any more. Alec and I had married. And what should have been Michael's didn't matter either now. Kitty and Steve would get everything, and then their children.

On the seventh of that December I had turned on the radio to get the symphony. There were a few bars of music, then the announcer's voice cutting in. I'll never forget how it sounded—as though all the harmony that had ever been in the world was broken and jangled forever.

Steve and Kitty had just left the house together, walking off in the pale winter sunlight. Let them go on. They didn't have to know yet; they'd find out soon enough.

We sat up nearly all that night, listening to the radio. After a while, Kitty slipped off. I went after her, and found her in her own room, crying. It was a pretty room, flowery and taffeta-hung. So fit for a girl who had been sheltered and indulged. It made me sad to think of Kitty having to face the real and difficult world she lived in.

"I know how you feel, child, but it's no use to cry. It won't get you anywhere."

She sat up, shaking back her blond hair. "I'll fix up my face and go down. I can't afford to waste a minute of being with Steve. He goes

258

tomorrow. But he's pretty sure he can get back for a day or so around Christmas. We've talked it all over, and we want to be married then. The day after Christmas."

They had planned the wedding for the spring. Kitty and I were never very articulate with each other. She didn't say, "It may be the last Christmas we'll ever have with each other." She didn't say it, but I knew she was thinking it. She only said, "I want it to be grand, and big—the grandest and biggest wedding this town has ever seen."

"How can I possibly fix all that by the day after Christmas?"

"Please, Mother. You know you can! You know 'Jane Lennerd can manage anything.' "

"All right. I'll try." The work involved would keep me from thinking. "Then what do you intend to do?"

"Go with Steve. Follow him around until he's sent out of the country. Something tells me it won't be so long, either."

"Oh, Kitty, stay at home. Stay here and wait. Don't go off to some dump; you'll be perfectly miserable."

It was really no use to argue; her mind was made up. "I always wanted you and Steve to marry, but I didn't picture it like this. I thought you'd have a lovely wedding when you were older, and settle down in the wing, and everything would be perfect. Not a hurried-up thing like this, with you leaving home, and Steve's going off to war." They were made for each other, suitable in every way, if only this wretched war hadn't come to spoil it all. I'd tried my best not to think about the war, tried to feel it would never involve us, and here it was, come into all our lives. It had really come into my life back in '37, when Mark had gone to China.

"It isn't perfect. I don't suppose anything is ever going to be any more. But sometimes you have to take what you can get on any terms you can get it."

I knew that. I had taken what I could get. Half a loaf. Sometimes, though, I've thought no bread, and a resignation to no bread, might have been better. But I knew that in Kitty's place I would have done what she was doing. I had been eighteen once myself, but of course she couldn't realize that.

We'd win this beastly business, but when I thought of all we'd have to plow through before we did win it, then scrabble around in the wreckage and try to put things together again—— Fine new world indeed! For the first time I really looked at the future with flagging energy. I was feeling the first whiff of old age.

I tried to busy my mind with practical details. "Why don't you ask Arland to give you Doña Ana's portrait for a wedding present?"

"We've got a God's plenty of portraits, Mother. Besides, Arland's fond of Doña Ana."

"She'd look wonderful in the front parlor."

Kitty smiled. "You've always hankered for her, haven't you? Besides, Steve wouldn't like it."

"Now's the time to ask for it."

"But Steve wouldn't like it. He'd think it was sort of snide—like Salome's asking."

Maybe Kitty was right. She handled Steve better than I had ever handled Mark. True, Steve was a lot easier to handle, but Kitty was better able than I was to bridge those deep chasms separating men from women, or, for that matter, one human being from another.

Kitty's wedding was big and was grand. I spared no trouble and no expense, and it was even finer than Arland's had been, and on just as traditional lines.

Kitty looked beautiful, and I was as gorgeous as possible in deep rose and silver. There was, of course, the usual little contretemps with Uncle Jeff. Seasons of high revel disoriented him, and when it was almost time for him to be arrayed in his dress suit, he was nowhere to be found. The thought of rummaging through the swamp for him on a cold December evening was disheartening, but it had to be done; the family had to be assembled.

"You better let me round him up," Alec offered. "That old fisherman he likes has come back to moor his boat at the point; that's where he is." So Alec went off. I was afraid he'd linger with the fisherman too—a salty character, teller of tall stories, but after a while he came back with Mr. Jeff in tow. We whisked Mr. Jeff into his finery, and he emerged stately and resplendent, and stalked down the aisle to his allotted place. With his crest of white hair and black eyebrows he looked an upholder of family dignity, and at the reception he drank his champagne with the air of never sinking low enough to consume any lesser beverage.

Alec gave Kitty away. Mark should have been here. He had cabled blessings. Hero he might be, but he had certainly put his family aside.

I had pointed out that fact to Kitty in no uncertain terms. Stephen and his best man and all the groomsmen were in uniform. The lights gleamed on gold braid and airmen's wings. They looked wonderful— so straight and tall and young, but it made everybody weepish.

All the old inhabitants and all the young gathered at Rosemont for the reception. I had followed all the traditions, only more so, but there were changes from Arland's wedding. All the young men in uniform were going to war, not coming back from it. There was too much ahead of us all. The phalanx of the aunts lacked dear Tee, and we all missed her. There was no Cousin Charlie and no Miss Jessie, and Miss Constance was too old and ill to leave her house. I had gone to see her not long ago. She had offered me cherry cordial, that potent brew of old ladies, and we had waxed sentimental over it. "I admire you, Jane, and what you've done. Now I wish I could go to Rosemont and see Kitty married. I hope and pray Steve will come back and they will have a full, happy life together."

The Querrell girls and Mrs. Van Delevan were no more. All these people I'd known so well had grown into before-the-fire legends to Kitty and her friends. Aunt Em and Cousin Olive were venerable fossils, and my generation was Old in Kitty's eyes.

Kitty was going away. One reason I had always been anxious for her to marry Steve was that she would live here. War brides all over the country were following their husbands. They were just war brides. Kitty was Kitty. She would come back, but would Steve? And what would it do to her if he didn't?

I knew Arland was worrying about him. Joyce was as blandly pink and white and gold as ever. Michael, she said, had told her not to worry, so she wasn't. Being a complete vegetable had preserved her. Just as Alec's growing laziness is what makes him so agreeable. His nerves are unstrained by continual striving. It's a fallacy that hard work is good for people; it's souring.

Gertrude had lived hard, and showed it, and didn't care. I'd lived hard, and tried not to show it. I still cared how I looked and continually struggled to look and seem young. But who was this raddled hag coming up to fling herself in my arms? Hollow eyes and wrinkled painted face . . . it was Claire. She lived in an unluxurious and narrow way up North. She had been divorced and had never remarried, though from Cousin Olive's reports on her, she had always been about to make a wonderful match. It had never come off. I accepted Claire's embraces as though we'd always been the best of friends. She gasped at the changes she found everywhere: Gertrude my satellite, the town revolving around me. I could afford to be amiable. She was the poor relation now. I wondered why I had ever been jealous of her. It had been such a waste of emotion.

The Delmans were on hand of course. The elderly couple, still handsome, stood together beaming on their grandchild and Kitty. Kitty's children would be part Delman, but it no longer seemed strange. Mr. Delman had returned to the hearth after his wanderings. After so many heartburnings the husband and wife were united, proud of their children and concerned for them. Rita had come for the wedding. She could have been just like her mother, but she had taken a different course. She still had her vigorous beauty and had evidently curbed her tendency to get too fat. She introduced her husband, a prominent doctor, and in her looks and her conversation and her marriage there was no trace of the early Delman atmosphere. Ellen and her husband had come too. He was a newspaper correspondent, about to leave for England, and Ellen's eyes filled with tears when he spoke of it. She was more like Joyce than like Rita, less pretty than Joyce, but with a thousand times more feeling and mind.

They'd heard from Robert—Butch to me—since Pearl Harbor. He was in the Pacific now. There was no reason Kitty shouldn't ally herself with the Delmans.

The firelight flickered over the walls, and above the crowds of people the eyes of the ancestors came alive. I was not given to worshiping them, but tonight they had a certain reality for me. It was a time to hold on to what you had and savor it a little, before it might be snatched away. How strange Wishmore would look to the Lennerd who'd fought in the Tripolitan war and won this land. In his day the passenger pigeons had gone winging over the point, darkening the sky. The pigeons had vanished, and the earth was pumping out oil. These young men grouped here, some of them in the Navy's blue, were talking of bombs and planes. Josiah Lennerd in his bobbing sail-spread ship had never dreamed of such things.

There was the slim dreamy-eyed Lennerd in Confederate gray, his gloved hand on his sword. Steve had found that very sword upstairs and had gone lunging around with it for days. This boy had never come back from his war. There was a batch of poems in the attic in a trunk. They were sentimental verses, written in his flowing hand, with curlicues around the letters. He looked like a poet, but he wasn't. Not from the stuff I'd found. He didn't look like a soldier or a leader, but war had made him one. He might have been among the very great ones, but he was killed too soon. War had been his art. It would have been so much better if he had never been forced to find it out. So much better if the questions of slavery and secession had never boiled up, or else had been thrashed out without fighting. It would have been nice if he had been able to keep on writing silly verses to young ladies no doubt equally silly.

If only Stephen and these other boys could stay safe and commonplace, and not have to go out and prove themselves. Among them were born soldiers and leaders. At least I hoped so, since we depended on them and others like them to save our hides. It was fantastic to think our fate rested in the hands of these children. We would win, but victory wouldn't bring back the ones who died winning.

Then I was upstairs, helping Kitty dress, then I was at the door, watching the car take her away. It was all the way I had planned for so many years. She and Steve were married. They were in love, and they were rich, and the Lennerd property would be united in them. Everything was just as I wanted, except for the dominant, unescapable fact of the war. I had thought of this wedding when they were safe in their happy childhood. Now they were no longer children, and they were no longer safe. There was nothing I could do to make them safe. The war was the monstrous unknown quantity looming up to spoil all my foresight. The guests went on drinking and dancing for a long time before they left, and long before they were gone the house seemed empty to me. Alec went upstairs, and I put my hand on Arland's arm. "Stay awhile. I know I won't sleep a wink."

She hesitated, then she said, "I have something I must tell you, but I was going to wait until tomorrow."

"Tell me now. I'm not going to bed anyway."

We sat on the love seats in the front parlor, facing each other. "Poor brats, why couldn't they have had all this and not have to go out and find the war facing them?" I sighed.

"It's hard to pick out the right time to be born. When we came into the world it all seemed quiet enough, but we got mixed up in two wars."

"Kitty argues we had a chance to live our lives between them. Only we're still here and have to get through with this one, and, though she seems to think we're old enough to be through with everything important, we don't think so at all."

Arland got up and stood with her hands on the mantelpiece. "Mark should have seen her tonight."

"He sent a cable."

"I know," she answered. "He's on his way to Washington on an important mission."

"How do you know, Arland?"

"He sent me a cable too."

"What on earth for?" I demanded.

"Jane, I'm going to tell you something that will sound completely fantastic to you, but I might as well tell you; there's so little time to talk. He wants me to meet him in Washington."

I could only repeat her words after her. They made no sense.

"He's going to be there a month, maybe longer. Jane, I don't know how to say this: he wants me to meet him there and marry him. And I'm going."

ᴥ§ Chapter Eighteen

The words spun around in my head. There she stood, telling me this. The firelight shone on half her face and half her body, leaving the other half in shadow. Like the moon she loved, she showed only one side of herself to the world and to me. I'd loved her, trusted her, counted on her, and she was a stranger, someone I'd never known at all and could not have loved. The size and shape of her treachery shocked me into numbness. I couldn't believe her. Yet I did believe.

All sorts of details, bits of talk, forgotten incidents, swam to the surface and confronted me. She—Arland—was the veiled woman of my dream, the presence I'd felt, the unknown star I'd never seen, pulling Mark away from me.

She turned and faced me. "Jane, you've got to listen. You must believe me. I never did anything against you deliberately, not ever." I didn't answer, and she went on. "You know I wouldn't try to hurt you. I never gave Mark a word or a look. I never even guessed—— After all, he never opened his mouth about caring anything for me until that night——"

"What night?"

"The night Miss Kate was murdered."

It came back again, its complications and implications still living. Everything in my life led up to that night and wound away from it again. "Go on, Arland. I might as well know." My face showed in the mirror. I looked hard and set and old. "You might as well start from scratch and let me know what it's all about—at last."

"I don't know where to begin; it's confused. You know I told you how it was with Tim and me. You remember you said you thought Mark guessed, and he did. Once, before Tim's death, in that Dasheel business, he told me if he could help, to let him know. That's all he said. Except, some time after Tim's death, I couldn't help noticing how Mark avoided me. So once I came right out and said, 'I suppose you're disgusted with me for being a hypocrite about Tim, pretending everything was perfect. Because you know it wasn't'. And he answered that he would have thought more of me if I'd picked up and left, but supposed I'd done the best I could with a bad situation. Then he left the room. I remember how abruptly he got up and went out."

I'd noticed, too, how Mark had stayed away from her, but, fool that I was, I hadn't thought much about it. "When did he tell you he loved you?" Here I was, old, and flung aside; and there she stood, older than I was in years, but blooming again, prepared to take up life again in another way, blooming in a love not rightfully hers.

"When did he tell you?" I repeated.

"Not until that night."

It always came back to that night.

"Of course I knew you and Mark were having a hard time with the place——"

"So you saw your chance to fish in troubled waters."

"Jane, you can't say that to me! You know it isn't true."

"Quit posing like something so damned noble. Makes me want to throw up."

"I don't. I wasn't. Because I didn't know he was in love with me. Maybe if I had known it, I wouldn't have been nice at all. But that night I was at Michael's when Mark came in. I knew he was upset, but he and Michael went into the other room to talk business. When he came out again, he said he'd take me home if I was ready to go. So he drove me home. On the way he told me he had borrowed from Michael and hated to."

"Did he tell you what a fight we'd had?"

"He didn't say a word about it."

"But you added two and two, I guess."

"I didn't think it was all peace and quiet, but I just asked him if I could lend him some money, and he said no, I couldn't. Then we began to talk about something of my own concern—something to do with Tim, and I asked Mark to help me, and he said he would, and then he left."

"You know where he went, don't you, that very night? He went straight to Ludie Daniels! There. I saw his car parked outside. I was trying to find him, to make up with him, and I saw his car! You think he was crazy about you then? Not crazy enough to keep him from her, I can tell you! You think that over. He was carrying on with her— maybe had been for years."

"Jane! My God, have you believed that all this time?" Her face changed and softened. "If you'd only told me——"

"Why tell? I didn't want anyone to know he was sleeping with her and making an utter damn fool out of me!"

"Oh, Jane, I wish I'd told you." She came and sat down by me and took one of my cold rigid hands, covering the flash of Miss Kate's diamond and sapphire ring. The warmth and life in Arland's fingers made me draw mine away. I didn't want her near me, or touching me.

"That business about Ludie—— I wish I'd told you all about it, but my own pride kept me from saying anything either! Mark went there that night because I asked him to. Of course I didn't know you saw him, or what you thought. You see, it wasn't Mark who was carrying on with Ludie for years, but Tim. You were right when you thought she was bad and dangerous, but not to you—to me."

"But Mark and Ludie—they did have an affair. She was crazy about him. I could tell by the way she looked at him."

"They did, when they were awfully young. And if she cared for any of her men, it was Mark. But when he came back from France he was through with her. Then Tim got entangled with her. He was seeing her that time right before we were married, but of course I didn't know it. It was on again, off again, but it kept up. She was the one I told you about—the one I was afraid of, the one Tim was afraid of. That night when Tim was killed, all of you were out at her place, remember? I wouldn't go, because by that time I suspected what was going on. Then I was sure. When he was killed, she was with him."

I made some kind of exclamation—it was so unreal.

"Yes, she was. When the car crashed, she wasn't hurt, and she scrambled out. Mark had begun to suspect what was going on; that's one reason he looked for Tim on that road. Then Mark knew she'd been with Tim, and so did Michael, because they found the heel of her shoe in the car. They didn't say anything until I came out and asked Mark if Ludie had been with Tim. Then he told me he'd found the heel of a shoe."

"Rhinestone studded. And she had on gold slippers!" They twinkled at me out of the past. "Go on."

"That night, the night you saw Mark's car out there, I'd sent him. Ludie had some letters from Tim. She knew poor old Mr. Laidlaw was getting out that panegyric. Since times were getting hard for her, too, she wrote me a nice little note telling me it would be embarrassing for the family if the letters got to the public eye on the heels of the book and when the governor was coming to dedicate a building to Tim. I couldn't pay blackmail, and I would simply have let her go ahead and do her damnedest: I was beyond caring. But there was Tim's family. You know how they worshiped and adored him; his memory was all they lived for. And it wasn't only a love affair. It was a lot worse. She sent me a copy of one of the letters. In it Tim said he was going to meet Jim Tate at the Owl's Nest at such and such a date. You know who he was? One of the people involved with Dasheel, very shady. The one who brought the money to Dasheel from somebody down in the swamp—the go-between. If Tim was going to meet him, and knew him, he couldn't be entirely innocent of everything connected with it."

"Tim was in it?"

"I don't know how much, and I don't know how much Ludie knew about comings and goings, but she knew a good deal. You see, her husband used to go down there to that house and probe for bullets, and bandage up the ones who were wounded. Mr. Laidlaw, with his bad heart, couldn't have stood all that made public.

"I didn't know what to do, or which way to turn, so that night I told Mark all about it, and asked him to go out there and see her and get the letters. None of us could afford to pay blackmail. We were all hard hit, and you never know where a thing like that's going to end. Mark said he'd fix her. He went off, looking grim, and I was sure he would."

He'd gone, looking grim, and I thought of what I'd felt seeing his car out there. If only I'd known!

"He told me later what happened. He said he'd reminded Ludie of early days. He said, 'But Ludie wasn't to be moved to tears by any memory of high old times.' Maybe she resented his not giving her high old times any more. Then he said he drew a complete picture of the Laidlaws and their state of mind. Of course that didn't budge her. She said she meant no harm, but she was broke. So Mark took to bullying her. He told her if she showed anything to anyone, or opened her mouth to utter one word, he'd see she would 'get it in the neck good and plenty.' He told her he knew enough, and if he heard the slightest echo of anything connected with Tim, he'd see she landed in jail. Of course Mark couldn't prove those men had met in her place, or that she knew who they were, but he scared her. I suppose she knew him well enough to realize he meant every word he said, that he could and would do it. So she turned the letters over to him.

"Then he went on back to Wishmore, rang me up and told me he had what I wanted and would bring the letters to me in the morning. I said to just burn them up; I didn't want to see them or touch them."

"Why didn't he tell me all that? Why did he let me go on thinking he was out there sleeping with Ludie? He could have explained!" I hated him all over again. "He was a beast—a nasty, cruel, hateful, mean beast!"

"It was mean of him. He should have told you. But you know he's hard sometimes. You made him mad, I suppose, and he wouldn't tell you."

The candlelight and the firelight blurred and mixed and swam before my eyes. "He only said he'd been there, but not for the reason I thought. And I didn't believe him. Why should I? Why in God's name should I? He let me go on saying everything, and he could have stopped me!"

He could have, but he hadn't wanted to. He was fed up with me—right to the gills. He wanted to leave me. He'd already decided to leave. In his heart of hearts he wanted to go to Arland and tell her he loved her. Explanations, a moment's reconciliation wouldn't have made any real difference. Sooner or later he'd have left me and gone to her. He'd been cruel with the inevitable cruelty of a man tired to death of one woman and wanting another. "He went straight to you, didn't he?"

"He came under my window and called me, and I got up and let him in."

I could hear him, standing outside in the dark, and see her, waking, listening, getting up and going down the curved stairs, her thin pale robe trailing behind her and her braided hair falling over her shoulders. She'd opened the door to him. They had been there in the quiet night, telling each other everything in their hearts.

"He told me about Miss Kate. Then he said he'd decided to leave Wishmore for good and all."

"And you were glad of it. You'd hoped for it, and you were glad as you could be."

"Not glad. But I didn't much blame him. I admit that. I thought you cared about him, but I didn't think it was doing either of you much good."

"You sat up there all these years at Holly Trees. And all the years when I was struggling to get along with Mark, you were making a picture of yourself, all patience and self-sacrifice, and he gobbled it up! He fell for it, and you wanted him to. You know damn well you did. Don't pretend to be better than anyone else!" My anger mounted. "No wonder I couldn't make a go of things! You were always there."

"I wasn't. I wasn't even around for years. If it was all my fault, why couldn't you and Mark get along then? Before I ever came home."

"But you came back. You may not have said or done anything— either of you—but you were always there, in his mind and heart. It was hopeless for me, and I was so stupid—so damned dumb!" So blind, thinking it was Ludie, that slut, when it was Arland. I saw now how little Ludie could have mattered, but Arland—— She'd had power over his imagination. That was her quality: she could stir imagination. She showed Kitty and Steve the kind of people they could become, cherished in them the traits they cherished in themselves. She reminded Alec of the sort of beauty he really craved. "You look like Doña Ana," he'd said. "You make me think of Homer's long-limbed women." It wasn't what she was; it was what she conjured up. For Mark she'd kept alive in him the idea that someday he'd find what he wanted.

"To think I loved you and told you everything—— Why weren't you at least honest?" I floundered for breath. "When did you fall in love with him?"

"I think I realized it after we talked so long, you and I, and I'd told you about Tim. Right after that."

"Did he fall in love with you then?"

She hesitated, and the color in her cheeks deepened to a burning rose. "Afterward he told me it was about then, but he didn't say anything—not a word. Not till that night, when he said he wasn't going back to Wishmore. He said it was hopeless."

"And he had loved you a long time. He said that, didn't he?"

"Yes, and that I might as well know." I could see them, there in the dim room, with the perfume of jessamine blown through the open windows, and the only light the round-globed lamp burning like a full moon, but etched with its happy pictures instead of the moon's sad face. His intensity of anger at me had been forgotten in the intensity of his love for her. I could see them so plainly, in each other's arms, exchanging long kisses, like starving people eating at last after desperate hunger.

"That's why you were so strange the day after Miss Kate's murder," I accused her. "I thought you had something on your mind, but, my God, I never guessed what! Mark had been to you—you had all that between you. No wonder you were no help or comfort to me."

"That night when he came, when everything was over between you anyway, why shouldn't he have told me what he felt? Why not? Why shouldn't we have that at least? Because that was all."

With the selfishness of someone in love, she didn't give a damn about me any more. Her face was flushed with warm color, her eyes shining and her mouth quivering.

"He told me he was leaving, he never intended coming back, and he loved me. He said he had nothing to offer me, but he loved me, and I might as well know it. And someday he was going to send for me. And I said I would come."

"Why didn't you tell me the truth long ago?"

"Would it have helped any? What good would it have done either of us? I wouldn't tell you now if I could keep you from knowing. Do you think it's been easy for me? When Mark told me he loved me I would have gone with him then and there but for you. But you married again; you remade your life. I had nothing—an occasional letter. And that night, when it was over as far as you and he were concerned, why shouldn't he have told me what he felt? We'd never had anything else."

There she stood, telling me this. That's why she'd never married again, and never seemed lonely. She had been sustained by a secret love like an underground spring, making its own fresh and blossoming oasis. A love enduring through time and space and change and war. The kind of love I had wanted from him for myself. It had been given to her and not to me. What had she ever done—so passive, and secret, and silent—to deserve it?

If it had all been in the past, maybe I could have forgiven it all and accepted it all. But it wasn't past. It was not. She was young again, in spite of time. She was in love, in spite of time and distance, and Mark loved her now, this minute. He was going to marry her.

Why hadn't time and waiting paled her and pinched her and aged her? It hadn't. Not at all. It had crowned her, given force to her mind and depth to her beauty. She would go—go there to meet Mark, and he would see all he had remembered, all he had imagined and more—a woman in the very full tide of living.

"We'll only have this little while together now, maybe only this little while out of our whole lives."

She astounded me. Under her softness there ran such tenacity and such daring. She had staked her whole life on just this little while. So rootless, and so threatened, yet worth it. How much it must be worth to them both!

"Jane, you can't begrudge us such a little bit of snatched-up happiness; you can't. Please kiss me good-by and wish us luck. We need luck."

She came over to me, but I flung off her outstretched hand and got up. "No, I won't kiss you, or wish you any kind of good luck! You were cruel and treacherous and lying, both of you. You were a snake in the grass to me. You ruined things for me. You deliberately took everything away from me—everything I wanted! I'll never forgive any of it, not ever!"

She picked up her cloak and folded the soft furs around her and started out of the room. Then she came back. "Jane, you're putting too much stress on all of it. Entirely too much. Mark loves me in his way. But with men like him love doesn't amount to an awful lot. It's never played much part in his life and never will. He never understood what you felt because he never will feel it. Look how long he's done without me. He went and left me, too, you know. And the real reason he cares for me, or thinks he does, is because I let him go and didn't try to stop him or ever ask him to come back. The trouble is, men women usually want most are men like Mark, and they really aren't very interested in the state of their own feelings. They have too much else on their minds."

I turned my back on her and didn't answer. She hesitated, then left the room, and I heard the front door close.

I stayed where I was, heaping lump after lump of coal on the fire and watching the blaze go leaping up the chimney until the windows began to go gray with morning.

❦ Chapter Nineteen

Arland drove to New Orleans the next day and took a plane for Washington. Mark met her there and they were married. The town burst with excitement over the sudden and unexpected romance. The progress of the newest oil well—the war itself—was relegated to the background. Mark was a hero now, and Arland made a very suitable heroine for a hero. At least the town thought so.

Of course I went about exclaiming, too, and hanging over pictures and reading news items. One paper even said they were early sweethearts. Nobody seemed to remember I had once been married to Mark myself. I had put up with him when he was poor and unknown. Now he was famous nobody gave me any share of him at all. Somebody asked me, "Did you ever guess any of it, Jane? You and Arland are so intimate."

"I knew they wrote to each other. I wasn't really surprised. There were straws in the wind. Then when it was all settled, of course she told me all her plans." My face felt frozen, saying it. When we were children, it was a family custom when anybody lied for the others to begin shuffling their feet—the young men coming to take out the bodies of Ananias and Sapphira. I thought of that while I was speaking, and my toes began to twitch at my own lies. Fortunately, no one knew how I had received the disclosure of Arland's plans.

"It seems strange," Mrs. Lews said wonderingly. "But everything seems topsy-turvy. You just aren't surprised at anything any more." I pretended I thought it was wonderful. And that I had laid a benign hand on the whole proceedings and was scattering benisons on the happy pair.

"Think how quietly she sat up at Holly Trees all this time," Gertrude said. "She told me once she heard from Mark. I didn't think a thing of that. They were such old friends. I suppose warmer feelings started by letter. And the war brought it to a head. Like all these other love affairs. Poor things, they don't have much time together, do they? Then I suppose she'll come back to Holly Trees and wait some more."

"It doesn't seem very satisfactory," I couldn't help saying.

"What is? These days nothing's comfortable. Arland's good at getting herself heroes, isn't she? She had Tim when he was on the crest of the wave. Now she's got Mark."

Now she had Mark. The thought ate into me. Everybody seemed to think as Gertrude did, that they had fallen in love with each other by writing all those letters. "No wonder," Aunt Em said. "Arland writes such charming letters."

"You never thought she would marry a divorced man, did you?" I couldn't resist that. She was so full of weepy romantic sentiments about the whole thing.

"Divorced?" she looked surprised, peering up over the edges of a helmet she was groping with fuzzily. A large ball of wool flopped out of her lap and I picked it up for her. "So he is. My, I'd forgotten; it's been so long ago. And so much has happened. But I can't hold it against poor Arland, with this awful war on."

So the aunts forgave. It wouldn't have been a bit of use telling them all Arland had been a sly and scheming little beast. They all loved her, and with their usual lack of facing up to facts they never believed what they didn't want to about the people they liked, while they swallowed the tallest tales about the people they didn't like. Besides, I believe they would rather have gloated if I had shown the smallest signs of discomfiture. In their eyes I was too continuously right and successful: lucky.

They discounted the planning and work I'd put in to get what I wanted. There were plenty of people who would have chuckled over my comeuppance. They wouldn't know. I'd learned to keep my pose of being brilliant and successful, of getting everything on earth I wanted.

I was particularly anxious for Alec not to guess how I felt. I was very wary when we talked over Mark and Arland. Alec had always thought she was so perfect. Much worse, he liked her looks, and when a man is taken by a woman's looks she can be a fiend and he won't know it. Or admit it. Or give a damn.

He speculated about the marriage. "She was wrapped up in Tim, though I sometimes think she wasn't as happy as she pretended. Then, too, I never saw Mark and Arland together much after Tim's death. I was away, and when I came back, Mark was gone. But she's Mark's type—the only sort of woman he ought to marry. She owns herself completely—perfect self-control. But never wants to own anybody else."

"I believe you're right," I answered evenly. Only one person, besides myself, guessed Mark had loved Arland a long time. Ludie Daniels.

She stopped me one day on the street. We never spoke, but when she hailed me, I paused.

"So Mark's married again," she started by saying. "You know, we were crazy about each other before he went to war—that first war. When he came back he didn't have much time for me. It kind of hurt. Hell, it hurt a lot! Once on the excursion boat he had a fight with Clem Burgess. Everybody thought it was on account of me." Now so completely beyond the ranks of the respectable, I wondered if Ludie would have liked to have held her place on the fringe and gradually worked in. If she'd used her talents a little differently, she could have done it.

She laughed a little and rolled her eyes, automatically taking on the tones and gestures of her young days. "I wish it had of been. I reckon it was, too, in a way. But not the way I wanted. I'd been having some dates with Tim just before he was married, and Clem was teasing me about him, and Mark fired up and told him if he didn't keep his mouth shut, he'd kill him. And Clem said he'd talk like he damned pleased, and Mark hit him. Mark didn't want Mrs. Laidlaw to know her brand-new husband was running around with me so close to his wedding day."

That was as near as Ludie ever dared come to broadcasting her little adventures with Tim. It didn't matter. Ludie had no more power. She was fat and no longer prospered. Tim was long dead, and others were claiming the limelight he had loved. His parents were dead, too, and no longer had to be shielded. Proclaim from the housetops now that Tim had had a long-drawn-out affair with Ludie, that he'd known all Dasheel's game and tried to hush it as long as he had dared, and people would hardly listen these days.

And Arland was married to Mark. Even then, on the excursion boat, he had cared enough about Arland to try to protect her. He had loved her then, whether he had admitted it or not.

I left Ludie abruptly and stood on the corner waiting to cross.

Cars were snarled up, tooting wildly. It was like our town to have an intersection with not two stop signs, but four, so that nobody stopped, or everybody did. I would give it my attention, and make the city fathers change it.

A long truck, laden with shining pipes, began to move. It nearly collided with a jeep overflowing with yelling soldiers. The bluish neon lights of a nearby store went on, and all the other lights. They glared down on the pushing crowd, making people look ghastly. It had all become modern, and I had helped make it so. But I felt like something crouching in a jungle a trillion years ago. Crouched and baring its fangs.

Six weeks passed, then seven. I knew Mark had set off for China again, but Arland still stayed away. Visiting friends, Bedelia said. Then Arland sent me a wire, saying she would reach home on a Thursday evening, driving herself up from New Orleans. I didn't know whether the wire was an outstretched olive branch or simply a warning of her imminent arrival.

I knew I had to behave—at least in public—as if there had been no break in our friendship, as though I were still as fond of her as ever. If I didn't, everybody would find out what I thought and felt. She had me in a crooked stick, and she, of course, would behave like a damn angel.

Thursday was cold and rainy. The war news was dreadful. I had a long mournful letter from Kitty, telling us she felt in her bones Steve was leaving soon. Then she would come home. One part of her letter was cheerful. She thought and hoped she was going to have a baby. She hadn't lost any time. A grandchild. It was absurd; Kitty was too young. Of course she'd leave most of its care to me, I'd see to that.

In my mind's eye I could already see the little thing, little Steve or little Kitty—maybe little Jane, best of all—flitting through Rosemont's rooms and gardens, smearing the brocade, wreaking havoc with ornaments, tearing up the flowers, smudging, and making a dreadful racket. A baby, that's what we needed! When I'd first craved Rosemont, I'd had visions of swarms of children leaping around the garden and tearing through the house. That's one reason I'd wanted it so much. Mark's children and mine. Maybe I'd have oodles of grandchildren though. It was again the fashion to have children thick and fast. They would be Mark's grandchildren and mine. Not

Arland's. That's one thing I'd have that she wouldn't, thank heaven.

"Aren't you going to Holly Trees to be there when Arland comes?" Alec asked. I hadn't told anyone she was coming, but he had seen the wire and had wanted to know what was in it. "Don't you think we all ought to go and cheer her up?" he suggested.

"She doesn't want a flock of people; she'd much rather be alone. Don't tell the others."

"Maybe you're right," he agreed. "But somebody ought to be there; it'll be pretty dreary for her driving up to Holly Trees all by herself on an evening like this. Particularly with the worry she has on her mind."

Since he prodded me, there was nothing else for me to do but drive over to Holly Trees myself Thursday afternoon. The house did look shadowy and deserted and too quiet under the sighing trees. The whole place was so different from its usual air of life and welcome. Bedelia let me in. She was gloomy, too, talking of Arland, her "po' chile," having to come here by herself.

"Mr. Mark done took hisself off again over yonder where dey's a-fightin', ain't he?"

I said he had, and she sighed. "An' she gotta come here and a-set and a-set."

Everybody always did feel sorry for Arland when anything was wrong with her. She set up a general current of sympathy, and people made her troubles and her joys their own. They thought of me as a brilliant example of material success—someone who always had her own way, was always lucky, and never had any troubles at all.

Bedelia left me for her kitchen, and I went from room to room filling vases with water, and fixing the camellias I had brought. I grumbled at them when their heads fell off and when they wouldn't group themselves the way I wanted them to. I lit the lights and made the reluctant smoldering fires burst into flames and roar up the chimneys. I was going to give the house a welcoming look, for Arland. Then I was going to take myself off. I wasn't going to stay and give her my welcome.

The house, though, began to affect me little by little. The longer I stayed in it the more it began to whisper to me and work on my nerves. It brought back too many memories. Parties, and quiet fire-lit evenings when a group of us talked and laughed together. Christmas dinners, and old family jokes, and Uncle telling me to look in his pocket, he had a surprise for me. Arland running down the steps, taking me off to her room, asking me to help her with her party. Or sitting me down in front of the mirror and working on my hair. "Now—now you look pretty!"

Now people said I was "fascinating" and dashing. When I was young, she was the only one who ever told me I looked pretty—or tried to make me so. In the library I put a low silver bowl of violets on her desk—the first violets. Then I looked at the desk. It was closed, and I wondered if it was locked. I tried it. It wasn't. It opened under my hand.

Mark's letters must be in it somewhere. Of course I'd been trained not to open desks or drawers . . . not to rummage through other people's things. But I had long ago given up being a refined gentlewoman of delicate sensibilities. And I wanted to see Mark's letters to Arland. Keeping a wary ear for sounds from the kitchen, and sounds outside, I began to go through the desk systematically. I took care not to disturb anything. I soon found what I wanted.

They were all together, arranged according to dates. One by one I read them all. What I wanted most to know was when he had begun to love her. They were love letters, of course, but I had steeled myself to that. Anyway, Mark was not given to long analyses of the nuances of feeling even to her. He could make love a damn sight better than he could hold forth on the subject.

What he told her most was what he was doing, and how he was living, and what he planned to do next. Blown by chance winds, not taking much thought of the future, yet he had gone on, and gone ahead. In one letter from South America he described the scenery, gave an account of a storm in the mountains, and the difficulties of flying through it. Another time he was in a town shaken by an earthquake. Sometimes he gave brief descriptions of the people he was working with. He wrote a good deal about Kitty. Arland evidently kept him well informed about her and everything that went on in the town. "I laughed a lot at what you told me about——" he was always saying. The letters from China were the most interesting, and the fewest. They had come by air. He spoke of "little brushes with the Japs," told another time of the airfield so laboriously built. "Now we have to pull out of here damn fast and leave it."

What I resented more than love passages was the way he'd let her share his life. Arland had told him about Kitty all the years he'd cut himself off so completely from me. He only mentioned me once, in a passage that referred to things past.

"I meant to settle down and do my best. I guess I should have tried harder, but Jane and I are so different. It just didn't work out well. I felt we'd both do better apart. I'm sure glad she and Alec married, and hit it off, and everything's turned out so well for them."

Then later he'd said, "I thought of you longer and more often than I knew. At your wedding it hit me all of a heap that you were really married and going away. I was an awfully lonesome critter. Not too much interested in anything." Over and over he thanked her for believing in him without explanation. And for waiting. "If ever you change your mind or meet someone else, you know I won't blame you. I'll never change toward you." And he hadn't.

Arland had been his dream, his image, but for a long time he hadn't realized it. It was the great resemblance between Arland and myself that had attracted him to me in the first place. Unconsciously he was looking for her. I remember the night he first made love to me. She had fixed my hair and put her clothes and her perfume on me. He'd said, "I thought you were Arland." I hadn't behaved like Arland. I had definitely proceeded under my own steam. I had been myself then, and he had liked it. Very well indeed. Maybe I'd deceived him by being like myself and not like Arland at all.

But he didn't know for a long time he had any feeling for her. That attraction he'd felt for me could have turned into love if I had been different. I could have adapted myself to him, gone with him where he wanted to go, and taken him away from her forever. He would have forgotten all about her. But I had made him stay at Wishmore, and the dim image had grown and had taken on life, and had burst into his mind and heart. Because she had come back. And she had no longer loved Tim, and Mark had sensed it. They were both grown-up then, Arland and Mark. They couldn't help seeing the truth—that they belonged together.

It was not his fault, or hers. It was Tim's and mine. Mine. If I had tangled my life, I could only blame myself. And for the first time, free from self-deception and self-delusions, I saw it all in its true light. They hadn't done me any injury. I had done it to myself. And sitting there in front of the closed desk, with the faint scent of the violets coming to me, my heart softened.

I had taken a long time with the letters, had become absorbed in them. I had forgotten to listen for the sound of the car. So I got up and stood by the window to watch for Arland. The rain had stopped, and a cold red sunset flushed the sky and colored the puddles. I knew now how I must meet Arland. I would tell her I was sorry for all I'd said and felt. I would tell her what I had found out. My enemies were not outside. They never had been. My enemy was within myself. That's what I must fight, and I would.

It was too late to undo the mistakes I had made with Mark. But not too late to undo my violence with Arland. She would forgive me, at once and forever. She had been happy, but not for long. I wondered why I'd ever had any resentment against her. The war was too real; it mocked all the feelings I had wasted.

Mark had been gone for years, and years had passed since he had been part of my life. I had Alec and Kitty, maybe a grandchild coming and Rosemont, plantations and oil wells. And maybe I could do some useful war work.

I had wished Mark dead often enough. I had even wanted to kill him. No, he was going back into the war, and I was free. I no longer hated him. He had never loved me or belonged to me. Arland had been right about his nature. He had loved her in his way, but he didn't belong to her either. That's why he had turned to her. She didn't demand him to belong to her.

I would telephone Alec and ask him to gather up a group of people and bring them here, so that Arland would find some cheerfulness when she came. And later, when we were alone, I would tell Arland everything, and we would love each other as we had before. She would need me now, and I would always need her. And for the first time in my life I felt I really needed Alec. Not to prove something to the world, but for myself. Maybe now we could at last find in each other what we each felt the other lacked. At least I would find sympathy and comfort with him. And I would no longer ask him to be what he was not, but be glad he was there. I would work on my life with him, work toward harmony and contentment and serenity: the fruits of old age. How tedious they sounded. My God! who wanted that!

I'd lost Mark long ago, so what could I be losing now? Being young. I knew I would never hate anyone with violence any more, or love anyone with passion. I would never give way to impossible yearnings, or conjure up wild visions of the future. All that was over.

I went to tell Alec to come here, and to wait for Arland.